AMADORO

Other books by Vincent McConnor

The French Doll
The Paris Puzzle
The Provence Puzzle
The Riviera Puzzle
*I Am Vidocq
Limbo
**The Man Who Knew Hammett*

*A Tor book

AMADORO

Vincent McConnor

A TOM DOHERTY ASSOCIATES BOOK
NEW YORK

This is a work of fiction. All the characters and events portrayed in this book are fictitious, and any resemblance to real people or events is purely coincidental.

AMADORO

Copyright © Vincent McConnor 1989

All rights reserved, including the right to reproduce this book or portions thereof in any form.

A TOR BOOK
Published by Tom Doherty Associates, Inc.
49 West 24 Street
New York, NY 10010

First edition: April 1989
0 9 8 7 6 5 4 3 2 1

This book is for
Miriam and John Ross

chapter one

ASHTON HENDRIE WAS AWARE OF HIS LEATHER HEELS echoing through the deserted marble corridors with such a hollow reverberation that he might be striding through a mausoleum. The closed doors on either side would fly open, at any moment, to reveal endless rows of vaults where forgotten skeletons were long immured. Citizens of Manhattan who perished in some monstrous catastrophe.

He'd never known such thoughts when he walked through here, hundreds of times in the past, before he met Sandra Saunders and heard her convincing arguments for life after death.

This was New York City. Alive, noisy and vibrant. Not an abandoned metropolis.

The streets, far below, had been dazzling in bright sunlight as his taxi brought him down Fifth Avenue from his apartment, where his wife was sleeping late.

Today was the first Sunday in June and he was on his way to have lunch with Tim Carrington, his editor in chief, along with half a dozen top staff members. Always happened whenever he finished a new cover story for *Metropole*. He did this four or five times every year and looked forward to meeting the old man with anticipation and a slight feeling, as always, of apprehension.

He would be given his next cover assignment, after he'd been congratulated for the job just finished. Recently he'd been unhappy about some of the proposed subjects. Either the individuals hadn't interested him or, in several instances, he'd known them personally and disliked them. When he turned a portrait subject down, it was not assigned to either of the other regular writers but was dropped and never mentioned again.

Sandra Saunders' face was on the cover of the new issue of *Metropole* that would be handed out today by Tim's secretary. Either a painting or a clever caricature. He hoped, this time, the caricature wouldn't be too eccentric or the painting too revealing, because he admired Sandra more than most of the celebrities he had profiled in the recent past.

On weekdays this public corridor was crowded with a noisy rush of people from many strata of city life because every suite was occupied. There were law firms, an advertising agency, a famous diamond importer and several tenants so important they had no identification on their doors.

He wondered about those anonymous suites. Did they belong to foreign governments in fear of bombings or were they hidden lairs for the alphabet boys? The FBI, the CIA or the KGB?

Today every door would be locked. He knew this to be a fact because, from time to time, he tried a few as he came in for these Sunday meetings.

Only the main street entrance to this impersonal skyscraper—the glass-and-marble atrium with its phony waterfall and artificial sunlight facing Park Avenue—was open weekends. Two uniformed guards were positioned behind a circular marble information desk, their backs to a long central corridor with rows of facing elevators broken by side corridors leading to the Fifty-first and Fifty-second streets entrances, which were never unlocked on Saturday or Sunday.

Today's brunch should be even more interesting than usual.

He'd done a fine profile of Sandra Saunders. Amusing, informative and slightly sensational. The three most important requirements. Much better than his last one. The egotism of symphony conductors was not conducive to the writing of an honest portrait. You could never dig out the man behind the silken mask. He'd done that arrogant Viennese conductor three years ago and had felt the same urge to add acid to his usual mixture of fact and satire. He'd resisted the urge and both profiles had been personal failures.

It was quite different with Sandra Saunders. For one thing, she had talked—openly and freely—about past and present and made some startling predictions concerning the future. His future as well as that of some famous people and the world in general. Some of which were confidential and had not been revealed in his article.

He'd come to like Sandra, without any reservations, although he'd been skeptical at their first meeting because he had no real understanding of either parapsychology or astrology. Now he knew a great deal about both and was convinced of their validity.

He hoped this new celebrity he would be assigned today would prove as fascinating a subject and as human. Unfortunately, so many of them were neither. Successful people seemed to lose their humility as they scrambled up their golden ladders.

His destination was now in sight, straight ahead, at the end of a long side corridor. A pair of teak doors held the familiar logo of *Metropole* magazine embossed upon a large enamel disk at the center of each. Simple, elegant and dignified, to suggest the very special qualities of the famous international monthly.

He pushed one of the doors open and saw the familiar red-haired beauty ensconced at her gleaming aluminum desk near the far wall. She never looked up but he was certain she knew who had entered and heard the door whisper shut behind him as he crossed the immense foyer with its eccentric modern sofas and chairs, everything designed to impress or intimidate the visitor. He still felt awed by its size, after five years of passing through here.

Checking the rows of framed *Metropole* covers hanging on the walls as he passed, to be sure that the famous people he'd written about were still there. He saw Kissinger first, then Jessie Norman and Woody Allen. Twenty of them now. Each representing at least three months of his life.

Miss Delaney, as was her custom, appeared to be absorbed in the Book Review section of the Sunday *Times*. He wondered if she really read it or only used it to impress the many doubters of her intelligence. She'd been hired, obviously, for her glorious red hair, large blue eyes and ravishing figure. She looked up, finally, and smiled sweetly as he passed her desk.

"Morning, Maggie."

"They're expecting you. In fact, you're the last."

"I intended to be." He didn't hesitate or turn from the straight path he always followed to reach the pair of inner doors with their smaller circular logo. Opened one of them and hurried down the inner corridor past more closed doors which led to various departments of the magazine, toward the single massive carved oak door at the end.

His wife wouldn't wake before noon. Her eyes, at this moment, were masked in pink satin, her ears silenced. Their housekeeper, Rosie, would nudge her awake when she brought a breakfast tray with one section of the Sunday *Times*. Mara only read the theater news. She had given two performances yesterday, with another coming up tonight. They rarely saw each other weekend evenings when she was working but he would pick her up tonight, after the play, and take her somewhere pleasant for supper to celebrate his latest portrait. Mara enjoyed celebrations.

The door to his editor in chief's sanctum held no logo or name. Everyone knew this was Tim Carrington's office.

Ash went in and hurried through the deserted outer office—Carrington's secretary, Miss Crevani, would be in the gallery waiting for her cue to produce copies of the new issue—and flung open the inner door.

Several people were talking at once but someone had noticed his arrival and begun to applaud. Others looked around and the sound grew until everyone was applauding.

This had never happened in the past.

He nodded his head as he crossed the paneled room, between half a dozen staff members in a circle of armchairs, facing the impressive white-haired man seated at the desk. Ash realized that he was jerking his head up and down in response to the applause, like Woody Allen. He stopped immediately.

Carrington rose behind his antique English desk, still applauding. "Good job, Ashton. One of your best. I've just been saying it should sell every copy of our June issue."

"Thank you, sir. I certainly hope so."

The others were on their feet as the applause died down.

"Afraid I don't have an acceptance speech prepared." His eyes moved around their smiling faces, all friendly, except for managing editor Tony Rufino. This was a special moment and Ash was touched.

"It is my considered opinion," Carrington continued, "that our cover stories—each succeeding portrait, but especially those by Ashton Hendrie—have become the absolute best of their kind."

Ash sank into an armchair that had been waiting for him, close to the desk, as the other staff members resumed their seats.

Carrington remained standing. "All three of our investigative reporters and the infrequent outsider brought in for a special portrait are, of course, excellent. And everyone concerned, in each department, is an essential contributor to the quality, but for this past year I've felt, and so has our esteemed publisher—my friend and colleague, Horace Bradshaw—that the cover portraits by Ashton Hendrie are outstanding. This latest one, I suspect, may be his best."

Another flurry of applause.

Ash laughed. "Am I about to receive my severance pay, sir?"

"God forbid! I hope, Ash, that you will continue with these brilliant jobs you're doing for as long as I am editor in chief of *Metropole*. And long after."

"Congratulations, Ash!" A light female voice.

He saw that it was Amanda Kwong, chief of the research department and his favorite associate. "Thanks, Mandy. We did it together."

"You're the best, Ash!" This voice was male.

Ash turned, recognizing the soft Louisiana accent of Cort Fontaine, and saw a flash of white teeth against his handsome dark brown face. Cort was the magazine's brilliant art director. "You always make my written portrait look better with your pictures."

Carrington laughed. "We could go on like this, my friends, but there is much to be done and brunch is waiting. Each of us has, already, enjoyed reading the portrait of Sandra Saunders but only Cort and I, as usual, have seen the June cover since it arrived from the printer." He sat down and pressed a button under his desk. "Miss Crevani is waiting with a stack of mint copies. *Metropole!* That sophisticated monthly devoted to the good life. The magazine for trendsetters and achievers!"

One of the north doors had opened and Carrington's secretary swept in from the gallery as though making a stage entrance, followed by a grinning youth bearing a pile of large white envelopes which he distributed, starting with Carrington and Ash, then handing one to each staff member as Miss Crevani observed his progress.

Ash smiled. This routine was the same every month. The only change was that Miss Crevani wore a smart new dress each time.

"That should be all for the moment, Miss Crevani." Carrington waved her away and slipped the thick magazine from its envelope.

All the others were doing the same thing while Miss Crevani and her assistant returned to the gallery.

Ash saw, as the glossy cover slid from its envelope, that the color portrait was a handsome oil painting of Sandra Saunders looking most impressive. Silver hair around the plump face, inquisitive blue eyes. She was smiling and the artist had slimmed a few pounds from her weight. "It's an excellent portrait. Sandra will be delighted."

"That's splendid!" Carrington exclaimed. "I said it was one of our better ones, Cort, when you showed me the finished canvas, but it's even more impressive in print."

"Thank you, sir." Cort darted a glance toward Ash, who nodded in agreement.

Carrington set the magazine down, gently, on his desk. "Let us know, Ash, what reaction you get from Miss Saunders."

"I'll very likely show her a copy this afternoon."

"Excellent! Our next item of business, as usual, is your next portrait."

Ash straightened apprehensively, prepared for another name he would reject. When that had happened in the past, it caused embarrassment because he always had to come up with acceptable reasons for his refusal. Thus far he had succeeded.

"The subject for your September assignment was decided, earlier this week, at a meeting of the board. We all know that our July cover features Iris Murdoch and the August portrait will be Placido Domingo. Only two staff members, at this point, know the identity of the person selected for September. Cort's been searching for pictures and Miss Kwong has been doing her customary in-depth research on the proposed subject."

"Without much success." Mandy frowned. "This lady is most elusive."

Ash smiled. "Another female subject?"

"You're very good with the ladies." Carrington rose from his desk. "No objection to two in a row, I trust?"

"Certainly not. That's happened before."

Everyone got up as Carrington came around his desk.

Ash joined him and they went ahead of the others toward the north pair of doors.

Carrington was a dynamic figure, tall and lean. Intelligent face under a thatch of unruly white hair. Brown eyes flashing with enthusiasm. Tanned from weekends in Bucks County, where he owned a small farm. He had the large and capable hands of a man who worked the soil. Surprising hands for an editor. It was Carrington's taste and enthusiasm that had made *Metropole* an instant success. What was he saying now?

". . . and, as you're about to see, Cort has come up with quite an interesting collection of photographs."

"Not so many as usual," Cort muttered, behind them.

"And a file of pertinent facts on the lady, prepared by Mandy and her staff," Carrington continued, grasping the knobs of both doors.

"Fewer facts than I've ever dug up on any subject in the past," Mandy responded.

Carrington pushed both doors back. "And here she is! Known as the most beautiful woman in New York City. Your portrait story, Ash, will call her the most beautiful woman in the world! Lyli Amadoro . . ."

"Amadoro?" Ash glanced at Cort again and the art director raised an eyebrow and grinned.

Carrington entered first, Ash following, into the spacious room that was the magazine's picture gallery, where spots of light focused on a single row of mounted photographs circling the walls at eye level.

Miss Crevani, beaming with anticipation, stood at a long conference table, like the hostess of a party. The youth who had handed out the copies of *Metropole* stood beside her near a stack of file folders.

Carrington had turned toward the left, the others at his heels.

Ash, as was his habit, went in the opposite direction, alone, moving along the line of color photographs and gray newspaper clippings framed by dark mats. He leaned forward to study each one intently.

Amadoro! Most beautiful woman in the world?

He had seen the lady several times in person. Once in some restaurant. He couldn't remember whether it was Le Cirque or 21. Twice in theater lobbies. Both shows were hit musicals. The first time he had been with his wife.

Mara had whispered, "There's Lyli Amadoro . . ."

He'd turned to see an incredibly beautiful woman with long blond hair talking to a distinguished older man.

His wife had murmured, "I don't think she's all that beautiful, do you?"

The second time he'd been alone because Mara was working. That night he had bumped into someone and turned to apologize. It was Lyli Amadoro. He'd been so surprised by her beauty, face-to-face, so overwhelmed by the unfamiliar scent she was wearing, that he had stammered his apology.

She had smiled and looked into his eyes. "Any time."

He had remained frozen as she moved ahead with a different escort.

Her perfume, again, had been unlike any scent he'd ever encountered. The most subtle, and certainly the most sensuous. It had tantalized him long after he was seated and trying to concentrate on his program.

She had been more attractive in person than in any of these photographs.

Amadoro leaving a Bond Street boutique, a scarf covering her golden hair and dark glasses hiding her eyes, but the exquisite nose and voluptuous mouth were unmistakable. Dining somewhere—the typed card said it was the Plaza—with another woman and two men in evening clothes, both women lavishly jeweled. A stunning shot of Amadoro walking in a silver-and-violet drizzle, hands thrust into a tailored white raincoat, long blond hair glittering with drops of mist. The captioned card, underneath, said it was the Tuileries. Somebody must've taken that shot with a telescopic lens, because she had obviously been unaware of the prying camera. Amadoro caught in a stunning pose, descending the grand staircase at the Metropolitan Opera on the arm of another handsome escort. This time her rose velvet gown and long metallic evening coat were striking because of their simplicity. The blond hair was wound on top of her head and threaded with jewels, which made it appear to be some fantastic sort of crown. Snapshot of a little girl with curly brown hair, posed with a small white dog, in front of a modest New England-type cottage. The card said it was New London, Connecticut. She was beautiful even then. He wondered if her name was Lyli Amadoro when she'd been that age . . .

Of course not! Amadoro was one of her husbands. The most recent.

"What do you think?"

He turned, still engrossed, and looked down to see Mandy Kwong's oval face—her unblemished skin like ivory silk—Oriental eyes and straight black hair with bangs touching her eyebrows. "What?"

"Will you accept this assignment?"

"Without a moment's hesitation. The dame's incredible."

"That's the only picture Cort could locate of Amadoro as a child. He sent one of his photographers up to New London, after I discovered she was born there, to dig up early pictures. Bought this from a filling station attendant who claimed he'd gone to school with her." Moving on, beside Ash, to a portrait shot of the adult Amadoro in a tailored suit and slacks. "Isn't she exquisite! Truly lovely . . ."

"Even more in person."

"You've met her?"

"Never. Only seen her." He continued to follow the line of photographs around the gallery, Mandy chattering softly beside him.

"She's noted for guarding her privacy. There've been incidents with those creepy paparazzi who tried to get shots of her. Cort had a difficult time finding this many pictures."

"These are quite enough to put me on the trail of the real Amadoro."

"Good luck, my friend."

"First an interview with the lady."

"She never gives interviews."

"I've met that type before. In the end they always talk. And talk . . ."

"From what I hear, she's more accessible at her office."

"What's the address?"

"Fifty-sixth and Fifth. You know I never remember numbers. It's in those file folders. All necessary addresses, including her parents' in Connecticut. They still live there."

"I'll tackle them after I talk to her."

"She's on the board of directors of Amadoro Associates, the corporation that owns the building where she has an enormous office suite. They also control the skyscraper where she has a condo."

"Sounds like a cozy tax shelter for the lady." He continued to study each photograph as they circled the gallery, glancing at Mandy, conscious of her exotic beauty. She always wore a high-necked and close-fitting dress, slit on the sides, called a cheongsam. During office hours it was partially hidden by loose white smocks with large pockets in which she kept slips of paper covered with notes on all current projects. Sunday she never wore a smock, and today her cheongsam was made of lime-colored silk. Her tiny hands, as she talked, made delicate birdlike motions.

"I had one of my assistants check all major newspapers and magazines," she was saying, "but Amadoro's never given an interview to any of them."

"Whose idea was it to call her the most beautiful woman in the world?"

"Carrington's, of course. But Cort agreed. Don't you?"

"I suppose . . . Can't think of any woman more beautiful. Maybe Garbo."

"Curious, isn't it? They're both known by their last names. Garbo and Amadoro . . ."

"They both had good press agents."

"I saw Garbo the other day. Walking on East Fifty-seventh."

"She still as beautiful?"

"Couldn't tell. She was wearing a hat and sunglasses, but I recognized her from the way she walked. Garbo and Vanessa Redgrave are the most elegant walkers I've ever seen. And maybe Meryl Streep." She peered around the gallery as Ash glanced at the final photograph. "Time for brunch!"

"And I'm ready. Didn't get any breakfast." He saw Carrington waiting for him near the open doors beside Miss Crevani and the boy with his stack of file folders.

Mandy walked beside him toward Carrington. "I look forward to working on this Amadoro story, Ash. It's going to be quite a challenge."

"You were very helpful with the Saunders portrait. Especially simplifying that parapsychological material in the beginning as I struggled to understand it."

"That's me! Mandy the great simplifier. Concentrate and define. Tell me, Ash, did the Saunders story affect you, personally? All those scientific papers on extrasensory perception and the rest . . ."

"It affected me profoundly. I plan to read more deeply in the whole psychic field."

"I've always been a believer."

"Have you?" He looked down at her with fresh interest.

"My father was Chinese, but my mother's Irish and psychic. I've been interested in parapsychology and astrology for years. I'm a member of the Parastro Society."

"I'll be damned!"

"So, working on the Saunders story was especially fascinating."

"Come along, Ashton!" Carrington touched his sleeve.

"We'll talk later, Mandy."

"Of course."

Carrington's eyes revealed his excitement. "What do you think, Ash? Another great portrait!"

"Fascinating." He walked with Carrington as Miss Crevani, still the hostess, led the way through the editor in chief's office, toward the south wing of the *Metropole* suite where double doors to the executive dining room stood open and the staff butler, Parkins, waited to greet each person by name.

"The big problem, of course," Carrington was saying, "is that Amadoro seldom gives an interview. Even *Fortune* couldn't get one. The few times she did talk to reporters she gave them a tissue of taradiddles!" He accepted two file folders from the waiting youth and handed one to Ash, who, as they talked, slipped it into the envelope with his copy of *Metropole*. "Mandy's come up with fewer facts than usual. Less background material . . ."

"She was just telling me."

"Lyli Amadoro is an enigma!" Carrington continued. "You must ferret out the secret at the heart of the Amadoro legend. And you're certainly the man to do it. I told Horace yesterday that you would charm her, as usual, and come up with the greatest portrait we've ever done."

"I'm flattered, sir."

"Good afternoon, Mr. Carrington." Parkins bowed and smiled. "And Mr. Hendrie."

"We're at opposite ends, as usual." Carrington paused, inspecting the attractive table. "I'm ravenous. Had breakfast at seven and drove in from the country for a conference on the Placido Domingo portrait we're having painted by a new young artist in Madrid. He sent color prints of what he's done thus far. Absolutely brilliant! They arrived Friday after I'd left for the weekend and I wanted to see them before brunch. We must find something special for your Amadoro cover. A really stunning portrait of the lady. Any suggestions?"

"Not offhand . . ."

"We'll talk to Cort about it." He headed for the far end of the table where he always sat, his back to a row of tall windows overlooking the distant East River.

Ash took his place at the other end of the table and, facing Carrington, stood behind the Chippendale armchair, glancing at his name on a place card as he wondered who would sit on either side of him. Woman on his right and man to his left but he hoped the man wouldn't be Tony Rufino. Impossible to check the two place cards unobserved.

As Carrington waited beside his armchair, the others spread out, looking for the cards with their names. Everyone talking.

Ash saw that one of the senior editors, Corina Curtis, who had worked with him on most of his portraits, had paused beside the chair to his right. "Good morning, Rina. Didn't get a chance to see you earlier."

"You were a bit late."

"Overslept and caught a laggard taxi."

"Aren't they always?" She smiled at Cort, who was standing behind the chair opposite. "That's a fascinating portrait of Sandra Saunders on the new cover."

Cort turned to Ash. "I hope Saunders likes it."

"I'll let you know." Ash saw that Carrington was peering around the table.

"Everyone found his place? Sit down, ladies and gentlemen."

Ash, like everyone else, rested his white envelope on the damask tablecloth as he sat. He was aware of Miss Crevani departing and closing the doors, conscious of clear blue sky visible through the windows behind Carrington, and of Parkins snapping his fingers at a waiter standing near what appeared to be an enormous many-paneled coromandel screen, but if you looked close, each panel held an amusing picture of a city where one of *Metropole*'s branch offices was located. At the same time he noticed that Mandy Kwong was seated on Carrington's left, with Bert Bemis, another senior editor, on his right. Tony Rufino was in the middle, next to Corina, and Sylvia Vernon, a bright associate editor, sat between Cort and Bert. All talking and laughing, even Tony, which meant they were genuinely pleased with his portrait of Sandra. Everyone, of course, had read the proofs weeks ago but hadn't seen it in print until today.

"Here we are!" Carrington exclaimed, welcoming the waiter, who had returned from behind the screen, bearing a silver tray holding magnums of champagne in Georgian silver coolers.

The waiter set his tray on an antique serving table, placed against the long wall, under a framed Renoir from Horace Bradshaw's private collection of Impressionists.

Parkins lifted one bottle from the ice, wrapped it in a napkin and proceeded to uncork the wine as the waiter performed the same ceremony with the other bottle.

"Congratulations on the Saunders portrait." Tony Rufino was looking toward him, smiling his customary sardonic rictus.

"Glad you like it," Ash responded. "Any reservations?"

"None about how you handled the story. Several about your subject. I still can't believe this Saunders dame is for real."

"I gather you don't accept parapsychology."

"Buncha crackpots manipulating credulous people who are afraid of dying. Simple as that!"

"Millions of people, according to one recent survey, do believe in psychic phenomena," Ash responded.

"Buncha fools."

"I'm a firm believer in extrasensory perception," Corina said quietly. "I have personally experienced demonstrations of its viability. Many times."

"I can't believe it!" Rufino exclaimed.

Ash reached out and touched Corina's hand, resting on the white cloth. "I believe you. I'm convinced, since meeting Sandra Saunders, that there is something else after we finish this present life. I was never absolutely certain before."

"And you are now?" she asked eagerly.

"Unexpectedly."

All conversation halted as Parkins filled Tim Carrington's glass and the waiter poured Ash's champagne. Everyone waited silently, familiar with this monthly ritual.

Ash's eyes moved from face to face. These were people he'd been associated with for five years, but, except for Mandy and Cort, he didn't consider them his friends. They were the daily strangers who touched one's life, day after day, yet you never really knew them. Not even Carrington or Corina . . .

Carrington rose, smiling, as the last glasses were filled. "I wish to propose an affectionate toast to our man of the month—that brilliant investigative reporter who writes our most subtle and provocative portraits—Ashton Hendrie!" Raising his glass. "To Ash!"

Everyone stood, reaching for his wineglass and holding it toward Ash, who remained seated. "To Ash!"

"Thank you. Every Ms. and man of you." He stood up as they drank. "I wish to propose a toast to that fascinating lady who is the subject of our June portrait." Lifting his glass. "To Sandra Saunders!"

"Sandra Saunders!" They raised their glasses.

Ash drank with them, his eyes moving from face to face.

In three months he would be standing here again, another glass of champagne in his hand, drinking a toast to Lyli Amadoro.

chapter two

ASH BOUNDED UP THE WORN WHITE MARBLE STEPS TO the double mahogany entrance doors with their gleaming silver knobs. Yanked the antique bellpull but, as usual, could hear no response from inside. Turned and looked down into Gramercy Park, holding the large white envelope in his left hand, knowing it would take Miss Cassie several moments to come from wherever she might be in the red brick mansion. Aware of his taxi continuing west on Twenty-first Street toward Fifth. Glanced around the fenced park, across the street, with its four grassy areas and tall elm trees. Children playing on the gravel paths, uniformed nannies watching them, seated on wooden benches beside shiny black prams. A few old men, far apart, dozing in the afternoon sunlight or reading. This was a relic of an earlier, more tranquil Manhattan that had survived among the apartments and office buildings looming on every side.

Before leaving *Metropole* he had stopped by his own office to check the contents of Mandy's file folder on Lyli Amadoro. Two typed pages held everything the research department had been able to discover. He would have to start digging for himself, using those two pages as a starting point. His first step would be to arrange a preliminary interview with Amadoro.

"Good afternoon, Mr. Hendrie."

He turned at the sound of the gentle Southern voice and saw that the door had been opened. Miss Cassie stood there in her dove-gray Sunday uniform with white collar and cuffs as well as a starched apron. Her thin figure could have stepped from a novel by Henry James, but then so could this old mansion. "How are you, Miss Cassie?"

"As usual, sir. Does no good to complain at my age."

He kissed her on the cheek before stepping inside, out of the hot sunlight, into the shadowy entrance hall that always seemed to smell faintly of roses.

"Miss Saunders expects you, sir."

"But I didn't tell her I was coming today. Wanted to surprise her."

"She's not one you're likely to surprise. Said it was you when the bell rang. 'That's Mr. Hendrie,' she told me. She's in the dining room eating lunch."

"Then I shouldn't disturb her."

"Oh, no! She said bring you right in . . ." Going ahead, through the high-ceilinged hall with its sturdy Colonial antiques, past the closed doors to the parlor and the curving staircase with its row of ascending portraits—severe, unsmiling Early American faces—in carved frames revealed by a spill of daylight from overhead. "Miss Saunders always has a late lunch on Sunday. Usually invites several guests. Today she's eating alone but I knew she was expecting someone. Guessed it might be you, sir."

"Miss Saunders isn't the only psychic in this house."

"I don't begin to glimpse what Miss Saunders does but I do have my own moments of clarity." She swung open one of a pair of tall doors. "Here he is, ma'am! Mr. Hendrie . . ."

"Come in, lover! You're in time for dessert."

"Just had brunch at the office."

"But you barely touched your food!"

"Oh?" He crossed the sunny dining room toward the smiling woman seated at the end of the long table in a bay window overlooking a brick-walled flower garden. "You were watching me?"

"For a bit." She held out both arms. "Give us a kiss!"

Approaching her he noticed the cordless white phone on the table, always within easy reach, the single yellow rose in a slim crystal vase. Saw the plate of unfinished salad.

"It was a fine brunch, even if you didn't eat much . . ."

He bent and kissed her lightly on the lips.

"All those champagne toasts and lovely compliments!"

"Several of those toasts were to you. Our portraits are a tremendous success. Yours on the cover and my written portrait inside." He placed his envelope on the polished surface of the table. "Here it is."

"How exciting!" Snatching up the envelope, eagerly, and opening the flap.

He sat at the table, behind her, as she slid the magazine out.

"Oh! How nice!" she exclaimed. "How very nice . . ."

Cassie was removing Sandra's plate, at the same time trying to see the portrait on the cover.

Sandra held it up. "Look at this, Cassie!"

"Very flattering." She carried the salad plate toward the kitchen.

"A splendid likeness." Sandra put the envelope aside and studied her painted portrait. "I was afraid the artist would make me look enormous, when you said he worked from photographs, but I do believe he's made me seem a bit thinner! And I like that antique astrolabe he's placed beyond my shoulder. A subtle touch! I only wish my hair really did look that attractive."

"You're pleased?"

"Absolutely delighted. We'll have some wine and drink a toast of our own." Glancing past him toward the pantry door and whispering something.

"What are you saying?"

"Telling Cassie which vintage I want." She opened the magazine and flipped through the pages. "I'll read this later." Setting it on top of the envelope. "May I keep it?"

"Of course."

"My copy will arrive in the mail on Tuesday and I'll have Cassie pick up several more copies from the newsstand."

"No need for that. The magazine will be sending you fifty copies. More, if you wish."

"How nice! There's so much I must say to you, Ash. All the things I've kept in my heart since that first day you came here. Told me *Metropole* had selected me for a portrait and you would be writing it. I was dubious, at first, whether such a portrait would be right and proper for me . . ."

"I knew you were."

"But as we talked that afternoon, I found that your sign was Sagittarius, so I knew everything would be all right. I've been reading *Metropole* since their first issue and knew they sometimes make a complete fool of their portrait subjects."

"Only when they *are* fools."

"I realized that as we talked, and I know now, without reading what you've written about me, how perceptive and kind you've been . . ."

"Better read it before you make a statement like that."

"I'll most certainly read every word, but I've come to know you these past three months. I respect and love you, Ash. I'm grateful, most of all, that it was you they assigned to write my portrait. And, of course,

I'm grateful to *Metropole* for doing a cover story on me at all. This portrait article will be read around the world! It will further establish my credibility, as well as that of my twin professions—parapsychology and astrology—which haven't always had the respect and approval of the public or the scientific community. Parapsychology, of course, is fairly recent—an extension of psychology—but astrology is older than most religions. It has been verified by clinical investigations and statistical laws. As you know, the name of the Parastro Society, which I founded, is a combination of both—*para*psychology and *astro*logy. Did you ever check those words—their origins—para and astro?"

"That's in my profile. They both come from ancient Greece. Para means, quite simply, a going beyond, and astro comes from aster—meaning star. So parastro means going beyond the stars."

"And that's exactly what parapsychology and astrology attempt to do. Search for unknown forces in those vast distances of time and space. We don't, as yet, comprehend what's there, but we've been able to reach into the darkness and touch an incredible life force or intelligence beyond present knowledge."

"I've come to understand some of this since I've known you."

"I know you have. Your portrait does me great honor and will, I'm certain, explain to people what I'm attempting to do in my work. Many outside New York—especially in Europe—have never heard of Parastro."

"They will now."

"I haven't sought or wanted publicity but this has been different. I accept it and believe it's for the good of my future work. I'm grateful to you, Ash. Deeply appreciative of what you've done."

"Here we are, ma'am."

They looked around as Miss Cassie returned, bearing a bottle of champagne in a silver wine bucket with two glasses on a tray.

"You said you wanted the nineteen forty-nine Cordon Rouge?"

"Yes, Cassie. You can open that for us."

"Certainly, ma'am." Setting her tray down. "You haven't had your raspberries."

"Couldn't eat another bite. Much too excited."

Cassie glanced at the *Metropole* cover again as she placed a wineglass in front of each. "Fine likeness! Makes you look a bit younger, but no woman could object to that. Remember, ma'am, I told you—first time Mr. Hendrie rang our bell—he was here to offer you a precious gift."

"I do remember and, of course, you were right. This portrait will change my life in ways I can't even begin to foresee."

"You'll be world-famous now!" Cassie wrapped the wine bottle in a napkin and proceeded to work on the cork. "Of course, you've been famous in America for years with your column in the newspapers, your books and lectures. Now Sandra Saunders will be known to everyone!"

"I haven't wanted such publicity before—which is why I've never appeared on television—but this is the time, I believe, to let people know about our Parastro Society."

The cork came out and Cassie quickly poured a swallow of wine into Sandra's glass.

She sipped it and nodded. "Lovely!"

Cassie filled the glass, then hurried around the table to fill Ash's.

Sandra raised her glass. "I wish to propose a toast . . ."

Ash was aware of Cassie leaving the room as Sandra talked.

"This is an important moment in both our lives. Yours, Ash, as well as mine. Your portrait will influence the future for us both. I never drink a toast to the past or the present. Only the future. This toast is to your future, Ash. And mine. And to the future of our world. As well as those other worlds far beyond this small planet we call Earth. I drink to that waiting golden world which man will, one day, know." She raised her glass. "To the future of the universe—a peaceful universe!"

"I will, most certainly, drink to that." He touched his glass to hers.

In the silence, as they drank, the song of birds flooded through the open windows.

"Several things I must tell you today, Ash . . ." Sandra took another swallow of wine. "After today, of course, we'll be seeing each other less frequently . . ."

"Nonsense! At least once a week."

"That's impossible, and you know it. We'll both be much too busy. We've been together constantly for three months. Less in the last month, of course, than in the first two, but we've talked on the phone every day. Now our collaboration is finished. You have another portrait to research and write."

"I was given my new assignment this afternoon."

"I know."

"You know the name of my next subject?"

"That I wasn't able to discover. What I'm saying is, you're about to start questioning and investigating a new subject." She hesitated. "There were several things I held back when you questioned me."

"I was aware of that and understood."

"Deeply personal things I didn't want you to print."

"I respect that."

"For instance, my marriage . . ."

"You never mentioned it."

"You didn't ask. I was married years ago but it was a great mistake. He was an Aries." She glanced at the magazine resting on the white envelope. "You accepted, from our first meeting, that I was psychic . . ."

"I did."

"There's nothing unusual about being psychic. I didn't say this before because, for the purpose of your portrait, I wanted you to believe I am unique."

"And you are."

"No . . . Many children are born with psychic powers. Most never realize that. Others do, but without comprehension. Still others, like us, sense there's something unusual about life. We become conscious of this very young, while those around us—even our parents—do not."

"Are you suggesting that I, too, am psychic?"

"I was aware of that the first day you came here, sensed you had more than the average person's knowledge, for instance, of what I do. That was another reason I permitted you to do my portrait. Aware of your understanding. Knowing you'd had personal experience with psychic phenomena."

"Yes." He tossed off the last of his wine. "I had."

"You wish to tell me about it now?"

"I don't think so. No . . ."

"Then I'll tell you something more about myself. Since it's too late for you to use any of this in the magazine. I was born with a caul over my face. Today that's believed to be a lucky omen for a child. In ancient times such a child was thought to have supernatural powers. Female babies born with a caul, in some civilizations, were said to be witches and were put to death. Such a child, even today, is thought to have special qualities." She finished her wine and set the glass down.

Ash studied her tranquil face as she folded her hands in front of her on the table.

"I was born in a small town on the Eastern Shore of Maryland. All four of my grandparents had settled in the United States from foreign countries. My grandfathers came from Scotland and Ireland but both my grandmothers were Latin, one from Italy, the other Castilian. All four of them lived into their late nineties, so I knew and loved them. Especially my grandmothers. A girl child is always closer to her female relatives, except for her father." She reached for the champagne bottle as she talked and replenished their glasses. "I had no suspicion, until years afterward, that both my grandmothers were looked upon by some of our neighbors as rather odd. There were stories of their seeing apparitions and making prophecies. I have no personal knowledge of this, only what I was told long after both of them died."

They touched glasses and drank.

"I learned, years later," she continued, "that I had done something incredible when I was only four years old and both my grandmothers were still alive. An aunt I'd never met—my father's youngest sister—was coming to visit us from another town. It was only a matter of fifty miles but there were no cars in those days. The journey had to be made by carriage, with an overnight stop at a hotel. My family had been preparing for Aunt Emma's visit, I suppose, and I must've watched cook baking special cakes and beating the dough for biscuits. Certainly, I'd heard my aunt's name repeated over and over but I'd never seen her. Two days before she was to arrive I danced through the house, from kitchen to parlor, singing three words. 'Auntie Em's dead! Auntie Em's dead!' My dear father was shocked. Wanted to punish me, but my grandmothers dissuaded him. They pointed out that I could have no idea what the word dead meant because no one in our family had died since I was born. Nobody in our town had a phone, but next morning, Papa received a telegram from the railroad depot informing him that his sister had died, after a heart attack, at the precise time I made my announcement. That, apparently, was my first experience with extrasensory perception . . ."

"Amazing."

"When was your first such experience?" she asked quietly.

He set his glass down. "I've never told this to anyone. Even my wife . . ."

"Then it's about time you told somebody!"

"Happened after I left Princeton and came to New York for a course in journalism. Found an apartment near Columbia University . . ."

The telephone buzzed softly.

Sandra turned to stare at it. "Forgive me, Ash, this is urgent."

"Of course."

She picked up the phone. "Yes, Nora?"

Ash watched Sandra's face as she listened to her secretary's voice. An incredible face . . .

"Of course I'll talk to him." She pressed a button. "Good afternoon, Howard. How can I help you?"

A face without a wrinkle. She was seventy-three and slightly overweight, but not fat.

"I understand . . ."

He studied her face as she listened to the voice on the phone—no longer aware of his presence—staring at the polished surface of the table.

The softly brushed silver hair had been red in her youth. Clear blue eyes that always held his attention. You couldn't look away from them. Intelligent face with a generous mouth and prominent nose.

Today she was wearing a simple dress of some light cinnamon-colored material with a single strand of pearls. Her clothes came from Paris and the pearls were real.

There was something comfortable and maternal about her. Was it her hands? They were plump and pink, nails carefully manicured, but they were hands that would be capable of kneading dough. Sandra was more motherly than his own mother.

"What sort of plane will it be?" she asked.

Ash rose from the table, careful not to disturb her. Walked to the open windows with their yellow-and-white summer draperies and looked down into the garden where Miss Cassie was walking on one of the paths.

She sensed his presence and lifted her head. Smiled and nodded before turning into a side path.

"My advice is, quite simply, you must not take that plane."

He turned from the windows, aware of the tone of authority in her normally gentle voice.

"Why not? Just a moment, Howard. Let me focus on this . . ."

Ash froze as she raised her head and closed both eyes. It was as though she was staring through the ceiling. Her face was impassive.

"There's something wrong with that plane. Some mechanical fault I don't understand. It will crash in deep water. Yes! Into the ocean. I see only darkness. Everyone aboard will perish . . ." She opened her eyes. "Do not take that plane, Howard."

He saw that her body was tensing, visibly, as she talked.

"Certainly not. It would be unwise for you to tell anyone else. They wouldn't believe you and would pay no attention to your warning. I will talk to you during the week." She set the phone down, folded her hands on the table and closed her eyes, visibly relaxing.

Ash walked toward her, silently, his eyes on the clasped hands—like a Holbein drawing—and sat at the table again.

Only then did she open her eyes. "You heard, of course . . ."

"Yes."

"What I said must not be repeated."

"Naturally."

"It was one of my clients. An important New York banker who always contacts me before taking any plane trip."

"The illustrious Howard Munger."

"Did I say his name?"

"Only Howard . . ."

"He was flying to Mexico City tomorrow with a group of economic and government specialists to discuss more loans for Central America. That plane will never reach its destination." She sighed. "At least Howard Munger will not be aboard. He's a brilliant man—a good man—and his life is important. To his family and to our country." Glancing toward the open windows. "Miss Cassie's walking in the garden."

"I just saw her down there."

"Something else I never told you. Cassie and I were both christened Cassandra."

"Cassandra? The Greek prophetess . . ."

"My grandmothers must've known something when they selected that name for me. When I came to New York, years ago, I dropped the first three letters of my given name. Kept only Sandra. Nobody would've listened to an astrologer who called herself Cassandra Saunders. Actually, Saunders is the false name. My father's name was Sanderson. I changed that, legally, to Saunders to protect my family. I didn't want any of this in your portrait."

"I understand."

"Cassie never uses her full name unless she's signing a legal document. Miss Cassie is, also, psychic . . ."

"I've discovered that."

"Dear Cassie! She told me, when she applied for the job as my housekeeper, that we had the same name—Cassandra—informed me that she possessed second sight."

"What's that?"

"An old-fashioned American way of saying one has the ability to foresee. She didn't need to tell me. Her first words were 'You need a housekeeper!' and I did. The woman who'd been with me for years had died the previous night . . . You were about to tell me, when the phone interrupted, about your first psychic experience. You'd found an apartment uptown . . ."

"The first night, after my furniture had been moved in, I was exhausted. Slept soundly but, in the night, something wakened me. I opened my eyes and saw the figure of a man sitting in an armchair . . ."

"Saw his face?"

"Not clearly. It was as though I was seeing him through a veil of mist."

"Were you alarmed?"

"Startled, naturally, to find a complete stranger in my apartment. Then I heard his voice. He whispered: 'Help me. Please help me . . .' I told him: 'I can't. I'm sorry. I can't help you.' I turned over and went back to sleep. I've felt guilty about it ever since. Telling him I couldn't help him."

"But there was no possible way you could help him."

"I saw him again, many times, in the two years I lived there. He was always seated and would say the same thing. 'Help me. Please help me . . .'"

"You never learned who he was?"

"The day I moved downtown. When the movers were carrying out my furniture. A neighbor stopped me, in the hall, to ask why I was leaving, and after I'd explained, she told me that the previous tenant had committed suicide in my bedroom."

"Poor soul . . ."

"That was, far as I know, my first psychic experience."

"And there've been others?"

"Oh, yes! It was because of them I was eager to write your portrait for *Metropole*. Wanted to find out and understand what it is you do in astrology and, especially, parapsychology. I learned, rather quickly, that you are absolutely honest."

"You thought I wasn't?"

"I had to be certain. Find out for myself."

"I was aware of that in your questions—your probing—trying to get at the truth. And I think you did. I, too, am always seeking the truth. I convinced you, I hope, that parapsychology is a new and expanding field in which I am a searching and questioning participant."

"You did. But why is it so many psychic phenomena are concerned with death? You've never explained that."

"There is no simple explanation. I can only tell you what I believe."

"Please . . ."

"Psychic phenomena involve both life and death. Equally! For instance, this plane that will crash tomorrow, causing many deaths. I will have saved Howard Munger but there's nothing I could do to save the others. For that matter, I'm not even certain that Howard won't take that flight. I can't prevent his doing so. Can only warn him. The decision must be his." She paused, hands clasped on the table again. "Life and death are like two sides of a playing card. They exist side by side, joined together. I believe it's as simple as that. We set out on the path that, eventually, leads to our own physical death the moment we are born."

"That I understand."

"I believe the psychic world exists around and within this visible world. They constantly touch."

"I keep having a curious experience I wish you would explain . . ."

"What's that?"

"It usually happens early mornings when I'm waking from deep sleep. I'm not completely awake and, suddenly, there's a glowing rectangle—like a small television screen—inside my closed eyelids. I see a sunny street or a brightly lighted room. With people moving about. Some familiar faces, but frequently, people I don't recognize. The first time it happened I saw an outdoor market that looked like Europe. Bright-colored vegetables and flowers. People shouting and laughing. A woman came close to the dark opening as though she was looking into the lens of a camera, but she was staring at me. I'd never seen that market before. Another time it was a deserted courtyard and the entrance to a magnificent old stone mansion with no sign of life. What does it mean? Am I dreaming when I have these visions?"

"You are looking through the window of your mind."

"I don't understand."

"Seeing scenes from your past or your future. Or scenes which you may never see in reality. I've heard of such visions through a window in the mind but have never experienced them myself."

"Enough of my personal experiences with the psychic! I shan't bore you with any more."

"Another time, perhaps." She reached out and patted his left hand. "I'm grateful it was you who wrote my portrait." Turning to study the

Metropole cover again. "I'll be waiting, eagerly, to see what it brings into my life. New people for me to advise and help." She filled their glasses as she talked. "And you'll be starting a new assignment. I saw you in that paneled office, with your associates, when you were told the name of your next subject."

He studied her face as they drank the wine. That open, questing Irish face with the inquisitive blue eyes. In his word-portrait he had described her face as compassionate, constantly observing the human race with anticipation but without prejudice.

Sandra set her glass down. "Your next portrait is, once again, a woman. I saw pictures of her as you walked around that gallery. She has long blond hair but I was unable to recognize her face. It didn't come clear to me . . ."

"I've never, in the past, told anyone the identity of a current portrait assignment. In your case, just this once, I'm going to break my rule not to reveal the name."

"Is that wise?"

"For this portrait I suspect I'll need more help than usual. The subject is, indeed, a woman—a famous woman—but our research department has produced fewer background facts than usual. This woman is constantly in the news—mostly in the business and social sections of the papers—but nothing of a personal nature is ever printed about her. She refuses to give interviews, and photographs are shot only when she's unaware of the camera. I must question as many people as I can find who know her and will talk. That's why I'm going to tell you her name. On the chance you might know something about her. Anything that would help me write her portrait."

"And who is this mysterious lady?"

"Lyli Amadoro . . ." He saw her eyes widen.

"I understand your problem."

"You do know her?"

"No." Sandra hesitated, and when she spoke, her voice was barely audible. "We've never met."

"I was hoping you might've done her horoscope."

"I never discuss the horoscopes with anyone but my staff."

"I'm aware of that."

"I did do Amadoro's."

"But you just said you hadn't met."

"We haven't." She set her wineglass down. "There was a phone call. Last winter. My secretary said a gentleman was calling who claimed to be a personal assistant to Lyli Amadoro. He demanded to speak to me personally. I took the call but he never told me his name. He sounded young, in his thirties, with a deep, rather musical voice—as though he might have trained for the opera—and he, much too obviously, tried to charm me with it. He said Madame Amadoro was aware of my important work in astrology and parapsychology. She'd read my books and followed my daily newspaper columns. Which always surprises me! The prominent people who read the column at breakfast . . . As you know, I don't write the daily column anymore. It has nothing to do with cosmic astrology. It's only a simple guide for the uninitiated. I did write the column years ago, when I was starting out, but for the past ten years my staff has done it for me. Extremely capable young people. And I do check every column for accuracy. My staff does all astrological charts for the general public.

"I only do horoscopes for people I know personally, as well as celebrities and prominent business executives, all of whom must come in for no less than two personal interviews before I consent to do their charts. Everything is based upon ancient principles of astrology, but some of what I do, personally, involves extrasensory perception. I'm unable to do that unless I meet the subject and question him.

"So I explained to Amadoro's assistant that I couldn't do anyone's horoscope without seeing them, in person, for two lengthy interviews in my office. Here in my home. He said that was impossible and tried to persuade me to interview the lady in her own office. I told him I could not talk to anybody at their place of business. Too many interruptions and distractions. He said he would, regretfully, report our conversation to Madame Amadoro."

"That's the last you heard?"

"Oh, no! In half an hour Amadoro herself was on the phone. Saying there were tremendous crises in her business and personal lives and she wanted to know what might develop in the future. I hadn't cared for the operatic sound of her macho assistant and didn't like her seductive voice any better. She begged me to do her horoscope. I explained that I would have to see her here, in my office, and question her about certain facts that it was absolutely necessary for me to know. What I really needed was to observe her in a completely silent room and get the psychic vibrations I must receive from every client before I can begin to function. Without that, it's difficult to go into any depth with predictions for their future."

"I wouldn't be able to write my *Metropole* portraits if I didn't talk to the subjects. Many times. Testing and evaluating them."

"Exactly! Madame Amadoro then began to plead with me. Told me there was a psychic in Paris—Fernand Maudru—who had helped her."

"You'd heard of him?"

"He's a dear friend. The field of parapsychology is not crowded. Most of us know each other and correspond. Fernand's in his eighties but still flies over here every year to see his friends and clients. He's in San Francisco at the moment but he'll be here in two weeks to lecture at Town Hall under the auspices of our Parastro Society."

"Would it be possible for me to meet him? Privately . . ."

"I'm sure that could be arranged."

"I'd like to ask him some questions about Amadoro."

"Fernand would never tell anyone about a client. You or me! But you should see him."

"And, I suppose, you won't tell me anything more about her."

"Lyli Amadoro was not a client. So I can tell you this . . . She offered me ten thousand dollars to do her horoscope. Said she could send me an elaborate printed brochure, containing the important facts of her life, which had been prepared by her own publicity people. She would answer all my questions on the phone.

"I agreed to read the biographical material and said I would attempt a rough preliminary chart from that. My fee would be one thousand dollars. Later, if I agreed to complete her horoscope—if the information in the brochure and from our phone conversations was satisfactory—there would be an additional charge of two thousand dollars. My standard fee for any celebrity.

"The brochure arrived that afternoon with her check for the full amount—three thousand. Such a nuisance! I glanced through the material, which told me nothing of any importance. Saw that it included the date of her birth—which I wondered about—but neither the place nor the time of day. Nora phoned Miss Amadoro and managed to get that information from her secretary after some discussion. I spent the following morning on Lyli Amadoro's preliminary charts but quickly gave up."

"Why?"

"Because it was absolutely impossible to tell her anything about the future. Meticulous birth data is necessary, and I had a feeling she wasn't giving me the true facts. I sent the brochure back, along with her check and a note saying the material wasn't satisfactory. I would be unable to do her horoscope."

"What did she say to that?"

"I never heard from her again."

"What did you learn about her from that brochure and what she told you?"

"Not a thing. All I knew was through psychic perception. It was impossible to tell Lyli Amadoro anything about her future because she had no future."

"What do you mean?"

"The unfortunate woman is, at any moment, about to complete her present life."

"Complete . . . When?"

"I can't tell you that, precisely, because I don't know. There is a void ahead for her. Only emptiness and darkness."

"Within the next three months? While I'm writing her portrait?"

"Possibly. I could see it would be within a year and that was last winter—November—seven months ago."

"Her portrait's to be in our September issue."

"Better work fast, my friend."

"What will be the cause of her death?"

"I was unable to understand when or how it would happen. Only that it appeared to be sudden and violent. Either an accident or . . ." Her voice trailed away. "It might be suicide. Or it could be murder . . ."

chapter three

A TAXI CARRIED HIM UPTOWN, BACK TO THE *METROPOLE* office, but he was unaware of the empty midafternoon streets, reviewing the few facts he'd learned from Sandra.

The possibility of Lyli Amadoro's sudden death would goad him to complete her portrait as quickly as possible. Especially with Sandra predicting it might be suicide or murder. Either way her death would cause an international sensation.

He hadn't met Amadoro but he knew she was going to die.

Not in twenty or thirty years, but within a matter of months. This knowledge would, inevitably, influence how he handled her portrait.

The same blank-faced guards at the information counter looked up as he crossed the deserted atrium with its splashing waterfall. "Back again, Mr. Hendrie?" The older guard made a note of the time on a leather-bound clipboard. "All the others from *Metropole* checked out more than an hour ago."

"Don't tell anyone I'm here." He took the express elevator and when he reached his office locked the door.

Glanced toward the wall of windows as he crossed to his spartan modern desk and saw the green expanse of Central Park far below. That view was the only thing he liked about this sterile air-conditioned compartment, the creation of some unknown decorator who had designed all the *Metropole* interiors. He preferred to do his writing in his small study at home on an old portable rather than on the big electric typewriter which watched him, ominously, from its wheeled metal table as he sat down and stared for a moment at the abstract painting hanging above the sofa. He'd never discovered what it was supposed to represent or replaced it with something more to his own taste. Perhaps a Gaugin or Cézanne reproduction. He hadn't gotten around to that and, very likely, never would.

Ash unlocked his desk and pulled the center drawer open. Lifted out the file folder with the few facts Mandy had dug up on Amadoro and settled down to read the two neatly typed pages again.

Mandy was right. This was the worst job her department had ever done on a proposed portrait subject. Not their fault, of course, but a sure indication that he was in for a difficult month getting all the necessary background material on Amadoro before he could start writing.

He'd read these notes and checked each clipping before he went downtown to see Sandra, but he studied them again, even more carefully. Making his own notes on a pad.

There was no intrusive sound to disturb him. The low hum of the air-conditioning was, fortunately, as familiar as his own pulse.

When he finished studying the final clipping—Amadoro wearing a bikini, with an unidentified man in bathing trunks, on the deck of a yacht the caption said was anchored in the Baie des Anges —he swiveled his leather armchair to face the electric typewriter and began to type out his notes in a more compact form on a sheet of paper.

He pulled his typed list from the typewriter and read what he had typed.

    Lyli Amadoro—age 43
    Born 1944—New London, Conn.
    real name—Leola Martin
    father—Hap Martin
    mother—Glenda Martin
    marriages:
    1—1960—Toby Towson
    2—1964—Lord Robert Craydon
    3—1978—Conte Alfredo Amadoro
    maintains homes: New York,
      London, Paris
    owns condo—New York—
      59th and Park
    office—Amadoro Associates—
      56th and Fifth

separate suites for her many
enterprises
including:
  Lyli Cosmetics
  Parfums Amadoro
  Lyli de Paris (fashions)
  Lyli de Venezia (fashions)
  Amadoro Motors (British)
  Amadoro Management (real estate)

He went over the other information he had stored in his mind.

Amadoro's parents still lived in New London. Father was Happy Martin, who'd been a football star, and her mother, Glenda, a New York actress. Father, for several years, with Wall Street brokerage. Retired and moved to Connecticut before birth of daughter. Only child, Leola, attended public school in New London, where she met first husband, Toby Towson, scion of old New England family. His mother, Clarissa Towson, eccentric socialite; father, Walter Towson, millionaire. Toby Towson drowned, swept overboard in storm from family yacht. Leola inherited fortune. Married, three years later, to Lord Robert Craydon, British, owner of famed Craydon Castle and founder of Craydon Motors. Leola lived in England until Craydon was killed testing a racing car. Inherited second fortune. Began to invest in American and foreign corporations. Kept town house in London, pied-à-terre in Paris. Established fashion house—Lyli de Paris—with woman designer. Married third husband in Venice. Conte Alfredo Amadoro. Lived in palazzo and established Lyli de Venezia fashion house. Count Amadoro died in skiing accident and Lyli Amadoro got a third fortune. Find out when and why she changed her name to Lyli . . .

All three husbands died in accidents. Look into that. Was Lyli with them when they died?

She had returned to New York after death of third husband and never married again. Always seen in public with extremely handsome men. She was on the boards of many important corporations. Recently organized international consortium, Amadoro Management, dealing in real estate, including hotels and office buildings. Possibly the richest woman in America. No record of any children . . .

He closed the file folder and locked it in the drawer again. Folded his typed list and slipped that into his wallet.

Amadoro led an unusually discreet private life, in spite of her constant public appearances. The press, apparently, never got close enough to question her. Who were the men in her life now? Was there one special man?

In the morning he would have his secretary arrange an appointment with Amadoro for midafternoon. He'd learned, from past experience, that women executives were always more agreeable after lunch.

Checking his desk clock, he saw that it was past four-thirty.

He didn't want to stop by the apartment at this hour because Mara was always nervous before every performance. She would have a bath followed by a nap, and Rosie would serve her supper on a tray. Sunday night she left for the theater in a taxi around six-thirty for an eight o'clock curtain. He would pick Mara up at ten-thirty and drive her somewhere for a quiet supper. She was always hungry after a performance. Remember to take a copy of *Metropole* to show her.

Better catch a cab to the garage and pick up his car. He would need it tomorrow morning to drive around the city, digging up more information about Amadoro.

Five hours to kill before he met Mara, but he was in no mood to see anyone else. Most of their friends spent Sunday floating from brunch to cocktails to dinner on a rising flood of alcohol.

What about a movie? He wasn't really in the mood for that.

Why not drive out to the end of Long Island? Park somewhere and sit for an hour staring at the ocean. Go over the few facts he knew about Amadoro and work out a tentative plan of attack for tomorrow's first meeting. Decide how to approach this elusive beauty . . .

Afterward drive back to Manhattan and stop by the apartment for a nap and shower. Get there around seven, after his wife had departed for the theater.

That's what he would do! The ocean air should clear his head and relax him.

In less than an hour he was parked at the edge of an unfamiliar dirt road, watching sailboats skimming back and forth.

Sat there, in the cream-colored Jag, for more than an hour. Thinking about Amadoro. Still planning his line of questioning.

Finally, locking the car, he walked along the shore, filling his lungs with fresh air.

A few old men fishing, teenagers running with a sheep dog.

He kept walking for half an hour, then returned to the Jag and got out the copy of *Metropole* from the glove compartment. Shook it out from the white envelope and smiled as he glanced at Sandra's face on the cover before settling down to read her portrait. Read it from start to finish, for the first time, without any interruptions.

This had to be the best of all his portraits.

He was smiling when he pushed the magazine back, in its envelope, into the glove compartment and, feeling relaxed and pleased, turned his car around and headed back to Manhattan.

At ten-thirty, he slowed the Jag across Forty-eighth Street toward the Biltmore Theater, through a rush of after-theater traffic, past several empty parking spaces. Probably occupied, all evening, by cars belonging to people who had been inside watching his beautiful wife. He pulled up to the curb and got out. Locked the car and strode down the familiar alley toward the stage entrance where some of the actors were already coming out.

"Mr. Hendrie? How lovely to see you!"

"Good evening." He wasn't certain of their names but recognized the ancient British character actress who played his wife's aunt in the comedy. "How'd it go tonight?"

"Full house. Your sweet wife got a new laugh she'd never found before."

"That should put her in a good mood for supper."

"I should hope so, dear boy! Enjoy yourselves." She lurched on her way, trailing perfume.

Ash went inside, past the doorman, toward the stairs.

"Evening, Mr. Hendrie! The wife's in her dressing room."

"Thanks." He went up the steps through a haze of mixed perfumes. It still gave him pleasure, the excitement had never diminished, visiting backstage after a performance. He knocked on the third door in the familiar narrow corridor.

"Come! I'm sufficiently decent."

Ash swung the door open and saw Mara hunched before the dressing-table mirror, rimmed with glaring bulbs, peering at her enchanting face as she removed a false eyelash from one of her blue eyes. "Ready for supper, my sweet?"

"Two minutes!" She pulled off the other lash, dropped it into a small box and wiped her eyes with tissue.

"That face is more beautiful than ever." He stooped to kiss the top of her head, breathing deeply of the subtle perfume she always wore.

"Wish I could do something about my nose."

"What the devil's wrong with it now?"

"Same thing. I've always thought it was too small!"

"Any larger and it would get in the way of things."

"I suppose . . ." She shrugged out of her robe and let it fall over the back of the chair as she rose from the dressing table.

His eyes slid down her delicious pink body, from the firm breasts to the graceful legs to the delicious feet in scuffy old slippers. "Lovely! Head to toe!"

She giggled. "You've seen it all before."

"Each time more enchanting!"

"Not so bad yourself. Even fully clothed." She held her face up, lips puckered, golden-red hair flowing over her bare shoulders.

He leaned down and kissed her, firmly and tenderly.

"Be ready in one minute." She slipped behind a screen.

Ash sat on the tufted pink satin chaise and inspected himself in the mirrors. Saw that he needed a haircut. "Good show tonight?"

"Had so many laughs we ran two minutes longer than usual."

"Passed that English actress, plays your aunt, as I came in. She said you had a laugh you'd never gotten before."

"No fault of hers. The bitch killed one of my best lines. God deliver me from aging British character actors. Their faintest whisper can be heard above a thunder of applause. It's all those years they spend in rep. I plan to have a little chat with the old girl. Oh! How stupid of me." Her face appeared around the edge of the screen, hair swinging free. "How was your day?"

"Just about perfect."

"Everyone liked the new portrait?"

"They applauded when I arrived."

"Congratulations!" She vanished behind the screen again. "When are you going to tell me whose portrait it is this time?"

"At dinner. I have a virgin copy in the car. You'll be one of the first, as usual, to see it."

"And you got your next assignment?"

"Start on it tomorrow. Tracking down all the intimate facts and secrets of the lady."

"I won't ask who it is. Knowing you won't tell me."

"Matter of fact, this time I just might."

"I don't believe it!"

"Phoned the Russian Tea Room. Made a reservation for eleven."

"Blini with caviar! You are a darling." She appeared from behind the screen. "Shall we go?"

Jumping up, he saw that she was wearing a summer dress he'd never seen before. Some sort of tan material with a rippling skirt, no jewelry, white slippers and carrying a white purse. "You look delectable." He kissed her on the cheek, before opening the door, and watched her legs under the flickering skirt as he followed her through the corridor.

As they went down the steps he wondered where Lyli Amadoro might be at this moment . . .

They entered Central Park through the Columbus Circle entrance, leaving the neon glare of the city behind.

Mara leaned back against the seat and stared at the stars.

As the Jag slowed along the curves, toward the Mall, they didn't bother to talk.

He always drove around the park before taking Mara to dinner.

Ash knew that his wife was unwinding after her performance. Should he tell her the name of his next portrait subject? She might have heard some Broadway gossip about Amadoro. He needed more information about the dame. Even gossip. There was, usually, some factual basis for gossip.

Mara would read the new portrait after she went to bed tonight. Fortunately they had separate bedrooms. In the beginning that had been because she liked to study her lines for every new play in bed and most nights, after a performance, was unable to sleep, so she read mystery novels until three in the morning. He, however, needed his sleep and he was unable to close his eyes if there was any light in the room.

He realized that he was hungry and looked forward to dinner. Mara devoured an enormous breakfast at noon but didn't eat again until after her performance.

Sandra Saunders had told him she was giving a small party tonight to celebrate her portrait on the cover of *Metropole*. Probably for the members of her family who shared that old mansion on Gramercy Park. He'd never found out how many there were but he'd met one sister, a nephew and a cousin and was aware that several other people he'd seen in the halls—faceless shadows who spoke with soft Southern accents —must be relatives.

"What are you thinking?" Mara whispered, sitting up and snuggling closer.

"My thoughts were wandering." He glanced beyond the trees to his left, as he turned the car south, and recognized familiar buildings on Fifth Avenue. "Hungry?"

"Ravenous."

"Me, too."

"The air seems cooler."

"Always cooler on the Fifth Avenue side of the park."

She giggled. "You mean upper-class apartments get a better type of air?"

"Always!"

"You are a snob."

"Now and again." He saw the dark bulk of the museum ahead and realized they would soon be passing their own apartment.

"Not many people in the park . . ."

"Probably thousands—happily mugging and robbing—but you can't see them."

"You haven't watched the park lately, from our windows, through those ancient binoculars . . ."

"Matter of fact, I had a brief look this evening. After my shower."

"You must see the damnedest things."

"Frequently."

"That's voyeurism."

"I prefer to call it investigative research." He glanced at the familiar row of cooperatives they were passing on Fifth. "If you look, quickly, you can see our lighted windows."

"Good to know Rosie left the lights on and, hopefully, turned down our beds. Makes me feel secure."

"I always want you to feel secure. Not enough security in this world. Very little in Central Park . . ."

He turned on Fifty-seventh and managed to park the Jag near the restaurant.

Their customary table was waiting and as vodka was served with a platter of pirozhki they glanced around, looking for familiar faces. Mara gave small waves to theatrical acquaintances and Ash nodded to several people he knew.

The pirozhki were hot and crisp, the vodka ice-cold.

Ash ordered supper. Blini with caviar, to be followed by Cotelettes Kiev with salad and a bottle of 1973 Perrier-Jouet.

And, as they drank their vodka, Mara asked again, "Who is it this time? Tell me before I collapse with anticipation. Who's on the cover of the new *Metropole?*"

"See for yourself." He picked up the white envelope from the table where he had dropped it as they arrived. Pulled out the magazine and handed it to her.

She stared at the rich colors of the painted portrait. "I still don't know who it is." Reading the caption under the picture. "*'Metropole* portrait of the month—Sandra Saunders!' The astrologer?"

"She's much more than an astrologer."

"I've always wanted to know more about her. One of the actors in our show belongs to the Parastro Society. He's always talking about Sandra Saunders and handing out literature from the Society. I've even read some of it."

"You never told me that."

"I don't tell you half the things that happen backstage." She leafed through the magazine searching for the written portrait. "What do you think of the lady yourself? Did you like her or detest her?"

"I liked her. Tremendously."

"You don't believe in what she does, do you? All this astrology and parapsychology . . ."

"I didn't at first."

"But you do now?" She put the magazine down. "Really?"

"Yes. I do."

"I am surprised." Her hands moved, as she talked, with the considered gestures of the professional actress. "The famous investigative reporter. Always suspicious and unconvinced . . ."

"This is a most convincing lady. In a month of interviews—during which everything she told me was double-checked by Mandy and our research people—we were unable to disprove anything Sandra told me about her work. She's been a psychic since she was a child."

"You believe in psychic phenomena?"

"Long before I met Sandra Saunders. One day I will tell you . . ."

"Believe in life after death?"

"I've always believed there's something. Had no idea what. Sandra's convinced me even further."

"I hope she's right." She hesitated, no longer smiling. "I'd hate to think, my love, that when I die I would never see your handsome face again."

"I'm convinced, now, there is indeed something more after this life."

"Maybe I'd better join the Parastro Society and get all their literature."

"I'll arrange for us both to join. Also, I'd like to have Sandra do your horoscope, now that she's done mine. I'd like you to meet her."

"You've never said that before, about any of the people you've profiled for *Metropole*."

"She's the only one who became a friend."

"Why don't we take her out to dinner?"

"We could. Although I think she'd prefer dining at the apartment."

"Lovely! Rosie can plan one of her special dinners and . . ."

Ash looked up as a small procession brought their first course. Two waiters served the blini while a third opened their wine.

They sighed, happily, as they tasted the first blin with its center of sour cream and caviar.

Mara spoke first. "And tomorrow you start on your new portrait."

"That's right."

"You've never in the past even hinted who any of your portraits were . . ."

"This new one, I suspect, will be more difficult than any of the others. I anticipate problems."

"Why do you say that?"

"Because, first of all, Mandy Kwong's been able to give me only two brief pages of background material on the lady."

"That's unusual, isn't it?"

"Never happened before. She always came up with a thick folder of facts, a biography in depth, for each previous subject. Nothing like that this time."

"Is this an unknown person?"

"This dame's a world celebrity. Frequently called the most beautiful woman in New York."

"Meryl Streep?"

"Certainly not! For her *Metropole* portrait Tim Carrington and the editorial staff have decided to call her the most beautiful woman in the world."

"Sophia Loren!"

"This woman's not an actress."

"The most beautiful woman in the world? But not an actress . . ."

"There are several beautiful women who are not actresses, you know . . ."

"I can't think of any."

He finished his last blin with a final swallow of wine.

"Your pauses are dramatic, but much too long. Who is this international beauty?"

"Lyli Amadoro."

"Should've guessed, when you said Mandy couldn't come up with much information. I know practically nothing about the lady. I've heard she refuses to meet anyone from the press."

"She'll see me."

"When?"

"Tomorrow."

"Good luck, my love . . ."

chapter four

ASH AIMED THE JAG DOWN A CURVING RAMP TOWARD AN unfamiliar but brightly lighted subterranean garage, then followed a line of red neon arrows to a booth where a uniformed attendant sat beside a computer.

"Floor, sir?"

"Ninetieth." He brought out his wallet.

"Park anywhere on this level."

"How much?"

"No charge, sir. You're going to Amadoro Associates?"

"Right." He slipped the wallet back into his pocket.

"They own the building. No charge for their visitors."

"Which elevator?"

"Straight ahead. Express elevator to the ninetieth floor. It's got Amadoro Associates in big letters."

"Thanks." He followed more red arrows until he saw a neon sign—"Elevators"—and parked in the nearest vacant space. Walked back toward a brightly lighted marble corridor with rows of elevators on either side where several well-dressed businessmen waited, some with leather briefcases, as their clones stepped out from elevators which they entered.

The elevator with AMADORO ASSOCIATES in bronze letters above it was in the center. He was aware that some of the business types watched him as he pressed the Up button and the elevator doors opened.

Stepped inside and saw there were only two buttons—Up and Down—so this elevator didn't stop at any other floors. He pressed the Up button.

The doors closed silently and he felt a suspicion of motion as the elevator began to rise.

Glancing at the mirrored walls, he noticed an antique brocade-upholstered bench at the rear and was surprised to see a small brown teddy bear in a corner of the seat.

He was looking forward to this interview with mixed emotions. There had been no difficulty when Miss Lundborg called for an afternoon appointment. She had spoken to Amadoro's secretary, male, who had said that Madame would see him at two o'clock.

He'd spent the morning in his office, studying his notes on the lady. He couldn't make a move in any direction until he talked to her. As yet he had no idea where he would start his personal investigation after he questioned her.

He had lunched at 21, alone, where he chatted with several casual acquaintances and planned his first questions for Amadoro.

Several people had already seen the new issue of *Metropole*—there was a special list of influential New Yorkers who received advance copies, by messenger, Monday morning and there had been a dozen calls before he left the office for lunch, complimenting him on the Saunders portrait.

Mara had roused him from a sound sleep last night to tell him it was the best portrait he'd written. He had thanked her, only half awake, and gone back to sleep.

The elevator doors opened silently, although there had been no sensation of coming to a stop.

He stepped out into an enormous high-ceilinged foyer where a sleek young man sat at a glass-and-metal desk reading a book. The desk was placed at the far end of the foyer in front of a row of tall plants in huge white pots, their green leaves reflected in the mirrored wall, behind them, in which he glimpsed himself and the closing doors of the elevator.

The young man looked up briefly, checked something on the desk, then returned to his book.

A stark gray-and-black-striped rug led from the elevator to the desk.

Ash glanced at his wristwatch as he followed the stripes. One minute past two. He never liked to arrive early for any appointment.

The long side walls, he realized, were sheathed in polished metal—probably aluminum—with elegant sofas upholstered in violet silk. The effect was austerely handsome. Three sofas against each wall with a low aluminum table in front of each, holding fresh flowers in crystal bowls and a selection of magazines. He was pleased to see copies of last month's *Metropole*. That, surely, had to be a good omen.

He saw, as he came closer, that the tanned young man at the desk was reading a novel with a lurid jacket. Macho type. Unusually handsome, with curly black hair and broad shoulders. Wearing a light gray summer suit, white shirt and Bronzini cravat. His hands, holding the book, were surprisingly large and muscular. The desk was bare except for an appointment chart with a list of typed names.

The young man, finally, looked up from his book and smiled, revealing perfect teeth. "Mr. Hendrie?"

"That's right."

"I'll find out if Madame Amadoro is free. She's having a busy afternoon, as usual." He reached down to lift a pale gray cordless phone from an invisible resting place and pushed a button. "Won't you sit down, Mr. Hendrie?"

"I prefer to stand." So her employees called the lady Madame.

"As you wish." Holding the phone closer to his mouth. "Foyer reception. Paolo speaking. Mr. Hendrie's here." He listened, briefly, to the response. "Thank you." Returning the phone to its hiding place and rising. "Madame will see you in a moment. Her appointments are running late again."

Ash moved away from the desk to avoid further conversation and stood with his back to the young man, who was surprisingly short when he stood up. Glanced around the foyer again and felt a brief sensation of claustrophobia. The metal walls seemed to be pressing toward him.

"No! I won't, Mommie! I won't . . ." A child's voice.

Ash turned as a small boy with curly black hair raced across the foyer toward the young man behind the desk, followed by a rather drab young woman. They had come through an opening in the mirrored wall where one section had slid open. Mother and boy seemed out of place in this luxurious setting. As she hurried in pursuit of her son, Ash glimpsed a long inner corridor before the panel closed again.

"Wait, Fredo," the young woman ordered. "Wait for me. You hear?"

"Want my teddy bear!" The boy darted behind the desk and kicked the swarthy young man in the leg. "You took my teddy bear!"

"No, Fredo!" She pursued him around the desk. "No!"

"I haven't seen your teddy bear," the young man protested.

"I'll punish you!" The boy's voice was hoarse with rage. "I'm a demon! I'll set fire to you!"

"Stop this, Fredo!" his mother commanded. "Stop it!"

"That's all right. No harm done." The young man continued to smile as he retreated from the small fists.

"Did your son lose a teddy bear?" Ash asked.

The boy looked at him. His lips were smiling but his eyes were fierce.

The young woman noticed Ash for the first time. "He's always losing his toys and he makes such a fuss."

He saw that she had a pale face and long brown hair. "I noticed, as I came up just now, someone had left a teddy bear in the elevator."

"Oh! Thank you." She smiled. "You see, Fredo? Teddy's in the elevator. Right where you left him."

"Want my teddy bear!" The boy scampered across the foyer toward the elevator.

"Wait, Fredo! Wait!" She hurried after him as he stood on his toes to reach the elevator button.

The doors opened and the boy saw his toy as he rushed inside. "Teddy! You ran away!" He picked up the bear by one leg and banged it against the bench. "Bad bear!"

The mother followed him into the elevator and the doors closed.

Ash turned to the young man behind the desk. "That child's a monster. Is he always like that?"

"Sometimes worse."

"Who are they?"

"The mother used to work here, I'm told. She comes back to visit one of the employees. I think there's something mentally wrong with the boy. Please, sir, forget I said that."

"I didn't hear a word!"

A buzzer sounded discreetly.

The young man reached for the phone. "Foyer reception, Paolo speaking." Listening briefly, his eyes on Ash. "Right away, sir." He put the phone down and pressed a button under the edge of his desk. The mirrored panel slid open again. "Madame Amadoro will see you, Mr. Hendrie."

"Thanks."

"There will be someone to escort you."

As he walked through the opening he had the curious sensation of stepping through a looking glass into a strange and unfamiliar world. Hesitated, facing the seemingly endless corridor.

No windows here, but the paneled walls glowed with soft light from a row of crystal chandeliers down the center holding tiny bulbs instead of candles. Pairs of closed doors on either side which, like the walls, were carved from some pale brown wood. Between the doors were console tables with pottery urns holding fresh flowers that were reflected in gilded antique mirrors.

Hurrying toward him, silently, on the rose-and-green Aubusson carpet was another muscular young man in a gray business suit.

"Mr. Hendrie?"

"Yes."

"Madame Amadoro regrets that she kept you waiting."

"Quite all right." Walking down the corridor, beside him, he saw that the youth's hair was light brown and he was even more handsome than the first. He wondered if Lyli Amadoro selected them personally. An executive's assistants revealed much about the personality of the executive—male or female. As did the physical surroundings. This French corridor was curiously ambivalent after the aluminum-sheathed foyer. The lady's private office should be even more revealing. Probably Louis XIV!

"Here we are, Mr. Hendrie." The young man opened one of a pair of doors and motioned for him to enter.

Ash strode into an attractive office with floor-to-ceiling windows which, to his surprise, was extremely masculine. More paneled wood, only this was dark. Comfortable English antiques with black leather chairs and a Chippendale table-desk. The man rising from the desk was even more handsome than the others. Slightly older, with gray hair, wearing a light tweed jacket. He should, certainly, have a British accent.

"Ah! *Bon jour*, Monsieur Hendrie. Madame Amadoro has been a longtime admirer of your fascinating portraits in *Metropole*."

"That's pleasant news." The accent was French, Parisian French.

"And so have I, monsieur. I am Clement Marnat, one of Madame's personal assistants." He came around the leather-topped desk and led Ash toward a pair of inner doors. "We go through here. You can appreciate that Madame's time is limited. She is happy to be able to give you half an hour."

"That will be more than sufficient, I think, for my first visit."

The Frenchman opened one of the doors and bowed for him to enter.

Ash had expected another office, but this was an oblong passage, low-ceilinged with walls covered in yellow silk above masses of white and purple flowers blooming in sunken marble basins. No windows, but overhead spots were aimed at the blooms. The effect was somehow joyous and lively. "How beautiful!"

"A bit theatrical for my taste, but Madame says the flowers are intended to welcome visitors." He walked ahead, across the black-and-white tiled floor, toward a pair of inner doors. *"Un moment."* He knocked, lightly, then swung both doors open. Stepped inside and bowed. "Monsieur Hendrie is here, Madame."

"Mr. Hendrie! Come in, please . . ." The voice was attractive in timbre, lilting and enticing.

Ash entered, passing the Frenchman, and found himself in a large windowless room—not an office—resembling an intimate theater, that seemed to float in diffused light. Hesitating, facing the incredibly beautiful woman seated at another modern desk. He walked toward her slowly, without speaking, as though drawn by some curious force, aware only of her long blond hair and exquisite smiling face. The air, he realized, was scented by the same perfume she had worn in that theater lobby.

"So you are Ashton Hendrie . . ." Gesturing toward a pair of massive armchairs facing her desk. "Do sit down, Mr. Hendrie."

He grasped the thick upholstered back of one cubelike chair to push it forward but discovered it wouldn't move. Either too heavy or secured to the floor. He sank down and found it comfortable but too low. Also, he would prefer to sit closer to this woman he'd come to interview. Seated, facing her, he realized that her stark blond wood desk was bare. It stood on a low platform, only a few inches high and barely noticeable, but it allowed her to look down on all visitors. And, for the first time, he noticed an enormous Irish wolfhound stretched out in the shadow at her feet. The dog's eyes were unfriendly.

"Haven't we met before, Mr. Hendrie?"

"I believe not . . ." Could she have remembered his face from that theater lobby? "The members of your staff who admitted me called you Madame. Is that what you prefer—Madame Amadoro?"

"Only in Paris." She laughed, tossing her golden hair back over one shoulder. "In London I am Madam Amadoro and in Rome I'm Contessa Amadoro, but in New York I prefer to be just—Lyli. And you? I'm told your friends call you Ash . . ."

"That's right." She'd been checking on him!

"I was surprised and, of course, intrigued when I learned that Ashton Hendrie of *Metropole* magazine had requested an appointment . . ."

As she spoke he decided that she looked much younger than the age given to him by the research department. Their report said Amadoro was forty-three, but she appeared to be at least ten years younger. The pale yellow hair hanging straight down, like lustrous silk, was extremely feminine. Her face was as carefully made up as that of an actress. Long artificial lashes over the most amazing eyes he'd ever seen. They were ice-green.

". . . and, of course, I've read *Metropole* since its first issue. That was, I believe, five years ago."

"Correct."

"You joined the staff, at the start, to write the monthly portrait feature . . ."

"Along with two other investigative reporters."

"But yours are the most outstanding. I look, each month, to see if Ashton Hendrie has written the latest portrait. When you are the author, I read it immediately."

"That's extremely flattering."

"I never flatter anyone." She smiled, her eyes searching his face. "I say precisely what I think and what I mean. At all times."

He realized, as she talked, that she was wearing a tailored summer suit made of some soft violet material and a white blouse. A silver chain encrusted with emeralds circled her throat. Under the desk her legs were in violet slacks over high-heeled white leather boots.

". . . and I especially enjoyed the latest issue of *Metropole* with your portrait of Sandra Saunders."

"How could you have read that? Subscribers don't receive the magazine until tomorrow."

"I like to see things ahead of other people and I usually have ways to do that."

"I'm sure you do."

"I was very interested in your latest portrait because I'm an admirer of Sandra Saunders. I read her column every morning."

"You believe in astrology?"

"I do not disbelieve . . . I am, by the way, a Scorpio."

"You know Sandra Saunders personally?"

"Unfortunately—" She hesitated. "We've never met."

He waited, thinking she was about to say that she had talked to Sandra on the phone, but she didn't bother to elaborate.

"I'm particularly intrigued by *Metropole* because you maintain offices in several foreign cities, and since I have business interests in those same cities, I am especially interested in your foreign editions. Many of my international companies advertise in *Metropole*."

"Do they? I wasn't aware." As she named several of those companies—some unfamiliar—he continued to study her face. The delicate nose and sensuous lips. The decidedly firm line of the jaw did not mar but accentuated her beauty.

". . . and so I was curious when I learned that you had asked for an appointment. Flattered that you are here. Still wondering why . . ."

He saw that she was waiting to hear his reason for this visit. Aware of the waves of sensuality the dame projected without moving a finger.

"You're an extremely attractive man, Mr. Hendrie . . ."

"I was just thinking how beautiful you are."

"Are you married?"

"For the past six years." He was distracted by an image of Lyli Amadoro in bed . . .

"Happily married?"

"Extremely."

"Lucky you!"

"My wife is Mara Moore. The actress . . ."

"I've seen her on the stage. She's quite lovely."

"I think so."

"I've had three husbands. Happiness survived, each time, for less than a year. All my husbands, fortunately, were accident-prone. I didn't have to divorce them. You still haven't told me why you're here."

"*Metropole* wants me to write a portrait of Lyli Amadoro for our September issue." He saw her straighten in the chair.

The dog growled softly under the desk.

"I was afraid this might be what you wanted. That's why I consented to meet the man who has written all those clever portraits. Your subtlety and wit intrigue me. Your knowledge of human nature is extraordinary! Each portrait brings out facets of character which are not evident in the public persona of your subjects. Many of them have been acquaintances, but your portraits were incredibly revealing. I saw them more clearly for the first time."

"You are known to the public and to the press as the most beautiful woman in New York."

She shrugged. "I could name a dozen women more beautiful than I. My so-called beauty bores me."

"*Metropole* plans to name you the most beautiful woman in the world."

She laughed. "But that's ridiculous!"

"It was the consensus of our editorial board. I wasn't even present. However, now I have seen you, I'm in complete agreement."

"I could name twenty women in Paris much more beautiful than I. My beauty, such as it is, has never truly interested me. When I was young and first came to New York, there were some well-intentioned persons who urged me to become a fashion model. I was more interested in the corporations which hired those models to advertise their products. I studied their pouty faces and skinny bodies in the pages of *Vogue* and analyzed the layout of each advertisement.

"Today I am a director of many of those corporations as well as chairperson of Amadoro Associates. And those models? Long since vanished! There's a new crop of empty faces every year.

"I discovered, at an early age, the one thing I wanted from life was money and decided the only way I could achieve that quickly was to marry a wealthy man. I managed to capture not one but three! Today I have a chain of Amadoro Boutiques in every major city. Branches of Lyli de Paris in London and New York, with one of my favorite young designers in charge of each. Every department store sells Parfums Amadoro. This year Amadoro Motors introduced Lyli One—the first luxury car designed especially for women—and next year will bring out Lyli Two. There's much more! At the moment, for instance, I'm creating a line of gourmet health foods—items which I, personally, find delicious—to be called Cuisine Lyli. Healthy but appetizing foods I eat myself . . ."

As she talked, animated and vivacious, Ash studied her face more carefully. Searching for the human being behind the mask. It was, indeed, an enchanting face. But, suddenly, he heard Sandra's voice. "It might be suicide. Or it could be murder . . ." Was it possible that this vital creature's life was in jeopardy? Within a few months!

Sandra must be wrong. She had told him during their early interviews that her predictions were not always accurate.

He recalled, as he analyzed Amadoro's face, a poem by some obscure French poet he had read years ago.

> She wore a mask of beauty
> But the lips dripped venom
> And her eyes held death . . .

Why had he remembered that now?

He looked at her eyes, twin pools of cold green, then at her lips, those soft pink lips, smiling as she talked.

AMADORO 49

". . . and, in addition to my personal companies, I serve on the board of directors for several international consortiums. I could never have achieved all this without marrying three very rich men and inheriting their fortunes. But I am boring you with this talk of business."

"Certainly not! In fact, I should like to question you, at much greater length, about your career in the world of international finance." He rose from the heavy armchair. "You are reputed to be one of the richest women in the United States."

"I wouldn't know about that."

"Our research people came up with the fact that you're on the boards of more major corporations than any other woman in the history of Wall Street."

"Your research people are already investigating me?"

The dog growled again.

"That's customary. To research the subject of any proposed portrait. Before I start writing."

"Please sit down, Mr. Hendrie."

"I'm more comfortable standing, if you don't mind. Prefer to think on my feet. Especially in these preliminary sessions . . ."

"Sit down, Mr. Hendrie." Her voice was sharp.

The dog barked.

"Very well. If it disturbs you."

"It does."

He returned to the chair but sat on an arm, facing her.

"You said 'preliminary sessions' . . ."

"Yes."

"There will be no preliminary or any other sessions." She continued to smile. "This is our only session. I do not wish to have my portrait in *Metropole*. Even written by Ashton Hendrie."

"Can't I persuade you? Convince you . . ."

"That would be quite impossible. I'm honored that *Metropole* would wish to print my portrait—flattered that you would be the one to write it—but I do not wish to have my portrait in any magazine. At this moment or at any foreseeable time in the future."

He knew that she meant what she was saying. The words were spoken calmly and coldly, without emotion. He kept his own voice low, his words precise. "I will write your portrait, even without your consent, and it will appear in the September issue of *Metropole* as scheduled."

"There's nothing I can do to stop you. I would not attempt to do so, legally, because that would only bring the most unwelcome sort of publicity to me and my associates."

"Then at least we don't have to worry about libel."

"Will your portrait be libelous, Mr. Hendrie?"

"We have never been accused of libel with any of our portraits. I would not wish to write anything that would displease you or do anything to detract from your public image. It's an exquisitely elegant image."

"It's been delightful meeting you, Mr. Hendrie. I'm honored that you wished to add my portrait to your gallery and regret my inability to comply."

"No chance you might reconsider?"

"None."

"Pardon, Madame." The Frenchman's voice came, softly, from an invisible speaker.

"Yes?" She glanced toward the dim ceiling, where the speakers must be hidden.

"Your next appointment is in five minutes."

"Mr. Hendrie is leaving. You can show him out."

Ash rose from the arm of the chair and walked toward her but stopped as the dog growled again and Amadoro moved back in her chair, leaving both arms outstretched, her hands flat on the desk. "This is a great disappointment. My inability to persuade you to cooperate in the preparation of your portrait."

"But you're still going to write it?"

"I am." He saw that both her forefingers were silently tapping the polished surface of the desk.

"I will send an immediate directive to all employees. Advise them that *Metropole* plans to do this story. Warn them that anyone who talks to you or any other representative of your magazine, if discovered, will be discharged. Without warning or discussion and without references. I will explain that I, personally, do not wish to have such a portrait printed in *Metropole* or any other publication."

He hesitated, before turning to leave. "I suppose this has all been taped."

"Naturally."

"Even so, I must ask you one more question. What are you trying to hide?" He saw her straighten, her forefingers no longer tapping.

"I have nothing to hide from anyone." The green eyes flashed and her voice was harsh.

The dog growled, deep in his throat.

Ash turned, suddenly, and strode across the silent room.

One of the doors had been opened and the Frenchman was waiting outside.

He didn't glance back at the woman seated on the low platform designed to put her above any visitor who occupied one of those low chairs. She could look down on them without their noticing.

Well! He had noticed. And she hadn't liked it when he stood up.

He wondered what she was hiding from the public. Whatever it was, he would find her secret and expose it in his portrait.

Ash was seething as he went through the open door.

Amadoro was, certainly, the most beautiful woman he'd ever seen.

Unfortunately, after a single encounter, he detested the bitch.

chapter five

HE HURRIED THROUGH THE ENTRANCE CORRIDOR, BACK at *Metropole*—avoiding the eyes of employees he passed but nodding if anyone spoke—straight toward the oak door at the end. Went in, leaving it ajar, heading for Carrington's secretary, who sat at her desk talking into a phone, past a distinguished-looking man seated on a sofa, his Gucci portfolio beside him. Paused at the desk as Miss Crevani looked up.

"Hold on a moment, please." Placing a hand over the mouthpiece and swiveling her chair to face him. "We tried to reach you earlier."

"Is Tim free?"

"There's someone with him. I'll tell him you're—"

"Ask him to call me when he has a moment. I'll be in my office."

"Shouldn't be too long."

He turned to leave as she resumed her telephone conversation, closing the door and hurrying down the side corridor to his own office.

His secretary, Greta Lundborg—serenely calm as a Nordic dawn—looked up from her typing when he burst in. "How'd it go?"

"Amadoro won't talk. Tell Mandy and Cort I must see them."

She reached for a phone.

"Any calls?"

"Carrington. Half an hour ago."

"Crevani just told me. He'll be calling again."

"Nothing else urgent." She began to dial.

He continued past her into his office, but instead of sitting at his desk went to the windows and looked down at the peaceful green expanse of Central Park. A breeze was moving through the trees, its presence visible west to east, making the young leaves dance. His view of the park always calmed him when he had a problem.

AMADORO

He'd never felt so completely discouraged about any portrait subject in the past. Amadoro was the first to refuse him. And she meant it. Her decision had been absolute and final.

The dame must be hiding something! A scandal in her business dealings? Something unpleasant in her personal life?

If he dug up anything scandalous out of her past—whatever it was—would he be able to use what he found? *Metropole* never printed scandal. That had been a matter of editorial policy from the first issue. At least no new scandals were ever revealed, only ancient ones which had long been public knowledge.

Well! He was going to dig. Starting tomorrow . . .

Tonight he'd have a quiet dinner with Mara at the apartment—she never gave a performance Monday night—and he should be asleep before eleven.

Tomorrow he would drive up to New London and talk to Amadoro's parents. She wasn't likely to contact her family tonight and order them not to see him.

A light tapping on his door.

He swung around. "Come!" Moving toward his desk as Mandy hurried in ahead of Cort. "I saw Amadoro and the bitch wants no part of us." He sank into the armchair at his desk as they sat facing him. "She told me—quite firmly—she does not wish to have her portrait in *Metropole* and will terminate any staff member who talks to us."

"Typical of the lady!" Mandy rested a pad on the arm of her chair and produced a thin gold pen from a pocket of her smock. "Everyone I've contacted says she's consistently difficult."

"We must get more information." He laid out twelve blank sheets of paper on his desk in double rows of six. "Facts about Amadoro, past and present—rumors and gossip—and more photographs."

"I've struck a complete dead end on pictures," Cort responded. "We've checked every major source. Newspaper morgues, archives and every commercial supplier. They've come up with nothing but duplicates of those we already have. I'm assigning a pair of photographers to follow the dame, day and night, for this next week. At least we'll get some fresh shots of our own."

"Contact your opposite numbers in our London and Paris offices," Ash suggested. "Both of you. See what they can turn up. Tell them it's urgent. I'm going to start my usual pages of preliminary notes with the few facts we now have. Feeling my way. Hoping to stir up some ideas—"

The phone interrupted him.

"This'll be Tim." He snatched it up. "Yes, Greta?"

"Mr. Carrington on line one."

"Right." He jabbed a button. "I saw her, Tim. The beauteous Amadoro."

"And is she agreeable?"

"The lady's a bitch."

"That is bad news."

"She wants no portrait in any magazine! I was unable to question her and she refuses to assist us in any way. Will fire any employee who talks to us."

"We'll do the portrait without her."

"That's what I told her. The curious thing is, she reads *Metropole*. Likes the magazine. Complimented me on my portraits. She'd even read the new one on Sandra Saunders. Thought it was excellent."

"Why do you think she doesn't want us to do her portrait?"

"I suspect the lady has a secret."

"Indeed!"

"Something she doesn't wish to have exposed. I'm driving up to New London tomorrow to dig into her past. Starting with her parents."

"That should produce something. You have carte blanche, as always. However, if you do come up with some lurid secret in the lady's past or her business affairs, we must be extremely cautious. Remember, Ash, we do not print scandal. We'll discuss whatever you do turn up with our legal geniuses. Is the lady really beautiful? Half as lovely as they say?"

"She's certainly the most beautiful dame I've ever seen."

"Most beautiful woman in the world?"

"I haven't seen all the beautiful women in the world."

"But we can call her that?"

"I suppose so . . ."

"You obviously don't like her."

"She's beautiful, intelligent—and a destroyer."

"She would have to be, to have achieved her present eminence in the masculine world of international business. I wish you luck in your dangerous endeavor. Keep me informed."

"I will, Tim." He set the phone down and looked at the others.

"This is going to be tough," Mandy murmured.

"Yes." He studied his two favorite associates as his mind raced. Aware that Mandy was wearing an immaculate white smock over a peacock-blue cheongsam and that Cort, his dark Creole face scowling, looked efficient in one of the tan linen jumpsuits he had designed for himself to wear during work hours. "Mandy, check on Amadoro's personal friends."

"She doesn't seem to have any."

"Every human being has one or two close friends. Check those pictures in our gallery and get the names of all her escorts." He turned to Cort. "Have blowups made of their faces and show them around. I want the name of every man."

"Good idea." Cort nodded.

"She must have one special friend. I suspect it would be a man. She's not the type to confide in another woman. Study those photos. See if there's one face that appears more often than the others. Get his name! And, Mandy—I've learned that Amadoro has some sort of fancy brochure she hands out that contains an authorized biography. See if you can get a copy."

"I'll make some calls." Mandy picked up her pad and got to her feet.

Cort jumped up. "Get back to you, Ash. Minute I have anything."

Ash reached for a marking pen as they departed and began to print thick black letters across the top of each sheet of paper. He always did this whenever he started a new portrait.

CHILDHOOD, PARENTS, FIRST MARRIAGE, SECOND MARRIAGE, THIRD MARRIAGE, NEW YORK, LONDON, PARIS, BUSINESS LIFE, SOCIAL LIFE, FRIENDS . . .

That left a single blank page.

He printed one more word. ENEMIES.

Enemies always talked. Usually at some length. In the past there'd been many times when hatred led to truth.

He began to separate the facts he had fixed in his mind from the unimportant background material and printed each one, in smaller letters, under the relevant headings.

As he did this he searched for some simple piece of information that might illuminate the life, private and public, of Lyli Amadoro.

What was her secret? Most famous people had at least one personal secret they never discussed. One shattering fact that could damage their lives and, possibly, the lives of others.

Amadoro's secret must be more damaging than most.

He unlocked the drawer of his desk and brought out Mandy's file folder with the two brief pages of background material. Listed each important fact under a heading on the sheets of paper. That done, he stared at the pages spread in front of him, no longer seeing the words, his mind searching for some key to Amadoro. That key must be found before he could begin to write about her.

He always planned his portraits step by step, start to finish, and had to know the ending before he could write the first sentence.

He'd known what he would write about Sandra Saunders—not the details but the overall plan—after their first meeting.

Ash gathered the sheets of paper together and placed them in the drawer, file folder on top, and locked the drawer again.

Checked his desk clock. After five-thirty.

Tonight he and Mara would have a quiet dinner at home. Maybe watch an early PBS show and get to bed early. Monday, when Broadway shows were closed, was their night for sleeping together, either in his bed or hers. He smiled. Some of Mara's best performances were not given onstage. He was a fortunate and happy man.

Except, at the moment, for Lyli Amadoro! Mustn't permit her rejection to influence and color the portrait he had to write. That must be done without prejudice.

He left his office abruptly and, after brief instructions to his secretary, took the elevator down to the garage for his Jag. Drove up Madison and stopped at a favorite patisserie—Rosie, their Puerto Rican housekeeper, had asked him to bring dessert for dinner—then continued on to his apartment. Left his car with the doorman, who would park it in a side street for the night, told him he would want it in the morning at nine.

The lobby and elevator, fortunately, were empty. He was in no mood for small talk with any of the neighbors.

When he unlocked the door to his apartment, he heard women's voices in the living room. Mara knew he didn't like intruders at this hour. Especially on Monday! One of her actress friends must've dropped by for cocktails. Then he recognized the sound of his mother's laughter. Millicent! That made him smile.

He hurried through the foyer, with its framed theatrical posters and small tables crowded with bric-a-brac—mostly French, which Mara had bought because they amused her—holding the box of pastry carefully as he went into the living room.

His two favorite women—wife and mother—were seated on the yellow sofa in the curve of the baby grand, giggling, talking and drinking cocktails. A copy of *Metropole* rested on the sofa between them. "Are those vodka martinis?"

The two faces turned as one.

"Ashton, luv!" his mother exclaimed.

"Martini for you?" Mara asked.

"Not at the moment. How are you, Millie?" He leaned down and kissed her on the cheek.

"Simply smashing, dear boy!" She put her drink down. "Wrote a whole chapter this morning. Any day I achieve that is a huge success. So I decided to treat myself to some window-shopping, then have a nice chitchat with Mara. Rang her up first, to be sure she was free."

"Thought I heard your voice, sir . . ."

He turned to see Rosie, holding out her hand for the pastry box.

"What did you get from the bakeshop?" she asked.

"Lemon cheesecake."

"Very nice, sir."

"Perfect!" Mara turned to his mother. "Millie, won't you stay for dinner?"

"Not tonight, luv. Alain and I are dining out with some new people from Beverly Hills. He thinks they may buy the little Daumier."

Ash sank onto the sofa at the end, beside his wife, and kissed her as Rosie carried the pastry box off to the kitchen.

"Mara showed me this new issue of *Metropole*," Millie was saying, "with your portrait of Sandra Saunders. I'll get my copy tomorrow in the mail. Can't wait to read it."

"I read it last night." Mara faced him again. "You've done a fascinating portrait of a very complex woman."

"Tell me, Ash. What do you truly think about her?" Millie asked. "Is she genuine?"

"I was completely convinced."

"I've heard that most astrologers are actually psychic. At least the better ones." She turned to Mara. "Did you know that, luv?"

"Not until I read Ash's portrait."

"I became involved with several in London, at a rather low point of me young life," Millie continued, "when I was a reporter. They fascinated me but I was never persuaded."

"My father certainly believes in them," Mara interrupted. "He has one in Philadelphia he calls every morning from his office."

"A stockbroker gets advice from an astrologer?"

"Many of them do. Papa says this man's better than *The Wall Street Journal*."

"I do believe in psychic phenomena," Millie went on. "I'm involved with it every morning. I sit at my typewriter with no idea what I'm going to write. Then it pops out in a rush, as though someone else's fingers are tapping the keys. Some psychic force tells me what to write. I'm frequently amazed by what comes out."

"Is this new book being written by Penelope Ashton or Cecil Cartwright?" Ash asked.

"It's good old Cecil again. Five luvly murders off the Kings Road in Chelsea."

"Not many sons have mothers who spend their days plotting murder!"

Millie laughed. "Very few mothers have sons who are investigative reporters. Which, in my opinion, is nothing more than being a rather elegant sort of detective. Of course, you've inherited my avid curiosity! Snooping about for clues to the character of the person whose portrait you're writing. But never getting involved with blood and bullets. Always associating with celebrities. No criminals or murderers. Unlike your mother."

"My new assignment isn't like the others. I've a feeling there could be murder."

"You're joking!" Mara frowned. "Aren't you?"

"If you do learn anything about murder, I want to be the first to hear." Millie's eyes salivated with anticipation. "I could use some firsthand knowledge. Your dear father's talking about four weeks in Europe, late this summer. Couldn't you two come along?"

"Four weeks?" Ash glanced at Mara. "We've been thinking about two weeks on the Cape."

"This would be a week in Switzerland, then down to Salzburg for a week of luvly Mozart and two weeks in Paris. Wouldn't you both enjoy that?"

"Sounds like heaven," Mara murmured.

"All expenses paid!"

"By whom?" Ash asked.

"If Alain sells that Daumior he can afford a month of luxe for all four of us! And he's going to Switzerland to look at an early Picasso—the rose period—he hopes to buy from some private collector."

"I can't make any plans until I see how this new portrait develops. We may not even get to the Cape."

"Well! Do think about Europe. Alain and I would enjoy the trip much more if you two came along." Millie rose from the sofa as she talked. "You know, Ash, I'd like to meet this Saunders woman. Maybe have her do my horoscope. Is she terribly expensive?"

Mara and Ash got to their feet.

"Ash is having her do mine," Mara said. "She's already done his."

"Has she? Perhaps she gives a family rate!"

He laughed. "I'll speak to her."

Millie kissed him and collected several parcels from a table. "Alain might want her to do his horoscope with the rest of us. Every owner of a New York gallery should consult an astrologer." Heading for the foyer. "I'm off!"

Ash switched on the television set as Mara followed Millie through the foyer. He wondered about those four weeks in Europe with his parents . . .

The television screen came alive and a newscaster reported the latest bombings in the Middle East, but his words were meaningless as Ash continued to evaluate the Amadoro problem.

"Millie's looking very fit." Mara crossed the big living room toward him. "Did you notice that ridiculous hat she's wearing?"

"No, I didn't. Millie always wears ridiculous hats." He took her in his arms and kissed her, firmly, on the mouth.

She snuggled and giggled. "If I had picked the perfect mother-in-law and father-in-law, they would've been Millie and Alain. Nice of you to have them waiting in the wings all those years we lived together."

"I thought so, at the time. No point in letting you meet them until you agreed to marry me . . ." His attention was caught by the newscaster's voice.

". . . chartered plane carrying a group of government officials and bankers is missing on a flight to Mexico City . . ."

He clutched her shoulders with both hands.

". . . has been learned from a confidential source in Washington that they were flying to attend an international conference on the financial problems of Central America . . ."

"What is it?" Mara whispered. "What's wrong?"

"Shhh!"

". . . here in New York City, it has just been revealed that one American member of the party, banker Howard Munger, was not with the group when it departed from Kennedy Airport. A spokesman for Mr. Munger told reporters that the banker had canceled because urgent business required his presence here. Mr. Munger is deeply concerned for his friends and colleagues who were on this flight. One moment, please . . ."

Ash moved away from Mara, closer to the television set.

"It is now confirmed that the airliner carrying a group of top financial experts to a Mexico City economic conference has crashed into the Gulf of Mexico. Rescue planes and Coast Guard ships are on their way to the scene of the disaster and it is feared—"

He snapped the television off.

"That's horrible!" Mara murmured. "All those people . . ."

"She said that plane would crash."

"Who?"

"Sandra. She warned Howard Munger not to take it."

"Warned him?"

"On the phone. He called yesterday, while I was with her. Munger's one of Sandra's clients. Always asks her advice before taking any plane. She told him he would die if he went on this flight. I'd better call her."

"I'll tell Rosie we'll dine at seven. Okay?"

"Fine." He snatched up the phone from a coffee table and dialed as Mara went toward the kitchen. Heard the phone ringing in the mansion on Gramercy Park. It was answered immediately and a familiar voice repeated the private number. "Nora, it's Mr. Hendrie. Has Sandra been listening to the radio or watching television?"

"Not at this hour."

"May I speak to her?"

"Hold on."

He glanced through the open windows toward the green trees, across Fifth Avenue, in Central Park.

"Yes, Ash?" Sandra's voice, sounding puzzled.

"I gather you haven't heard the news . . ."

"What news?"

"A flash, just now. That plane to Mexico City crashed in the Gulf of Mexico . . ."

"Dear God!"

"All aboard believed lost. They say one person had canceled. Didn't take the flight. Howard Munger."

She sighed. "I wish, somehow, I could've saved every one of them, but I can only help those who seek my help. Howard must be in shock. Thank you, Ash . . ."

He set the phone down, then, preoccupied, went to the record player and raised the lid. Bent to check the disc that was already in place. One of Mozart's sonatas for two pianos. He snapped the lever and, as the disc revolved, walked to one of the windows overlooking the avenue. They were open because it wasn't yet warm enough for air-conditioning. He endured that all day in window-sealed offices and preferred fresh air at home until midsummer.

The shimmering sound of two pianos filled the room.

He stood there, looking down at the early evening traffic, his eyes following a crowded bus.

Once again he had witnessed a demonstration of Sandra's psychic powers.

He reached for the binoculars, in a corner of the window ledge, and focused them on the people strolling on the other side of the avenue, along the edge of the park.

"Rosie's fixing that veal casserole you like . . . You have a good day?"

"Frustrating."

"You saw Amadoro?"

"Oh, yes!" His binoculars followed a smartly dressed old lady walking up Fifth, unaware that she was being trailed by two teenage boys who were getting ready to snatch her handbag. He saw this same scene played at least once a week. Different cast of characters but identical plot. Some evenings the victim fought back, but most times she only screamed as the teenagers ran off with her purse. There was no chance of catching them.

He smiled, beginning to relax, watching the familiar scene.

"Did Amadoro talk to you?"

"Long enough to say she wanted no part of a portrait in *Metropole*."

The teenagers had snatched the old lady's handbag and were escaping, as usual, in opposite directions. The woman, surprisingly, produced a whistle and was blasting on it. The sound was shrill but nobody bothered to turn and the boys had vanished.

"How was your day?" he asked.

"My agent sent me down to see Joe Papp about a part in some play he's doing. I've met Joe before and like him."

"Hope it works out. What about the play you're in now?"

"They think it may last through July. Is there a chance we could go to Europe with Millie and Alain?"

"I doubt it. This Amadoro portrait's going to be difficult . . ." His binoculars followed an attractive girl jogging down Fifth Avenue. She passed the old lady, who was no longer blowing her whistle but talking to an elderly man who had removed his hat and was shaking his head in disbelief.

"Then you are going to write it? Amadoro's portrait . . ."

"Of course I am." He wouldn't have time to jog tomorrow morning before he drove up to New London. He'd overslept today and missed his Monday jog. Must make up for that on Wednesday and no excuses.

"How will you dig up the facts if Amadoro won't help you? Is Mandy doing that?"

"Mandy and her researchers haven't come up with much." He saw a blonde in a smart white dress walking with an older man. Why didn't more women wear white in hot weather? White always looked cooler than bright colors. A child ran past the blonde and her friend, down the avenue, a small boy with curly black hair.

"Dinner should be ready in ten minutes . . ."

"Good. I'm hungry."

A woman was hurrying after the boy.

Ash leaned forward as he recognized her. That young woman who'd been at Amadoro Associates! She was trying to catch her son again. Perhaps she could tell him something about Amadoro!

"What are you watching?"

He turned from the window, leaving his binoculars on a table, and, hurrying now, strode across the living room toward the foyer.

"Where are you going?"

"Someone I must see. Across the street. Be right back!"

"But, darling! Dinner . . ."

Ash was running now, through the foyer—the sound of the two pianos following him—and, leaving their front door open, down the empty corridor to the elevator. Waited impatiently as it rose from the lobby. The elevator doors opened and closed in slow motion and it seemed to take much longer than usual to reach the ground floor.

He hurried past the doorman to the street and ran toward the downtown corner. Waited for the lights to change before he dashed across Fifth Avenue. Stood, briefly, peering up and down the crowded sidewalk but saw nothing of the young woman or her son.

People were strolling before dinner, others walking home from jobs in the skyscrapers below Fifty-ninth. The sun had dropped behind the tall apartments on the far side of the park.

Ash ran south, to Sixty-third, where a vendor was selling ice cream.

Several children waiting in line to be served with a circle of mothers and nursemaids watching them. He paused beside the wheeled cart. "Excuse me . . ."

The vendor looked around. "Yeah?"

"See anything of a small boy with curly black hair? Five or six years old . . ."

"You lose him, mister?"

"He's not mine. Saw him a minute ago. Running ahead of his mother. He's a little monster."

"They're all monsters!" The vendor handed a cone piled with chocolate ice cream to a small girl and took money from her hand. "Aren't you, honey? All monsters!"

"Yes. They are," one of the nursemaids answered. "Monsters!"

"No, mister, I didn't see that perticaler monster." The vendor rang up his sale on the cash register. "Now whicha you monsters is next?"

Ash moved away from the cart, hesitating, looking up and down Fifth and into the park, but there was no sign of the boy or his mother. They must live in the neighborhood. He would watch for them when he drove through the side streets and mornings as he jogged.

That young woman would, surely, be able to tell him something about Amadoro. The receptionist at Amadoro Associates said she had worked there. A former employee should know what the other employees thought and said about their boss. Would have heard the office gossip.

He frowned and started back, up the avenue, toward his apartment.

Hadn't learned much today.

Must do a hell of a lot better, tomorrow, in New London.

chapter six

HE SLOWED THE JAG TO A STOP IN FRONT OF A WHITE picket fence surrounding the white cottage where young Leola Martin had posed with her small dog. The photograph was in his wallet but he didn't need to check it because nothing had changed. Except the house was larger than it had appeared to be in that snapshot and seemed farther back from the street.

He left his car and stood for a moment on the sidewalk, looking up at the white clapboard house with its dark green door and shutters.

Swung the gate open and no dog barked as he started up the brick walk. The lawn had been mowed recently and flowers bloomed in neat beds edged with more bricks. He had expected the house might be shabby but, of course, this was New England, where people cared for things.

He went up the steps to a shallow porch and fingered the button beside the door. No sound, music or voices, came from inside. Only the distant response of a bell. Then footsteps hurrying toward the door.

It was opened by a plump, middle-aged woman with gray hair and a flushed Irish face, wearing a voluminous apron. "Yes, sir?"

"The Martin residence?"

"You sellin' somethin'?"

"I've driven up from New York to ask Mr. and Mrs. Martin some questions about their daughter."

"Miss Leola? What's that girl been up to now? Don't tell me! None of my business. Never seen her, never want to." She laughed. "I'll find out if Mr. Martin will talk to you. What's the name?"

"Hendrie."

"Hen . . . Wait here, sir."

Ash turned away, as the door closed, and looked back toward the street. Wondered how many times that small girl who became Lyli Amadoro had danced down this walk toward the gate. Had she been scheming and planning, even then, to be rich and famous? Surely she had never expected to be the most beautiful woman in New York. Much less the world! He turned back as he heard the door open.

"You can step in. I'm Annie, their housekeeper." She held the door wide for him to enter. "Mr. Martin's in the parlor." Closing the door and scurrying ahead of him.

He followed her across a bare floor gleaming with polish, past some attractive American antiques and a green-carpeted staircase, toward an open archway. Noticed a stair lift slanting up the steps, its padded seat resting at the bottom.

Annie came to a stop under the archway, facing into the room. "Here's that gentleman, sir."

"Come in! Come in!" The welcoming voice was deep and rough.

Ash stepped into the parlor and faced an enormous gray-haired man with a shattered face whose massive body, in a loose tweed jacket, sport shirt and slacks, was slumped into a tremendous chintz-covered wing chair. His nose looked as though it had been smashed many times and never reassembled properly.

"Don't let my face startle you, friend. This handsome profile's the result of football, amateur boxing and ice hockey, mostly the latter. You want to question me about Leola?"

"I'm told that was Lyli Amadoro's name—Leola Martin."

"It's the one Glenda and I gave her but she's had a few others since." His eyes narrowed. "Did Leola send you to see us?"

"Quite the contrary. Miss Amadoro refused to answer my questions. I was afraid she might've contacted you. Told you not to see me."

"Have a seat." Flapping a beefy hand toward a Windsor chair. "What's the name?"

"Hendrie. Ashton Hendrie."

"Sit down, sir. I'll call my wife. She'll want to be in on this."

Ash sank into the chair.

Martin turned toward the hall and bellowed. "Annie! Fetch Mrs. Martin. Tell her we've got a visitor."

There was no response to his orders.

"Ashton Hendrie?" Martin faced him, scowling. "You're the guy writes those portraits in *Metropole*."

"Guilty. I'm doing one, for our September issue, on your daughter."

"I'll be damned!" His scowl faded. "Glenda and I read *Metropole* every month. Keeps us in touch with New York. So you're doing a portrait of Leola! Don't know that she'd want you to see us, but then we haven't talked to her in a long time. Wouldn't know what she might want . . ." He looked toward the archway. "Come in, sweetheart. You'll never guess who this gentleman is! My wife, Glenda . . ."

Ash got to his feet as he saw an erect figure seated in a compact wheelchair, propelling herself across the room. Their eyes met and she smiled. She had Amadoro's green eyes. Only these eyes were friendly.

"This is Ashton Hendrie. He writes those—"

"I know what Mr. Hendrie writes." She held out her right hand. "I'm a great admirer of your *Metropole* portraits, Mr. Hendrie."

"Thank you, Mrs. Martin." He took her hand in his, gently, aware of the long fingers and delicate bones.

She revolved the wheelchair and came to a stop beside her husband, facing Ash.

He sat down again as Martin explained his presence. She appeared to be tall, even seated in the wheelchair, but that could be because she was so thin. Exquisite face, pale skin, without a wrinkle. No makeup, except for the lips. White hair, smartly arranged. Or was it an expensive wig? Wearing a light gray summer suit which, from the way the slacks draped over her knees, must be silk. Feet in silver slippers. Smart striped blouse, no jewelry.

She turned to Ash as her husband finished his explanation. "But what can you expect to learn from us? We know nothing about this person who calls herself Lyli Amadoro. We've not heard from Leola —our daughter—in years. I suspect she doesn't even exist. I'm afraid there's nothing we could say that would help you with your portrait."

"You can tell me about Leola Martin. What she was like . . ."

"Leola was a dear child." Turning to her husband. "What can we tell him, Hapworth?"

"Tell me about yourselves. Your lives. When your daughter was here. Anything you remember from those years . . ."

"I see no reason why we can't talk to Mr. Hendrie," Martin said, his voice a husky growl. "We can only tell him the truth."

"Naturally, dear." She smiled as she turned back to Ash. "Will Leola know we've talked to you?"

"Not unless you tell her."

"Then she'll never know," Martin said emphatically. "Leola's rich and famous now. Surrounded by people who protect her."

"We read that in *The New York Times* several years ago," Glenda said. "And I find it very sad that she has to be protected. Have you seen our daughter?"

"Yesterday afternoon."

"Is she well? How does she look?"

"Very beautiful. In fact, she's said to be the most beautiful woman in New York City."

"She was always a beauty." Martin smiled. "Even when she was a kid. Got her looks from my wife, as you can see. Glenda was a Broadway star, back in the thirties."

"Not a star, Mr. Hendrie. I was featured in some of the big musicals. Cole Porter and Jerome Kern. Sang and danced, but I danced much better than I sang. Most of us did. Except Ethel—Ethel Merman. She was the top."

"And I was in college," Martin said.

"What were you studying?" Ash asked.

"Business administration at Yale, but I majored in football."

"He was a football star," Glenda explained. "Happy Martin. Everybody called him Happy instead of Hapworth, which was his first name. Happy! And he certainly was. Still is . . ."

"Went down to New York most weekends. Having fun and raising hell. Glenda was dancing in a show at the Winter Garden. Prettiest girl I'd ever seen. Longest legs! Took her out to supper."

"The Stork Club. I fell in love with Happy that first night."

"Wasn't my face!" He chuckled. "And she had no idea my folks were rich."

"I fell in love with his eyes—and his heart. Happy has the most beautiful eyes, if you really look at them, in that battlefield of a face. And the kindest heart. But I refused to marry him until he finished college. That's when I found out his mother was one of the Boston Hapworths and both his parents were wealthy. His father was Walter Martin—"

"Dad founded a bank in Boston," Martin interrupted. "He was into everything. Real estate, chemicals, New York hotels—you name it!"

"So your daughter inherited her business expertise from you and your father," Ash observed.

"You might say that, I guess."

"She certainly didn't get it from my side of the family." Glenda laughed. "My folks ran a dancing school in Trenton, New Jersey. Mostly tap dancing. They were always broke."

"She must've gotten her artistic temperament from you, Mrs. Martin." Ash was relaxing, pleased with the material he was uncovering about Amadoro's parents.

"I saw no sign of that," Glenda continued, "when Leola was a child. We sent her to a dancing class here in New London, but she found that boring. Later, after she left high school, she went to a dramatic school in New York. They told us she showed promise but had one tremendous problem. She wanted to be a star. Nothing less! An instant star. Immediately."

"She is a star. In the world of business and as a figure in New York's social life. One of Manhattan's top celebrities."

"Wouldn't know about that." Martin frowned. "I read, somewhere, she's a millionaire several times over." He smiled again. "Thank God she inherited her mother's looks, not mine. You should've seen Glenda singing and dancing, in a spotlight, the whole cast around her . . ."

"Now, Hapworth! Mr. Hendrie doesn't want to hear about us."

"But I do, Mrs. Martin. That's why I'm here. For instance, how long have you lived in New London?"

"Since the year before Leola was born. That was . . ." Glancing at her husband again. "Don't suppose she'd mind our telling her age."

"Been printed in the papers often enough," Martin replied. "So I don't see why not."

"My information," Ash said, "is that she was born in 1944."

"That's correct." Glenda nodded. "We'd found this house the year before."

"Was there any special reason for your leaving New York?"

"Oh, yes! I didn't want to raise a child in the city. New York had changed during those war years. Both of us, Hapworth and I, wanted to leave." Turning to her husband. "Didn't we, dear?"

"We sure as hell did."

"You see, Mr. Hendrie, we'd become alcoholics. I'd left the stage when I married Happy and, with nothing to do, began to drink. Happy was with a brokerage firm on Wall Street and was drinking heavily because of the pressures. We became alcoholics, together, before we realized what was happening to us. So we decided, with a baby on the way, we would never drink again."

"And we never did!" Martin exclaimed. "I haven't had another drink to this day. One of Glenda's doctors told her, recently, she wouldn't be alive if she hadn't cut out the booze when she did. Wouldn't have survived when she smashed her car into a tree and crushed her spine . . ."

"That's more than twenty years ago," Glenda explained. "I do very well, but I'll always be in this wheelchair. We came to Connecticut, before Leola was born, to change our lives for the sake of our child. So she would have a happy life. And she certainly did."

"You see, Mr. Hendrie"—Martin straightened in his chair—"I inherited not one but two fortunes. The first from my maternal grandfather, the second from my father."

"But we've always lived modestly," Glenda continued. "For years Leola had no idea her father was wealthy. We selected this house because it wasn't ostentatious. Our lives were comfortable but never extravagant. We weren't interested in traveling, so we never went to Europe or vacationed in Bermuda. We loved Connecticut. Winter and summer! We still do."

"Leola didn't suspect we had money," Martin muttered, "until some snotty kid in high school told her, 'Your old man's filthy rich.' She asked me, that night, at dinner, 'Are we filthy rich, Daddy?' . . ."

"How old was she when she found out?" Ash asked.

Martin shrugged. "I wouldn't know."

"She couldn't have been more than fourteen," Glenda answered. "Because she dropped out of high school when she was fifteen."

"Didn't finish?"

"She hated school, unfortunately. Wanted to go to New York and study acting. I'd always heard the Neighborhood Playhouse was one of the best schools in the city, so we agreed to let her go there."

"Paid all the bills," Martin said, "including a furnished apartment near Greenwich Village with a live-in companion." Turning to his wife. "You recall her name?"

"Mrs. Winston—Laurie Winston. I found her through a fancy employment agency. Her husband had been killed in World War Two and she never remarried. This was nineteen fifty-nine. She'd made a career for herself as a paid companion, mostly for elderly Park Avenue widows. We both found her intelligent—an attractive, sophisticated woman—and we hoped she might be able to control our daughter . . ."

Ash looked from face to face. "Had she been difficult?"

Glenda frowned. "She had, increasingly, shown us that she possessed a strong personality."

"She still does, Mrs. Martin."

"When Leola wanted something she usually got it. We never refused her anything within reason, but we did want her to appreciate the value of things. People as well as possessions. We didn't suspect what she was up to in New York . . ."

Martin shook his head. "And never found out until we had a phone call from the Towsons—Walter and Clarissa, the wealthiest man in New London and his wife—inviting us to tea. We'd never met the Towsons but we went, of course; drove to their estate on the edge of Long Island Sound—not far from here—and while we had tea we were informed that their only son had just married our only daughter. We were aware, naturally, that she'd known Toby Towson in school but didn't suspect she'd been seeing him in New York. Nor did Mrs. Winston, who was supposed to be watching her. We learned, later, that Leola had been cutting her acting classes and meeting Toby every day."

"What was young Towson doing in New York?"

"He was studying at Harvard—his second year—but he spent weeks at a time in the city. Most of that time with our daughter. They were married by a justice of the peace after Leola discovered she was pregnant."

Ash smiled. "I suppose both families, eventually, approved of the marriage. The joining of the two families . . ."

"Wasn't much else we could do," Martin answered.

"They did seem to be in love, Leola and Toby," Glenda went on, "and we—all four of us—wanted a grandchild, I suppose."

"So you had a grandchild."

"We've never seen it!" Martin exclaimed.

"Why not?"

"We only saw Leola once after her marriage." There was a sudden mist of tears in Glenda's eyes as she turned to her husband.

He shook his head, the battered face solemn. "We thought we'd see the newlyweds when they came to New London after their honeymoon. Read an item in the local newspaper that they were staying at the Towson mansion. Glenda phoned and asked to speak to Leola . . ."

"I asked for Mrs. Toby Towson," Glenda continued, "and whoever answered—she sounded like a maid—told me to wait. When Leola came on I knew right away, from the sound of her voice, that something was wrong. She told me she never wanted to see us again. That she was now Mrs. Towson and was starting a life of her own. They would be living on the Towson estate with Toby's parents and have their own apartment in New York. When I asked about her health she said they would be in Paris when the baby was born. She and her husband were leaving for Europe the following week."

"The baby was born in Paris?"

"In 1961. Toby's mother called and told us it was a girl. Mrs. Towson was very sweet. Said she was sorry Leola hadn't seen us before she and Toby left for France. Apparently, at that point, she had no idea we hadn't seen Leola after her marriage."

"We saw our daughter only once after that." Martin's voice was husky with emotion. "Soon after Toby died."

"She drove here in a shiny red Mercedes," Glenda explained. I saw the car stop at our gate but had no idea who it was as she came up the walk. Her hair, which had been light brown and curly, was pale blond. Long and straight."

"That's how she wears it today."

"I opened the door before she rang the bell. Didn't recognize her until she spoke. She walked past me as she said, 'Where's Happy?'"

"I was in here," Martin continued, "having a nap before dinner. The sound of Glenda closing the door roused me. And there she was—our daughter—standing in front of me. A stranger! Tell Mr. Hendrie what she said, honey. You remember better than I . . ."

Ash saw that Glenda was frowning, troubled by the memory.

"Well . . . right off, she said she was leaving New London for good. Told us she wanted no part of the past. That she would probably never see the Towsons or us again."

"And she hasn't," Martin murmured.

"Said she wanted nothing from us. She was going to have a fortune of her own."

"I asked her what she meant," Martin went on, "and she said we would have to read about her in the papers."

"Leola looked around this room." Glenda glanced from side to side as she talked, seeing the room as Leola had seen it that day. "Said she hated our house and would never step foot inside it again. She was going to have her own home. Not one but several!"

"We were shocked." Martin sighed. "Dumbfounded."

"Said she hated all parents, including Walter and Clarissa Townson!" Glenda's hands clenched in her lap. "She had a plan to start a business in Paris. Didn't say what it was. Like a fool, I said, 'But, Leola, you loved your husband, didn't you?' 'Loved his money,' she said. 'Didn't have to love him.'"

Martin shook his head. "Then she turned on her heel and left."

"We never heard from her again," Glenda whispered. "And that, I'm afraid, is all we can tell you about our daughter, Mr. Hendrie."

"Both the Towsons have passed on," Martin said. "I'm told that Leola got all the Towson money, since Toby was their only child."

"Is there anyone who can tell me about their marriage?"

Martin shrugged. "I wouldn't know."

"There's Cap Larson," Glenda said. "He was with them more than anyone. Whenever Toby and Leola spent weekends at Best of Times. Before the baby was born."

"Best of Times?"

"That's the name of the Towson estate. It's never been sold. Leola owns it now."

"Cap Larson's the caretaker. Lives in the old guest house. He was captain of the Towsons' yacht—*Sea Sprite*. Towson sold the *Sprite* soon after Toby's death. He was washed overboard in a storm and drowned. You should see Cap Larson. Ask him about Leola." Martin laughed. "Cap'll tell you everything for a hundred-dollar bill. Although you can't believe all he says."

"What about the dog your daughter owned? When she was a child . . ."

"Which dog?" Glenda looked puzzled. "Leola always had one."

He pulled a print of the snapshot from his pocket and handed it to her. "Our research people found this."

She stared at the picture. "I remember the day this was taken."

Martin chuckled. "Leola was never one to play with dolls. Only dogs."

"This was a stray she found in the street," Glenda explained. "Leola named him Prince. She liked to read stories about handsome princes." Handing the picture to her husband. "This one was her favorite of all the dogs. Remember, Happy, how she hugged and kissed him?"

"I remember."

Glenda sighed. "Guess she always loved her dogs more than she loved us . . ."

chapter seven

AN OVAL BRONZE PLAQUE EMBEDDED IN THE STONE WALL beside the tall iron gates held three gleaming brass words: BEST OF TIMES.

Ash parked the Jag and tried the gates. They weren't locked. He pushed them open and returned to his car. Backed up and slowly drove inside, leaving the gates wide for his return.

Followed the curving drive between a jungle of overgrown grass under tall trees in need of pruning. A strong smell of decay rose from dead leaves and rotting branches that had fallen to the ground. The only sound came from the birds, disturbed by his car.

The drive continued to curve until he lost all sense of direction.

He braked as the Jag shot out from the drive into bright sunlight and came to a stop facing the distant mansion. Best of Times was an impressive sight. The drive had been designed so that an intruder never glimpsed the house until he came around this final curve. The shock of coming upon it so suddenly would halt any visitor.

The mansion appeared to be nineteenth-century. Or was it a copy of some older structure? Red brick with white trim. All the shutters were closed, but the great house didn't appear to be in disrepair. At any moment one of those tall mahogany entrance doors would open and someone would step out. The white marble steps were like old ivory in the sunlight, the lawn and flower beds immaculate. This sunny picture was a pleasant surprise after the drive, dark as twilight, with its chilly reek of decomposing leaves and dark earth.

When the newlyweds, Leola and Toby Towson, returned from their honeymoon, this drive must've been lined with neatly trimmed trees, glimpses of green lawns and gardens between their trunks.

"You're trespassing here, sir." A man's voice, coming from the shadow under the trees, deep and menacing.

Ash turned to see a tall figure wearing a dark blue shirt over dungarees. His white hair was thick and unruly, rugged face deeply tanned. He was holding a rifle in one muscular brown hand. "Captain Larson?"

"That's right."

"My name's Hendrie—Ashton Hendrie. I work for *Metropole* magazine."

"Never heard of it. What you after here?"

"I've just come from seeing Mr. and Mrs. Hapworth Martin. They suggested I see you."

"Happy and Glenda?" He lowered the muzzle of his rifle. "Haven't seen the Martins lately. How are they?" He moved into the sunlight. "Glenda was in a wheelchair last time I saw her."

"She still is, but she seems fine."

"I drive into town to pick up rations and booze but always do that early mornings, so I never see anybody. Why'd the Martins send you to me?"

"I'm writing a story about their daughter and they—"

"Leola?"

"—and they thought you'd be able to tell me about her life here. After she married young Towson. Said you'd know more about it than they did. They, apparently, only saw their daughter once after her marriage."

"Writing a story about Leola, are you? I often wonder what's happening to her. Haven't seen her myself for several years."

"I saw her yesterday."

"Saw Leola?" He came closer to the Jag.

"I'd like to ask you some questions."

"She still pretty as ever?" He switched the rifle to his left hand. "Leola Martin was the prettiest girl I ever saw."

"She's a strikingly beautiful woman."

"I've seen her pictures in the New York papers. Calls herself by another name now."

"Lyli Amadoro. Amadoro was the name of her third husband, Count Amadoro."

"Picture didn't look much like Leola. Not the way I remember her."

Ash brought out the hundred-dollar bill he had folded into a pocket after leaving the Martins and held it up for Larson to see. "I'd be willing to pay for any information you can give me. About Leola when she was living here. Those first months after her marriage . . ."

Larson reached out and slipped the bill from between his fingers. "No reason I shouldn't tell you what I know. It's not all that much. Did her folks answer your questions?"

"They couldn't tell me much, either. But they did talk to me."

"Come inside."

"Thanks." Ash got out, quickly, leaving the car door open.

"I live in the guest house." Larson motioned toward the right, where one arm of the drive circled the side of the mansion. "When the Towsons were alive I had an apartment over the garages with the rest of the staff." He carried his rifle, pointed toward the ground, as he walked beside Ash. "Leola suggested I move into the guest house when she inherited this property from old man Towson. Made me caretaker. I see to repairs and guard the property. She offered a good salary, so I accepted. After all, I'd been with Toby's father ten years as captain of the *Sea Sprite*. That was the old man's yacht. My father came from Norway but I was born in Brooklyn. Joined the merchant marine during World War Two and when that was over went back to sea—avoiding all the other wars—until I got to be captain of my first private yacht. Here we are, sir . . ."

Ash saw that they were approaching an attractive vine-covered house, surrounded by a neat garden in full bloom. "What's become of the Towsons' yacht?"

"The old man sold the *Sprite* when Toby died. His wife, Clarissa, wan't interested in boats. She liked horses." He opened the front door and went ahead, through a low-ceilinged hall where he rested his rifle on an antique chest. "I'll leave this here. It's not loaded." He led the way into a pleasant room with paneled walls, an elaborately carved bar and comfortable armchairs.

The room reminded Ash of an English pub.

"This is where Mr. Towson liked to do his drinking after an afternoon's sail. Always had a few friends staying here in the guest house." He went behind the bar. "Sit there, by those windows. I'll fix us something to drink. You look to me like a Scotch-and-water man."

"Splash of water, please."

"That's what I like to hear."

Ash sat in one of the armchairs and saw that the open windows faced a stretch of lawn with a view of the distant Sound. He turned to watch Larson pouring generous drinks. "Did Leola—Mrs. Toby Towson— join the others in this room?"

"Nope. Never saw her here." He came from behind the bar with their drinks, set them on a low table and sank into a chair. "This was mostly for the older men who drove up from New York for a weekend. Leola and young Toby did their drinking in the main house and aboard the *Sea Sprite*. I got to know Leola pretty damn well when they had me take them out for a cruise. Just the two of 'em . . ."

"Was that often?"

"Several times a week, those first months after their marriage." Raising his glass. "Your good health, sir."

"And yours."

They drank, enjoying the whiskey.

"I liked Leola," Larson said.

"Did she get along with Toby's family?"

"Couldn't say from personal observation how Toby's mother felt about her new daughter. Rarely saw them together because I seldom went into the big house. Spent most of my time aboard the *Sea Sprite*. But I heard the servants gossiping—there were ten in help here then—and they said Mrs. Towson and Leola were always picking and digging at each other. Never actually quarreling, you understand, but looking for an advantage, you might say. On the other hand, the old man was mighty fond of Leola. Inviting her into the library after dinner. Showing her his first editions and talking about books. Seems Leola had always been a great one for reading. She could talk about books by the hour. Which is more than Toby could do, with all his education. Though he never went back to Harvard after their marriage. Old man Towson collected rare editions—Trollope and Dickens—and he was always telling Leola to read them. Especially Dickens! The name of this estate—Best of Times—was, I'm told, taken from one of Mr. Dickens' books."

"Yes, I know."

"Leola told me that. When the old man died, she inherited everything as Toby's wife and the mother of his child. Mrs. Towson—Clarissa—had died first. With the two of them gone, Leola sold all their fine antique furniture. Today the house stands empty, except for some broken junk. And, maybe, a few ghosts."

"So Mr. Towson got along with Leola? Better than his wife . . ."

"I noticed, when there was a party aboard the yacht, most women seemed to avoid Leola. It was the men who gathered around her, while their wives watched them."

"What became of Leola's child?"

"I've no idea. Never saw the kid. One of the servants said there was something wrong with it."

"Wrong?"

"She didn't say what it was and I never asked."

Ash hesitated, as they finished their drinks, deciding how to ask Larson about Toby Towson's death. He liked to spring an important question without warning. "Were you aboard the *Sea Sprite* the night young Towson drowned?"

"I was standing right beside him when it happened. My mate was at the wheel. Toby and I had gone on deck to check the weather. Barometer had been dropping all evening. We'd been fighting a gale for half an hour, but we weren't in any real trouble. Then all of a sudden there was this tremendous gust of wind. I grabbed the rail and yelled at Toby to do the same. Looked around and saw him go over the side as the *Sprite* rolled with the storm."

"What did you do?"

"We dropped flares right away and circled the spot, but there was no sign of Toby. I knew there wouldn't be until after the storm."

"What about Leola?"

"I went below to their cabin and, when she didn't answer my knock, opened the door and went in. Leola was asleep in her bunk. I couldn't rouse her."

"Had they been drinking? Leola and Toby . . ."

"Champagne with dinner and brandy after. I knew, when Toby came on deck, that he wasn't sober, but I thought he'd be all right. I'd seen him drunk before. Many times."

"When did you manage to wake Leola and tell her what had happened?"

"Not until morning, after we berthed at New London. She got hysterical. We all knew she was six months pregnant. So I carried her up to the house in my arms and Mr. Towson sent for their doctor."

"Was Toby's body found?"

"Washed ashore."

"Was there an autopsy?"

"And a Coast Guard inquiry. Leola hadn't seen what happened, so she wasn't required to testify. I was the only witness, along with my mate. Told them I saw the boy lose his balance and go overboard. Nothing I could do to save him. Had to say he wasn't exactly sober."

"Nothing suspicious about Toby's death?"

"The verdict was accidental death by drowning." Larson paused. "There's been other deaths on the *Sprite* before the old man owned her. Some of the crew thought she was a haunted ship. There were stories of fatal accidents to members of the crew, and the man who designed the *Sprite* is said to have killed himself on her maiden voyage with a bullet in his head." He set his glass down. "In the old days the word sprite meant ghost."

"Did it?"

"Mr. Towson never knew. The *Sprite*—wherever she is and whoever owns her—will always be a ghost ship. The new owner may not suspect, but every crew will find out . . ."

chapter eight

ASH PASSED CARRINGTON'S SUITE AND TURNED DOWN the side corridor to his own office. Pleased, as he opened the door and his secretary looked up, to see that no one was waiting for him.

"How was New London?" she asked.

"Interesting. Discovered several fascinating things about Madame Amadoro." He passed her desk, heading for the inner door. "Tell Mandy I'm back."

"She was looking for you earlier."

"Want to pin down on paper what I've learned while it's fresh in my head." He grasped the knob of the door and turned it. "Don't put any calls through."

"There's been a man asking for you. Phoned three times."

"Name?"

"Wouldn't give it. I asked each time and he said it's a personal matter. That you know him. He has a foreign accent. French, I think."

"If he calls again, let me talk to him." He opened the door and went into his office.

"I'll find Mandy for you."

Ash closed the door and went straight to his desk. Sat down and unlocked the top drawer. Brought out the Amadoro file, opened it and separated the sheaf of loose pages. Laid them out—in two rows of six again—and began to make notes of what he'd learned from the Martins and Cap Larson. Added each brief item to the pages headed CHILDHOOD, PARENTS and FIRST MARRIAGE.

Kept at it until he heard a familiar light tapping on his door. "Come in, Mandy!" He put his pen aside as she entered.

"Sorry I couldn't make it right away. The usual Carrington post-lunch conference."

He observed, as she came toward him—pad and pen in hand—that she was wearing one of her smocks over a dark green cheongsam with matching slippers and there was some sort of booklet under one arm.

"What did you learn in New London?" She sank into an armchair facing him, resting her pad on an arm, the booklet on her lap.

"Several things I need you to check. In 1959, still known as Leola Martin, subject studied acting at the Neighborhood Playhouse. Contact fellow students and talk to instructors. Find out what they thought of her. She was living in Manhattan with a companion—paid by her parents, Hapworth and Glenda Martin. The companion was a Mrs. Laurie Winston. Trace her and talk to her . . ."

Mandy was making rapid notes.

"I need to know more about the parents. Hapworth Martin, called Happy—football star at Yale, later worked for a Wall Street brokerage. Mother a featured performer in Broadway musicals of the thirties. First name Glenda. What was her name before she married?" He glanced at what he'd printed under FIRST MARRIAGE. "I want a copy of all documents—autopsy report and Coast Guard inquiry—pertaining to the drowning of Leola's first husband—Toby Towson—lost from family yacht, the *Sea Sprite*. Should be able to locate all this in New London." He watched as she made more notes. Aware of the subtle, barely noticeable perfume Mandy always wore. It wasn't possible that she could be forty. Her unlined face looked more like twenty.

She looked up from her pad and smiled. "Well! You've turned up several leads."

"Which may lead nowhere."

"I've only this one small item for you, I'm afraid." Pushing the booklet across the desk. "That public relations brochure Amadoro hands out when anyone asks for her biography."

He stared at a large photograph of Amadoro on the cover. The green eyes and long blond hair.

"Expensive color plates and slick copy." Mandy giggled. "But read this and, like a TV newscast, you want more facts."

Ash laughed as he put the booklet aside. "I'll read it later. One other thing. I'd like to see a copy of the birth certificate—better contact our Paris office—of Leola's child. A girl. Born Paris, around 1961. I want to know her name and what's become of her."

"I'll call Paris in the morning."

"That's about it."

The phone rang.

Mandy rose, snatching up her pad. "I'll get started on these other items right away."

"Thanks, Mandy." He picked up the phone as she departed. "Yes, Greta . . ."

"That man's calling again."

"Man?"

"With the French accent."

"I'll talk to him."

"Line three."

He jabbed the button. "Ashton Hendrie speaking."

"Good afternoon, Monsieur Hendrie . . ."

"Sorry I was out when you called before, Monsieur Marnat."

"So you recognize my voice?"

"Your accent's unmistakable. And fresh in my mind from yesterday."

"I would like to see you."

"To what purpose?"

"There was a staff meeting this morning. Every employee of Amadoro Associates has been warned not to talk to you or any other representative of *Metropole* magazine. There are several things I could tell you about Madame Amadoro. Rather important things . . ."

"In spite of an official warning not to talk?"

"Because of that warning. I am a Frenchman, monsieur. I resent anything that encroaches upon my freedom as an individual."

"When do you wish to see me?"

"As soon as possible. Preferably after dark."

"Tonight?"

"If that would be convenient."

"Where can we meet? I have a car—a cream-colored Jaguar."

"Rather conspicuous. No matter! The conspicuous is seldom suspicious. I will walk east when I leave the office and have an early dinner in some restaurant, in case I'm followed—which is unlikely—then continue on to First Avenue and Fifty-second. I will be there at eight o'clock, the northwest corner. Lyli never ventures east of Park."

"Eight o'clock."

"I shall be waiting, monsieur. À *bientôt* . . ."

Ash set the phone down.

So Marnat was willing to talk! This might be the break that would open up everything. Which frequently happened when he was working on a portrait. One person would hold a key to the private life of his subject. Pray God, Clement Marnat would have a key to Lyli Amadoro . . .

He began to check over the notes he'd made on the sheets of paper and studied the two pages of material from Mandy's department. Went over everything, again and again, but came up with no fresh ideas.

Miss Lundborg departed before six, after switching off his phone so that no calls would come through.

Finally, he examined the booklet on Amadoro but, except for several glamorous studio photographs of the lady, there was nothing new or revealing. He locked everything in the top drawer of his desk.

Mara was working tonight and he would eat dinner alone somewhere. Maybe Costigan's, after he saw Marnat.

Right now he wanted to pay a visit to his father. Alain would surely have heard gossip about Amadoro. Art dealers always knew a great deal about their potential customers—the very rich.

He made his way through the emptying offices to the elevator and went down to get his car. Eased the Jag through streets suffused with a golden haze of light from the west, where the sun made black silhouettes of the tall buildings. Found a parking space on Fifty-seventh beyond the Galerie Hendrie.

The sidewalk was crowded with smartly dressed men and women, released from their jobs in nearby offices, hurrying to some urgent and, hopefully, pleasant rendezvous.

He paused to inspect his father's small display window where a single beam of light focused on an excellent Utrillo—a familiar Paris street—handsomely framed and placed against gray velvet to enhance the colors of the painting.

A buzzer sounded, far away, as he entered the gallery, passing an attractive young woman, probably a student, studying a Monet garden and an older couple standing in front of a large Picasso drawing. Continuing toward the arched passage at the rear, he saw his father's assistant, Miss Mortlake, materialize from the dimness.

"Ash! Haven't seen you in weeks."

"Been rather busy."

"I read the new portrait this morning. Simply fascinating! I'd always wanted to know about Sandra Saunders."

"Delighted you enjoyed it. Is the great man available?"

"In his office. He'll be most pleased to see you."

Continuing on through the passage, he wondered if his father was still enjoying the charming Miss Mortlake's beautiful young body. She was British, slim and blond, with the creamy skin of someone who had spent her life in an English garden. He wondered how she achieved that in grimy New York. Like her many predecessors, she was having an affair with Alain. Each assistant lasted a few years, but Ash's mother, who wrote her clever detective novels, never suspected. Or had she, long ago, decided to overlook Alain's liaisons and never mentioned them in order to preserve their marriage? He'd discovered, at an early age, about his father's amorous adventures and was amused by them.

The private office, as he pushed the door open, was unchanged. One of the most comfortable rooms he'd ever known. Walls hidden behind bookshelves and paintings.

Alain, seated behind his Louis XVI table-desk, glass in hand and reading, looked up and smiled. "Ashton! *Mon fils* . . ." He set his glass down, closed the book and got to his feet. "What brings you here?"

"Was in the neighborhood." They embraced, brushing cheeks, right and left. "Thought I'd stop by for a drink."

"I'm having a dry vermouth. You'll join me?"

"Avec plaisir."

"Sit down! Sit down . . ." He went to an antique cabinet and opened a pair of carved doors to reveal a well-stocked bar.

Ash sank onto a fauteuil—most of the furniture was French—and glanced around at the familiar paintings on the walls, his father's personal favorites and not for sale, as he listened to what he was saying. Alain was half French, half American and spoke with a very slight accent.

". . . and I find that a dry vermouth relaxes me at the end of the day. Gives me enough energy to walk home for dinner. Your mother tells me she saw you and Mara yesterday . . ."

"Millie was at the apartment when I got home." Reaching for the vermouth. "Apparently her new book's going well."

"Is it?" Alain sat at his desk again. "I never ask about her writing anymore. Except for the incomparable Simenon, all detective novels bore me."

They drank, studying each other, relaxing.

"Millie and I have agreed, after all these years, that I don't have to read her books and she doesn't question me about the gallery. I know nothing about murder and she knows less about French painting. Millie tells me your latest portrait's about that Saunders woman.

Obviously, an incredible person. Had a client some years ago, wouldn't purchase a painting—it was a first-rate Lautrec—unless Sandra Saunders assured her it was authentic. She said it was and I made a handsome sale. I've just been reading a new biography of Lautrec. One rather amusing anecdote. Seems he got lost, one rainy night, hunting for a pissoir. Too much absinthe, I suppose. And while he was wandering through an unfamiliar alley he could wait no longer . . ."

Ash studied his father, only half listening to the Lautrec story, wondering if he would look like Alain when he was sixty-six. Doubted he would live to that age and, for that matter, wasn't at all certain he cared to, unless his life was as satisfying as his father's. The Galerie Hendrie had been a success since the day it opened, shortly after the war. He wondered if he really did look like Alain—Millie thought so—but he'd never been convinced. They were the same height, tall and lean. Both had straight black hair and brown eyes. Alain's hair was graying at the sides. Millie claimed she fell in love with him because his voice reminded her of Charles Boyer. They had met in London during the war years, when Alain was in uniform. His father's hands were thin with tapering fingers, while his own hands were embarrassingly muscular, the fingers blunt. Alain was wearing a summer suit—pale brown linen—with a white shirt and handsome tie. Their tastes, certainly, were alike. Simplicity, comfort, muted colors. He realized that the Lautrec anecdote was finished and Alain was sipping his vermouth. "Afraid I didn't hear the end of your story. My mind was wandering."

"I was aware of that."

"Thinking about the next portrait I'm writing. Tell me, *mon père*, what do you know—personal or otherwise—about Lyli Amadoro?"

"Amadoro?" Alain set his glass down. "So Amadoro's the subject for your next one."

"I didn't say that."

"But she is, isn't she?"

"You mustn't tell anyone. Even Millie."

"Word of honor. Especially Millie."

"What gossip have you heard about Amadoro? I talked to the lady yesterday and she refuses to cooperate. Doesn't want her portrait in the magazine. Ordered her staff not to talk to me or anyone else from *Metropole*."

"There's very little gossip about her and even that, I suspect, is mostly rumor. Several people have said that she married three times for money and, in each marriage, the husband died. Left her a fortune. Three fortunes! That's how she was able to buy her way into the business world. She's reputed to have a remarkable talent for turning money into more money. Some say—like one of those amorous insects which destroy their mates after copulation—Amadoro killed all her husbands."

"Killed them?"

Alain chuckled. "Wore them out sexually, so they were too exhausted to swim, ski or test a racing car. That's how they died. By water, earth and fire. While Lyli piped her magical flute. According to this legend, she killed them with excessive pleasure. Which must be a rather cozy way to die."

"Is there much talk about her?"

"I wouldn't know. I've heard Amadoro discussed at parties. The more elegant affairs . . ."

"You met Amadoro at these parties?"

"I only see her from a distance. Making a spectacular entrance. Preferably down a flight of steps. She never remains for long. But I have met the lady and talked to her."

"Where was this?"

"Here in the gallery. We discussed a painting she considered purchasing."

"What was she like?"

"I could only see her nose and mouth. Quite lovely! Her hair was covered by some sort of hood, eyes hidden behind sunglasses. There were others in the gallery but nobody recognized her. I found her extremely shrewd when it came to the price of a painting."

"Who was the artist?"

"It was a small but very fine Renoir. Young girl with a dog."

"A white dog?"

"Matter of fact, it was. How could you know that? She told me it reminded her of a dog she once owned. Years ago. Said she preferred dogs to people. You could trust a dog . . ."

"She bought the painting?"

"Unfortunately, in the week she was trying to make up her mind, I sold it to a collector from Texas. Then, of course, she wanted it. Furiously! Tried to buy it from the new owner but he wouldn't sell. Like most very rich people, she had objected to the price. That's how the wealthy keep their money. Always trying to persuade you to give them something for less. In my opinion, most of them buy pictures as investments, not for the beauty of the painting. Every time they look at it they see thousand-dollar bills framed on their wall."

"Have you ever met a man—a Frenchman—named Marnat?"

"Clement Marnat? It was he who arranged for Madame Amadoro to see the Renoir. He'd noticed the canvas when he was in the gallery and thought she might like it."

"What else can you tell me about her?"

"That's it, I'm afraid."

"And Marnat?"

"He used to be a familiar figure in Paris and London."

"You knew him then?"

"Before I came to New York. He hung around the galleries and was seen with some of the most beautiful women. And the wealthiest."

"A gigolo?"

"*Mon Dieu!* No. Much more elegant—and intelligent—than that type. He actually did work on staff for several of the better-known Parisian art dealers and, because of his social connections, made sales to his wealthy friends. Marnat came from an old and titled family; most of them were in politics. His credentials were impeccable but, unfortunately, he had absolutely no ambition. There are men like that, you know."

"He has a job now. With Amadoro Associates."

"Does he? I had no idea. Of course, he's not so young anymore. Nor as handsome. He would require a regular source of income. I wonder if he was on Amadoro's staff when he brought her to see that Renoir. If so, I was not informed and didn't suspect."

"Are you going home presently?"

"Any moment. Miss Mortlake can close up shop and switch on the alarms."

"Good. I'll drive you."

"That would be most pleasant. Perhaps you'll come in and see your dear mother."

"I've an appointment at eight but I'll stop by for a drink."

"Millie still likes sherry before dinner. Disgusting British habit!"

They drank vodka martinis instead of sherry—even Millie—and relaxed in the luxurious living room overlooking upper Park Avenue.

At two minutes before eight Ash slowed his car toward the curb at the corner of Fifty-second and First.

The Frenchman was waiting.

Ash leaned over to open the car door. *"Bon soir!"*

"You are prompt, monsieur." Marnat folded himself into the Jag.

"Where can we talk?"

"I think, *peut-être*, we might drive through the park." He closed the door and sank back against the seat. "Unlikely that anyone would recognize either of us there at this hour."

Ash swerved west on Fifty-first, through deepening twilight, toward a distant streak of sunset, barely visible at the horizon.

Marnat remained silent, facing straight ahead.

Ash turned the Jag again, up Third. "Your call was a surprise."

"I'd considered contacting you since yesterday. Then when we were ordered, this morning, not to talk to anyone connected with *Metropole*, I decided to phone you. I'm delighted that you agreed to see me."

Driving west on Sixtieth, he wondered if he should tell Marnat that he was aware he knew Alain. Better keep that to himself for the moment. He glimpsed trees in the park, at the end of the street.

"Perhaps I should inform you. I've . . ." Marnat hesitated.

"Yes?"

". . . known your father, casually, for many years."

"Have you?" Ash smiled.

"We met frequently during the war years in London and later in Paris. Then, more recently—here in New York—I introduced Alain to Lyli. He had a painting, an exquisite Renoir, I thought she might wish to buy. She saw it but was unable to make up her mind, and Alain sold it before she could decide. Such a pity! It was a masterpiece—first quality—but Lyli hates to spend that much money on anything."

Ash caught a green light and shot across Fifth into Central Park, heading toward the Mall. This was the dinner hour and there was no traffic. The benches along the walks were empty, only a few pedestrians hurrying through the dusk like lost shadows. He noticed a young woman with a small child running ahead of her. Could it be? No. This woman was slightly taller, and it wasn't a boy but a girl.

"There is much I can tell you, monsieur . . ." Marnat's voice sounded impatient.

"I'm sure there is."

". . . about Lyli. Her personal life. About Amadoro Associates."

"How long have you known the lady?"

"I was a friend of her husband's, Conte Amadoro. I knew him long before she met him."

"And where did they meet?"

"Gstad. They'd gone there with separate parties for a week of skiing. I was with Alfredo's party, but I knew most of the people in the other group, so the two became one. I introduced them—Lyli and the Conte—because I knew they were both excellent skiers. In fact, Alfredo was a champion in Italy. So they quickly became partners. When we flew back to Paris, Alfredo gave a supper at Maxim's for Lyli to meet all his friends."

"What can you tell me about their marriage?"

"Everything." He laughed quietly. *"Eh bien!* Almost everything."

"And about the Conte's death?"

"I was there when he died."

"Were you!"

"I witnessed the accident. Along with several other skiers." Marnat stopped abruptly. "I will tell you all that I know about Lyli. There is much that only I know."

"I'm sure there is."

"I will tell you everything. For a price, of course."

Ash slowed the Jag and glanced at the lights around the distant lake. "How much?"

"Ten thousand dollars."

"I would have to consult my editor in chief."

"How long might that take?"

"I can see him tomorrow morning."

"I'm the only person who can tell you about Lyli's private life. The absolute truth."

"Shall I phone you?"

"It would be better for me to contact you again."

"I'll be in my office. Tomorrow afternoon."

"Two o'clock?"

"Fine."

"I will have a late lunch and phone you from a public booth while I'm out. It is dangerous to make personal calls from Amadoro Associates."

"Your phone's bugged?"

Marnat shrugged. "One can never be certain."

Ash saw that they were passing the reservoir. "When I came to see Amadoro yesterday afternoon, there was a child in the outer reception room."

"Child?"

"Small boy with his mother. The attendant at the desk told me the young woman was a former employee. Who is she, do you know?"

"I only come in contact with persons who have appointments to see Lyli and rarely encounter any of the employees. There are several hundred. This young woman may have been employed, at one time, as a typist or secretary . . ."

Ash turned the car right, toward the Ninety-sixth Street exit of the park. "There was a dog with Amadoro while I talked to her. Crouched at her feet, watching me."

"He's always there when she sees a stranger. Trained to growl when anything is said that displeases Lyli. He knows from the sound of her voice."

"What's his name, do you know?"

"Prince. All Lyli's dogs are called Prince."

Ash restrained a smile. He was learning things.

"You can drop me at Park, if you will. I prefer to walk, rather than risk our being seen together any longer."

"Of course." He drove across Fifth and continued on Ninety-sixth toward Park.

"You haven't asked me what I want with ten thousand dollars."

"None of my affair, is it?"

"But I don't mind telling you. I intend to return to Paris and spend the remainder of my life there. I've never cared for New York. Compared to Paris this is a cold and unfriendly city. Ten thousand American dollars will provide me with enough money to live on for more than a year. Until I can find myself a new project."

"Another rich woman?" Ash was sorry he had asked that, as soon as he spoke.

"That becomes more difficult each year, monsieur. I do not resent your question. I've always managed to survive because of my love for beautiful women."

"And did you—love—Lyli Amadoro?"

"For a brief time, in Paris. Yes . . . I adored her. This was after the death of my dear friend Conte Amadoro. Before Lyli became so impossible. She's quite a different person now. Completely changed.

I'm speaking of her private self. I no longer feel at ease in her presence . . ." He leaned forward as they reached Park Avenue. "This corner, please."

Ash slowed the car to a stop. "I'll do what I can about that money. Is what you know about Amadoro worth ten thousand bucks?"

"Oh, yes! Probably much more." Marnat opened the door and got out. Closed it again, then leaned through the open window. "I have good reason to believe that Lyli killed her second husband, the Englishman."

"And her third husband? Amadoro?"

"Certainly not! But the Englishman . . ."

"Robert Craydon?"

"I also knew Robbie Craydon. A charming man . . . One night in Paris, when Lyli and I were enjoying—golden dreams . . . This was at her apartment and we had fallen asleep on divans. *Au pays des rêves d'or!* She wakened, trembling and sobbing. I placed an arm around her to comfort her and she whispered in my ear, 'I killed my husband. The English one. But I've just seen him again. He comes back to haunt me. In my dreams . . .' She continued for half an hour, weeping as she explained. How she had killed Craydon and was now seeing his ghost. I thought she was hallucinating because of the opium but, later, I began to wonder . . . She has no memory of what she said. Isn't that worth ten thousand dollars? I'll tell you everything she said that night and much more. *Eh bien!* I shall call you tomorrow afternoon. If you have the money I will tell you all I know about Lyli Amadoro. *À bientôt,* monsieur." He turned away from the car.

Ash sat there, puzzled and shocked, watching Marnat disappear into the night.

The Frenchman's hands had swooped and darted as he talked. There was an obscenely large ring on the little finger of his right hand. Ash always looked at hands because they revealed hidden clues to character, and he was suspicious of men who wore enormous rings.

Would the magazine pay ten thousand for Marnat's information? This sort of thing had never come up in the past. He couldn't believe Lyli had killed any of her husbands. Cap Larson had been present when young Towson was washed overboard and tried to rescue him.

Marnat was a con artist. He would take the ten thousand and fly to Paris on the first jet. His information would either be false or unprovable . . .

He drove on, still evaluating what Marnat had said.

The Frenchman, probably, knew much more than he had hinted about Lyli. Certainly he should have firsthand information about her marriage to Amadoro, her Paris years, as well as her business affairs there and in New York. But was it worth ten thousand bucks?

He would have to justify such an expenditure to Carrington, who, in turn, must get approval from the board of directors.

The Frenchman was smarmy. Informing on a woman with whom he'd had an affair and, even now, he was accepting a salary from her. The guy was a slimy creep.

chapter nine

TURNING DOWN SECOND AVENUE, ASH REMEMBERED that he hadn't eaten any dinner. Tonight he wanted a quiet spot where he could consider what he'd just learned from Marnat. That meant Johnny Costigan's.

Mara could find a taxi after tonight's performance. He hadn't remembered to phone her. No matter. She always arranged for Rosie to leave a cold supper in the kitchen when he didn't call, or she would go to Sardi's with some of her actor friends.

He drove west on Fifty-fifth to Third Avenue, where he found a parking space across from Costigan's.

There was no lurking doorman smoking a furtive cigarette and no windows facing the avenue. No striped canopy from curb to entrance. Only a neat silver sign on the door with one engraved word: COSTIGAN'S.

He'd voted on all these items when Johnny showed him the first plans for his new restaurant. No doorman, no canopy, no garish sign.

Ash pushed the door open and went inside, conscious of the inviting aroma of food and a sense, as always, of comfort and relaxation. This was his place. His home away from home.

Hesitating in the softly lighted circular foyer, facing into the dining room, he glimpsed Johnny talking to people seated in one of the alcoves toward the rear. He liked to stand here, this brief moment before Johnny noticed him, and look around the restaurant with a proprietary feeling. And why not!

The hatcheck girl was invisible in her cubicle, to his right, beyond the foyer. She was Johnny's youngest, Sheila, who would be engrossed in another textbook. All Johnny's kids were in college, Sheila studying journalism at Columbia.

On his left, opposite the checkroom and parallel to the street, was an old-fashioned bar presided over by a genius with a face like an aging pink baby whose name was Danny Casey. In spite of his smiling face, Danny could handle any emergency, physical or psychological. If you were a regular, your favorite potable would be served by Danny as Johnny seated you at your table.

In the dining room the colors were muted browns, tans and yellows. Autumnal colors. Each banquette was in a shallow curved alcove, so you couldn't see who was dining on either side of you or hear their voices. That had been Johnny's idea and a smart one. The alcoves made the ceiling look as though it was scalloped. Regulars sat in an alcove but strangers were offered tables in the center or escorted to a larger dining room at the back.

Some of the center tables were empty. Tuesday nights were slow even in the most popular Manhattan restaurants.

Shaded candles lighted small yellow and white flowers, in low bowls on each table, without revealing the identity of the diners.

He saw that Johnny was coming to greet him and moved forward to shake his hand.

"Ash! Good to see you."

"I'm alone tonight."

"Your usual table's free." Johnny led him toward an alcove.

Ash waved to Sheila, who looked up as he followed her father past the checkroom.

"People are talking tonight." Johnny lowered his voice. "About your latest portrait."

"That's good to hear."

"Read it this afternoon in my office. It's the greatest!"

"Thank you, my friend."

"My wife reads Sandra Saunders' column every morning, and three people tonight told me they're her clients." He eased the table out for Ash to sit on the cushioned banquette, as he talked, placing a menu within reach. "From what you write about her, you apparently think Saunders is on the level."

"I certainly do. She's an incredible person."

"Enjoy your dinner. I'll tell Georges you're here."

"No hurry. Thanks . . ." As Johnny moved away he saw Danny hurrying from the bar with a glass on his silver tray. "Danny! How are you?"

"No complaints, sir." Setting the drink in front of him. "Here we are . . ."

"Not a moment too soon!" He smiled as he glanced at the double whiskey in the sparkling Waterford glass.

"Read your portrait of that Saunders dame . . ."

"Did you?"

"Terrific! Everybody's buzzin' 'bout it t'night. Do you believe in this psychic stuff y'rself? Astrology an' para-what's-it . . ."

"I most certainly do."

"Glad t' hear it, sir." He bent down, eyes solemn, to whisper, "Me wife's grandmother, in Dublin, is a witch."

"Is she?"

"At age ninety-seven, if you can believe it! Enjoy your dinner."

Ash picked up the glass of whiskey as Danny returned to his bar and, gratefully, took a large first swallow. Saw the tall figure of his favorite waiter, a middle-aged Frenchman who had the poise of an archbishop, coming toward him. *"Bon soir,* Georges."

"Monsieur Hendrie . . ." He bowed slightly. "People are discussing your new portrait in *Metropole*."

"Johnny just told me."

"Congratulations, sir. Once again."

"Thank you."

"Would you care to order now?"

"Yes, but don't serve anything until I've had a second drink. And I know what I want for dinner."

"Very good, sir." He brought out a gold pencil with his pad.

"First a slice of the country pâté . . . then the broiled halibut with no sauce, as usual. And one green vegetable. Anything but spinach."

"The chef has baked zucchini tonight with a crust of Camembert."

"That's for me. And, with the fish, a split of champagne."

"Certainly, sir." Giving another of his almost invisible bows before heading toward the kitchen.

Ash took another swallow of whiskey and, eyes darting around the restaurant, resumed his consideration of what he'd learned from Marnat . . .

Wondered, briefly, where Lyli Amadoro might be dining tonight. Thank God she went to more fashionable spots than Costigan's . . .

Would Sandra Saunders be having dinner at home, alone in that pleasant old-fashioned dining room facing her rose garden? He'd dined there several times while working on her portrait. Just the two of them. He suspected all those relatives who lived with Sandra ate in some sort of communal dining room in the basement. He should have phoned her today when he returned from Connecticut. Do that tomorrow . . .

Ask Sandra to do horoscopes for Mara and his mother. He would like to be present when she interviewed Millie. His mother, author of a dozen detective novels, would ask more questions than Sandra!

As he drank the whiskey he began to relax. The pleasant room with its susurrant voices—there was never any music—always did this when he was overtired.

"Evening, Ash."

He looked up to see Desmond McCorkle. "How are you, Mac?"

"Would I be intruding?"

"Certainly not." He saw that the detective held a double whiskey.

"Wanted a private word with you." Picking up a chair from an empty center table with one hand, he placed it facing Ash and sat down. "Your health, pal!"

Ash raised his glass and they drank.

"Noticed you come in but thought I'd better let you enjoy a few swallows of Danny's best before I bothered you."

"No bother, Mac. Any time."

"Off duty tonight. Hunting doe, as usual. Costigan's watering hole gets a better class of doe than the singles spots. Bit too intellectual, at first sighting, but they bed down like the others."

"When are you going to find yourself another wife?"

"Never again, pal. I've stopped looking for the perfect dame. Found her twice. Wrong twice. Twice divorced. My son's in college, studying to be a shyster. So what do I need with another wife? How's your lovely lady?"

"Still in that same play. How's murder in Manhattan these days?"

"Nothing big at the moment. Only four homicides today. Run-of-the-mill stuff. Things'll pick up as the weather gets warmer. Always more homicides in July and August."

Ash wondered why McCorkle had joined him. He usually didn't leave the bar unless it was with a girl. Handsome guy. Must be in his early forties but looked ten years younger. Only the regulars in Costigan's would recognize the famous Inspector Desmond McCorkle —known in police and criminal circles as Mac the Cork—because his picture rarely appeared in the newspapers. Although his curly silver-red hair, rugged face and the physique under that expensive summer suit would attract the eyes of every woman. He wondered what his "does" said when he introduced himself. Did he tell them who he was when he sighted them at the bar? Maybe he waited until later. Much later . . .

". . . and only learned recently," McCorkle was saying, "you own a piece of this joint."

"Very small piece. A hundred of Johnny's friends put up a few thousand each when he decided to open his own restaurant."

"Must be a gold mine!" McCorkle drained his glass and set it aside. "To get to the point . . ."

Here it came! Ash finished the last of his whiskey.

"I've read your latest portrait in *Metropole*."

"Have you?" This was, certainly, unexpected.

"About that Saunders dame. I'd always thought she was some kind of phony."

"She's on the level, I promise you. Her clients are among the most prominent people in this city."

"So I learned from your profile. Couldn't put it down! The incredible things this dame's predicted. That came true . . ."

"Everything in my portrait was thoroughly checked."

"I always read Saunders' column in the paper."

"Do you?"

"Like to check what it says under my astrological sign. I'm a Leo."

Danny, without a word, set fresh drinks in front of them and removed their empty glasses.

"You said in your portrait," McCorkle continued, "this Saunders dame is a Leo."

"That's right."

"Well! Since we both have the same sign, and now that I've read your article about her and you tell me she's the real McCoy, I'd like to meet the lady. Maybe have her do my horoscope."

"That could be arranged. Quite easily. My wife and my mother plan to have Sandra do theirs. She's already done mine."

"I'd like to talk to this dame. Ask her some questions."

"About the past or the future?"

"Don't give a tinker's damn about the past. That's over and finished. It's the future interests me. My future." He paused. "For instance, how long I am going to live . . ."

"This worries you?"

"Didn't used to bother me—maybe because I never thought about it—but recently I've been wondering if there's a bullet waiting round the next dark corner just for me. I've been lucky all these years but luck eventually leaks out. I'm no kid anymore. Been thinking a lot about death lately. You suppose Saunders would see me?"

"Of course she would. You want me to call her? Arrange an appointment?"

"I can do that. I'll phone her from the office. How much would this set me back? Coupla hundred?"

"I suspect Sandra might do your horoscope for nothing."

"Yeah?"

"She's worked with police departments all over the country. Locating missing persons and criminals . . ."

"I know she's worked with Manhattan Homicide, but never on a case when I was involved. Okay! I'll call her."

"You'll like her, Mac. She's quite a dame." So this was all McCorkle had wanted, to question him about Sandra. He picked up his fresh drink and raised it toward the detective, who reached for his. They touched glasses and drank. Perhaps he could learn something from McCorkle, catch him off guard in this moment of mutual confidence. "Tell me, Mac. What do you know about Lyli Amadoro?"

"That phony dame!"

"You've met her?"

"Never. I've seen her arriving at some of the big charity affairs. Surrounded by her personal Mafia. She's the most carefully guarded dame in this city."

"I've been wondering, for some time, if she'd be a good subject for one of my portraits. You heard any rumors about her? Police talk?"

"Nothing. Very few murders on Park Avenue. Never heard anything about Amadoro being involved with criminals."

"What about drugs?"

"Not to my knowledge, but that, thank God, isn't part of my job. When drugs turn up in a case of homicide—and it happens all the time—I call Narcotics in a hurry. I've no use for bums involved with drugs. Too much respect for the human body—especially mine."

"I'm the same way."

"Waiting for your wife?"

"Not tonight. Mara's working. I'm going to have a quiet dinner, then head home."

"And I've disturbed you long enough." McCorkle drained his glass and set it down. Got to his feet, lifting the chair back to the other table. "Thanks for the conversation, pal."

"Anytime, Mac." Extending his hand across the table.

McCorkle shook it, firmly. "I'll let you know if I see this Saunders dame."

"Have to phone her myself tomorrow. I'll tell her you'll be calling."

"That would be great. I'll check Danny's bar again. In case any fresh does turned up. See you, pal."

"Sure, Mac." He watched the detective as he left the dining room, shoulders straightening, his walk becoming more of a swagger. McCorkle must've sighted an attractive doe at the bar.

He'd made a decision while they talked. He wouldn't say anything to Carrington about that ten thousand Marnat wanted for his information. When the Frenchman called tomorrow, he would tell him he wasn't interested in what he knew about Amadoro. Say he hadn't consulted his superior but had made the decision himself. He didn't care to pay money to an informer.

chapter ten

EACH MORNING THE GREAT CITY WAS BORN AFRESH. Every day was like the start of a new world.

Central Park was divided by curtains of sunlight stretching across Fifth from between the tall buildings.

Heading north, Ash passed from warm sunlight through cool shadow and into sunlight again. He could feel the change in temperature through his jogging suit.

The early morning air was cool and sweet.

This was the first chance he'd had to jog since last Friday. He never bothered on weekends. Only three weekdays—Monday, Wednesday and Friday—but this past Monday he'd overslept after his late supper with Mara at the Russian Tea Room.

He wondered if Marnat was asleep this morning. After staying awake all night and planning what he would do with that ten thousand bucks.

Only a few joggers in sight, far ahead.

He always entered the park at Sixty-fifth and turned north. At the moment he'd reached that part of the drive where he could see the open windows of his own apartment and the elegant mansion, in the distance, housing the Frick Collection.

Not many cars at this hour. A few riders on rented horses, mostly pairs, although there was one bearded older man on a sleek black mare, obviously not rented, who always rode alone.

He'd reached the one lonely spot, in sight of the lake, that always made him slightly uncomfortable. There was talk that several joggers had been mugged in this area. The drive was edged with bushes tall enough to hide a man.

He was a fatalist about muggers. Kept twenty bucks folded in a breast pocket for easy access and carried no other money. They said if you tossed a twenty-dollar bill at a mugger he would leave you alone.

His mind was running faster than his feet.

Thinking about Amadoro. Amadoro of the green eyes. Those eyes of death! What was she like behind that Helen of Troy façade? He had to find out. The real Amadoro . . .

And Marnat! He'd driven along here last night with Marnat . . .

He disliked men who were too handsome. When the Frenchman called he would tell him he didn't want what he was selling.

McCorkle! Worrying about death . . .

Everyone had to die. Most people didn't think about that inevitable fact of life. Perhaps because they never considered such a possibility for themselves. Only other people died . . .

Increasing his pace as he passed the high shrubbery, he was aware of a car approaching behind him. Nobody would attempt to mug him when a car was in sight.

He looked around and saw a black Volkswagen with two athletic types in jogging suits. As it passed he noticed that the license plate was covered with dirt, the car hadn't been washed in weeks.

The car slowed to a stop, several yards ahead.

One of the guys must be getting out to jog while the other drove ahead until his friend tired. They would take turns. Driving and jogging.

Both of them got out. Left the car doors open and came toward him. They wore identical black jogging suits with white stripes.

Ash glanced behind him. No cars approaching and the other joggers had disappeared. One man walking a dog around the far side of the lake.

As they came closer he saw that they were young, short, heavyset. Powerful shoulders. Curly black hair, glistening with oil. Handsome, empty faces, so alike they could be plastic masks. Clones of Paolo's face. The receptionist at Amadoro Associates! Their eyes were on him. Fists already clenched. And they were smiling in anticipation.

He stopped jogging and waited. Realized he was taller than either of them, his arms longer, which gave him an advantage.

The guy on his left swung first.

Ash ducked. Felt the fist go past his left ear.

The force behind the blow carried his attacker off balance.

He gave the second guy a hard left in the nose. Felt cartilage collapse. Swung a right into his gut. The muscles were softer than he'd anticipated.

Nose spurting blood, the guy dropped onto the grass.

Ash turned back to the first jogger as the same fist grazed his right cheek. Ducked but straightened fast with an uppercut that sent the guy sprawling. Whirled to face the other one, who was pushing himself to his feet, mouth and chin covered with blood. Started toward him but the guy backed away, eyes dazed. "Let's get outa here!" he shouted, stumbling ahead of his clone toward their car.

"Give my best to Amadoro!" Ash called.

They threw themselves into the Volkswagen, slammed the doors and sped off.

Ash fingered his cheek and found the skin was broken. Pulled a clean tissue from a pocket, wet it with his tongue and wiped the blood away.

He'd been concerned about muggers along here but hadn't given any thought to the possibility that Amadoro might send someone after him. Muscle boys who were probably good at persuasion but nothing to fear in close combat. His knowledge of boxing, from college, had saved him this time, but he wouldn't care to meet this pair at night on a dark street, when they would be sure to have guns or, more likely, knives.

After a final dab at the cut, he stuffed the tissue into his pocket.

As he resumed his jogging, there was no sign of the Volkswagen and the man across the lake had disappeared with his dog.

Now there was a spurt of cars past him, as though a red light had been holding them at the south entrance to the park.

He turned right toward the Seventy-second Street exit, then right again down Fifth. Crossed the avenue to his apartment building, where the doorman was helping a woman into a taxi. Wiped his cheek with the back of his hand and saw that the trickle of blood had stopped.

The doorman noticed him as the cab drove off. "Back already, Mr. Hendrie?"

"Cut it short this morning. Did you happen to notice a black Volkswagen around here earlier? Two men in it."

"Funny you should ask! I saw them guys drive past half a dozen times. Before you came down to jog."

"You won't be seeing them again." He jogged through the lobby to the elevator.

Safe in the apartment, he examined his cheek before he shaved. The skin was barely scratched.

Showered and dressed, he made coffee and drank two cups—their housekeeper seldom wakened before nine and Mara never opened her eyes until noon—and took a taxi down to his office, where Miss Lundborg had a list of phone calls waiting.

He took it into his office and was checking the names when a light tapping interrupted. "Come in, Mandy!"

She slipped in, wearing a vermilion cheongsam under her smock and gold slippers. In one hand, a pad and pen with a sheaf of typed notes and Teletypes. "You busy?"

He put the list of calls aside. "Only just got in."

"Greta told me." Sinking onto her usual chair, facing him. "I've turned up one or two things."

"I was confident you would." He sat at his desk.

"Talked to Paris and London. Came in early to catch them at the end of their day. London, by the way, was dripping and Paris was smiling."

"Comme toujours!"

"Now, then!" Glancing through the typed pages and Teletypes. "Both London and Paris say they have very little on Amadoro in their files. These Teletypes came later. One from each office." Handing them across the desk. "I told both offices to assign a researcher to the Amadoro project. See what they can find. Especially about Amadoro's marriages. And all official reports and news stories on the deaths of her second and third husbands . . ."

Ash looked at the two brief Teletypes as she talked. "Nothing important here."

"I've explained we need more background material and pictures than usual. Should get something by Friday."

He dropped the Teletypes on his desk as Greta brought coffee. "I'll have mine black this morning, please."

"And you, Miss Kwong?" She set the tray on his desk.

"Cream, as usual. Two sugars."

Ash watched his secretary pour the steaming brew, prepared in the executive kitchen, from a Georgian silver pot into large Wedgwood cups as its dark aroma filled the room.

"I've sent one of my girls up to New London this morning. Folksy type," Mandy continued. "To get a copy of that autopsy report from the police and check out the Coast Guard inquiry. Told her to talk to the locals. Pick up anything she can about Leola Martin's parents. Especially that car accident which put her mother in a wheelchair.

Thanks, Greta." She accepted the cup—after resting papers, pad and pen on the desk—and began stirring her coffee. "I did learn one thing when I talked to London. Their executive editor, Giles Redfern, flew over here this past weekend."

"He's in New York?"

"At the Stanhope. He's here for a meeting with Carrington."

Ash reached to take the cup of coffee from his secretary. "What's happening, Greta? You're wearing your Mona Lisa smile. Are we repainting our London office? Or closing it?"

"Nothing like that. Mr. Redfern, I'm told, is taking a leave of absence to write a novel. He arrived Monday morning, for a week of discussions with Mr. Carrington and the board of directors to find someone who could replace him as head of the London office."

"Greta always knows everything!" Mandy exclaimed. "Long before my spies find out."

"Not really." Greta laughed and headed for the door.

"Greta!" Ash called.

She looked back, still smiling, hand on the doorknob. "Yes?"

"Arrange for me to get together with Giles Redfern. Perhaps lunch somewhere . . ."

"I'm sure that can be fixed." She opened the door and departed.

"I told Paris to get a copy of the *certificat de vie*," Mandy continued, "for Leola Towson's baby. The daughter's name and where she can be located. Told them to contact the American Embassy. Question staff members who knew Amadoro in Paris." Glancing toward the door and dropping her voice. "I learned, from London, that Giles Redfern's wife is a close friend of Madame Amadoro."

"That could be useful."

"They dined together frequently when her second husband—Lord Robert Craydon—was alive. Lyli sees the Redferns whenever she's in England. She still keeps a town house in Knightsbridge."

"Redfern should be able to give me personal information about her marriage to Craydon. His death . . ."

"You see! Another source opens. I should think lots of fresh information will pour in, eventually, from London and Paris—as well as from other sources we can't anticipate. Always happens."

A brisk series of knocks.

Ash glanced toward the door. "Come!"

Cort Fontaine hurried in. "Got a moment?"

"Of course." He saw that the art director held a photograph.

Cort sat on the arm of the other chair facing Ash. "I've put photographers on Amadoro's trail, as you suggested."

"Learn anything?"

"Nothing, as yet. They're watching her on eight-hour shifts. She spent yesterday in her office, except for a two-hour lunch at Twenty-One. Drove there in a chauffeured black Rolls . . ."

"That's her personal car and chauffeur," Mandy explained.

"Apparently had a lunch appointment with an unidentified man who was with her when she left Twenty One and drove back to the office with her. The black Rolls returned at the end of the afternoon—approximately five-thirty—and took her, alone, to that fancy new apartment complex at Fifty-ninth and Park—"

"She lives there!" Mandy interrupted. "That's only five blocks. She could've walked."

"Amadoro didn't come out again. Only picture they got, yesterday, was a shot of the lady leaving Twenty One." He handed the photograph across the desk. "With friend."

Ash took it and saw the familiar 21 entrance, where Amadoro had just come up the shallow steps to the street and was pushing her long blond hair away from her face. Wearing a simple tailored dress, soft green with matching slippers and purse. She had paused in bright sunlight before getting into the Rolls. Her smiling friend stood behind her. Good-looking man, tall, curly blond hair. His face seemed familiar. Ash snatched up a magnifying glass and held it over the photograph. The man's gray suit was unmistakably British. "I'll be damned!"

"You know the guy?" Mandy asked.

"It's Giles Redfern." He put the magnifying glass aside.

Cort looked surprised. "I didn't recognize him. I'd heard he was in New York."

"Everybody heard but me!" Mandy set her cup and saucer on the desk.

The phone shrilled.

Ash reached to pick it up. "Told Greta not to put calls through unless they're important." Lifting the phone to his ear. "Yes?"

"Thought you'd want this." Greta's voice. "Miss Saunders on two."

"I'll take it." He glanced at the others. "Sandra Saunders." He pressed the button. "Good morning, dear lady."

"Ash? Are you all right?"

"Couldn't be better. Tim Carrington wanted to know if you'd gotten any reactions from your portrait."

"They've been pouring in. Complete strangers and dear friends. People I've not heard from in years . . ."

"Are they favorable?"

"All wonderfully positive."

He placed a hand over the mouthpiece. "The response has been terrific. She's delighted."

". . . phones haven't stopped ringing," Sandra was saying. "Never had such a response to anything I've ever done. I'm very grateful to you, Ash. And to *Metropole*. Tell Mr. Carrington and all your other associates."

"I certainly will." He saw Mandy gathering her pen and papers as she got to her feet.

"See you later," Mandy whispered.

He nodded and watched her leave with Cort as he listened to Sandra.

". . . and this national recognition, in your magazine, will have a tremendous effect on public opinion and acceptance of my work. Several of my colleagues have contacted me. Delighted with what my portrait in *Metropole* will do for the entire field of parapsychology. This should help get more endowments for the study of psychic phenomena. Duke University and many others. But that isn't why I'm calling you this morning. I must warn you, Ash . . ."

"Warn me?"

"There is danger for you today. Early this morning, while I was in the garden, I had a premonition of two men threatening you. There seemed to be grass and trees. I came in and checked your charts, and there is an indication of danger for you today while you're in motion."

"That already happened. This morning while I was jogging in Central Park."

"Someone attacked you?"

"Two men. Just as you say."

"Were you hurt?"

"Only a slight abrasion on my cheek. I chased them away."

"Thank God! I should've called at once, but I knew you wouldn't be in the office so early and I didn't want to disturb you at home."

"Your interest in my welfare is very kind. I'm grateful. And touched."

"I'm interested in the well-being of all my clients. And you're much more than a client, Ash. You're a dear friend."

"I planned to call you this morning, but I've been busy. By the way! Now that I've finished your portrait, my wife and I want to join the Parastro Society."

"I thought you might."

"And Mara and my mother would like you to do their horoscopes."

"My pleasure. Have them contact Nora. She arranges everything. Better still, your Miss Lundborg could call Nora and, between them, they can fix dates. Your mother writes detective novels . . ."

"That's right."

"You told me about her when I was doing your charts. I especially enjoy doing horoscopes for writers. They're so complicated."

He laughed. "Millie's will be the most complicated, I promise you. I'll have Greta call Nora."

"Lovely!"

"There's someone else wants you to do his horoscope. You may have heard of Inspector Desmond McCorkle . . ."

"Mac the Cork? I've read about him in the papers."

"He's a friend of mine. I'll pay for it, if you'll do his charts. But don't let him know. Cops don't get that much salary and I owe him for past favors."

"There'll be no charge. I like cops. Always enjoy working with them. All over the country. I've done horoscopes for many of them, several in New York, and I've never charged a fee. Inspector McCorkle called me ten minutes ago."

"Did he?"

"I'm seeing him this afternoon. Many policemen are preoccupied with dying. It's a common fear. I'm sure I can help him."

"He told you he's afraid of death?"

"Didn't need to tell me."

"You are a witch."

Sandra laughed. "Only get my broom out one night every year."

"Perhaps I'll see you later in the week."

"I certainly hope so."

"And what about dinner next week at our apartment? Mara wants to meet you."

"I'd love that."

"Has to be Monday, the one night she doesn't work. I'll have her phone you."

"I shall look forward to that. Good-bye, lover."

"Good-bye, Sandra." He set the phone down and, as he glanced at the photograph of Amadoro and Giles Redfern, reached under his desk and pressed the button twice, the signal for his secretary to come in.

Giles Redfern should be extremely helpful on Amadoro's years in London. Perhaps there would be someone in *Metropole*'s Paris office who knew her when she lived in France.

The door opened and Greta came toward him with her pen and dictation pad. "I found Mr. Redfern in Mr. Carrington's office. He'll drop by later to see you."

"That's fine."

"Doesn't have an office of his own while he's here."

"I expect to be in all day. Sit down."

She sank into an armchair, resting her dictation pad on an arm.

"Phone Nora Sanderson. Arrange for Mara and Millie to have separate appointments with Sandra to have their horoscopes done. This will take some calling, back and forth, to determine when all the parties concerned will be free . . ."

She made notes as he talked.

"Also arrange for all of us—my wife and I, and both my parents—to become members of the Parastro Society. Better consult my father, I suppose, and find out if he wishes to join. I know Millie does, but we'd better ask Alain. Tell Nora to send all bills here to the office and mail everything else—the monthly *Parastro Journal* and any other material—to our apartments."

"I understand."

"Call my wife this afternoon. Tell her I've invited Sandra to dine with us next Monday night. Also, she should call Sandra and invite her personally. Tell my dear wife it should be a rather simple dinner because Sandra's supposed to be on a diet. And that, I believe, does it."

Greta rose from the armchair with her pen and pad. "Is the Amadoro material interesting?"

"Fascinating! But I've no idea, as yet, what direction it will take in relation to her portrait. Oh! Meant to tell you as I came in. That man who phoned yesterday. The one with the accent . . ."

"I remember."

"He'll be calling this afternoon. Around two. I'll talk to him."

"More coffee?"

"No, thanks. You can take these cups."

She piled the cups and saucers carefully.

"I suspect I won't start writing the Amadoro profile as quickly as I began the Saunders portrait. That was probably the easiest portrait I've ever done. And Amadoro's may be the most difficult."

"I certainly hope not." She carried the cups and saucers back to the outer office.

Ash unlocked his desk. Took out the file folder with the sheets on which he had listed the few facts he'd learned about Lyli Amadoro. Spread them in front of him, in the same double rows of six, and opened the folder. For the next hour he went over every word again, making brief notes on each page.

Should his portrait start with Leola Martin's happy childhood in Connecticut? Both parents thought it had been happy, at least the early years. He wasn't so certain.

Why had Leola Martin turned on her parents and never seen them again?

Children frequently rejected parents, but not so suddenly as that.

Had the Martins told him all the facts?

chapter eleven

ASH ORDERED LUNCH FROM THE EXECUTIVE KITCHEN after his secretary left for a luncheon appointment. Walked up and down, considering how to organize the Amadoro portrait from the few facts he now knew about her.

Paused to look down at Central Park from his windows, unable to locate the spot where those thugs had attacked him this morning.

He wondered about Amadoro's reaction when they reported back to whoever was in charge of them. They would certainly say they'd given him a rough time. Never admit he had won that round.

When the waiter brought his lunch he ate half the chicken salad without tasting it and drank the cold Mexican beer standing at the window again. Didn't bother pouring it into a glass because it tasted better from the bottle.

He always thought more clearly, solved problems and worked out his most complicated ideas, looking down at this peaceful green expanse of park . . .

Someone knocked on the door and he gulped the last of his beer. Damn! Couldn't they leave him alone during the lunch hour?

He faced the door. "Who is it?"

The tall man in the blowup with Amadoro came in, smiling and looking very British in another Savile Row suit.

"Giles! How are you?" Ash placed his empty beer bottle on the silver tray and extended a hand as Redfern came toward him. "Only learned, this morning, you were in town."

"Flew over Sunday night." Shaking hands, briskly.

"Sit down . . ." He circled the desk and, casually, slipped the picture of Amadoro and Redfern into the folder. Closed it as Redfern sank into an armchair. "I suppose you'll be discussing your temporary retirement with Carrington and the board of directors." He sat, facing him.

"I've not told them, as yet, I'm departing permanently."

"Are you?"

"That's off the record for the moment. Until I drop my bomb and resign."

"Why are you leaving?"

"As head of the London office, I've absolutely bloody nothing to do unless Carrington needs a feature on some British locale or celebrity. My staff is extraordinarily competent. They can handle whatever's needed without supervision from me. My salary's considerably better than average but not enough to pay me for being bored. And I have been bored for the past year. I've some novels laid out that I'm eager to write. Which is what I was doing, five years ago, when *Metropole* asked me to head their London office. So! I've decided to opt out. My wife and I plan to live in the country. She will grow mums and marrow while I'm at my typewriter."

"Sounds like the good life."

"Not for a young chap like you. But it's what Julia and I want."

"I wish you well."

"Thanks, dear boy. Now, then! I was told by Carrington's secretary —the ubiquitous Miss Crevani—that you wished to see me."

"I do, indeed. Had my secretary send out word the moment I heard you were here."

Redfern gestured with one elegant hand. "I am at your command."

"I suppose you heard, before departing from London, that I'm doing a portrait of Lyli Amadoro." He was aware that Redfern straightened slightly in the armchair, raising his handsome head as though on the defensive. "For our September issue."

"I must've been above the Atlantic, somewhere, at the moment you were being told the subject for your next portrait. I believe it's always announced at a special Sunday brunch."

"That's right."

"We never get the word, in London, before Monday."

"I've learned, quite by chance, that you are a personal friend of the lady."

"Amadoro?" Redfern shrugged. "I suppose I am . . . Lyli doesn't really permit close friends. My wife and I saw her rather frequently when she was married to a British subject and living in London.

Actually, Julia knows her much better than I. Lyli's rather suspicious of anyone connected with a magazine or newspaper. I usually see her at some dinner party or social function."

"I was hoping you might be able to give me a personal slant on Amadoro's life in England. Her marriage . . ."

"Of course, she wasn't Amadoro then. We knew her as Lady Leola Craydon. Saw her, most frequently, prior to the unfortunate death of Robbie Craydon."

"Anything suspicious about that?"

"Suspicious? What the devil do you mean?"

"All three of her husbands seem to have been killed in accidents. Craydon was burned to death testing a racing car."

"There was a thorough investigation by New Scotland Yard and the customary official inquest. I read everything they printed in the London press because we were genuinely fond of Robbie. I'd known him for years. Long before he married the beautiful Mrs. Towson. Robbie was always testing those new motors he designed. Would never leave that to a subordinate. He'd had several earlier accidents with rather severe injuries but always survived. Until that last one. The official verdict was quite simple. He was burned to death when the car crashed into a wall and exploded."

"Did his wife testify at the inquest?"

"She wasn't required to attend. No need for her to testify, since she hadn't been present at the scene of the accident. In fact, she rarely watched Robbie test his new models. Lyli doesn't even drive. She's always chauffeured everywhere. In London or when she was staying at Craydon Hall, their country place. I must warn you, Ash. I'll not help the magazine, in any way, to find out the facts of Lyli's life in London. I will not tell anyone—Tim Carrington or you—anything I know at first hand or have heard from others. That would, in my opinion, be terribly bad form. Absolutely unthinkable!"

"I respect that, Giles, and understand. My mother, you know, was born in London."

"If I knew, dear boy, I'd forgotten. So you do appreciate my position?" Redfern rose from the armchair. "And not a word to Carrington about my leaving permanently. I prefer to inform the old boy myself."

"Of course." He got up and extended his hand again.

Redfern shook hands across the desk. "Perhaps we'll have another chat before I fly home."

"I'd like that." He remained standing as Redfern headed for the open door. "Good luck with Tim Carrington."

"I'm having lunch with him and Horace."

"Any idea who's to replace you in London?"

"Not the foggiest! And don't, quite frankly, give a damn." He went out, leaving the door ajar.

Ash sank into his chair.

Would Redfern phone someone at the London office and order the staff not to provide information to New York about Lyli?

He had a feeling it would be several weeks—perhaps a month—before he could start to write the Amadoro portrait.

"You didn't eat your lunch!"

He looked up to see his secretary frowning at the unfinished salad. "Wasn't hungry."

"I called your father. He doesn't wish to join the Parastro Society."

"I suspected he mightn't. Alain never was a joiner."

"Says he'll hear enough about it from your mother. Miss Kwong's hovering. Told her I'd just come back from lunch and didn't know if you were free."

"Have her come in. Hope she's turned up more on Amadoro than she had this morning."

"She has a fistful of notes."

"That's a hopeful sign." He watched Greta pick up the tray with the debris from his lunch before glancing at the pages spread out on his desk. Nothing more he could learn from them.

"Ash! I'm getting some dribbles of information . . ."

He looked up and saw the scraps of paper and glossy photographs in Mandy's left hand. "Into every life a few dribbles must fall."

She perched on an armchair and glanced at the top scrap of paper. "First of all! We've been unable to track down Leola Martin's paid companion during the years she lived in Manhattan."

"Mrs. Winston?"

"Was able to trace where they lived through the Neighborhood Playhouse. Leola Martin rented a two-bedroom apartment on Morton Street."

"Where the devil's that?"

"Below Greenwich Village. Narrow street between Hudson and Seventh. I used to know a poet who lived there. One of my researchers talked to the present manager of the building, but he'd never heard of

Leola or Mrs. Winston. We've contacted employment agencies that cater to a Park Avenue clientele. Companions and housekeepers. Found an office on Madison that, for years, placed Mrs. Laurie Winston in jobs. Including this one with Leola Martin. The owner came up with the following . . ." Eyeing her notes again. "After Leola Martin married young Towson and moved to London, in 1960, Mrs. Winston retired. She said that Winston—as she called her—told her she would never work again."

"If she was retiring she may have moved away from the city." He made several notes on his pad.

"I've contacted some actor friends who were at the Neighborhood Playhouse the same year as Leola Martin, but they don't remember her. Probably in different classes. The Playhouse office tells me one of their instructors may know something. He was a student when Leola was enrolled. I'm sending one of my girls to see him tomorrow when he breaks for lunch."

"What else?"

"We've identified most of the handsome guys, in these photographs, who escort Amadoro around town. Park Avenue and Wall Street types. Some are married. Several are in two pictures with her. Only one man's in half a dozen."

"Which man?"

Mandy picked out two photographs and shoved them across the desk.

Ash studied them. Amadoro laughing, walking down Fifth, on the arm of a smiling young man with red hair. He was strikingly handsome. Both in evening clothes. Amadoro with the same young man, drinking champagne at Regine's. He remembered both photographs from Sunday's exhibition in the gallery. "Who is this guy?"

"One of those we haven't, as yet, been able to identify. Tonight I'm having one of my kids take his photograph to every smart club. Some doorman or paparazzo will recognize him." She rearranged her papers, pulled out a Teletype and studied the message. "This came in, ten minutes ago, from our Paris office. They're always more prompt than London."

"Which reminds me! I've just talked to Giles Redfern."

"He should know all the gossip about Amadoro's years in London."

"I'm sure he does, but he's not talking."

"Whyever not?"

"Amadoro, it seems, is a personal acquaintance. I can understand his feelings. Not wishing to inform on a friend. I only hope he doesn't order his London staff to refuse us material on Amadoro."

"Don't worry. Most of his staff are American."

"That's true."

"And they detest Redfern."

"Do they! Why?"

"They think he's pompous."

"He is, rather . . . You were about to tell me what came in from Paris."

"Oh, yes." She glanced at the Teletype. "The head of our Paris office—"

"Philippe de Guermond!"

"—knew Amadoro when she was married to her third husband—Conte Alfredo Amadoro—according to his secretary. She'll inform him, when he returns to France next week, that we're doing a cover story on Amadoro. She thinks he could make a large contribution to the Paris material on the lady."

"Where the devil is he?"

"Morocco. With the fashion editor and a photographer, doing a feature on Moroccan food and social life for our October issue. The Paris office is having trouble getting a copy of that *certificat de vie* for Leola Martin's baby because we don't have a birth date or the child's first name. French bureaucracy is being difficult, as usual." She shuffled her papers together as she rose. "I did learn one thing from Paris. Rather sad . . ."

"Oh?"

"They located a woman at the American Embassy who was working there when the baby was born and she helped with all those complicated documents an American must fill out. Including arrangements for its baptism at the American Cathedral. She's checking the date but can't remember the name the child was given. The horrible thing . . ."

"Yes?"

"This woman attended the ceremony. She says the baby was covered by a lace veil to prevent its being seen by the curious, but at one point, as they were leaving the cathedral, the veil dropped and she saw the baby's face. It was disfigured."

"What do you mean?"

"A large birthmark over one cheek. She only caught a glimpse before Leola covered the baby again, but she thinks it was the right side of the face."

"The beauteous Amadoro produced a disfigured child? Imagine how that must've shocked her."

"This American woman remembers that the young mother wept all through the baptismal service." Mandy headed for the door. "See you in the morning."

Ash looked down at Lyli's exquisite face in the photographs.

Cap Larson had heard there was something wrong with the child.

Giving birth to an imperfect baby would have been a shattering experience for Leola Martin. Had the child died, or was she hidden away in some expensive foreign clinic?

He checked his notes.

The baby was born in 1961 but he didn't have the exact date, day or month. She was no longer a child. Twenty-six years old! Nine years older than Leola had been when the baby was born . . .

The child was now a young woman.

He left his desk and walked to the windows.

Central Park was golden green in the afternoon sunlight.

Sad that a beautiful woman could produce a disfigured child. The press had, apparently, never learned about Lyli's daughter.

Could this daughter be the secret Amadoro feared might be discovered in her past?

Ash felt a sudden surge of compassion for Lyli Amadoro. Certainly he wouldn't reveal the daughter in his portrait. Some secrets should remain hidden.

He wondered how McCorkle was doing with Sandra this afternoon. She always interviewed new clients in her office overlooking Gramercy Park. That's where she had questioned him and he had answered every question, frankly and completely. He'd done that before she would consent to being interviewed. How would McCorkle feel being questioned? He was the one who usually did all the grilling.

"Ash! Got a minute?"

"Certainly." He turned from the windows, recognizing the voice, and faced Tony Rufino. Surprised, as the managing editor came toward him, to see that he was smiling. First time he'd seen Tony smile in months.

"I've come to apologize."

"What the devil are you talking about?" He crossed the office to meet him. "Apologize for what?"

"The ridiculous way I've been acting."

"I don't understand."

"There were rumors, months ago, you were after the London job."

"You mean Redfern?"

"I heard about it last winter, when Giles was here before Christmas, that he was taking a leave of absence this summer. There was a rumor you wanted his job."

"I'd no idea Giles was leaving until this afternoon. He stopped by and told me."

"Everyone said you would get it. I resented that because you've never been involved with management. I thought my qualifications were better."

"And, of course, they are. Immeasurably! You mean this is why you suddenly became antagonistic?"

"I suppose I did. Without realizing it."

"I'd no idea why we were so frequently at odds. For no reason. I don't want that London job. My future's here, in New York. My wife has a career of her own in the theater. I wouldn't leave her."

"But isn't one of your parents British?"

"My mother."

"I thought that might be part of the reason you wanted to move to England. Your family."

"Both my parents live in New York. I've been to London many times but have no desire to live there. Don't like the food."

"I've been an idiot!"

"I sincerely hope you get the job. Carrington and the board are meeting today. Why don't you talk to Giles? Let him know you'd like to take over while he's—on leave."

"For how long do you suppose that'll be?"

"I've no idea. Take him out to lunch tomorrow. Sell yourself."

"I will! I certainly will! Wish I'd done this six months ago. Come to you and told you . . ."

"I'm sure you'll do a splendid job in London."

"Thanks, Ash." Tony turned and hurried toward the open door. "Let you know what develops."

Ash went back to his desk and checked the clock. Pressed a button under his desk and picked up the phone.

"Yes, Mr. Hendrie?"

"Didn't that man with the French accent call at two o'clock?"

"No. He didn't."

"That's odd. It's after three now. Thank you, Greta." He put the phone down.

Had Marnat forgotten to phone, or had he changed his mind?

He jabbed the button again, twice this time. Sat down, facing the door, and waited for his secretary.

She came in swiftly with her dictation pad.

"I'd like you to make a call for me, if you will."

"Certainly."

"Sit here beside me. So I can listen." He pushed the phone toward her as she sank into the chair where she always sat for dictation. "Call Amadoro Associates. Ask for Mr. Clement Marnat. He's the man with the French accent. If he isn't in his office, find out where you can reach him."

"Right." She rested her pad and pen on the desk.

"If they want to know who you are, tell them you're a personal friend. Don't give a name. If they insist—hang up."

She dialed and waited for the connection. "Mr. Clement Marnat, please . . . Thank you."

Ash studied Lyli's smiling face in the two photographs.

"Mr. Marnat's office? Is he there at the moment? . . . I see. When do you expect him?"

Ash turned to watch her reactions.

"Really! I had no idea . . . Oh! Just a friend. Thank you." She returned the receiver to its cradle. "Mr. Marnat left, last night, for Paris."

"Did he!"

"He'll be away for several weeks on company business."

"I'll bet he will! Check the Manhattan directory." She rose, picking up her pen and pad.

"See if there's a listing for Clement Marnat."

"Be right back." She headed for the door.

Ash frowned. Something had happened to Marnat or he would've called. Had someone overheard their conversation yesterday on the phone? Had they been watching from a car when he met Marnat last night? Followed them through the park? Trailed the Frenchman after he dropped him on Park Avenue?

Greta returned with a slip of paper. "He's in the directory. East Fifty-fourth. Here's the address and phone number." She handed him the piece of paper. "Want me to dial the number?"

"I'll do it."

"Anything more?"

"Not just now." He checked the phone number as she left. Reached to pull the phone closer, pressed an outside button and dialed. Heard the phone ringing. Let it ring several times, then dialed again.

Marnat's phone rang and rang but nobody answered.

chapter twelve

ASH DIDN'T LEAVE THE *METROPOLE* OFFICE UNTIL AFTER six and, when he reached the street, decided to walk a few blocks up Park Avenue before thinking about dinner. The fresh air might clear his aching head.

Mara would be asleep, after the midweek matinee, on that pink chaise in her dressing room at the Biltmore. She would have a light supper, served by a waiter from Sardi's or some other nearby restaurant, before her evening performance.

He'd gone over his notes again, adding new ones from the information Mandy had given him. Most important was the fact that Leola Martin's daughter by Toby Towson had a disfigured face. That could have had a traumatic impact on the mother.

Did he need to know what had happened to the daughter? Probably not. He would never mention her in his profile of Amadoro. Or would he? Perhaps say there was a daughter but nothing more . . .

And what about Marnat? Why hadn't the Frenchman called him? He had needed that money to escape from Amadoro and live in France. Could he have persuaded her to transfer him to the Paris office in return for his silence? Or had he been ordered back to France, unexpectedly, for legitimate business reasons?

This side of Park Avenue was comfortably cool, but the opposite side looked hot because the sun, sinking in the west, still had enough power to turn the taller buildings bright orange, their windows flaming.

A stream of attractive young women hurrying to escape from their jobs. Smiling in anticipation of the evening. Several smiled at him.

He was glad he hadn't told Carrington about Marnat. The idea of paying that much money for information disgusted him and, he felt certain, would have been distasteful to the old man.

Ash saw he was approaching Sixty-first Street, as though he were heading home, away from Marnat's apartment.

Why was he avoiding it? He knew he must go there and find out, for himself, whether Marnat had departed for Paris yesterday. There would be someone—a manager or neighbor—who could tell him.

But first, he'd have dinner.

He turned left on Sixty-first and walked west to Café Lavendou.

The restaurant was crowded but the headwaiter found him a table. Dinner was excellent, including saumon en brioche, the service unobtrusive. He nodded to several acquaintances and realized he was the only diner eating alone.

After dinner, before he had time to change his mind, he found a taxi and told the driver to take him to Fifty-fourth Street.

Marnat's address was between Park and Lexington.

He paid the driver and walked east.

Most side streets, at night, were dark and silent like this one. Nobody walking. Not a car moving.

He felt a brief and unexpected frisson of apprehension.

More than seven million people on this small cluster of islands which were New York City, but he knew no more than a few hundred of them. Perhaps only twenty or thirty intimately.

He looked up at the windows of the buildings. All dark or curtained. New York was a secret city. A dangerous city.

Turn an unfamiliar corner and you could face sudden violence.

The address he sought was displayed in gleaming metal numerals above a lighted boutique window filled with golden evening purses and jeweled scarves. The shop was dark for the night.

Walking past the entrance, he saw the street number repeated on a brass plate beside a door under an archway several steps below street level. Going down the steps, he glanced up at the façade of the building and saw that it was a renovated brownstone. The original high front steps had been removed, the three-story structure turned into apartments.

He tried the knob and the door opened into a long hall lighted by a single overhead globe. As he went toward the carpeted staircase he noticed a row of mailboxes, each with the number of an apartment. The manager—Mrs. Lacey—was number 1 and Clement Marnat had number 6.

Ash went up the steps, aware of the silence, to the second floor, where a large shaded lamp was lighted on a table between small white pots of pink azaleas. Continued on, to the top floor, where an identical lamp cast its light on similar pots of flowers. Three apartments on each floor.

Not a sound in the building. Either the tenants had gone out for the evening or they were relaxing after dinner, although he didn't hear any television sets. All these old houses had thick walls.

Apartment 6 was at the rear. There was a small card with Clement Marnat written in green. Why did the French like green ink?

He pressed the bell button and heard a buzzer respond.

A woman laughed, suddenly, in one of the front apartments.

Ash fingered the button again and, after a moment, knocked several times. Tried the knob. The door was locked.

He returned the way he had come, down to the second floor, and found number 1 in the front. The card, under the bell button, had Mrs. Ferne Lacey neatly typed, and there was a faint blur of voices from inside. Pressed the button and heard another buzzer.

The door was opened by a plump woman with inquisitive black eyes and a mass of chestnut hair hanging to the shoulders of an attractive housecoat, holding a tall glass in her hand. "Yes?"

"Mrs. Lacey?"

"That's right."

"I'm looking for Clement Marnat. Phoned several times this afternoon, but there was no answer. I've just rung the bell and he seems to be out."

"I never know when Clem's home. Matter of fact, I haven't seen him since last night."

"Did he say anything about leaving for Europe?"

"Not a word! You wouldn't be Mr. Hendrie, would you? Ashton Hendrie . . ."

"How could you know?"

"Well, I'm not psychic, if that's what you're thinking." She pushed the door back for him to enter. "Come in, Mr. Hendrie."

He saw a living room crowded with furniture, and the voices were coming from a large television set.

She closed the door and moved ahead of him across the room. "Let me turn this damn thing off." She leaned down and the television screen faded to emptiness.

Ash noticed a copy of *Metropole* on a sofa. So Mrs. Lacey had been reading his Saunders portrait!

She rested her half-empty glass on a coffee table and went toward a small desk near a window overlooking the street.

"How'd you know my name?" he asked.

"Been expecting you. Sooner or later."

"I don't understand . . ."

"Clem left an envelope for you."

"Did he?"

She opened a drawer in the desk and pulled out an envelope. "Said I was to give this to you and nobody else. If I didn't see him before the weekend, he said I should call you. Tell you I had it. Which worried me." She faced him. "He wrote your name on the envelope with a phone number where I could reach you." Handing the envelope to him.

Ash saw his name, written in green ink on the white envelope, with the phone number for his office.

"When did he leave this?"

"Last night. Around ten, I think." She sank onto a sofa and reached for her drink. "I hope nothing's happened to Clem. Such an attractive gentleman . . ."

He turned the envelope over, saw that it had been sealed, the flap secured with transparent tape.

"Would you care for a drink, Mr. Hendrie?"

"Not at the moment. Thanks." He ripped the envelope open and pulled out a folded sheet of expensive notepaper. Unfolded it and saw several lines written in the same green ink. "Forgive me . . ."

"Go right ahead."

His eyes quickly absorbed the words.

              Tuesday night

  Monsieur Hendrie:
  I've just returned from our meeting and, as
  I entered this building, noticed a man standing
  in a doorway across the street.
  Came upstairs but wanted to see if he was
  still there.
  Went out again and there was a different man
  in the same doorway.
  Unable to see their faces, but the second man

was shorter than the first.
Walked over to Lexington and bought a paper.
Second man followed.
Was able to get a look at his face. A rather
ugly Mediterranean type. Never saw him before.
Someone knows I talked to you. So my life
may be in danger.
I will call you tomorrow afternoon, at two
o'clock, as I promised.
If you do not hear from me at that time,
you will know something happened.
I'm leaving this with the manager, Mrs. Lacey,
because I'm sure you'll try to contact me
if I don't call you.

No signature.

Ash folded the note and thrust it into a pocket with the torn envelope. "He wants me to pick up something from his apartment. Says you have a key."

"Of course." She put her glass down again and pushed herself up from the sofa, chestnut hair swaying. Went back to the desk and pulled out another drawer. Turned to face him, key in hand. "I never give keys to strangers, but since Clem asked you to get something from his apartment . . ." She held out the key and smiled.

He slipped it from between her fingers. "I'll return this as I leave."

"Leave the door open." Sinking onto the sofa and pushing the curtain of hair away from her face. "Maybe you'll have a drink later."

"Be back in a moment." He left the door ajar and returned upstairs. More slowly this time, reluctant to enter Marnat's apartment, certain he would find something unpleasant behind that locked door.

The upper corridor was silent as he turned the key in the lock.

Pushed the door open, cautiously, into darkness. Stood there, senses alert, listening. Not a sound.

He found the usual wall switch inside the door. Snapped it and two shaded lamps came alive in a small living room.

Removed the key from the lock, dropped it into a pocket and shut the door. Saw that most of the furniture was French—either antiques or good reproductions—and framed travel posters with photographs of familiar Parisian streets hung on the walls. As his eyes darted he noticed that every drawer was pulled out from a desk and sofa pillows had been scattered on the floor.

He crossed the living room toward an inner door standing open into a dark bedroom. The only light came from the lamps behind him.

First thing he saw was the unmade bed. Sheets tossed back, pajamas flung across a chair. Tall French armoire against one wall, doors wide open, a row of expensive suits on hangers.

Something stirred beyond the armoire.

He stepped back, startled, then realized it was only a thin summer curtain moving in a current of air from an open window.

As he went toward the armoire, eyes adjusting to the dim light, he saw something on the floor.

A man was sprawled there.

He found a wall switch and clicked it.

Lights came on in a reading lamp on a bedside table and in a large lamp on a chest of drawers under an ornately framed mirror.

Ash glimpsed himself in the mirror, like a stranger, as he passed the chest and approached the body.

The face was turned away but he could tell that it was Marnat.

There was no blood but the man was, obviously, quite dead.

He reached down but withdrew his hand with distaste, before touching the back of the Frenchman's neck.

Mustn't touch anything here.

He straightened and glanced at the row of expensive suits hanging in the open armoire. Twenty or more! He'd never known a man who had that many suits.

What should he do now? Call the police, of course . . .

No! Call McCorkle.

chapter thirteen

MRS. LACEY WAS SITTING ON THE SOFA AS HE ENTERED, holding a fresh drink. "You found what you were looking for?"

He closed the door and went toward her. "I found something I wasn't looking for. A body."

"You don't mean . . ."

"Monsieur Marnat, I suspect, has been murdered."

"In my building?" She gulped her drink. "Oh, my God . . ."

"I must call the police."

She gestured toward a pink telephone on the desk.

He went to the desk, snatched up the receiver and dialed.

"Thank God you found his body. Not I . . ."

"Police Emergency." The voice sounded young and alert.

"I want to reach Inspector Desmond McCorkle."

"McCorkle works out of the Seventeenth Precinct. They'll be able to tell you where he is at the moment. I'll connect you."

"Thanks."

"I think we'd both better have a drink." Mrs. Lacey rose, unsteadily, from the sofa and went to a compact bar where she took two highball glasses from a shelf.

Ash could hear the phone ringing.

"Straight Scotch, Mr. Hendrie?"

"That would be fine." Pray God he would be able to reach McCorkle. He didn't care to explain his presence here to anyone else. Why didn't they answer the damn phone?

"Seventeenth Precinct. Officer Gratz."

"Where can I reach Inspector McCorkle?"

"At the moment? Let me think . . ."

"This is urgent. I'm a personal friend."

"Everybody's a friend of the Cork. Hold on, sir. Lemme see can I locate him."

Mrs. Lacey lurched toward him and held out one of the glasses.

He saw that her hand was trembling. It was the wrinkled hand of an old woman. "Thanks." He tossed back a large swallow of whiskey.

She returned to sink onto the sofa and began to gulp her drink. "Mr. Marnat was such an elegant man. Always so thoughtful! Why would anyone want to kill him?"

"I couldn't hazard a guess." He set the glass down.

"Was there a weapon? A gun or . . ."

"I didn't take the time to look."

"You still there, sir?"

"Yes!"

"McCorkle's workin' day shift. That bein' the case, you better try a bar over on Third. We often reach him there. I'll check the number . . ."

"Costigan's?"

"You do know McCorkle!"

"Thanks." He dialed the familiar number as he glanced toward the silent woman on the sofa. "I should've called this number first . . ."

"Costigan's. Good evening."

He recognized the voice. "Johnny, it's Ash Hendrie."

"Mr. Hendrie!"

"Is McCorkle there?"

"Relaxing at the bar, as usual."

"Let me speak to him, please."

"Hold on."

He heard muted voices in the restaurant as Costigan carried the phone into the bar. Realized, suddenly, that he would have to show McCorkle the note from Marnat to prove his reason for being here. Felt in his pocket and found the folded sheet of paper with the envelope.

"Good evening, pal. McCorkle speaking."

"Thank God! I've just found a dead body."

"Happens all the time. Somebody you know?"

"Matter of fact, yes, I do know him. A Frenchman named Marnat. He worked for Lyli Amadoro. Or did, until very recently."

"You mentioned the Amadoro dame last night."

"And you were right, Mac. What you asked."

"Amadoro is your next portrait?"

"You guessed it."

"Where are you now?"

"The building where Marnat lived. I'm in the manager's apartment. Number One, on the second floor. Fifty-fourth between Park and Lexington, and you're at Fifty-third and Third."

"I could walk it in five minutes but I have a car."

Ash gave him the street number, set the phone down. Reached for his drink and finished the whiskey.

"Another drink, Mr. Hendrie?"

"No more, thanks." He put the empty glass down and sank into an armchair. Realized that her face was an expertly painted mask which, in the past few minutes, had developed cracks.

"I've read about Inspector McCorkle in the papers."

"I've known Mac for years."

"And you know Sandra Saunders! I read your portrait of her this afternoon. And here you are, in my apartment! This could only happen in New York . . ."

"With a dead man upstairs and a detective on the way." Jumping up. "Better leave your door ajar." He opened the door again.

"I do hope this won't give the building a bad name. Having a murder here."

Ash paced aimlessly, avoiding the furniture, as they talked. "I would imagine there are certain people who might want an apartment where someone's been murdered. You may even get more rent for it."

"I wouldn't want that sort of creep on the premises!"

"You own this building?"

"Got it in my second divorce. Tell me, Mr. Hendrie, what's she really like? Sandra Saunders . . ."

"Miss Saunders is an amazing woman."

"You think she's on the level? All this parapsychology stuff."

"I do. Yes."

"I've always wanted to have my horoscope done but was never sure whether or not I really believed in astrology. I do believe in some of it, but not everything. I'd like to know what the stars say about my future. You must've gotten to know Miss Saunders quite well while you wrote your portrait. What did you think of her, personally?"

"I started out with disbelief but I became convinced she's on the level. Before I began to write her portrait she did my horoscope. Gave me much valuable advice about my future."

"Did you have any psychic experiences of your own while you were involved with her?"

"Yes, I did."

"How fascinating!"

"I've arranged for both my wife and my mother to have their horoscopes charted by Miss Saunders. Which tells you what I think of the lady. We're also, the three of us, becoming members of the Parastro Society."

"I've several friends who belong. They've told me amazing things about their meetings. There's to be one at Town Hall—I forget just when—with some famous French psychic."

"I know. Miss Saunders has mentioned him."

"He made the most incredible predictions, last week, in San Francisco! About the future of the whole world."

"How well did you know Clement Marnat?" Ash asked abruptly, watching for her reaction.

She lowered her eyes. "I knew Clem quite—intimately."

"Did he have many visitors?"

"Well, I—I don't spy on my tenants."

"Any Latin types? Men, I mean. Short and muscular . . ."

"Not to my knowledge. I never saw any men friends."

"Women?"

"Oh, yes. I've seen him with several attractive young ladies. Noticed them from my windows, getting out of taxis—"

"Here you are!"

Mrs. Lacey gasped and dropped her empty glass.

Ash turned to see McCorkle looming in the doorway.

"Didn't mean to startle you, ma'am." He picked up the glass, which had rolled toward his foot, and set it on the coffee table.

"This is Inspector McCorkle," Ash explained. "Mrs. Lacey, who owns the building and rented an apartment to Marnat."

McCorkle nodded. "Mrs. Lacey . . ."

"I've read about you, Inspector. Never thought I'd see you."

"How long did this Marnat person live here?"

"Three years, I believe. Or was it four? I'll have to check."

"Has he ever, to your knowledge, been in any sort of trouble?"

"Oh, no! He was a gentleman."

McCorkle turned to Ash. "Where's the body?"

"Upstairs, in his apartment."

"I'll have a look. You better come along."

"I've got the key."

"And I'll want to talk to you later, Mrs. Lacey." McCorkle went ahead of Ash toward the open door. "Ask a few questions . . ."

"I'll be right here."

Ash closed the door and led McCorkle toward the stairs.

"Another lush," the detective grumbled. "You said this guy—Marnat—worked for Amadoro?"

"One of her personal assistants. She brought him from Paris. From what he told me, they'd had an affair after the death of her last husband."

"Were they still . . . ?"

"He didn't say."

"How'd you get involved with the guy?"

"Met him two days ago, when I went to interview Amadoro."

"Where was this?"

"Her office at Amadoro Associates." Climbing the steps, he quickly explained their meeting and as he turned the key in the lock, was telling McCorkle about his drive through Central Park with Marnat. He opened the door into the lighted apartment.

McCorkle went in first. "Where is it?"

"On the floor in the bedroom. I left the lights on." He closed the door as the detective went toward the inner room.

"Don't touch anything!" McCorkle called back.

"I didn't and I won't." He placed the key on a coffee table near the phone and, suddenly weary, sank onto a fauteuil. Leaned back, closing his eyes.

Did Amadoro have Marnat killed to prevent his talking? Amadoro was capable of using violence to achieve what she wanted or prevent what she didn't want. Her fortune could eliminate anyone who got in her way. Frightening thought . . .

"He's dead, all right."

Ash straightened and opened his eyes.

"It's murder. I can smell it. Taste it." McCorkle sank onto the sofa, reached for the phone and dialed. "Looks like the guy struck his head on that big clothes cupboard. Then again, maybe he didn't."

"I saw no blood."

"It's soaked into the rug." He moved the receiver close to his mouth and lowered his voice. "Inspector McCorkle speaking . . ."

As the detective gave orders, Ash wondered, unexpectedly, if his own life might be in jeopardy. Would Amadoro go that far to prevent him from writing her portrait? This was ridiculous! But suddenly, to his surprise, he knew fear—genuine fear—as never before in his life. His palms, he realized, were cold. He noticed, as McCorkle talked, a copy of *Metropole* resting at the far end of the sofa. Sandra's face. Still smiling.

The detective set the phone down. "They'll be here right away."

"Who?"

"Homicide detectives, forensic boys, coroner's assistants. The lot! Obviously, pal, you didn't kill this guy."

"Quite obviously." He was startled by the idea. "I promise you I did not."

McCorkle saw the magazine on the sofa. "That dame sure gets around. Met her this afternoon. She asks questions like a shrink. Or a detective."

"You liked her?"

"She's something special. I'm seeing her again tomorrow for another session. Tell me, pal, what was this Marnat guy like?"

"He was a smarmy creep. Willing to tell all he knew about Amadoro. Her personal life and business affairs. For a price."

"How much?"

"Ten thousand bucks."

"That's a nice price. You think he knew something that Amadoro didn't want you to find out?"

"He implied there were several things. Told me last night, to whet my curiosity, that Amadoro confessed to him, one night in Paris, that she had murdered her second husband."

"In France?"

"England. Burned to death testing a racing car he'd designed and was testing for Craydon Motors. That was his name—Sir Robert Craydon—he owned the company. There was an official investigation which called his death accidental."

"Then how'd the dame kill him?"

"She apparently didn't explain that to Marnat. They were at a party in Paris when she told him. *Au pays des rêves d'or . . .*"

"What the hell's that?"

"Land of golden dreams. They were smoking opium."

"I'm getting damn tired of drugs turning up in every murder investigation! No nice, simple murders anymore."

"Amadoro had two of her thugs attack me this morning while I was jogging in Central Park."

"They hurt you?"

"I chased them away."

"How'd you happen to find Marnat's body?"

"I suspected something was wrong when he didn't phone me this afternoon. He was to call me at two for my answer."

"What answer?"

"Whether *Metropole* would pay him the ten thousand bucks. That had to be approved by my boss."

"Was it?"

"I didn't tell him about Marnat. Decided I didn't care to be involved with an informer. Never happened before on any of my other portraits. I was going to tell Marnat I'd decided, myself, I wanted no part of it, but he didn't phone. That's when I became suspicious, because he'd been desperate for the money. Needed it to get away from Amadoro and go back to France."

"He told you that?"

"Oh, yes! So when he didn't call, I was certain something was wrong. Had my secretary phone Amadoro Associates and try to contact him. She was told he'd returned to Paris on company business. I had her check the directory and he was listed. Called several times but got no answer. So, after dinner, I came here. The manager hadn't seen him since last night, but she had a note Marnat said to give me if I came looking for him. With my office number on the envelope where she could reach me if I didn't show up before the end of the week."

"You've got this note?"

"Of course." Ash pulled the note and envelope from his pocket and handed them over.

McCorkle glanced at the name and phone number on the envelope, then unfolded the sheet of paper and read Marnat's note. He finally looked up. "I'll keep this."

"Of course."

He folded the note into the envelope and slipped it into his breast pocket. "I'll check with a pal at New Scotland Yard tomorrow. Get their official report on the death of Amadoro's second husband. What did you say his name was?"

"Craydon. Robert Craydon."

"How many times has this dame been married?"

"Three. Far as I know and all three husbands died in accidents."

"That's worth looking into."

"I talked to a man yesterday who saw Toby Towson—her first husband—killed."

"Witnessed his death?"

"So he says. I went up to New London to talk to her parents. They suggested I see Cap Larson—captain of the Towsons' yacht—who was standing on deck beside young Towson when he went overboard in a gale. Tried to save him."

"And the third husband?"

"Alfredo Amadoro died in a skiing accident. Marnat claims he saw it happen. He and several other skiers."

"Three husbands—three fatal accidents?"

"The lady, apparently, inherited three fortunes."

"Money is always a primary motive for murder. I think I'll have a look into all three of those deaths. What else did Marnat tell you about the Amadoro dame?"

"That's about it. And I can't be certain he was telling the truth when he said Amadoro confessed to killing Craydon. That may have been a come-on to get those ten thousand bucks."

"Someone followed Marnat last night, after he left you. Trailed him here and killed him. Maybe Amadoro found out he'd talked to you on the phone and had him followed from the time he left his office."

"I didn't see a car tailing us through the park."

"Maybe you weren't looking. I'll have a talk with this Amadoro dame tomorrow."

"Good luck, pal."

"Unfortunately, we've lost twenty-four hours. Good thing Marnat left a note for you. If you hadn't come here he might not have been found for several days."

Ash heard feet thudding on the stairs, a rising murmur of men's voices and laughter.

McCorkle got to his feet. "Of course, there's a possibility Marnat's death has nothing to do with this Amadoro dame. He may have surprised some guy robbing his apartment."

"You think that?" Ash rose from the fauteuil.

"No, I don't." He went to open the door and a crush of men poured into the room. "Straight ahead, gentlemen." Motioning toward the bedroom. "Be my guests!" He turned back to Ash. "You needn't stay."

"I'm heading home to bed."

McCorkle held out his hand. "Want to thank you for phoning me tonight. This looks like the first interesting murder of the summer. I'd have been contacted later, but I like to be on the scene early."

Ash shook his hand. "You'll keep me informed? Anything you learn about Amadoro. Remember, off the record, she's my *Metropole* portrait for September."

"Call you tomorrow."

"Don't know where I'll be."

"I'll find you. Good night, pal."

"Good night." As Ash went toward the open door he heard the sound of voices from the inner room. Some were laughing. McCorkle closed the door but Ash could hear their laughter as he went down the silent corridor toward the stairs.

The laughter was, somehow, obscene.

chapter fourteen

ASH SAT AT HIS DESK, THE AMADORO FILE OPEN AND ITS contents spread out in front of him, staring at the blue sky beyond his windows.

So much to be done but, as yet, no real idea what direction his portrait of Amadoro would take.

His eyes dropped to the double rows of pages listing all the known facts and paused at the final two. FRIENDS and ENEMIES. Did Amadoro have any real friends in New York? Who were her enemies?

He reread each page, starting with CHILDHOOD.

Under SECOND MARRIAGE he wrote:

> Did she murder Craydon?
> Or did Marnat say this to get ten thousand dollars?

Under ENEMIES he wrote one name:

> Clement Marnat

Returned to the previous page and under FRIENDS listed:

> Giles Redfern and wife (London)—won't talk
> Philippe de Guermond and wife (Paris)—?

Giles would be dropping his bomb today. He must see him again before he flew back to England. There must be some way he could be persuaded to talk about Amadoro. Perhaps Carrington might put pressure on him.

One morning paper had carried a brief item about Marnat's death. Body of Clement Marnat, employee of Amadoro Associates, had been found in East Side apartment. No address. Cause of death under investigation. No mention of murder or McCorkle.

There was a light knock on the door and he turned to see his secretary. "Yes?"

"Told Miss Crevani you'd like Mr. Redfern to join you for lunch. She just called back to say he won't be free."

"I suspect he's avoiding me."

"Crevani says they're having meetings all day."

"If McCorkle calls, put him through."

"Right."

He watched her leave, then glanced at the Plexiglas clock on his desk—time ticking silently in a cube of ice—and saw it was past eleven. He'd been sitting here nearly two hours, accomplishing nothing.

Returning to the pages spread in front of him, he wondered if the clue to Amadoro was buried in these typed and written words, the secret she'd hidden for years and didn't want revealed.

Could it be she had murdered her second husband and gotten away with it? When did he die?

He checked under SECOND MARRIAGE and saw that Craydon was killed in 1972. Fifteen years ago. Surely if that had been murder someone would have exposed the truth long before this. Except he'd read somewhere that most murders were never solved.

His train of thought was interrupted by the phone. Cort Fontaine reporting that his photographers had turned up nothing more on Amadoro. She hadn't left her apartment last night and had returned to Amadoro Associates this morning in her chauffeured Rolls.

Setting the phone down, he wondered if she had waited in her apartment all night for word that Marnat's body had been found.

He'd watched the morning news on television but there'd been nothing.

The phone rang again.

He picked it up. "Yes, Greta?"

"Mrs. Hendrie calling."

"Wife or mother?"

"Wife. On line two."

"At this hour!" He pressed the button. "Aren't you up early, my love?"

"Couldn't sleep."

"Bad audience last night?"

"Oh, no! We had a lovely house. Went right to sleep but wakened around five. No idea why. Heard you depart at nine. I've just talked to Sandra Saunders and she is a darling. She's coming to dinner Monday night. Seven o'clock. Thought we'd dine at eight. The three of us, comfy-cozy! Rosie and I are going to work on the menu this afternoon."

"Keep it light. Sandra's on a diet but she likes desserts."

"Rosie will have something delicious. After we decide on the food, you can order the wines."

"I'll select them, myself, Saturday."

"How's the Amadoro portrait going?"

"Slowly and painfully."

"You always say that when you're starting a new one."

"Don't you have a matinee today?"

"I'll be leaving in an hour. Bye, lover . . ."

Ash set the phone down, but before he could return to his notes there was a faint tapping on the door. "Come in, Mandy!"

Today she was wearing a yellow cheongsam under her smock. Holding a clutch of papers in one hand. "Morning, Ash!"

"I hope to God you've something interesting for me today."

"I most certainly do." She sat facing him and spread the papers out on her lap. "First another Teletype from Paris. They found the *certificat de vie* for Nicole Towson."

"So that's her name. Nicole?"

"It doesn't mention any birthmark on her face, and the American Embassy has no record of where Nicole Towson is today."

"Keep digging. Somebody must know."

"Unfortunately, Monsieur de Guermond will be held up another week in Morocco. Some sort of festival in the desert—rarely witnessed by foreigners—he wants to get photographs."

"I'll call him when he returns."

"We've been more successful in New London."

"You sent one of your girls up there yesterday?"

"She talked to everybody!" Checking notes. "Managed to get copies of the autopsy report and the Coast Guard inquiry on Toby Towson's drowning." Handing several Xeroxed pages across the desk. "Nothing suspicious about it."

He ran his eyes down each page and saw the words "accidental death" in both reports as Mandy talked.

"She found some clippings in the New London public library about the wedding of Leola's parents. The bride's name was Glenda Darling when she was on Broadway."

"Obviously a stage name."

"There was also a clipping about Mrs. Martin's accident."

"What accident?" He looked up as he set the reports aside.

"You wanted to know why she's in a wheelchair."

"Oh, yes."

"She was in a car. Driving alone in a snowstorm and hit a tree. Car was wrecked and she had severe spinal injuries. This was 1972. The clipping said she lost control on a stretch of icy road, but my girl questioned several people about the accident and two of them said Glenda had been listening to her car radio and heard a report that Sir Robert Craydon, husband of the former Leola Towson, had died testing a racing car in England. The news, apparently, distracted Mrs. Martin and she crashed into the tree."

He made a brief note on the page headed PARENTS.

"Another of my girls had lunch yesterday with an instructor at the Neighborhood Playhouse who was a student there with Leola Martin. Took him to lunch in a pub on Third Avenue—the school's on Fifty-fourth—and he remembers that Leola Martin had some talent, but more ambition than talent. Said she wasn't liked by the girl students but all the guys pursued her. She was a beauty, even then, and she had more money than most students. The most interesting thing he said was Leola tried out for a part in a play her class was performing but didn't get it. When they began rehearsing, the girl who won the part was ill and couldn't be there. Leola said she knew the lines. The director let her do several scenes and she was terrific. Knew every word! So they gave her the part and she was a tremendous success. Months later the other girl came back from Europe and told everyone Leola paid her to say she was ill. That's how the girl could afford a trip to Europe!"

"Even then she was buying people to get what she wanted."

"We've traced this man." Mandy handed a glossy color photograph across the desk. "You wanted to know his name."

Ash saw that it was the red-haired young man who had been photographed with Amadoro more often than her other escorts.

"His name is Burke Benedict. He's a model."

"That name for real?"

"His agent wouldn't say, but he did give me this picture with the guy's credits on the back."

Ash turned the photograph over and saw that Benedict was six feet three and had been born in Montana. Long list of top advertising agencies that had used him as a model and half a dozen off-Broadway credits.

"His phone number and address are at the bottom. Shall I contact him?"

"Maybe I'd better do that. His red hair and handsome face might confuse you."

Mandy sniffed. "I don't like men that tall and handsome. Instead of looking at me, he'd be looking into the mirror behind me."

"Have you talked to any of the other men who escort Amadoro?"

"Only identified three of them. Well-known tycoons. Tried to reach them but can't get past their secretaries. When I said *Metropole* wanted to interview several prominent men who were personal friends of Lyli Amadoro, they put me on hold. When they came back, each told me her boss wasn't interested."

"Another stone wall."

"That about does it. Any other leads you want us to follow?"

"Nothing at the moment."

Mandy glanced at another slip of paper as she rose from the chair. "Almost overlooked this . . ."

"Yes?"

"I've found Mrs. Laurie Winston."

"Where?"

"Right here in New York. As a last resort—I should've done it before—I checked the Manhattan directory and there she was. On East Seventy-third Street." Handing the slip of paper across the desk. "Phone number and address."

"Mandy, you're a genius! Why didn't I think of the directory?"

"Too easy. It's always the last place I look."

"I'll check both of these myself. Laurie Winston and Burke Benedict." He watched her head for the door. "You've been a big help. As always."

chapter fifteen

BURKE BENEDICT LIVED IN A DECAYING APARTMENT HOtel on Central Park West that was a favorite residence for theatrical people. There was a legend that, years ago, it had been owned by a famous firm of producers and, even today, some old stars from musical comedy still lived here.

A middle-aged blonde at the elaborate reception desk told Ash the number of Benedict's apartment, without insisting that she phone upstairs to announce him, and fluttered her jeweled fingers toward a row of elevators.

Ash went up to the fifth floor, where he followed an arrow pointing to apartments 510 to 520.

He found 519 painted on a door at the end of a corridor. A small metal frame contained a card with two typed names.

Cindi Adaire
Burke Benedict

He pressed the plastic bell button and waited.

Several television sets were turned on in nearby apartments, each to a different station.

He pushed the button again.

"Who is it?"

The voice was deep and so close, behind the door, that he was startled. "Mr. Benedict?"

"Who cares to know?"

"My name's Hendrie—Ashton Hendrie. You don't know me, but . . ."

The door was opened by the red-haired young man from the photographs.

His first reaction was that Benedict must be taller than six feet three.

"Ashton Hendrie from *Metropole* magazine?"

"That's right." He relaxed, relieved that he wouldn't need to identify himself. "I'd like a few words with you . . ."

"Whatever for? Come in, sir . . ."

Ash stepped into a narrow foyer lined with framed pictures. Color photographs of Burke Benedict, the professional model, between portraits of composers. He recognized Bach, Mozart and Schubert. "Forgive my intruding, without calling, but . . ."

"No matter. Come along inside. We'll have a drink. I suppose, before lunch, you'd call it a morningcap."

"Nothing to drink. Thanks." Following Benedict into a neat and pleasantly comfortable living room with open windows facing another apartment building across the side street.

"Please . . ." Benedict motioned toward a sofa.

As Ash sat down he was aware of crowded bookshelves and several excellent reproductions—Van Gogh and Gaugin—in simple frames. The painters surprised him. And so did an antique music stand in a corner near the windows.

"I read your latest *Metropole* portrait last night. That amazing Saunders woman."

"This simplifies what I've come to ask you." He hesitated as Benedict sank into a large armchair. Saw that he was wearing a light summer suit, white shirt, expensive cravat and highly polished brown boots. Intelligent blue eyes and incredible golden-red hair that had to be for real. Tanned and freckled. Even more handsome than in those photographs with Amadoro. The boots had four-inch heels that would make him six feet seven.

"And what do you wish to ask me, sir?"

"You've been photographed, many times, with Lyli Amadoro . . ."

"So it's about Lyli, is it? You're doin' a portrait of her for the magazine?"

"I'm not supposed to tell anyone when I'm preparing a cover story. Sometimes, to get at the facts, I'm obliged to confess the purpose of my questions. I am, indeed, preparing a portrait of Amadoro."

"I'll be damned." He picked up a silver box and raised the lid. "Cigarette?"

"I rarely smoke."

Benedict selected a cigarette, closed the box and returned it to the coffee table. "Does Lyli know 'bout this?"

"I saw her, Monday afternoon, at Amadoro Associates. Told her *Metropole* wished to feature her portrait in our September issue."

"What did she say?" Benedict snapped a silver lighter, held it to the cigarette and exhaled smoke toward the open windows.

"She wants no part of it. Refuses to be interviewed."

"That's Lyli! She's a great one for privacy. I've known her a couple years now, but she's never discussed her personal life with me."

"Did you ever meet a man named Marnat—Clement Marnat—who worked at Amadoro Associates?"

"Never heard the name. You've come t' me for information about Lyli?"

The direct question made Ash pause. "I always question people close to my subject, hoping to learn something of his or her personal traits and idiosyncracies. The subject usually suggests several close friends for me to contact. Lyli Amadoro is the first ever to refuse any cooperation. Sandra Saunders sent me to a dozen people who, she said, would be very frank about her and, indeed, they were. Thus far, I've found only one person who would talk about Amadoro."

"And you thought I might?"

"I hope that you will."

Benedict shrugged. "I would be able t' tell you nothin' personal 'bout the lady 'cause I don' know nothin' of that sort."

"*Metropole* never prints anything scandalous or libelous. Only the truth."

"I'm aware of that. I read your magazine every month." He hesitated. "Would Lyli find out I talked t' you?"

"Certainly not."

"Very well, Mr. Hendrie. What do you wish t' know?"

"Anything you can tell me."

He crushed out his cigarette in a free-form pottery ashtray. "Where t' start?"

"How did you meet Lyli Amadoro?"

"Through my agent."

"Agent?"

"I work as a model. I'm not particularly proud of that but it pays well. Someone, I never found out who it was, phoned my agent and asked t' see several tall male models t' work as an escort for a celebrity."

"You're paid to be Amadoro's escort?"

"Two hundred bucks a night. Usually twice a week. All expenses paid by Amadoro Associates. My weekly check comes from them."

"So she pays her escorts!"

"Only me. All the other gents are friends or business acquaintances. Wall Street, mostly. I've met some of 'em. I'm the only one gets paid, but Lyli introduces me t' everyone as her friend."

"How were you selected?"

"Apparently there were twenty of us. From all the top model agencies. We went to Amadoro Associates and, one by one, were asked t' walk across a low stage—I suppose it's used for fashion shows—in front of a dozen people who sat in shadow, so we couldn't, none of us, see their faces."

"And she chose you from those twenty models?"

"Somebody did, not Lyli. She told me, later, she only saw photographs of three guys who were selected from the twenty. Lyli picked me from those three. I have t' tell you, Mr. Hendrie, I never wanted t' be no male model. I came t' New York, from Montana, to study at the Art Students League. Started paintin' back on the family ranch. My God was Mr. Peter Hurd. After two years at the League I realized I'd never be half as good as Mr. Hurd. Burned every canvas I'd painted and looked for somethin' else t' do. I'd gotten married, my first year in the East, and my wife was makin' good money. She's a fine musician. Plays fiddle with the Philharmonic."

"Really!"

"So I had t' find somethin' t' do that paid as much as Cindi makes. I'd known a lot of models—male and female—and several told me I could make it as a model. Didn't think much of the idea, at first, but then I got a few jobs and, eventually, landed some television commercials—mostly as cowhands—and the money got bigger. On top of that I make at least a thousand bucks a month workin' for Lyli. I'm savin' t' buy a small ranch in New Mexico . . ."

"Would your wife like that?"

"She's the one suggested it. Cindi has a standin' offer t' join the Santa Fe Symphony. We hope t' pull it off in another year. Then Cindi won't have t' go on tours the way she does now, with the Philharmonic —weeks at a time—and I'll never have t' pose for another goddamn camera."

"You enjoy working for Amadoro?"

"Most of the time. I get t' eat at expensive restaurants. Places I can't afford. See all the Broadway shows and sit in the best seats at Avery Fisher Hall to hear my wife playin' on her fiddle."

"Does Amadoro know you have a wife?"

"Told her, right off, I was happily married an' didn' plan makin' no changes."

"Will you paint again? When you move to New Mexico . . ."

"My wife says I will. That's another reason she wants t' live there. She says anything you learn in music or painting you never forget. It's always there, waitin' t' come out."

"I'm sure that's true."

"By the way, sir, I'm meetin' Lyli tonight. Her black Rolls is pickin' me up at seven."

"With Lyli in the Rolls?"

"Oh, yes! And always punctual. I'll be waitin' downstairs. She was furious, the one time I wasn't there. Never did that again." He chuckled. "Tonight we're havin' dinner at the Four Seasons and drivin' down t' see some new play at the Cherry Lane."

"Do people recognize her?"

"All the time. Come up an' talk t' her."

"Is she gracious? Friendly with strangers?"

"Completely. She's a charmin' lady. When she wants t' be."

"You enjoy these evenings on the town?"

"It's a world I never knew. I've learned a lot about good food and the filthy rich. Vintage wines and headwaiters . . . I suppose I'll remember all this in New Mexico, but without ever wantin' any part of it again."

"Does the Rolls bring you home at the end of the evening?"

"Lyli drops me off before she returns to her condominium."

"Have you ever been there?"

"Sure have."

"What's it like?"

"Fanciest place I ever saw! She's got a duplex penthouse. With a bigger library than our town has back in Montana."

"You've been to her apartment frequently?"

"Several times t' parties. I'd see people I'd already met at the opera or in a restaurant. Some mighty famous people. I'm sure most of them think I sleep with Lyli . . ."

"And do you?"

Benedict grinned. "From time t' time. Maybe twice a month. She's the most exciting female I've ever known."

"More exciting than your wife?"

"My sweet wife's plenty excitin'. And more comfortable than Lyli. More affectionate. I love my wife but I don't love Lyli Amadoro. What's more, Cindi and I have an understandin'. She knows all about Lyli. I tell her every time I sleep with her, and Cindi tells me about her conductors and fellow fiddlers. You know, after a performance, a musician—includin' my wife—needs to come down to earth and most of them prefer to land in bed. That's simple, urgent rabbity sex. Nothin' t' do with love. I've never loved any woman but my wife. Never will. Rabbity sex is fine but it's not permanent, like marriage. The wife and I plan t' have kids when we get our ranch. Lots of kids! Lyli's a passionate woman but I don't think she knows one damn thing about love. I've talked about that t' my wife. I get a feelin'—end of the evenin'—that Lyli has used me. And discarded me." He frowned. "I wonder if she's ever loved anyone."

"Has she talked about her husbands?"

"Never. I told her, one night, that I'd heard she'd been married three times. 'But not for long,' she said. Changed the subject in a hurry."

"Does she discuss business? Amadoro Associates?"

"Not after the first time I met her. I escorted her to the opera that night. Think she wanted t' see how I looked in tails. And so did I. Had t' rent some in a hurry. As we sat in the box, during the overture, she told me she had only two rules for me t' follow. I must never ask questions about her private life or her business, and she never wanted t' hear anything about my wife."

"You agreed?"

"Never mentioned Cindi t' her again. Funny thing! Lyli sends Cindi expensive presents, every year, for her birthday. We've no idea how she learned the date."

"You've been very helpful, Mr. Benedict."

"Have I?"

"Given me a picture of Amadoro I would never have gotten from my research department or from her family." He rose from the sofa. "Perhaps we could have another chat, after I get deeper into the Amadoro story."

Benedict jumped up. "Been a great pleasure. Where did you see Lyli's family?"

"New London, Connecticut. They still live in the house where she was born. Her name then was Leola Martin."

"I never knew that."

Ash walked ahead of Benedict toward the entrance. "Has Lyli ever mentioned her parents?"

"Only once. Told me she hated them."

chapter sixteen

ASH FOUND A TAXI AND GAVE THE ADDRESS, ON EAST seventy-third, to the driver.

Only half a dozen blocks from his own apartment. Curious that so much of this Amadoro story was located in the upper East Side. Even Benedict's apartment was on the opposite side of the park. He could probably see it from the windows of his own apartment.

His taxi came to a stop in the block between Madison and Park.

The apartment had a striped canopy protecting an unimpressive entrance, and there was no attendant in the lobby.

Double row of mailboxes, one marked "Manager."

The name he sought was hand-printed on a card inserted in the slot of 43: Mrs. Laurie Winston.

He rode a small elevator to the fourth floor.

There were ten doors, five on each side, but the space between the closed doors indicated that these were larger-than-average apartments.

There were no name plates on the doors, only a number.

He pressed the bell button of 43 and heard a faint response of chimes inside. A child squealed and light footsteps seemed to run through a hall, away from the door, into the depths of the apartment.

No other sound. No television sets chattering here.

He fingered the button and heard the chimes again. This time there was no sound of the child, but a door opened and closed.

Ash wondered if Mrs. Winston had a servant . . .

The door opened a few inches, with the rattle of a chain.

A woman's face was partially visible in the narrow vertical space. White hair and one cold eye.

"I'm looking for Mrs. Winston."

"She's not here at the moment."

Her voice was cultured, speech precise, but the tone wasn't friendly. "Do you know when I could find her at home?"

"Who are you?"

"My name is Hendrie. Ashton Hendrie. I heard about Mrs. Winston from Mr. and Mrs. Martin in New London. The parents of Leola Martin. They suggested I contact Mrs. Winston. I found her address in the directory . . ."

"Mrs. Winston is away. Out of town!"

"You're Mrs. Winston, aren't you?"

The door banged shut.

Ash turned, reluctantly, and headed back to the elevator.

That woman, he was certain, had to be Mrs. Laurie Winston.

He wondered if she would report his visit to Amadoro . . .

Back in his office, Ash stared at the pages of notes he'd left spread across his desk.

Must consider what he'd learned from Burke Benedict and plan how to approach Mrs. Winston again. She would know about Leola Martin's early years in New York, her marriage to Toby Towson . . .

Benedict had confirmed what Glenda Martin had told him about their daughter's hostility.

Why did Amadoro hate her parents so violently?

He reached for the phone, pressed the button for an inside line and dialed Mandy's private number.

"Amanda speaking."

"I'm back."

"Any luck?"

"Saw them both. Benedict and Mrs. Winston. She closed the door in my face but I'm sure it was she."

"Shall I send someone to see her?"

"Not just yet. I want to try again. Benedict, however, was most helpful. Learned some interesting personal facts about Amadoro."

"Then it wasn't a total loss!"

"Quite the contrary."

"Anything more I can do for you today?"

"Don't think so. I'll spend the afternoon collating my notes. Trying to make some sense of them."

"I've heard nothing more from London or Paris. They've closed for the day, so I don't expect anything before tomorrow. I'll be leaving at five. Carrington wants a feature for the December issue on how New York celebrities vacationed this summer. I'm having cocktails with a woman who arranges offbeat holidays for the very rich and the super-sophisticated. Famous or infamous . . ."

"Have fun!"

"I doubt it."

Ash put the phone down and resumed his inspection of the sheets of paper in front of him.

The meager facts collected on these twelve pages and in Mandy's folder didn't amount to much. Certainly not enough to start a portrait of Amadoro.

His eyes moved across the double rows of pages until he reached the final two.

Picked up a pen and wrote "Burke Benedict" under the names he had already listed beneath FRIENDS. He wondered if Amadoro realized the young man was a friend.

Still only one name on the last page under ENEMIES. A dead man. Clement Marnat . . .

He suspected Amadoro might have many more enemies, but were there any other friends?

The buzzer sounded beneath his desk.

He lifted the receiver. "Yes, Greta?"

"Inspector McCorkle's here."

"Here?"

"Says it's urgent that he see you."

"Send him in." He put the receiver down and, quickly, shuffled the sheets of paper together. Slipped them under the file folder and stood up as the door swung open.

McCorkle entered, scowling, peering around. "Fancy office you got, pal."

"What the devil are you doing here, Mac?"

"Some things've turned up." Closing the door and coming toward him. "Like a few words with you."

Ash held out his hand and, as McCorkle grasped it, motioned to an armchair. "Care for a drink?"

"This is not a social call." He collapsed, wearily, into the chair. "It's the Marnat investigation. I need advice . . ."

Ash sat at his desk again, facing him. "What's happened?"

"Nothing's happened and I'm feeling goddamned frustrated. First of all, the coroner's report agrees with what I told you last night. Marnat was murdered. But he wasn't attacked where you found him. After you left, I noticed drops of dried blood leading from the living room into the bedroom. Marnat was struck, over the head, in the living room. The murder weapon's missing. Could be anything. His body was carried into the bedroom—probably by two people—and placed against the foot of that cupboard."

"It's an armoire."

"Whatever it is, I'm keeping it, for the moment, out of the newspapers. That this is murder. Spent most of the morning at Amadoro Associates. Trying to find someone who could tell me about Marnat. Nobody would talk. After questioning several fancy types and learning nothing, I saw the woman in charge of personnel and asked if any of their employees hadn't shown up for work today."

As Ash listened to the detective, he was aware of his curly red hair streaked with silver and remembered the young man with golden-red hair he had questioned earlier.

"At first, the dame wouldn't tell me a damn thing. I threatened to get a search warrant to look at her records and she turned me over to a little guy in a big office lined with metal files and computers who is their head accountant. He told me two men hadn't appeared for work this morning. Showed me their records, reluctantly. Both born in Italy. I lifted their present addresses from the records—one in Brooklyn, the other in the Village—and sent a man to check on them. Then I asked to see the big boss. Lyli Amadoro . . ."

"You saw Amadoro?"

"I was informed the great lady was out of the city. Another snotty dame with a fancy accent told me Madame Amadoro wouldn't be available before next week. She's away on business. Knew the dame was lying but nothing I could do about it. Told her I was investigating the death of an employee—Clement Marnat—who'd been murdered in his apartment. Said she'd never heard of Marnat and doubted that Madame Amadoro could be of any help. It was impossible for her to know all the employees by name. I pointed out that Marnat was one of her personal assistants and, at some point, she had surely met him. This arrogant bitch sent me to her twin. Just as uncooperative."

"Mac, you have encountered the high steel wall that business maintains around all large corporations. Impregnable! Impossible to crash."

"I'm going to crash this one if I have to go back with a platoon of cops!"

"Take a battering ram."

"Funny thing about Amadoro Associates. All the top people are dames. Men have the lower positions. Secretaries, receptionists and assistants . . ."

Ash laughed. "Amadoro is for women's rights. All the way, including bed."

McCorkle grunted.

"If you want to question Amadoro . . ."

"I certainly do. About this guy Marnat!"

"I happen to know she's having dinner tonight at the Four Seasons with a young man named Burke Benedict."

"Who's he?"

"The guy who, most frequently, acts as her escort. They'll arrive at the restaurant around seven and, after dinner, are driving down to the Cherry Lane to see a show."

"I'll catch her at dinner. The lady may never get to the Cherry Lane. Thanks, pal."

"Go easy on Benedict. He's a decent guy. Amadoro pays him to be her escort."

McCorkle's eyebrows went up. "One of those?"

"He's six feet seven in cowboy boots. He and his wife are saving to buy a ranch in New Mexico."

"Okay. I'll tell him to get lost while I talk to Amadoro."

"You seeing Sandra today?"

"Had to cancel my appointment. Explained I'm busy with a new investigation. She understood. Now there's a real dame!"

"That she is."

"Talked to Marnat's landlady again, last night, after you left."

"Mrs. Lacey?"

"Informed her we were sealing Marnat's apartment. She'd had several more belts of Scotch while I was upstairs. Kept repeating that Marnat was one of her best tenants. A gentleman. She had a thing for the guy but, far's I could tell, never got to first base."

"His tastes were somewhat more sophisticated."

"I called New London this morning. Spoke to Cap Larson about the death of Leola Martin's first husband. Confirmed what you told me. No way Larson could save him." Rising from the armchair. "Gotta get back on the job. I've five men working on this Marnat case."

Ash stood up. "You won't tell Amadoro how you learned she'd be at the Four Seasons tonight?"

"Trust me, pal! I'm damn grateful for the information." He started toward the door but looked back. "I've sent an inquiry to New Scotland Yard for a report on the death of the dame's second husband."

"Our London office is already checking on that."

"We'll compare notes."

"By all means! And good luck on this Marnat business."

"Right now, I've gotta find somebody who knew him. Somebody who'll talk." He continued to the door. "See you at Costigan's tonight?"

"I never know where I'll eat dinner until I get hungry."

"Just like a detective!" McCorkle laughed and swung the door open.

Ash sat at his desk again, as the door closed, and pulled the sheets of notes from under the file folder. Arranged the twelve pages in two rows again.

The phone rang.

He lifted it to his ear. "Yes, Greta?"

"Miss Saunders on two."

"Thanks." He pushed the two button. "This is a pleasant surprise."

"Know you're busy, lover, but . . ."

"Just finished a session with McCorkle."

"He had an appointment with me this afternoon but had to cancel."

"He told me."

"I'm calling to tell you I've just talked to Lyli Amadoro."

"What?"

"She phoned me. No secretary this time. She's apparently facing new crises in her life. Begged me to reconsider. Offered ten thousand dollars for me to do her horoscope."

"What did you say?"

"The only thing I could. I will never do her chart."

"Was she furious?"

"More hurt than angry. At least that's how she sounded. All an act, I'm sure. The lady likes to get what she wants and she's gotten nowhere with me. I can't do her horoscope because she has no future. And that's what she wanted to know. Her future . . ."

"Have you had this experience before? Other clients without a future?"

"Many times."

"What do you say to them?"

"Same thing. I will not tell anyone that this present life is ending for them. That would be a cruel thing to do."

"You still feel Amadoro has no future?"

"I do. In fact, I've just checked the notes I made when I worked on her charts, briefly, that first time she called. There's no indication of anything ahead for her. Only an empty void."

"Where was she when you spoke to her?"

"She didn't say. I assumed she was in her office. She asked if I knew where Fernand Maudru would be staying when he arrived in New York. I avoided answering that."

"Maudru will be here next week?"

"He's to appear at Town Hall a week from tomorrow night. Always arrives several days earlier, in order to have time for rest and meditation before his lecture."

"I wonder if I could talk to Maudru before his public appearance. Question him about his experience with Amadoro in Paris."

"I should be able to arrange that for you. Fernand always stays at the Plaza. Don't know when he'll arrive. I should think Wednesday. I'm not sure he would care to be involved with Lyli Amadoro again. Only hope she doesn't turn up at Town Hall. Fernand answers questions from the audience and she might try to reach him that way. People have done that before. Fernand's in his nineties and his health is somewhat precarious. That's why I wouldn't tell her where he'll be staying. I hope the papers don't name the hotel."

"He could go to a different one. Use another name."

"Fernand's been staying at the Plaza for years. He travels with a small group of disciples. Once he's in his hotel suite, no strangers can reach him without a lengthy interrogation. And I must go now. I've a client waiting."

"See you Monday evening! Dinner . . ."

"Seven o'clock. Bye."

Ash set the phone down and stared at the clear blue sky beyond his windows.

He hoped to learn something about Amadoro's life in Paris from Fernand Maudru. Something important . . .

chapter seventeen

ASH HURRIED THROUGH THE EMPTY ENTRANCE CORRIdor of the *Metropole* suite, uncomfortably warm in his old Burberry.

He had overslept—after a long and humid night that had kept him awake—and had opened his eyes to see a steady drizzle falling beyond his open bedroom windows.

His mind, through the night, had been occupied with Amadoro. So many important pieces missing from the lady's portrait, and only one person knew all the answers—Amadoro herself.

He strode past Carrington's office and turned down the side corridor.

Today he would stay at his desk, going over those notes again. Hoping for new information from somewhere . . .

"Ash! Wait a second!"

He turned to see Tony Rufino hurrying out of his office and coming toward him with outstretched arms. "You told me to have a talk with Giles Redfern and it worked!" Engulfing him with a bear hug. "I've got that London job!"

"Congratulations!"

"Not for a few months, but permanently. Redfern's resigned, won't be returning."

"Has he?"

"The wife and I always wanted to live in London."

"I'm delighted for you."

"I hear your Amadoro project's struck a hitch."

"Only hitch is the lady. Pronounced bitch."

Rufino laughed. "I'm sure it'll work out. I'm on my way to another meeting with Carrington. Making definite plans, now that Redfern's returned to London."

"When did he leave?"

"Last night."

"Damn! Wanted to talk to him." Ash continued toward his office. So Redfern had avoided further discussion about Amadoro. Had she warned him not to talk? Redfern had resigned, so, of course, he had no further loyalty to *Metropole*.

Ash flung his door open and saw Greta opening the morning mail. "Did you know Redfern flew home last night?"

"Heard when I came in. Was going to tell you."

"And I'm late this morning. Couldn't sleep."

"Coffee?"

"Had three cups or I wouldn't be here." He stalked into his dim office, the only light from his desk lamp, removing the Burberry and tossing it over a chair. Instead of going to his desk he went to the windows and looked down at the ghostly city.

The drizzle appeared to be heavier. Gray walls of rain hid the streets and Central Park was a dark blur.

He shivered, remembering what had happened last night.

He'd finally managed to fall asleep around three o'clock but had wakened, suddenly, in a cold sweat. Exactly like those nights, years ago, when he woke to find that ghostly figure seated in a chair. He pushed himself up in bed and peered around his bedroom, but there was no misty figure. He was shivering and pulled the sheet over his head.

Then he squeezed his eyelids, but no bright image appeared.

He'd been certain that something important was happening, somewhere, at that moment. Something that would affect him.

Was Lyli Amadoro dead?

Sandra said it could happen at any time . . .

How would that affect his portrait of the lady? Surely it might make things easier. People would talk. Tell him what they knew about the girl, Leola Martin, and Lyli Amadoro, the woman . . .

He had fallen asleep while considering the idea of Amadoro dead. And had overslept.

Rosie was up and fixed him a large breakfast as he listened to the morning news. Nothing about the death of Amadoro, but a prediction of showers all day. Clearing in the evening.

Staring now at the curtains of rain whipping between the tall buildings, he wondered what his experience in the middle of the night could portend. In the past it had always meant something.

Before leaving the apartment he had slipped into Mara's bedroom. She was snoring gently, as was her habit, eyes covered with a pink satin mask. He had kissed her on the forehead.

Every window in the visible skyscrapers was lighted.

He always felt marooned up here, looking down at the city during a storm, as though Manhattan were slowly sinking, leaving his office suspended in the air with nothing solid underneath.

Ash turned, suddenly, and went to the row of wall switches near the door. Snapped them until every light was on. This made the sky seem darker beyond the windows and even more ominous.

He sat at his desk, unlocked the middle drawer and brought out the pages of notes with Mandy's file folder. Spread them in their customary order and scowled at them.

Today was Friday! He'd spent four days on the Amadoro project and this was all that had been achieved.

As his eyes moved from page to page, he continued to have a strong feeling that something positive would develop today. From some unexpected direction. Perhaps it had already happened. Was taking place, last night, when he felt that presence in his room. Not a physical presence, but a psychic force.

He stared at the Amadoro notes, without touching them, until someone knocked on his door. He knew the personal knock of all close associates, their tempo and sound. "Come in, Cort!"

The art director hurried in with photographs in his hand. "Only have a moment." Sitting on the arm of a chair. "The old man's selecting the final artwork for the Domingo profile today. Wanted to tell you, Amadoro went out last night in the black Rolls. Chauffeur took her to an apartment on Central Park West where that red-haired guy who frequently escorts her was waiting. They had dinner at the Four Seasons. Left there, after eight, with another man. Also red-haired, but slightly older. He didn't get in the Rolls but had a car of his own. A gray Plymouth. Amadoro and the first guy drove down to the Cherry Lane. Came out at intermission. She seemed to be arguing with him and they didn't stay for the second act. Drove back to Central Park West where Amadoro dropped the guy, then went on to her own apartment. Didn't come out again last night."

"Most interesting."

"My guys got some pictures." Rising and handing them across the desk.

Ash reached for the photographs and glanced at each one as Cort talked. Amadoro and Benedict going into the Four Seasons. Coming out with McCorkle. Amadoro and Benedict leaving the Cherry Lane. Getting into the Rolls on a side street. Amadoro was wearing a tailored pale green outfit, jacket and slacks. No jewels.

"No decision, as yet, on an artist for the Amadoro cover," Cort was saying. "Won't be anything until Philippe returns from Morocco. Talked to Paris this morning, and that may not be for another two weeks."

"Keeps getting longer. I'm still having trouble finding personal material on Amadoro, but I've a feeling something will open up. Maybe a new source of information."

"I hope so. See you later."

As Cort left, Ash collected the photographs, put them aside and began to go over his notes once more.

He wondered what McCorkle had learned from Amadoro.

The buzzer sounded under his desk and he reached for the phone, hoping it would be McCorkle reporting. "Yes, Greta?"

"Your wife on line two."

"Thanks." He pressed the proper button. "You're up early!"

"Good morning, my love. Rosie says you slept late. You don't have a cold?"

"No, but I spent a miserable night. Too hot to sleep, then I overslept."

"I went right to sleep but wakened early. This humidity made my sinuses thrum. I've been inhaling steam from that vaporizer thing. Clears my head for a while. Will use the other one in my dressing room, tonight, before the performance. I'm calling to find out if you had any more ideas for Monday's dinner. Something Sandra might enjoy . . ."

"I know she doesn't eat much meat. Prefers fish or chicken."

"I'll see what Rosie suggests. She won't market until Monday. Will you be in the office this weekend?"

"Depends upon what happens on the Amadoro project today."

"Still having trouble?"

"This is a rough one."

"I'm seeing Sandra this afternoon. First interview before she starts my horoscope. Second session, middle of next week."

"What about Millie?"

"Your dear mother goes in for her first next Tuesday. Have to run now! Rosie's waiting."

"Bye, my love!" He set the phone down and looked toward the windows. Saw that the sky had disappeared behind the rain and the light seemed to be withdrawing. Glanced again at the photographs of Amadoro with McCorkle and Benedict. That incredible face . . .

A staccato tapping on his door. "Come in, Mandy!" He saw that she had several sheets of paper and was wearing a pale violet cheongsam under her smock.

"Didn't have anything for you earlier." Sitting in an armchair and resting the papers on her lap. "Several things just came in. Teletype from *Metropole*-London." She picked up a flimsy and glanced at it as she explained. "Précis of New Scotland Yard report on Robert Craydon lists death from explosion of petrol tank while deceased was testing new motor. Craydon so badly burned, no point in conducting autopsy."

"No autopsy?"

"This says dozens of people witnessed the accident. They're sending me a Xerox of the full report. Should get that tomorrow or, more likely, Monday." She pulled out another flimsy. "Teletype from *Metropole*-Paris. Unable to trace Lyli Amadoro's daughter, Nicole Towson. Last record they could locate, through American Embassy, she was staying in Switzerland—this was 1968—with a female companion. That's nineteen years ago."

"How old would she have been?"

"Seven years of age. Which makes her twenty-six today."

"If she's alive."

Mandy slipped the second flimsy under the first. "More clippings from London. Nothing really important, I'm afraid." Handing everything across the desk. "Some pictures of Lord Craydon."

Ash glanced at each clipping, aware that Mandy was getting up to leave. "He looks British. Short and blond. Lyli's at least two inches taller."

"She wasn't called Lyli then. The captions say Lady Leola Craydon and Lord Robert Craydon . . ."

"Did rather well, didn't she? An English lord, then an Italian count."

"About as high as a girl can go these days." Mandy giggled. "She can still call herself Contessa Amadoro, can't she?"

"I suppose . . ."

Mandy turned toward the door. "Will you be in tomorrow?"

"Don't know." He heard the door close as he studied the faded newsprint. Lady Craydon in a flowered hat at a garden party and, with her husband, at Epsom Downs. With Craydon again, in formal attire, at some charity performance in the West End. Lord and Lady Craydon sitting in a sleek sports car which the caption said was parked in front of Craydon Hall.

Lyli looked so young in these pictures. Her hair still light brown, arranged in curls. Oddly, she wasn't looking at her husband in any of the photographs but was staring into the camera. As though Craydon wasn't there. Maybe that's how she had wanted it. The social life, ancestral mansion and motor cars, but without Robert Craydon.

Ash remembered something as he put the clipping down. Glenda Martin had said Leola was driving a red Mercedes that last time she came to see her parents. Now she always rode in a chauffeured Rolls. Why and when, he wondered, had she stopped driving? And why had she changed her name to Lyli?

He added these questions to his notes.

The buzzer sounded under his desk.

He snatched up the phone and pressed the button for an inside line. "Yes, Greta?"

"Inspector McCorkle to see you again."

"Of course! Send him in." He set the phone down and got to his feet. McCorkle would have news! Facing the door, hopefully, as it opened. "Good morning, Mac!"

"I seem to be dropping in every day."

"The bearer of good news, I trust."

"Afraid not. Didn't cable New Scotland Yard until yesterday. Won't hear anything for several days. They always take their time."

Ash sat down, deflated. "I just had word, through our London office, there was no autopsy when Sir Robert Craydon was killed."

"No?"

"The body was so badly burned, an autopsy was impossible."

"That's not surprising." The detective walked up and down, in front of the desk, as he talked. "I've come to thank you for telling me where to find that Amadoro dame last night."

Ash saw that McCorkle's hat looked soggy, his raincoat dark with moisture. "You found her?"

"I'd never eaten at the Four Seasons. Heard about it, of course, and planned to go there sometime for dinner. Last night seemed like the time. Reserved a table for six-thirty and was enjoying the food when Amadoro showed up with her young man."

"What happened?"

AMADORO

"That woman's eyes miss nothing. They raked the restaurant like a double-barreled shotgun. Was afraid she'd seen my photo somewhere, but she went right past me. Nobody looked suspicious, I guess, because she swept across the restaurant to a table, her escort trailing. I finished dinner as I watched them. Amadoro didn't eat much. Rich dames always pick at their food to keep their skinny figures. Paid my check and waited in the lounge for them to come out. Women always head for the powder room to see if there's a spot of something on their pretty chins. Amadoro went in, and her escort into the john. He was the first to come out. Passed me on his way to have the doorman send for the Rolls. I was waiting when the lady appeared, every hair in place. Nobody else in the lounge, so I held my badge under her nose."

"What did she do?"

"Looked insulted. Told her my name and she said she'd heard of me. Informed her I was working on an investigation involving one of her employees—Clement Marnat—and that I'd tried to see her earlier at her office. Said she'd been told about the unfortunate accident but could be of no help. Claimed she couldn't know most of the people who worked for her and barely remembered the deceased. Only saw him once or twice."

"She's known him for years!"

"I let it go at that because, by this time, her escort was back and looking unhappy. Flashed my badge at him and he headed outside again. Didn't want to question the dame about Marnat until I have his record. I've sent an inquiry to the Préfecture in Paris. Told her it looked as though he'd been killed by two of her other employees. Gave her their names."

"Did she know them?"

"Claimed she never heard of 'em. So I told her they came from Italy and I was checking with the police over there. Also with our Immigration and Passports people."

"Was Amadoro furious?"

"Looked as though she could spit fire but she didn't. Said she was sorry she hadn't been in her office but would check on this Marnat character next week. If I would call her office she would, hopefully, have information for me. Nothing more I can do. Can't search a multimillion-dollar setup like Amadoro Associates. Wouldn't know where to start. She'll produce some scapegoat who'll talk but won't say much. I may never find out who killed Marnat."

"You didn't question Benedict?"

"No point. He stayed in the background until Amadoro was ready to leave. Had one of my men tail them down to the Village."

"They only stayed for one act of the show. Amadoro dropped Benedict at his apartment, then drove home in the Rolls."

"How'd you know that?"

"I have my spies."

"I'll bet you do!" McCorkle laughed. "I'm grateful to you once again, pal. Tipping me off where to find Amadoro. At least I met the dame and she'll know me next time."

"No other leads in the Marnat case?"

"Nothing. I'm on my way downtown to check with the Feds, but those two missing Italians may never be traced."

The telephone rang.

McCorkle scowled. "They're probably heading for South America with phony passports. Thanks again, pal!"

"Sure, Mac . . ." Ash watched him leave as the phone continued to ring. Picked it up when the door closed. "Yes, Greta?"

"You won't believe who's on the phone!"

"Surprise me."

"Lyli Amadoro."

"You're quite right. I don't believe it."

"In person, not a secretary. I told her you're in conference but I would try to reach you."

"You've reached me."

"She's on line two."

"Thanks." He punched the two button. "Good morning, Madame."

"I told you, Monday, I prefer to be called Lyli."

"So you did."

"This is only Friday and you've forgotten . . ."

"Let's say I put it out of my mind because I didn't expect to see you again."

"I've given much thought to our conversation . . ."

"That, at least, sounds hopeful."

". . . and have decided we should discuss this matter of my portrait more fully . . ."

"I would be happy to discuss it. Your office?"

"I'd prefer we meet in more casual surroundings."

"Wherever you say. Perhaps Twenty One or Le Cirque? I believe you patronize both."

"I think somewhere even more private . . ."

"Name it. I shall be there, at your convenience."
"My apartment would be most convenient."
He hesitated, completely surprised. "When?"
"Supper, tonight?"
"That sounds delightful."
"Eight o'clock?"
"Eight o'clock."
"I shall look forward to seeing you, Mr. Hendrie. À bientôt . . ."
"À bientôt!" Ash smiled as he set the phone down.

Better say nothing about this to anyone. Carrington or any member of the staff. Even his secretary!

He got to his feet and walked to the windows.

Had Amadoro decided in the middle of the night, when she was unable to sleep, that she would see him again?

Had he wakened at the instant she'd made her decision?

He leaned on the cold metallic sill under the windows and looked down, through the rain, at the dark streets.

Not yet noon, but the city appeared to be in twilight.

The rain wasn't as heavy.

Traffic, far below, was moving slowly. Headlights turned on in every car. They were like tiny black insects with angry electric eyes.

chapter eighteen

THE ELEVATOR ROSE WITHOUT A SOUND OR ANY SENSE OF motion.

An attendant in the elegant lobby had been expecting him when he asked for Madame Amadoro's penthouse and led him to this unmarked elevator, where he pressed a hidden release, high in a decorative metal column, to open the elevator door. Three buttons on a panel, in the elevator, marked Penthouse, Lobby and Garage. He had pressed Penthouse.

The elevator was like an exquisite jewel box. Mirrored walls with an antique French settee upholstered in golden silk and a thick carpet of darker yellow. Shaded crystal electric fixtures.

Ash glanced at himself in the mirrors. He'd gone home to shave and shower. Selected a dark gray linen suit he had bought last summer in London. White shirt and a favorite silk tie with pale gray-and-violet stripes. Perfect for a summer evening.

Fortunately, the rainstorm had passed over the city and he had glimpsed a fiery sunset between the tall buildings from his taxi.

Not a sound as he rose to the eighty-fifth floor. Imagine having one's own elevator! Living in a tower high above the metropolis. The lady had no need for drawbridges or protective dragons.

He wondered what her apartment would be like. Pretentious, undoubtedly. The work of some decorator who had pilfered treasures from all over the world.

He preferred his own modest apartment to this awesome perch in the sky. On a clear day Amadoro should be able to look down at Harlem in one direction and Coney Island in the other.

Checking his watch, he saw that it was one minute past eight.

The elevator doors opened suddenly and silently.

He faced a long vista lighted by crystal chandeliers, straight ahead, which appeared to extend through several spacious rooms. The effect was decidedly European.

"Good evening, Mr. Hendrie." A young and very proper British butler materialized, smiling and bowing.

Ash stepped from the elevator into a shallow foyer. "Good evening."

"Madam suggested I show you into the library. She will join you there."

"Thank you." He followed toward the lighted vista of rooms which turned out to be sections of a seemingly endless central corridor divided by tall doors that, at the moment, stood open. Closed doors, on either side of the corridor, each section of which had its own exquisite Aubusson rug with identical patterns in rose and gray. The paneled walls were hung with framed paintings, with shaded overhead lights, above rare commodes holding bowls of fresh flowers. He recognized the paintings as priceless cinquecento Italian, their scarlets glowing as though freshly painted.

The air was uncomfortably chilly.

He detested air-conditioning but realized the air would have to be kept stable here to protect these fragile paintings from all the noxious chemicals rising from the city below.

"Here we are, sir." The butler went toward the third pair of closed doors, on their left, and swung them open.

Ash stepped across the threshold into a world of books. No paintings here, only carved shelves filled with books—some in fine bindings, but many popular novels and even shelves of paperbacks.

He wondered if some of these books were from old man Towson's library. Cap Larson said Leola had sold everything . . .

Larson had said Leola Martin was a great reader. There were no reading lamps here, only large shaded lamps on tables, behind enormous sofas. The lady would have to do her reading elsewhere.

Straight ahead, between tall, tapestry-curtained windows, was a huge black marble fireplace, with garlands of carved flowers and fruits dripping from the arms of floating putti. There was a white marble bust of Voltaire on the mantelpiece, and logs were burning on a massive pair of andirons. "That fire looks most inviting. After today's miserable weather."

"May I offer you a drink, sir?"

"Whiskey and water, please."

"Certainly, sir." The butler turned toward an antique sideboard partially hidden behind one of the open doors where a large selection of bottles and glasses reflected the fire. "Ice, sir?"

"Yes, please." Ash moved closer to the fire and extended his hands toward the flames. "You're from England . . ."

"Afraid I haven't lost my accent."

"Don't ever lose it."

"I worked for Madam in England. Both the town house and the country estate."

"Craydon Hall?"

"That's right, sir. Madam knew I wanted to come to America, so she transferred me here last year." He offered a large crystal glass on a silver tray.

"Thank you."

"Madam will be down in a moment, sir." He bowed and, after leaving his tray on the sideboard, left the room, silently closing the doors.

Ash smiled as he faced the fire again.

So Amadoro also liked handsome men to serve her at home! This one could have stepped out of a drawing room comedy by Maugham or Coward.

Could he use that in his profile? The handsome men, of every age and nationality, who surrounded Lyli at home and during business hours. Perhaps mention it casually . . .

Sipping the whiskey tentatively, he realized it was the best Scotch he'd ever tasted.

He hadn't yet decided on his attitude toward Amadoro for this second meeting.

She would sweep in from the corridor, wearing another tailored outfit, holding out her hand. Playing Lady Craydon or Contessa Amadoro! As though he should bow and kiss her damn hand.

Americans didn't kiss hands, thank God! Not yet.

He would disregard her hand by keeping this drink in his own right hand.

Would she start to talk about the *Metropole* portrait at once or wait until after supper? Probably wait, hoping to put him in a relaxed mood with food and wine. She would, undoubtedly, have a French chef in her kitchen, and the wines should be superb . . .

It would be wise not to bring up the subject of the portrait. Let Amadoro speak first. After all, she'd invited him here. This was her party. Let her playact from her own script. He would follow her lead until he knew what she had in mind. Would be agreeable, of course, but businesslike—

"I hoped you might enjoy the fire."

Ash whirled, ice cubes rattling in his glass, to see Amadoro seated on the nearest sofa facing him, holding a tall drink in one hand. "You startled me."

"Did I? I'm terribly sorry." She smiled. "I ordered several secret passages installed when these interiors were designed. So that I can move from room to room and floor to floor, unobserved, whenever I wish. It amuses me to surprise visitors. Is your drink all right?"

"What? Oh, yes. It's perfect." He was conscious, once again, of her perfume.

"It was good of you to come here this evening."

"My pleasure." Glancing at the shelves behind her. "You must have thousands of books . . ."

"And I've read most of them. I prefer to do my reading in bed."

"Doesn't everyone?" He realized she was not wearing a tailored suit, but a dinner gown that appeared to have been wrapped around her body with alternating spirals of green-and-silver cloth. Bare shoulders with an exquisite emerald necklace. Her blond hair was arranged in a chignon at the back. Silver slippers on her feet. As he inspected her, she had been complaining about today's weather, and now, he realized, she was studying him.

"Do you always prefer to stand, Mr. Hendric?"

"Certainly not. I found that monstrous modern chair in your office rather uncomfortable."

"That is its purpose. This will be much better." She patted the sofa. "Modern furniture is only suitable for an office."

He walked to the sofa and, glass in hand, sat beside her. Took another swallow of whiskey before resting his glass on a low marble-topped table.

"Seemed to me this would be the best place for us to talk. My office is too frantic, a restaurant much too public."

"I agree."

"Here we can relax at supper and talk afterward."

"Sounds perfect." She was setting her rules for the evening. Letting him know she didn't care to discuss business until later.

"I've told my staff I want no interruptions. No phone calls. Business or personal."

"I've seen no phones since I arrived."

"All calls are taken in the servants' quarters, and if one is important a phone is brought to me wherever I may be. The cordless phone is a marvelous invention. Although I detest all phones."

"I'm inclined to agree. Casual callers never get past my secretary." He was aware that they were making conversation and wondered if he could sustain this until after supper.

There was a faint knock on one of the doors, barely audible, and the butler returned. "Pardon, Madam. Supper is served."

"Thank you, Denis." Placing her glass on the table. "Tell chef we're coming. Straightaway."

"Very good, Madam." He pushed both doors open and disappeared through the corridor.

Amadoro smiled. "Shall we, Mr. Hendrie?"

He got to his feet as she rose and walked beside her into the corridor.

The butler had vanished.

"We go this way." Amadoro gestured down the wide corridor. "I had no lunch today."

"Nor did I."

"Then we should both have an appetite. I canceled a luncheon appointment because of the weather, but I refuse to eat lunch in my office. We're having supper on the south terrace. It should be comfortably cool after the rain. I find it more pleasant for an intimate supper than either of the dining rooms. Complete privacy! This is the tallest building in the area, so no one can look down at us from a higher terrace."

"Sounds perfect." He was even more aware of the perfume now, walking beside her. That sensuous scent.

Was it possible this woman had ordered the death of Clement Marnat? Had she really killed her second husband? She had, certainly, sent those two Latin types to attack him in the park. Yet here he was, about to have supper with her.

"Through here . . ." She indicated another pair of open doors.

He followed her into a spacious dining room with boiserie walls. Soft light from hidden sources overhead. Comfortable French country furniture. Armchairs against the walls and a table in the center, large enough to seat six, bare except for an arrangement of white roses in the center reflected in the polished wood surface. No pictures on the walls.

"This is the smaller dining room."

"Smaller?"

"Actually, the other dining room is the same size but the table seats twice as many people." She went ahead, through open French windows, onto the terrace.

The butler was waiting. He bowed and walked ahead of them.

Ash followed Amadoro. He saw a glass-topped table set for two with squat candles lighted in silver holders.

The terrace was wide and the view, looking south, was spectacular, with the lighted windows of the World Trade Center visible at the tip of the island. Beyond that was darkness.

"This is like being suspended in infinity." He turned and saw she was seated, the butler waiting behind the other chair. "Forgive me! I've never seen anything quite like this."

Amadoro laughed. "It overwhelms most people. Especially guests from Europe."

Ash sat down as the butler pushed his chair forward.

"We're having a rather simple supper. I don't like complicated food in warm weather."

"Nor do I."

Unfolding her napkin as she talked. "As your eyes adjust to the darkness you will see a pinpoint of light far away."

He turned in the direction she indicated and glimpsed a tiny light which seemed to flicker against the black sky. "I see it."

"I'm told that's the torch on the Statue of Liberty."

Ash peered overhead and saw a canopy of twinkling stars. "I can see the stars now."

"Later, as we sit here, the sky becomes much lighter." She glanced around as the butler returned, pushing an aluminum cart on wheels with two silver-covered dishes under a glass dome.

The butler slowed his cart to a stop and rolled the dome back. Placed one dish in front of Amadoro, removing its silver lid, and served the other to Ash.

He saw an incredible salad but had no idea what it was, except for a row of anchovies arranged across the top.

The butler was serving Amadoro some kind of cracker from a napkin-covered basket of golden wire.

When he offered it to him, Ash saw that they were seeded pumpernickel crackers crusted with cheese. He picked one up and set it on his butter plate. Aware that Amadoro was attacking her salad with appetite.

The butler rolled his cart away, up the terrace, behind Ash.

As he dug his fork into the salad, Ash saw that it was an elaborate combination of several things. Avocado quarters under slivered leeks, topped by strips of red pepper under the anchovies. He could taste walnut oil and mustard in the dressing, but there were other ingredients he couldn't name. "This is delicious!"

"You like avocado?"

"I do, indeed."

"Mine own invention. Avocado Amadoro . . ."

"I'm analyzing each mouthful and shall describe it to my wife."

"I'm certain it was an avocado in the Garden of Eden that caused all that trouble. No other fruit could have tempted Adam like an avocado. It is, of all fruits, the most voluptuous."

He laughed. "You mean they were kicked out of their garden because they ate an avocado?"

"Something like that."

"Perhaps they left Eden to search for this dressing. It's excellent."

A sudden sound of barking came from inside.

Ash looked toward the open windows as a small cream-colored dog came bounding onto the terrace, growled when it saw a stranger, then ran straight to Amadoro.

"Somebody's left a door open." She leaned down to pat the dog, whose tail was now thrashing with pleasure. "This is Prince. He likes to sit beside me when I'm dining. Tonight he's supposed to be kept upstairs in the kitchen. You don't mind him here?"

"Certainly not. I like dogs."

The dog ran around the table and sat, looking up at him.

"Very handsome. That café-au-lait color. I've never seen the breed. What is he?"

"A miniature sheep dog. Not many of them in New York, I'm told. He was bred in California. Found him when I was out there on business. He's two years old now . . ."

"So your name is Prince?" Reaching his hand out, cautiously.

The brown eyes studied him.

"Once he inspects you he'll come back and sit beside me. Won't bother you again."

The dog came closer and, tail wagging, touched Ash's forefinger with the tip of his pink tongue.

"You've been accepted, Mr. Hendrie. Come, Prince!"

He returned to her at once and stretched out beside her chair.

"There was a dog, the other day, in your office . . ."

"He's my office dog. This is my house dog, my favorite. He never goes to the office. Would be too confusing for them because they're both named Prince. All my dogs are. The black poodle in Paris and the corgi in London. Named for a dog I owned when I was a child. I loved him, that first one, more than I've loved any other."

"I believe I've seen a snapshot of that one."

"Have you?" There was a brief flash of surprise in her green eyes.

He immediately regretted mentioning that photograph and changed the subject. "Did you say your kitchen is upstairs?"

"An elevator connects it with a serving pantry between the two dining rooms and food is brought down, as you've seen, in heated or refrigerated carts. The servants' quarters are also up there. A self-contained wing with its own private terrace and swimming pool."

Ash finished the salad and set his fork down. He realized that he had eaten too quickly. Had hurried, anticipating their after-dinner conversation, eager to learn why Amadoro had invited him here. Her mood at the moment, seemed relaxed and friendly.

She glanced at him as she put her fork down, salad unfinished.

"I suppose your chef is French . . ."

"Oh, no! I think Swiss chefs are the best. Many French ones, you know, perfect their talent in Switzerland. Some of the finest in Paris spent years in Zurich. That's where I found Carl. In addition to being handsome and young, he's the greatest chef I've ever known. He goes with me wherever I travel. Flies ahead when I visit my other homes."

"You have a town house in Knightsbridge, I believe, and a duplex in Paris?"

"Also a small chalet in Gstad and a very damp Venetian palazzo. Carl is king of all my kitchens. And for good reason! I find English food dull, Austrian too rich and Italian boring."

The butler returned, pushing a larger aluminum cart.

Amadoro remained silent as he removed their salad plates and served the next course.

Ash saw slices of fowl in a dark sauce and fresh asparagus lightly covered with a mousseline sauce.

"I hope you like duck, Mr. Hendrie."

"I do, indeed!"

The butler placed individual gold baskets with napkin-covered rolls at each place and, as they began to eat, lifted a wine bottle from a silver bucket, uncorked it quickly and poured wine into Amadoro's glass.

She tasted it and nodded.

He proceeded to fill both glasses.

"I drink only white wine, Mr. Hendrie. Never red! Even with duck. This is a sparkling Cortese that I import from Tortona." Raising her glass.

Ash picked up his glass and touched it to hers.

The butler departed as they drank.

Ash studied her face, savoring the wine. She even spoke of her chef as handsome and young! He wondered how many men she had slept with. Three husbands and Marnat. How many others in Paris? London, Venice and New York . . . ?

He was reminded of Don Giovanni. A thousand and three in Spain . . .

Was she a Dona Giovanni?

He smiled at the thought and set his glass down.

"You are smiling . . ."

"Some wines make me smile."

"I'm delighted that this one pleases you." She began to eat.

Ash picked up his fork and took his first taste of the duck. "This is quite the best duck I've ever eaten!"

"A few days ago this bird was flying above some Scotch Highland."

"Aviation has done much to change the world's eating habits."

They ate in silence, for a moment, enjoying the superb food.

Ash found her face even more exquisite in the soft light from the candles and thought of that poem again.

> She wore a mask of beauty
> But the lips dripped venom
> And her eyes held death . . .

Impossible to think of this vital woman dead.

She looked up, aware of his gaze, and smiled. "What are you thinking, Mr. Hendrie?"

"How very beautiful you are. What else could any man think, sitting across from you?"

"Most men think of money. My beauty, as you call it, has been quite useful—especially in business—but I've reached an age where it bores me. Anything that's too beautiful, like a perfect Greek amphora, soon becomes dull and you never look at it again."

"My father claims that perfection in a painting tires the beholder."

"I've met your father."

"Yes, I know."

"You do seem to know everything."

"No man knows everything. About anything."

"I know a woman who's said to be the most perfect hostess in Paris, but her parties are so dull nobody accepts her invitations anymore."

As she talked about social life in Paris, he considered what he would say, after dinner, when she granted him permission to write her portrait.

Dessert was a superb raspberry mousse, with which they finished the bottle of wine.

Amadoro continued to talk, superficially—now it was about her life in Manhattan and London—always social, never mentioning business affairs—and told the butler to serve coffee in the drawing room.

The dog bounced ahead of them through the long corridor toward the front of the duplex.

Ash saw that another pair of doors stood open—they had been closed earlier—into a lighted room.

Prince ran inside and they followed.

His first impression of the drawing room was that of colors. Yellow and white. Sunlight on ice and snow.

Amadoro went ahead of him across the enormous room.

It was, obviously, designed for entertaining. At least two stories high, with a false glass ceiling that had an elaborate design etched into the glass. Diffused light, soft and mysterious, filtered through from above.

"Sit here, Mr. Hendrie." She sank onto a large white satin sofa.

"This room is amazing!"

"A dear friend in Paris designed it for entertaining. It can accommodate a hundred people comfortably. Or two people."

Ash sat beside her as the butler brought a modern silver coffee service on a silver tray, which he rested on a low table in front of Amadoro, and poured the coffee.

The dog stretched out on the sofa, beside Amadoro, almost invisible against the white satin except for his black nose.

Ash realized that they were seated in an oval grouping of identical white sofas, three on each side, between columns which appeared to be made of large Plexiglas bubbles rising, as though from some magic sea, to support the false ceiling. Larger sofas, placed at intervals against the walls, were covered with golden moiré silk and separated by lustrous panels consisting of glass and ivory figures that seemed to be floating toward the ceiling. There were only two paintings—huge Picasso abstractions in white frames—hung opposite each other on the two long walls of the room. Enormous flat yellow silk cushions on all the sofas and floor-to-ceiling yellow curtains at tall windows standing open onto another terrace. There was an ebony baby grand, on a low platform, in one corner near the windows. Towering plants with gigantic green leaves in white pots, at intervals, against the walls. Tall white and yellow gladioli in crystal cylinders on several of the tables, which held an incredible assortment of objets d'art scattered between statues and abstract forms in glass lighted by large white pottery lamps with golden shades. The room was like a stage set designed by Lalique.

He was relaxed after the excellent dinner. Aware that Amadoro was still making small talk—he was only half listening—as the butler finished serving their coffee.

"Would you care for brandy, Mr. Hendrie?" Amadoro asked.

"Thank you."

The butler left the room as they sipped their black coffee.

Ash leaned back against the pillowed sofa. This had, indeed, been a perfect dinner. Now Amadoro would say that she had done much thinking, since their previous meeting, had decided to permit him to do her portrait for *Metropole*. She was not going to talk seriously until the butler had completed his duties. He could feel tension building as he finished the coffee and set his cup on the table. "You have a superb chef."

"I'm delighted you enjoyed supper." She was scratching the dog's head.

The butler returned with a bottle of brandy and a single crystal snifter on another silver tray. Poured a large brandy and placed it on the table in front of Ash.

"Thank you."

The butler turned to Amadoro. "Will there be anything more, Madam?"

"Nothing else tonight."

He bowed and went toward the doors.

Ash reached for the snifter and cupped it in his left hand. Watched the butler leave, without closing the doors, and noticed, for the first time, carpeted marble steps in a far corner leading to a landing, with more steps continuing out of sight upstairs. Ideal for Amadoro to make an entrance when this room was crowded with people. "I suppose you have more secret passages here?"

"Oh, yes! I like to slip into this room unnoticed when there is a large party and many guests. Suddenly I am here, in their midst. I prefer not to make an entrance. So theatrical." She stroked the dog's head as she talked.

He became aware that the light was fading overhead, all the table lamps dimming.

The butler must be doing it.

Ash looked around and saw that they were now seated in an oval oasis of light from overhead spots. The only other illumination came from the distant entrance hall and the lighted terrace beyond the open windows, but bright pinpoints of light were reflected from many of the glass objects on the tables.

He felt, suddenly, that he and Amadoro were opponents again.

"You said you saw a snapshot of my first dog. I must've been in that picture . . ."

"You were."

"Perhaps I should tell you. I killed that dog."

"What do you mean?"

"Haven't you found out about that?" She smiled. "I was only seven, but I remember it vividly. It was just before Christmas. I gave Prince a hot bath and locked him in a box outside the kitchen door. Left him there all night. He froze to death. I didn't mean to harm him. Nobody had told me that a dog could die. My father called me a murderer. I loved Prince. Didn't mean to harm him, but I killed him. Since then every dog I've owned has been named Prince. That way I keep him alive. I didn't kill him. You understand? Prince is alive."

"Yes, of course . . ."

"I suppose that was the first time I realized how much I disliked my father. Because he said I'd murdered Prince."

"Was this why, later, you rejected your parents?"

"How could you know that?"

"I've talked to them. Drove up to New London . . ."

"I hated both my parents from the day I learned they were rich and had never told me. For years they'd led me to believe they were not. I knew they weren't poor, but I'd no idea my father had inherited two fortunes. I detest them both. My father was a stupid football player, my mother a vulgar Broadway dancer. I never took a dime from them after I married Toby Towson. And I owe them nothing! You've seen that miserable house where I was born? Where they still live! With their money they could live anywhere. But they like it there!"

"I also saw Cap Larson when I went to New London."

"That fool! I offered him a job when I bought my first yacht, but he turned me down. A beautiful new yacht, anchored in the Aegean Sea, but he prefers to stay at Best of Times. I will pay his salary as long as he lives—because Toby liked him—but I don't ever wish to see him again." She straightened on the sofa. "You couldn't have learned much about me from them. Who else have you questioned?"

"I've located Mrs. Winston but haven't talked to her."

"Who?" She looked puzzled.

"Mrs. Laurie Winston. Your mother told me she was your paid companion when you first came to New York."

"Was that her name? I'd forgotten. So long ago! I don't recall any of the people from my past."

He realized that her right forefinger was tapping on the upholstered arm of the sofa.

"Did you send the police to question me last night?" she asked.

"Certainly not!"

"Inspector Desmond McCorkle turned up at the Four Seasons and questioned me in front of my escort."

So Benedict hadn't told her he'd seen him, or she would be even more angry.

"Inspector McCorkle asked me about one of my employees who seems to have been attacked and killed in his apartment."

"Clement Marnat. That was in the paper. I met him when I was at your office."

"So you did! Well, Inspector McCorkle learned nothing from me because there was nothing I could tell him. I invited you here tonight, Mr. Hendrie, to inform you that I still refuse to have my portrait in your magazine."

"I hoped you had changed your mind."

"Several of your people have contacted Amadoro Associates and requested interviews with my assistants."

"One of those would be our Miss Kwong, head of research."

"All were refused." She hesitated, making an effort to restrain her anger. "I want this investigation of my public and private lives stopped."

"That is, I'm afraid, impossible."

"Nothing is impossible, Mr. Hendrie. I'm prepared to offer you one hundred thousand dollars not to write my portrait."

"You—what?" He put the snifter down, brandy unfinished.

"The money will be given to you by my attorney. One hundred thousand dollar bills. Delivered by hand, wherever you wish it brought."

"So you invited me here for supper to offer me a bribe?" He rose from the sofa.

"A gift. Not a bribe. Such an unpleasant word! One hundred thousand dollars is more than you will ever make in a year."

"That's very likely."

"One hundred thousand—tax free! There's no way the money could be traced."

"I don't want your money, Madame." He kept his voice low. "I'm going to write your portrait and there's no way you can stop me. The police, at the same time, will be working on the Marnat investigation."

"Clement Marnat's death will never be traced to anyone at Amadoro Associates."

"Are those two Latin types who killed Marnat the same pair who attacked me in Central Park?"

"I know nothing about that."

"I'd talked to Marnat just before he was killed." He saw her eyes widen with surprise. "He informed me that, at one time, you and he were lovers. That you confessed to him that you had killed your second husband . . ."

"He lied! Robbie was burned to death when his car crashed. Hundreds of people witnessed the accident. You can get the autopsy report."

"We have already contacted New Scotland Yard. They say the body was so badly burned there was no autopsy."

"I suppose Monsieur Marnat tried to sell you what he claimed to be information about me."

"He did, but I wasn't interested. I am going to do your portrait, however, and it will be published in *Metropole*." He saw that her forefinger continued to tap without making any sound.

"Is there nothing I can say to persuade you not to do this?"

"Nothing. I shall tell the truth about you. Every fact that can be authenticated. Even if it is murder. My thanks for a most interesting evening, Madame." He turned and strode toward the open doors.

"I will destroy you, Mr. Hendrie." Her voice was cold and harsh.

The words were chilling.

Ash paused in the open doorway, considering how to reply, before turning and looking back.

She was no longer seated on the sofa.

He glanced around the room, but there was no sign of her.

A faint scratching noise came from his left.

He turned toward the sound and saw the dog scratching at the base of a glass wall panel.

She had escaped through one of her hidden passages!

The dog ran toward the steps, in the corner, and bounded upstairs. He would know where to find her.

Ash continued on, into the lighted corridor, and went toward the foyer.

No butler to show him to the elevator.

He pressed the button and the doors parted.

Stepped inside and jabbed the Lobby button.

The elevator doors closed silently.

She had threatened to destroy him!

This woman who was about to die . . .

chapter nineteen

"I WILL DESTROY YOU, MR. HENDRIE . . ."

Ash stood at the windows of his silent office, looking out at the morning sun flooding Central Park, as the words continued to echo in his brain.

He had heard them over and over, all night, unable to sleep.

When Mara returned from the theater, after midnight, she tiptoed into his room and whispered his name, but he hadn't answered. Heard her moving about in the kitchen, then silence as she ate the cold supper Rosie had left for her in the refrigerator. She had stayed in the kitchen longer than usual, and he had discovered the reason when he made his breakfast coffee. A note listing the menu for Monday night and suggesting he call her, before she left for her matinee, if he wanted to change anything or had any suggestions.

He would phone Mara, before twelve, and congratulate them—his wife and Rosie—on the menu. Tell her he had stopped at his favorite liquor shop on Madison Avenue and selected several excellent French wines. Better than that sparkling Italian he had drunk last night with Amadoro.

"I will destroy you, Mr. Hendrie . . ."

The threat, spoken so quietly, had chilled his blood.

After he left Amadoro's penthouse, he had walked the few blocks to Costigan's, hoping McCorkle might be at the bar, but his usual stool was empty and Danny Casey hadn't seen him for two nights.

Ash had sat on McCorkle's stool and ordered a double whiskey. Danny, fortunately, was too busy for more than a few words and sensed that he didn't wish to talk. Johnny Costigan stayed in the dining room, where every table was occupied and people were waiting to be seated.

He had sat there for half an hour, going over his second meeting with Amadoro from the moment of his arrival to her final words.

"I will destroy you, Mr. Hendrie . . ."

Not that she would, actually, have him killed. Or would she?

Was it possible for anyone—even with Amadoro's power and wealth—to kill and get away with it?

He'd finished a second double and barely remembered finding a taxi to take him home from Costigan's.

Should he call McCorkle? Arrange to meet him somewhere.

Tell him about Amadoro's threat. That she had invited him to her penthouse for supper. Offered him a hundred thousand not to do her profile and he had refused. Then she had said she would destroy him . . .

Ash went to his desk, where he had spread out the pages of notes again, snatched up the phone and jabbed the outside button. Dialed 911.

"Police Emergency."

"Good morning. I'm a personal friend of Inspector McCorkle. Could you tell me where I might reach him?"

"Hold on, sir. Lemme check . . ."

Ash stared at his notes as he waited, those same twelve pages with their headings. Reached for a pen and printed a second name under ENEMIES:

Ashton Hendrie

Printing his own name made him smile. He didn't, really, feel antagonistic toward Amadoro, but, of course, they were enemies . . .

"You still there, sir?"

"Yes."

"Nobody seems to know where McCorkle is today. I'll have him contact you if he checks in."

"That won't be necessary. Thanks." He set the phone down.

Amadoro must have many enemies. No way to know how many . . .

He left his desk and returned to the windows. Glanced down at the Saturday morning traffic in the dark canyons before focusing on the open sweep of park.

Lots of people there now. The bright sun and clear sky, after yesterday's rain, would bring thousands out today. He could see tiny figures swarming across the grass. Later some of them would picnic with their children and the walks would be black with strollers.

A faint sound, behind him, made him whirl as the door opened.

The muscular figure of a uniformed guard came in and the darting eyes saw him. "Didn' know you was in this morning, sir."

"Had some work to do. Anyone else in?"

"Nobody, sir. Sometimes Miss Kwong works Saturday, but I ain't seen her today. Sorry I disturbed you."

"That's okay." As the door closed he returned to the windows. There had been several robberies in the building and Carrington had been worried enough to hire armed guards to patrol the *Metropole* suite, nights and weekends, because of the valuable paintings and the technical equipment in various departments.

Mandy probably wouldn't be coming in today, and there was nothing more he could do here.

He checked his watch. Ten past twelve.

Returning to the desk, he picked up the phone and dialed his apartment. It only rang twice before it was answered.

"That you, love? I'm just leaving."

"Been working. Wasn't aware of the time."

"Doesn't matter. You caught me. The wines were delivered and they look lovely. You approve the menu?"

"Sounds perfect."

"I'll tell Rosie to go ahead and make her shopping lists. How was supper with Amadoro?"

"Excellent supper, but trouble afterward." He couldn't tell Mara about the offer of money. "She still refuses to give me any cooperation."

"Then why did she invite you for supper?"

"I suppose to threaten me and the magazine if we go ahead."

"Can she do that?"

"She can threaten, but it won't get her anywhere. I'm still doing her portrait and I told her so."

"That's my love! Now you've called, I must get to the theater."

"Give 'em a good show!"

"Always! Will you be free for supper tomorrow night? After the performance?"

"Have to let you know in the morning."

"Breakfast?"

"Hopefully."

"Bye, love! I'm off."

As he put down the phone his eyes were caught by a name on one of the pages—Mrs. Laurie Winston.

He should go back and see Mrs. Winston.

She must know many things about Amadoro.

This time he would persuade her to open the door and answer some questions.

He walked to Seventy-third Street, took the small elevator to the fourth floor and fingered the bell button of apartment 43. Heard the chimes inside but no other sound. Rang again, then rode down to the empty lobby, where he found a door marked "Manager." Rang the bell twice before footsteps sounded inside.

The door was opened by a white-haired fat man in neat coveralls. "Yessir? What can I do fer ya?"

"I'm looking for Mrs. Winston in number forty-three. She doesn't answer the bell."

"She ain't gonna be answerin' that bell no more, mister. Moved out, yesterday."

"Any idea where she went?"

"Mentioned somethin' 'bout Europe but didn' say where in Europe an' I didn' ask no questions."

"Were there any other people living in the apartment?"

"Mrs. Winston's daughter an' gran' child."

"Did they have their own furniture?"

"It's still in there. She said somebody would come for it before the enda the month. Rent's paid till then. You here for that furniture?"

"No, but I'd like to have a look in the apartment."

"Well, now, I don' know . . ."

Ash pulled a twenty-dollar bill from his wallet.

The man's eyes observed this, greedily. "You're not police?"

"Nothing like that. I write for a magazine and I'm a friend of Mrs. Winston's."

"Been here before?"

"Oh, yes. Saw her day before yesterday." He watched the twenty-dollar bill slide from between his fingers.

"Okay, sir. Guess I can let you in." He reached a key down from a wooden panel and, closing the door, headed for the elevator.

Ash followed. "How long had Mrs. Winston and her family lived in your building?"

"They been here a coupla years. Thought you said you knew the lady?"

"I do, but not well." He followed the manager into the elevator. "What's the daughter's name? I don't know her."

"She's Mrs. Winston, too, same's the old lady. She married her son, but he died."

The elevator took them to the fourth floor, where the manager unlocked the door and switched on lights in the apartment.

As they crossed the foyer Ash became aware of a ghostly trace of Amadoro's perfume. When they reached the curtained living room, the familiar scent was much stronger.

The manager snapped another wall switch, lighting several table lamps.

Ash saw that the furniture was comfortable but inexpensive, the pictures on the walls reproductions of famous paintings. Cheaply framed. "Have you ever seen a young woman here? Very attractive. Long blond hair . . ."

"No, sir. Can't say I have."

"She would've arrived in a black Rolls with a chauffeur."

"Nobody like that. Matter of fact, I never seen nobody visit the Winstons. Whole time they lived here."

"Did they go out much? Mrs. Winston and her daughter . . ."

"I've seen the old lady come in with shoppin', although they had most of it delivered. An' the daughter takes the boy out t' walk in Central Park."

"Boy?" His senses came alert. "How old is the boy?"

"Mebbe five or six. Little devil, that kid."

"You know his name?"

"Don't rightly remember. Odd kinda name."

"That perfume . . ." Ash sniffed the air. "Did Mrs. Winston wear that? Or her daughter?"

"I don't smell no perfume. Kinda stuffy in here. Mebbe I oughta let a little air in." He walked to the nearest window, shoved the curtains aside and raised it.

Ash saw that the apartment faced a blank wall. "Did Mrs. Winston's daughter go out to work?"

"Couldn't say. I got the impression the old lady had dough. They always paid their rent on time and there was never nobody after them for unpaid bills."

"Who signed the rent checks?"

"Mrs. Winston herself."

Ash moved around, casually, inspecting everything but finding nothing of interest. Except for that faint presence of Amadoro's perfume. He wondered if she had come here and told Mrs. Winston to move out in a hurry. Maybe after he saw the old woman two days ago . . .

"Care t' see the bedrooms?"

"If I may." He followed the manager through a narrow hall. "Were they pleasant—Mrs. Winston and her daughter—when you talked to them?"

"Kinda distant. Only time I seen 'em was when I'd be workin' in the halls an' they'd pass me. They would speak, friendly enough. It was the grandson was unfriendly."

"How do you mean?"

He turned around, his hand on a doorknob. "The kid's mother was always havin' trouble with him. He was a handful! Runnin' an' screamin' in the halls. If I didn' watch out he would kick me, but most times I was too fast fer him. A gen-u-wine little monster." He opened the door and went ahead into a sunny bedroom.

Ash frowned, remembering the small boy he had seen with his mother at Amadoro Associates and, later, running ahead of her along the edge of Central Park.

As he went into the room he was overwhelmed by Amadoro's perfume. A sparsely furnished bedroom with sunshine coming through the open windows. The dressing table had been stripped. "Whose room was this?"

"The young Mrs. Winston's. I was in here once, last winter, when a window got stuck."

So it was the younger Mrs. Winston who used the same perfume Amadoro wore. Had she bought it somewhere or had Amadoro given it to her? She had worked at Amadoro Associates in the past. Would be easy for the older Mrs. Winston to arrange for her daughter-in-law to get a job there. Paolo, at the reception desk, said the boy's mother was a former employee.

He had to find those two Mrs. Winstons. Talk to both of them.

Ash followed the manager across the hall to another closed door. "You have no idea where they might've gone? Mrs. Winston and her daughter . . ."

"No, sir. Only what I awready tol' ya. The old lady said somethin' 'bout goin' t' Europe. That's why she couldn' leave no forwardin' address." He opened the door and went inside. "This here's where the boy slept."

It was a smaller room, flooded with light from two open windows.

The first thing he saw was a child's bed that had been stripped down to the mattress. A closed door that, probably, led to a cupboard.

Ash opened the door and saw the cupboard was empty. Then he noticed something on the floor.

A small brown teddy bear, facedown, with a knife thrust into its back.

chapter twenty

THIS WAS THE STRANGEST DAY HE HAD EVER EXPERIenced.

As Ash walked through the hot afternoon sunshine toward Madison Avenue—his mind on that teddy bear—he noticed several unpleasant faces. Swarthy Latin types. He looked behind him, after they passed, but none turned to glance back and nobody seemed to be following him.

"I will destroy you, Mr. Hendrie . . ."

Was it possible to destroy someone on the crowded streets of the city? Of course it was! Happened every day . . .

Hadn't those two guys followed Marnat? Or had they only waited near his apartment? No matter. They had destroyed him.

He had an urge to get away from this area, which was his daily scene of activity.

No point in going home. Mara would be at the theater, and Rosie always went to a movie Saturday afternoon.

The empty apartment would be even worse.

Better stop at the garage and pick up his car. A long drive should relax him and, for a few hours, he could forget this overpowering sense of danger.

His panic, he realized, came from the fact that there was nothing he could do to protect himself. Only wait for Amadoro to make a move . . .

This was ridiculous! That she would, personally, do anything to harm him physically.

Perhaps Amadoro had only meant that she would, somehow, destroy him at the magazine. That was more likely what she had in mind.

There was no danger of losing his job. No way she could get him fired. Unless she bought the magazine! He knew, for a fact, that every offer in the past—and there had been several—were rejected by Carrington and the board of directors. Maybe she would offer so much money they couldn't refuse. In that event she could, certainly, arrange for him to be terminated.

So what! They would have to settle his contract and he would have no difficulty finding another job. Also, there was enough money in his bank account for him to survive.

He realized that he had changed directions, automatically, and was approaching his garage in the side street off Fifth.

While someone went to get his car, he called McCorkle from a public phone booth, again without success.

When the attendant brought the Jag, he eased out of the garage into heavy Saturday afternoon traffic without any idea of where he was going. He was in no mood for Long Island today, or New England. Where could he go for a few hours of peace?

Atlantic City!

He had talked, for years, of driving down there to have a look at the gambling casinos, but Mara could never be persuaded.

Checking his wallet at the first red light, he found that he still had several hundred dollars from his last visit to the bank.

Amadoro's voice drove with him all the way to Atlantic City.

"I will destroy you. Destroy you. Destroy you . . ."

He left the Jag in an immense garage under a hotel and took an elevator up to the boardwalk. Strolled for an hour. Inspecting the garish casinos and the unpleasant-looking people desperately searching for a good time. All of them looked hot, tired and unhappy.

Conscious of several young women staring at him. He was, of course, better dressed than most of the men he passed with their wives and girlfriends. A few older men without women. Seedy types that would live in the rows of rooming houses he'd noticed in the narrow side streets leading to the beach.

He finally went inside one of the less gaudy casinos, bought some chips and sat at a roulette table with a sleek young croupier in an ill-fitting dinner jacket.

His father had taught him to play roulette one summer, long ago, in Monte Carlo, and he had always enjoyed the excitement of the game. For a few hours. He had won then and he was winning now.

Continued winning, small amounts, and let his chips pile up

through the afternoon—as people left the table and were replaced by others—until he was distracted by a swarthy middle-aged man who kept passing the table and staring at him.

Could he have followed him from New York? One of Amadoro's thugs? Not likely! Too old . . .

The man's feral eyes, in their wrinkled pouches of flesh, began to distract him. His attention was drawn away from the clicking wheel whenever the man passed. Why did he continue to stare? Some sort of security guard who was given a signal by the croupier when anyone started winning? He counted his chips and saw they added up to more than a thousand dollars.

He had started with two hundred and had done rather well, playing carefully but not caring whether he won or lost.

The man's eyes drew his attention again and again, and he wasn't surprised when the wheel began to go against him. The pile of chips began to melt and he continued playing until all were gone.

Ash got up from the table, tipped the croupier and headed out into the lobby. Feeling relaxed and, to his surprise, hungry.

Checking a clock in the lobby, he saw it was past six. He'd spent several hours at the roulette table.

No sign of that inquisitive-eyed little man.

Leaving the casino, he crossed the boardwalk to the railing and looked beyond the beach toward the ocean. Several sailboats offshore against a clear blue sky. Not as warm as it had been when he arrived. The sun would sink in another hour but the neon boardwalk wouldn't come to life until after dark, when he would be driving back to New York and Amadoro. She would be waiting for him . . .

"Nice evenin' . . ."

The low voice, unpleasantly close, startled him and he turned to see the feral eyes again. "What the devil are you after? Staring at me in that casino. Made me lose a thousand bucks!"

The little guy shrugged. "Look like you can afford it."

"You're from New York." The accent was unmistakable.

"That's right." The unpleasant face attempted a smile. "Knew you was from the Big Apple, minute I seen ya. Can always tell! Been livin' in Atlantic since they opened the gamblin' joints, but I get back to the big town every month."

"What do you want from me?"

"I got somethin' fer you." He pulled a printed card from a pocket and held it up. "Good-lookin' young guy. Alone on the boardwalk . . ."

Ash glanced down at the small card, careful not to touch it, and saw a drawing of a nude girl with enormous breasts on roller skates. Large type said "The Pink Rink," and underneath, in smaller letters, was an address and phone number. "You shill for this place?"

"The wife owns it, mister. Best girls in Atlantic . . ."

He looked out at the rolling waves and saw they were brown with filth. "Get lost. All I want is some dinner. Then I'll drive back to New York and my wife."

"Had a fight with her, dincha?"

"Wasting your time, fella. Go back inside and find another sucker." He leaned on the railing, staring at a distant yacht, reminded of the *Sea Sprite* and a young man swept over the side . . .

Lyli Amadoro, whose name was Leola Martin then, had been asleep below deck in her cabin. Or had she?

"I will destroy you . . ."

Back to that again!

And a teddy bear with a knife stuck in its back . . .

Ash turned from the railing and looked around.

The creepy little man had disappeared.

Heading back, across the crowded boardwalk, he found the hotel with the underground garage where he'd left the Jag.

Drove carefully, in heavy traffic, until he reached the outskirts of the city. Ugly flatland that had once been marshes was now even uglier with rows of small restaurants, fast-food shops, used-car lots.

He swerved off the highway and parked outside the cleanest-looking restaurant. This one seemed to be the largest and had valet parking. He ordered a seafood dinner that turned out to be much better than he'd anticipated, with a split of champagne.

The return trip to New York seemed shorter. There was less traffic, so he could make better time.

Left the Jag with his doorman and took the elevator to his empty apartment.

Enjoyed a long, hot shower and went to bed.

Slept immediately, probably because of the fresh ocean air, and didn't hear Mara when she came home from her evening performance.

Couldn't remember having any dreams or nightmares when he finally awoke and heard birds singing, in the distance a faint clanging of church bells. Sunday morning . . .

He turned over, buried his face in the pillow and went back to sleep. Only wakened when he heard a familiar voice whispering in his ear.

"Would my love be ready for brunch in fifteen minutes? Omelette, sausages and brioche. Strawberries in champagne. Black coffee and more champagne!" She bit the lobe of his ear.

He grabbed for her but she had fled.

"I give you fifteen minutes, lover! Not a second more."

He smelled the fragrant scent of her bath soap. So she'd had her shower.

Ash sprang out of bed and without reaching for his robe ran into the bathroom.

In fifteen minutes he crossed the living room—shaved, showered and wearing a brown pongee summer robe—toward Mara, who was seated at the breakfast table, already eating.

"You made it!"

He kissed the back of her neck.

"One in front, if you don't mind."

"Good morning." He leaned down, kissing her lightly on the lips, and smelled the strawberries she was eating.

"You were sound asleep when I got home."

"Had a terrific night's sleep." He circled the small breakfast table, placed in front of an open window facing the park, and sat across from her. Filled their glasses with champagne and poured it over his strawberries. Mara preferred hers without wine, with powdered sugar.

"I had bad news yesterday," she announced.

"Oh?"

"There was a rumor backstage. Our play's finally closing."

"We'll be able to take that vacation with Millie and Alain!"

"It's not definite yet, but suddenly, business is way off. Matinee only half full and not much better last evening. I dread going to the theater tonight. Everyone's depressed."

He picked up his glass and waited as she reached for hers.

They touched glasses.

"To the closing of your play and our glorious holiday in Europe!" As they drank he saw that her face was troubled. "What's wrong?"

"You know how I hate a play to close . . ."

"But you've had a long run. More than a year. We'll take our vacation—all expenses paid—and you'll find a new play for next season."

"That's what worries me. Looking for another job. There just aren't that many good parts. Everyone says Broadway's finished."

"They've been saying that ever since I can remember."

"I'm calling my agent first thing in the morning. Eat your strawberries . . ."

As he ate, the crystal bowl of berries reminded him of Amadoro's glittering drawing room. He wondered if McCorkle would be working on the Marnat case today. Even a detective had to have Sunday off! Maybe taking his son—"the shyster"—to a baseball game . . .

They ate their strawberries in silence for a moment.

"You picking me up for dinner tonight?" Mara asked.

"I thought we'd go to Costigan's."

"Lovely! Haven't been there for weeks."

"I'll reserve our table." He'd suggested Costigan's because McCorkle might be there.

Mara stood up and collected the empty bowls. "I'll make the omelette. Back in five minutes."

"Where's Rosie?"

"Gone uptown. She was meeting her family for early Mass. Told her to take the day. You know how she likes to spend Sunday with her grandchildren." She carried the crystal bowls toward the kitchen.

Ash put his napkin down and, securing his robe, strode across the living room, leather sandals smacking on bare floor between the rugs, through the entrance hall to unlock and open their front door. Scooped up the *Times,* which he carried back to the breakfast table. Poured himself a cup of black coffee and settled down to glance through the Book Review after pulling out the theater section and setting it beside Mara's place. Glanced toward the park as he turned the pages and saw the usual throng of late morning strollers in dappled sunshine under the trees edging the avenue. Put the Book Review aside as Mara returned bearing a tray that she placed in the center of the table.

"You can divide the omelette. Smaller half for me, please." She lifted two plates from the tray as he reached for the silver spatula. "I'm looking forward to tomorrow night." She sat at the table again and refilled her coffee cup. "Dinner with Sandra."

"So am I." Slicing through the omelette and watching the melted cheese ooze out. Lifted the two halves onto their plates along with a pair of small baked sausages for each.

"Rosie's excited about meeting Sandra. I had no idea! She reads her column every morning."

"What's Rosie's astrological sign?"

"I've no idea. Will we make love, tomorrow night, after Sandra leaves?"

"Don't see why not."

They ate silently, enjoying the omelette with the warm brioche slathered with sweet butter and a mirabelle marmalade.

"You make a better omelette than my mother," Ash observed.

"I think so, too. You never said that before."

"Been meaning to, for years."

"Have you seen the posters they've put up, around midtown, with a picture of Maudru?"

"Who?"

"Fernand Maudru. That French psychic. You're going to his lecture, Friday night, at Town Hall."

"I'd forgotten his name."

"Wish I could go but I don't dare skip a performance. Rest of the cast would think I was deserting a sinking ship, with this rumor that the play may close. You are going, Friday night, aren't you?"

"I plan to. Sandra's arranging for me to see Maudru, hopefully, the day before his lecture."

"Why are you seeing him?"

"To find out what he knows about Amadoro. Her life in Paris."

"His picture's on all the posters. I looked at one in the window of a restaurant. Handsome old man with lots of white hair. Very thin, with piercing eyes. Like a magician!"

"Magician?"

"Didn't you ever notice a magician's eyes?"

"I've never seen a magician."

"They look straight at you, holding your attention, so you won't notice what their hands are doing. Somebody told me that's the secret of every magic act."

They ate with appetite as Mara chattered about the theater and, when they finished, she refilled their cups with hot coffee.

Ash reopened the Book Review section as Mara rose and placed their breakfast plates on her tray.

The phone rang.

"You get it." She lifted the tray and carried it toward the kitchen. "I don't want to talk to anybody. Unless it's Millie. This is one of my silent Sundays."

He got up from the table as the phone continued to ring. "Millie and Alain will be out at this hour, having brunch somewhere." Picked up the phone as she went into the kitchen. "You have reached a badly disconnected number."

"Have I, indeed!"

"Sandra? Wasn't expecting you to call. Mara just said she's having a silent day."

"I, too, like quiet Sundays, lover. In fact, I'm not taking any calls myself, but I had to talk to you. You saw Amadoro, didn't you? Friday evening . . ."

"She invited me to her penthouse for supper."

"Is that where you were! I saw you with her, briefly, in a place which appeared to be very cold. Snow and ice around you . . ."

"We were in her drawing room, after supper, and everything was white and glittering. White sofas with glass columns holding up a false glass ceiling . . ."

"Is that what it was!"

"A chilling experience. In every way."

"She threatened you."

"So you know, do you?"

"I didn't understand most of what she said, but I could tell from her attitude and the way her eyes flashed."

"She threatened to destroy me."

"Her threats can't harm you, lover. The lady doesn't have much time left to threaten anyone."

"You still think . . ."

"I most certainly do."

"She refused, again, to give permission for me to do her portrait."

"You will do it without her permission. She offered you a small fortune not to write it."

"Yes, she did."

"And you turned her down."

He laughed. "I feel better. Knowing you were watching."

"I had a sudden feeling about you, Friday evening, as I fell asleep. Saw you with Amadoro but only heard snatches of what she said. Couldn't hear your voice at all."

"Because of her threat I've been feeling extremely vulnerable. Aware that she may have someone watching me. Following me . . ."

"She won't."

"You make me feel much better." He was aware of Mara returning to sit at the breakfast table and picking up the newspaper as he talked. "We'll see you tomorrow night?"

"At eight. I'm looking forward to our evening together. There's one thing more. I talked to Fernand Maudru yesterday in Beverly Hills. He gave a lecture there last night and he's relaxing today, with old friends, in Palm Springs. He'll be flying to New York on Wednesday and I've arranged for you to see him Thursday afternoon at the Plaza. He said you could drop by around two. He never eats lunch but takes a nap at noon. Call his suite from the lobby. His secretary, Jean Clair, will be expecting you."

"That's perfect."

"Fernand thought your portrait of me was excellent."

"He'd read it?"

"While he was in Vancouver. Thinks you did a fine job explaining parapsychology for the public. And he's pleased you're coming to his lecture. His secretary will leave your ticket at the box office."

"Splendid!"

"My love to your dear wife."

"She's right here."

"Wouldn't think of disturbing her on a silent day. We'll talk enough—the three of us—tomorrow night."

"We both look forward . . ."

"Don't let Amadoro's threats disturb you."

The line went dead.

Ash set the phone down. "That was Sandra."

"So I gathered."

He went back to the breakfast table. "She talked to Fernand Maudru in Beverly Hills and arranged for me to see him Thursday afternoon at the Plaza."

"This is strange . . ."

"What?"

"Here's his picture." Handing the open theatrical section across the table. "Same one that's on all those posters."

He looked at the photograph in the center of a page surrounded by advertisements for concerts. A single word—MAUDRU—across the top and information about his lecture underneath.

Maudru's head was impressive, illuminated against a dark background. Long face, surrounded by an aureole of white hair curling like small feathers. The face was lean and ascetic, prominent cheekbones, eyes in deep sockets. Thin French nose, the kind Clouet had painted. His eyes were startling.

"What an incredible face," Ash murmured.

"I thought so, too. Felt his eyes following me from all those midtown windows. I told you! The eyes of a magician."

"Or a prophet . . ."

chapter twenty-one

ASH SAT WITH SANDRA, AT OPPOSITE ENDS OF THE SOFA, and Mara, who had been seated in a low chair on the other side of the circular coffee table, was now at the piano playing a Chopin.

The air-conditioning had been turned on for the first time this year. Mara insisted it would be more comfortable for their guest as well as for Rosie in the kitchen. It had been a warm day, but not hot enough for air-conditioning. Tonight, before he retired, he would turn it off and open all the windows.

Dinner had gone smoothly, with a minimum of fuss, and Rosie had looked dramatic in her best black uniform with a white lace apron, which she hadn't worn in more than a year. For casual parties she wore a gray uniform and no apron. Tonight was special, even for Rosie.

They hadn't left the dinner table until after nine o'clock.

Sandra had eaten everything and complimented Rosie after dinner.

He had poured a Chartreuse for Sandra, Framboise on the rocks for his wife and a snifter of Otard for himself.

Sandra had closed her eyes and was enjoying the Chopin.

Ash smiled. It had been a happy evening and he was completely relaxed, for the first time in several days.

Usually, after a dinner party, Mara complained about the clatter of pots and pans or the sound of a dish breaking, but Rosie had been so pleased to cook dinner for their famous guest that she wasn't making a sound in the kitchen.

Sandra had overwhelmed her. Told her that her latest grandson, Pedro, would soon recover from his allergy, warned her not to let him eat eggplant and assured her that he would live to be an old man.

Ash leaned back and, closing his eyes like Sandra, considered the long and futile day he had spent at the office. He'd been certain that something important would develop on the Amadoro story, but there had been nothing. Mandy had found no new information and Cort reported his photographers didn't see Amadoro all weekend. She, apparently, hadn't left her penthouse. He was beginning to wonder if she might have a private entrance through another wing of the skyscraper.

He'd tried to reach McCorkle twice today, without success.

Last night he had picked Mara up at the theater and, after circling the park for a breath of cool air, which they never found, driven to Costigan's. They had enjoyed a quiet dinner, but there was no sign of McCorkle at the bar and Danny Casey hadn't seen the detective all evening.

Should he take a quick trip to London and Paris—three or four days in each city—check on Amadoro himself? Use his personal contacts and avoid the two *Metropole* offices. The London staff would be disorganized with Giles Redfern turning the operation over to a new man, and the Paris office wouldn't be operating at peak form with Philippe de Guermond in Morocco. He could certainly turn up more about Amadoro's life in both cities through his own contacts. Discuss this with Carrington . . .

He opened his eyes and glanced at Sandra. Her eyes remained closed and she was smiling faintly as she listened to the music. Or was she asleep? She looked unusually attractive tonight. Wearing a smart dinner gown patterned with gray-and-violet flowers. A string of pearls around her throat. The silvery hair more attractively arranged than he'd ever seen it. What a comfortable human being she was!

He wondered what Amadoro was doing at this moment. On the town with one of her favorite escorts? Perhaps Burke Benedict . . .

Or alone in that extravagant penthouse? Standing on the terrace and staring down at the lights of the city far below? Maybe pacing in her glass-pillared drawing room. Sandra had called it ice and snow . . .

The piano was silent after a final crescendo.

Sandra opened her eyes and applauded.

"I'm terribly out of practice." Mara rose from the piano.

"You play like a pro." Sandra sighed. "Wish I could play Chopin like that. Or, for that matter, 'Three Blind Mice.'"

"My parents wanted me to be a pianist." Mara joined them and reached for her unfinished drink. "Mother taught piano at Curtis, gave concerts in Philadelphia, but she was never famous. I wanted to be an actress even then and escaped to New York. By the way, since I saw you, there's been a rumor my play's closing."

"Yes, I'm afraid it is." Sandra picked up her glass and sipped the Chartreuse.

"Can you tell me when?"

"I should think very soon. You'll be informed, officially, next week."

"At least I can make other plans now." She glanced toward Ash. "You know how I hate rumors and indecision, love."

"I was going over your preliminary charts yesterday," Sandra continued, "and I promise you'll be signed for a new play in early October."

"I will?" Mara's eyes gleamed with excitement.

"It should open on Broadway before Christmas. The best part you've ever had. It will have a long run. Perhaps two years . . ."

"Dear God! That's a hit!" Turning back to Ash. "Two years!"

"Meanwhile," Sandra went on, "you're going to Europe this summer. With your parents, Ash. But you already know that."

"We've been invited, yes."

"You're going. Both of you."

"Only if I can finish the Amadoro portrait by the middle of August!"

"You'll finish it. Although you'll be taking a brief trip to Europe yourself to get material."

"Will you, Ash?" Mara asked.

"That's possible . . ."

"It's quite definite," Sandra stated firmly. "I would think the first week in July. You're going to Paris and London. After Amadoro completes her present life . . ."

Ash straightened on the sofa.

Mara set her glass down. "Lyli Amadoro is going to . . . die?"

Sandra frowned. "That is a word I never use."

"I'm shivering." Mara clutched her bare upper arms, dramatically, with both hands. "Can you be certain, Sandra?"

"It is in Lyli Amadoro's horoscope."

"You've done her horoscope?"

"Only briefly. A few preliminary charts. When I came to the sudden completion of her present existence, I refused to continue the charts or tell her what I'd discovered. I never tell a client anything like that."

Ash set his brandy snifter down. "If what you're saying is true—and I'm sure it is—her portrait in *Metropole* should cause a sensation. I feel like a ghoul saying that, but I must make plans in anticipation of her death. Hadn't occurred to me before. This has to be the most complete portrait I've ever done. The obituary of a world celebrity! I must be aware of this, constantly, as I write."

"Let's talk about something more cheerful!" Mara exclaimed.

"Your vacation in Europe," Sandra responded, "and the new play next season. Those are positive and happy thoughts."

"Another Chartreuse, Sandra?" Ash asked, rising from the sofa.

"I won't be able to finish this, after those lovely wines we drank at dinner."

"We saw a picture of Fernand Maudru in yesterday's *Times*," Mara said, "advertising his Town Hall appearance. I'm so sorry I'll be working. You'll be there, of course."

"Oh, yes. I always introduce him when he appears in New York. As usual, it's going to be sold out. Which pleases Fernand. The proceeds from his American tour go to the Institute Parapsychologique he heads in France. Our Parastro Society is affiliated with them, and there are branches in England, South America and India. Each one, of course, independent of the others."

Ash moved around the room as they talked. "My parents would like to attend the lecture, but they have a previous engagement with one of Alain's clients. A dinner party to celebrate the opening of his private gallery. Many of the paintings were sold to him by my father."

"What is Fernand Maudru really like?" Mara asked.

"What is anyone really like, my dear?" Sandra sighed. "He is one of the most complex human beings I've ever known. An incredibly strong man, in spite of his age. A leader who attracts followers with his humility and compassion. I've known Fernand for many years and he's a true friend. I respect and revere him and look forward to continuing our relationship when we complete our present incarnation." She smiled. "We plan to keep in touch."

Mara got to her feet, facing Ash. "Darling, why don't you show Sandra your study? That's where he always writes the final draft of his *Metropole* portraits."

"I'd like, very much, to see where you work." Sandra rose from the sofa.

"It's the most cluttered room in the whole apartment." Ash went ahead, Sandra following.

"And I'll see if Rosie's nearly finished in the kitchen." Mara headed in the opposite direction.

"This is the one room Rosie doesn't step foot in unless I'm here." Ash led Sandra through an inner corridor. "Twice a year she dusts but I watch. So nothing's displaced." He opened a door and reached inside to snap on a wall switch. "Please . . ." Motioning for her to enter first, as lamps came alive.

"How nice!" She stepped inside, eyes darting. "I can understand why you would prefer to write here."

Ash took out his handkerchief and, after moving some books from the seat, dusted off a comfortable armchair. "Be my guest, dear lady!"

She sank down but continued to look around.

Ash sat on the tapestry-covered armchair at the table-desk on which his typewriter rested, in the center of a mass of books and magazines, an open cardboard box of fresh typing paper, a pewter shaving mug crammed with pencils and all the other paraphernalia of a working writer. "I've written all my *Metropole* portraits here. The final draft that goes to the printer. These windows are closed tonight and curtained, but they face the park. I keep them open when I'm working. No phone in here to disturb me. My whole life is in this room. At least my life as a writer. That steel file contains everything I've written. Since before college . . ."

Sandra glanced from side to side as he talked.

"These shelves hold books I've enjoyed and respected. Starting with those I read as a kid. Especially Mark Twain. The French writers I discovered in college. Balzac, Flaubert, Proust. All here!" His hands indicated different shelves as he went on. "Dickens, Conrad and Joyce Cary. Hemingway and Fitzgerald, but not so many Americans. I suppose that's because my roots aren't American. And this is my favorite picture."

She turned to inspect a framed watercolor.

"My father gave me that, for my eighteenth birthday. Cézanne painted it, long ago, in Provence. Sunlight on a green hill. A small piece of eternity. I look at it, constantly, as I type and try to be a better writer than I am . . ."

Sandra realized, as Ash talked, that her attention was wandering. Something was happening somewhere that concerned her. Something tremendously important. She felt a curious and unfamiliar constriction in her throat at the same time a chill swept down her arms. She let her muscles relax as her senses sharpened.

Ash saw the expression on her face. "What is it, Sandra?"

She shook her head, unable to speak. The sensation in her throat became more intense and she clutched at her neck with one hand.

"Let me get you some water!" He got to his feet.

She put out her other hand to hold him.

Ash sank back into the armchair and faced her. Saw the hand drop away from her throat. "You've seen something?"

"Felt something. Something—horrible . . ."

"Your throat?"

"Something—swallowed . . . Amadoro!"

"What?"

"She's—dead . . ."

"Where?"

"Don't know." Her eyes closed. "I saw nothing. Only felt my throat constricting. Heard voices—calling her name. Amadoro . . ." She opened her eyes slowly. "I've never had such a strong physical sensation before." Straightening in the chair. "Well! You can write your portrait without interference now. Lyli Amadoro is no longer any threat to you or anyone else." She rose and Ash jumped up from his desk. "I must get home. It will take several hours for me to relax enough to sleep."

"I'll get the car and drive you downtown."

"Certainly not. Don't fuss. I'll take a taxi."

Ash opened the door and she went ahead.

"Say nothing about this to your dear wife."

"Of course."

"At least for the moment . . ."

Mara was at the piano but stopped playing when she heard their voices.

Sandra departed in a flurry of compliments for the dinner.

Ash escorted her down to the lobby and helped her into a taxi. "You're all right now?"

"Of course." She smiled. "First time I've performed in public. Hope I didn't frighten you. It will be in the paper tomorrow morning, I should think. About Amadoro."

He lowered his voice. "Is it suicide or . . . ?"

"Or murder?" She frowned. "I don't know."

"Good night." He closed the taxi door.

She waved as the taxi sped away.

Ash returned to the apartment, where Mara was standing at one of the front windows looking across the avenue toward the park. As he joined her he realized that she had already turned off the air-conditioning and opened the windows. "What a pleasant evening!"

She smiled. "I thought dinner went rather well."

"Rosie surpassed herself." He leaned down to kiss her on the cheek.

"Let's skip sex tonight. I'm tired and still thinking what Sandra said about my finding a new play. And a hit!" She snuggled against his shoulder. "My mind's darting and diving."

"So's mine."

"Sandra's a truly remarkable person."

"You don't begin to know."

"Good night, my love." She raised her head and looked into his eyes. "I do love you."

He kissed her on the lips and walked beside her through the apartment to her bedroom, then continued to his own room. Stood at the open windows, looking north across several rooftops, and faced the fact that Amadoro was dead.

Writing her portrait would be much easier now.

This would open up fresh sources of information. People would talk who, until now, had refused. Perhaps even Giles Redfern and his wife would tell what they knew about Amadoro. All the more reason he should take a fast trip to London and Paris. Track down anyone who had known her. Now he must trace her missing daughter. That could mean several additional days in Switzerland . . .

He wouldn't get much sleep tonight. Thinking about the Amadoro portrait and making plans. An endless night of tossing and turning. Reliving that scene in his study when Sandra had suddenly clutched her throat.

Ash slept immediately and was wakened from deep sleep by the telephone. He checked the electric clock on his bedside table and saw it was just past two o'clock.

The phone kept rining.

Amadoro was dead!

He scrambled out of bed, flung the door open and ran down the hall to the living room.

The phone continued to ring as his bare feet smacked the floor.

Mara wouldn't hear it because she always plugged her ears for the night, and Rosie had orders never to answer the phone after they retired. He snapped on a light but couldn't remember where he had last used the phone.

It rang again.

He looked toward the sound and saw the white phone on the bar. No memory of when he had left it there.

It rang once more before he could pick it up. "Yes?"

"Mr. Hendrie?"

It was McCorkle. "Yes, Mac?"

"Thought you'd want to know, pal . . ."

"Amadoro's dead."

"How could you know that!"

"It's quite a story. Let's just say I knew. Where'd it happen?"

"In her apartment. Looks like a drug overdose."

"Suicide?"

"Or an accident. I thought, since you're writing the lady's portrait, you might like to have a personal look at things."

"Are you saying I can come there?"

"That's the idea. They haven't removed the body yet."

"I'll be right over."

"It's a penthouse at the corner of—"

"I've been there. Had supper with Amadoro. Friday night."

"Did you!"

"Been calling you ever since. Wanted to tell you about it."

"You left a message?"

"Matter of fact, I didn't."

"Well, pal. Looks like I'll have a few questions for you."

chapter twenty-two

THERE WERE THREE POLICE CARS AND AN OMINOUS windowless van double-parked at the foot of the skyscraper when Ash got out of his taxi and paid the driver. He looked up at the great tower but could see only a few lighted windows before the upper floors of the black marble structure were swallowed into the night sky.

He entered the partially lighted lobby, where groups of men were gathered near the information desk. Some held mobile television cameras. Others had press cards pinned to their lapels. They came crowding toward him.

"Who are you, mister?" "What's your name? "You police?"

He strode past them, avoiding the eyes of the night attendant at the desk, and headed for the private elevator to Amadoro's apartment.

There was a young cop on guard who watched his approach and, as he came closer, saluted. "Mr. Hendrie?"

"That's right."

"Inspector McCorkle said I should senya right up." He turned to the elevator and felt along the metal column at the side.

"It's higher, I believe."

"Yuh been here before?"

"That's right."

"Got it!" He pressed the hidden release and the elevator doors slid open. "McCorkle's upstairs, sir."

"Thanks." Ash stepped into the elevator and pressed the Penthouse button.

Again no sense of rising, only a faint hum from the powerful cable that was lifting him through space.

Little did he suspect when he came down in this elevator Friday night, raging at the woman he had just left, that he would be returning to view her dead body.

Must call Sandra in the morning. She had been correct in still another prediction.

Lyli Amadoro dead! The most beautiful woman in New York. Most beautiful woman in the world? Not anymore . . .

The elevator doors opened and he stepped out into a glare of light. Every bulb in the long central corridor had been turned on.

Another uniformed policeman, older than the first, jumped up from an antique chair. "Mr. Hendrie?"

"Yes."

"Inspector McCorkle said you're to come upstairs. You can go through here." He went toward the open drawing room doors. "There's some steps in the corner."

"I know." Ash moved ahead, into the brightly lighted drawing room, and as he turned toward the steps, realized that the lights above the false glass ceiling had been turned up and every lamp in the room was lighted. The white sofas glared and spears of light were reflected from the bubble columns and the glass objects on the tables.

The marble staircase turned and became a broad flight of red-carpeted steps leading to the upper floor.

He wouldn't tell McCorkle about those secret passages. Not yet.

Far away, in the depths of the apartment, a dog was howling.

Prince? Mourning for his mistress . . .

A trio of detectives, in the upstairs corridor, stopped talking and stared.

"Inspector McCorkle?"

One man pointed. "In there . . ."

Ash went toward a pair of doors standing open onto another brightly lighted room but hesitated before entering. Straight ahead a second pair of doors was open. He saw McCorkle, in the distant room, with several men.

Properly lighted, this sitting room—Amadoro would have called it a salon—must have been intimate and attractive, but with every lamp and chandelier lighted it was as artificial as a stage set. Beautifully designed and decorated, but unreal. There were no shadows, no feeling of intimacy. Everything seemed exposed and revealed. An exquisite Degas painting of ballet girls, above a white marble fireplace, looked tawdry, and the delicate Louis XVI sofa and chairs were cheapened. As he crossed the salon, slowly, he glimpsed the night sky beyond a row of tall windows standing open onto still another terrace.

McCorkle had noticed his arrival and hurried to meet him. "Just in time, pal. They're about to remove the body."

Ash walked beside him, uncertain how he would react to his first dead body.

"Because of this profile you're doing on the dame, I thought you'd like to be in on this."

"Yes, of course." As he entered the boudoir, Amadoro's perfume was overwhelming. "I'm very grateful, Mac . . ."

McCorkle motioned for the other men to move aside.

Ash saw that the bed was gold and ivory, white satin sheets tossed back.

Amadoro in death, as in life, was incredibly beautiful.

He stood at the foot of the bed, with McCorkle, looking down at her, aware of the others observing him.

Her body, deeply tanned, was partially covered by a white chemise of the most delicate lace he had ever seen. Long strands of blond hair flowed over her shoulders and spread across white satin pillows. Arms straight down beside her body. One hand was clenched but the other lay flat, the fingers splayed out. Her long scarlet nails were, somehow, ridiculous. The forefinger was not tapping angrily now. She had removed all makeup before retiring, even the false eyelashes, and her face looked more naked than her body. The mouth seemed smaller, lips thinner, without lipstick, and it was slightly open as though she had just spoken. The green eyes were wide but their color seemed to have faded, or was that because of the glaring lights?

Ash sighed. "They called her the most beautiful woman in New York . . ."

McCorkle nodded. "Prettiest corpse I ever saw. You had enough?"

"Yes." Ash turned away from the bed.

"Okay, you guys!" McCorkle raised his voice. "You can have her."

Ash saw two heavyset young men in white, whom he hadn't noticed before, start toward the bed, unfurling a wheeled stretcher. He realized that the walls of the boudoir were covered with gold moiré satin.

"We can talk in the other room." McCorkle went ahead of him. "Nothing more I can do here. Still have to question the servants more carefully." He motioned toward a pair of fauteuils in the salon.

Ash sank down onto one and the detective, rather gingerly, settled onto the other.

"How the hell did you know the dame was dead?" McCorkle asked. "Before I told you."

"Sandra Saunders came to the apartment tonight for dinner. We were alone in my study, Sandra and I, when she started choking and clutching at her throat. She gasped: 'Amadoro. She's dead . . .'"

"I'll be damned. What time was this?"

"Around ten, I should think."

"That's just about when the guy from the coroner's office says she died. Between nine and twelve. The maid didn't find her body until one o'clock. That's when she comes in here, every night, to check the lights. The dame had a habit of falling asleep and leaving them on. Especially that reading lamp on her bed table. If she left that on, the light would wake her during the night, so the maid had strict orders to check. Tonight she thought the dame looked strange. Stretched out on her back. Seems she always slept on her right side. When the maid went close she saw her eyes were open and knew something was wrong. Called the police."

"Why are you here, Mac? I thought you only investigated murder."

"Case like this, when it could be suicide, accident, or murder, they send an inspector to cover each. Coroner's office tracked me down. Said it could be murder. They always call me if there's a celebrity involved. When I heard Amadoro's name, I hopped out of bed in a hurry."

"You think it is murder?"

"Doesn't look like it, but I'm not convinced it's suicide. More like an accident."

"Why do you say that?"

"There was a pill bottle and a water glass on her bed table. The glass, apparently, hadn't been used but the pill bottle was more than half empty. We've contacted the doctor who prescribed them. His name and address were on the label. These Park Avenue doctors do a big business in sleeping pills. Claims he warned the dame never to take more than two. That's what it says on the label. If she gulped half the bottle, they could've killed her.

"The servants told me she dined out tonight. They don't know where. They say she's been irritable for several days. Unable to sleep nights . . .

"Guy from the coroner's office thinks she may have been tight and kept swallowing the pills. Thinking she hadn't taken any earlier. Drank water each time. That's why the water glass is empty."

"So you think she killed herself unintentionally?"

"That's how it looks at this moment. Something may turn up, during the autopsy, that could change the whole picture."

"Where are the servants?"

"Waiting in the kitchen until I finish here."

"Could I talk to them?"

"Don't think that would be such a good idea. Not at the moment. Maybe tomorrow."

"I understand." Ash rose from the fauteuil. "I'm very grateful, Mac. That you called me."

McCorkle got to his feet. "I knew you would like to see, firsthand, what had happened to the dame. No reporters allowed, but I thought I could bend the rule for you."

"I appreciate that." He realized that McCorkle was walking him toward the corridor, probably eager to get on with his investigation.

The detective motioned for him to wait as the two white-uniformed men rolled their covered stretcher from the boudoir and crossed the salon to the corridor.

Ash saw the outline of Amadoro's body under an ugly plastic sheet. The head, breasts, hips and feet.

Lyli Amadoro! Most beautiful woman in the world . . .

She no longer wore a mask of beauty, but her eyes, now, certainly held death . . .

As they turned right, in the corridor, he became aware of her perfume again. Little more than a trace, lingering behind, but unmistakable.

He glanced at McCorkle. "You'll keep me informed?"

"Sure will, pal. Call you tomorrow."

"Thanks." Ash was conscious of McCorkle returning to the boudoir as he went toward the corridor. Heard the dog howling again when he turned left toward the stairs.

Lyli Amadoro was dead.

He could write her portrait without interference.

chapter twenty-three

"HE'S WAITING FOR YOU, MR. HENDRIE. ASKING, EVERY fifteen minutes, if I've located you."

"Thank you, Miss Crevani." He continued past her desk and knocked on the inner door.

"Come!"

Ash swung the door open and saw Carrington glowering behind his desk.

"Where the devil have you been hiding?"

"I overslept." He crossed the office and collapsed into a leather armchair.

"Had Miss Crevani ring your apartment every half hour but she kept getting a busy signal."

"Took the phone off the hook when I got home last night."

"I heard on the early news that Amadoro was dead. I presume you heard the late news?"

"I didn't get to bed until after three. I was at Amadoro's apartment. Saw the body."

"You what!"

"As a guest of the police. My friend, Inspector McCorkle, knew about the Amadoro portrait and thought I might like to visit the scene of the—tragedy . . ."

"My God, man! This gives us an exclusive."

"I would think so. Yes . . ."

"This is tremendous!"

"I was present when the body was removed."

"Was it an accident or did she take her life?"

"They don't know yet. I'll hear more today, after the autopsy.

McCorkle promised to keep me informed." He couldn't tell the old man that Sandra thought it was murder.

"Must confess, when I heard the first report, I had a brief hope it might be . . . murder."

"Murder, sir?" His reaction was genuine, surprised that Carrington would suspect murder.

"Couldn't help wondering how it would increase our sales if Lyli Amadoro were murdered while you were working on her portrait and you, the investigative reporter, could solve the case before the police. What a scoop—as we used to say—that would be!"

"Nothing like that, I'm afraid."

"No matter! You'll have an exclusive on Amadoro's death with a firsthand account of the actual scene. The only one who can describe it from personal observation. This will add a final brilliant touch to your portrait."

"Before I do any actual writing I would like to pay a brief visit to London and Paris—now that Amadoro can't prevent people from talking. Interview her friends and associates in both cities."

"Excellent idea! How long do you judge that might take?"

"Perhaps three days in each city. I'll arrange in advance, through our offices over there, to interview people. That can be done ahead, appointments set, before I arrive."

"You'll wait, of course, until after the cause of her death is established officially."

"Oh, yes!"

"I suppose there'll be some sort of funeral ceremony . . ."

"I've no idea."

"Something elaborate, I should think. After all, she was an international celebrity. You'll be there, of course. Assign photographers to cover the affair. Did she have relatives?"

"A daughter, but we've been unable to locate her."

"She'll turn up now! You must question her privately. Find out about her relationship with her mother."

"Whoever's in charge of Amadoro's legal affairs will know where the daughter is." Ash got to his feet. "Looks as though this will be a fascinating portrait."

"Could be the most important we've ever printed. I'm glad you're the one writing it, Ash." Carrington smiled, flashing his too-perfect dentures. "Should have tremendous impact, since there's never been a feature story on Amadoro. It would be a tremendous plus if this is murder and you can pinpoint the killer . . ."

"That's rather unlikely."

"I can dream, can't I?"

"Yes, sir." He turned and strode toward the door.

Miss Crevani looked up as he hurried past her desk. "Miss Kwong's looking for you."

"I'm sure she is."

"What does Amadoro's death do to our portrait?"

"Makes it even more important." He escaped her inquisitive eyes and hurried to his own office.

Greta was opening the morning mail. "We're late today."

"I stopped in to see Carrington."

"Lots of calls!" She picked up a list as she rose from her desk and followed him into the inner office.

"Let me have that list." He sank into his armchair and took the slip of paper from her. "Tell Mandy I'm here."

She picked up the phone, pressed a button and dialed. "It's Greta. Tell Miss Kwong he's available."

"Inspector McCorkle didn't call?"

She set the phone down. "Not this morning."

"See if you can reach Sandra for me."

Greta snatched up the phone again, got an outside line and dialed.

"Nothing urgent here." He dropped the list on his desk.

"Will you be taking calls?"

"Let me know who's calling."

"Right." She spoke into the phone. "Nora? Greta . . . Oh, is she? I'll put him on." Handing the phone across the desk. "Miss Saunders was expecting you to call."

"Of course!" Taking the phone. "Well, dear lady! You did it again."

"It's rather frightening, isn't it?"

"I've only just come in. McCorkle phoned, middle of the night, said I could join him at Amadoro's apartment."

"McCorkle's handling the investigation?"

He swiveled his chair to face the windows as his secretary departed. "Only if it turns out to be murder. He won't know until after the autopsy. McCorkle thinks it could be accidental death or suicide."

"It is murder." Her voice was hushed now. "But don't ask me who the murderer is. I can't tell you that."

"Won't tell?"

"Can't. I've no idea who."

"But it was sleeping pills, wasn't it?"

"I'm not certain."

"They found an empty pill bottle."

"I'm afraid there's something else involved."

"But you're certain it's murder?"

"Yes, dear friend. I am certain."

"Then that's how I'll treat it—no matter what McCorkle says."

"Do be careful, Ash. I mean you, personally."

"I certainly will."

"That was a lovely dinner last night. I'll tell Mara, when she comes for her next appointment, how much I enjoyed the whole evening. Sorry I made a scene in your study."

"You said Amadoro was dead. And you were right."

"Such an unpleasant way to leave this life. Wish I could have helped her, but that was impossible. See you Friday night, at the Maudru lecture."

"Or sooner." He set the phone down and stared at the sunny sky beyond his windows. Seated at his desk, he couldn't see the park, only small white clouds sailing across the blue sky.

"So Amadoro's dead?"

He turned to see Mandy perched on an armchair and swung his chair around to face her. "How long have you been here?"

"Two seconds. You were putting the phone down as I came in. Looking terribly solemn. Didn't want to interrupt your chain of thought."

"Amadoro's death is going to change things. Our portrait must be definitive when it appears in September. Her death should open many new channels of information. We'll be able to get at the true facts of her private life. Past and present. People will talk more freely."

"I should think so."

"I've seen Carrington. Told him the police don't know whether her death was suicide or an accident."

"What about murder?"

"McCorkle doesn't think it was."

"The morning papers are vague as to cause of death."

"This is going to be exciting, Mandy. Peeling off the layers from Amadoro. Getting at the heart of two mysteries. Her death and her life . . ."

"I had one Teletype this morning from Paris. It arrived Saturday, but I wasn't in the office. From the assistant art director. She says Amadoro had a well-known Parisian painter do her portrait three years ago. She apparently hated it and wouldn't accept it. Refused to pay the artist. The Paris office wants to know if we'd be interested in seeing a color print of the painting."

"By all means! This could be the picture for our cover. Particularly if she didn't like it. The artist may have seen too much. Revealed the inner woman. Tell Paris to take an option on the portrait. Exclusive rights for reproduction. We might even buy the painting! But don't say that just yet. Better tell Carrington what you're doing. He's in a good mood because of what Amadoro's death will do to publicize our portrait, so he'll agree to anything. I've already told him I'll be taking fast trips to Europe for additional material."

She got up from the armchair. "Need an assistant?"

"That's not a bad idea. I'll see what can be arranged."

Mandy smiled as she departed.

Ash rose from his desk suddenly, went to the windows and stared out toward the park. The green expanse of grass and trees looked peaceful in the morning sunlight.

He had just remembered the cold frisson of apprehension that had wakened him just after four o'clock this morning. His first thought had not been of Amadoro, but of Nanny Eke in London.

That dear old lady! She had been his beloved nanny for five years.

He had known, at once, that something was wrong. These chills in the night had happened before. He'd gone back to sleep and when he got up had forgotten about Nanny Eke in a rush of thoughts about Amadoro's death.

Ash returned to sit at his desk and, as he reached for the phone, glanced at his desk clock.

Early evening in London.

He pushed a button for an inside line and buzzed his secretary.

"Yes, Mr. Hendrie?"

"Would you get Mrs. Eke, in London, for me? You have the number."

"Right away."

He put the phone down and stared at the blue sky again.

Visualized the small Hampstead cottage he had visited so many times with Nanny Eke when he was a child. She had taken him there to have tea with her daughter, Mrs. Jepson. He always found time, whenever he returned to London, to visit the cottage with flowers and presents for Nanny Eke, who had lived with her daughter since she retired.

Always, in the past, when he had one of these frissons in the night, it concerned death or dying.

He dreaded making this call . . .

The phone rang, startling him.

He picked it up. "Yes, Greta?"

"I have Mrs. Jepson on two."

He pressed that button. "Mrs. Jepson? It's Ashton Hendrie."

"Oh, Mr. Hendrie! How could you know? Mama passed away in the night."

"I am so sorry."

"She was talking about you, just last evening, wishing she could see you . . ."

He realized that she was crying softly. "Had she been ill?"

"Only a few days . . ."

"She seemed fine when I talked to her at Christmas."

"Mama always felt better when she heard your voice. Doctor says she didn't suffer at the end. Such a blessing . . ."

"Is there anything I can do? Anything you need?"

"Nothing, Mr. Hendrie. Thank you. Everything's taken care of. Mama managed to save quite a bit, much more than my husband and I had realized, from all those years when she worked. Especially the last years, with your family . . ."

"She was a fine woman. Some of the happiest memories of my childhood include your mother. Give my best to your husband."

"I will, Mr. Hendrie."

"Can't get over there at the moment, but I will be in London for a few days later this month. Perhaps you and Mr. Jepson will have dinner with me."

"That would be lovely! We'll see you then."

"Good-bye." He set the phone down as tears filled his eyes.

His childhood had vanished, forever, as he talked. His beloved "Eekie" dead. She never liked him to call her that, insisted it should always be "Mrs. Eke," but he had realized she would smile whenever he did, even though she continued to protest. Dear "Eekie" . . .

The phone rang.

He pressed the inside button and picked up the phone. "Yes, Greta? What now?"

"Someone to see you. Mr. Denis Nair . . ."

"Never heard of him."

"He claims he was Lyli Amadoro's butler."

"Good Lord! Of course . . . Send him in. And no calls while he's here. Not even McCorkle! Especially McCorkle."

"Right." The line went dead.

He faced the door as he got to his feet, remembering the sleek young Englishman in impeccable livery who had served dinner so deftly. The dark blond hair and long fingers with their carefully tended nails.

The youth who entered was a shock. Tousled hair, apprehensive eyes, pale face. Shorter than he had seemed in uniform. Wearing a cardigan, over a sport shirt and creased slacks.

Ash extended his hand. "This is, certainly, most unexpected." He saw that the fingers were long, the nails clean. They shook hands.

"Terribly sorry to bother you, sir."

"Not at all."

"I had to talk to someone. After last night's tragedy. Someone who knew Madam. And I could only think of you."

"Glad you did." Motioning to an armchair as he sat at his desk again.

"Thank you, sir." Nair sat down, rather tentatively. "You were the only person I could think of to contact. It was pleasant, last week, serving you. The usual people who dined with Madam were not so appreciative, if I may say so."

"Tell me, what sort of people did dine there?"

"Mostly business executives, with no interest in the food they were served. They barely noticed what they were eating, only the project they were trying to sell Madam. She always instructed me, ahead, to keep filling their glasses. Unlike when you were there. Madam told chef that you were, probably, a gourmet. She discussed the menu with him and told me which wines to serve."

"Dinner was superb."

"I could see you enjoyed it, sir. I told Carl. He's the chef."

"What did Madame say after I left? We had something of an argument."

"I don't mind telling you, sir, she was furious. Didn't say a word to any of the staff. Went upstairs to her private suite and slammed the door. We heard it from the kitchen. Her little dog howled most of the night because Madam wouldn't let him into her boudoir. Mrs. Dainley, the housekeeper, had to take him to her room."

"I understood, from Madame, that the staff has its own quarters."

"Oh, yes! Quite separate. The connecting door, from the kitchen, is locked every night. Mrs. Dainley's the only one has a key. She locks it—after Madam's maid checks the lights—and it isn't unlocked until next morning when Mrs. Dainley prepares our breakfast."

"I'm told it was the maid who found Madame's body when she checked the lights in her boudoir."

"She screamed but nobody heard her. So she had to come running to tell us Madam was—dead. We all went in to look at the poor lady. You could see from her eyes there was no life."

"Your name is Denis—Nair?"

"That's correct, sir."

"And why did you come to see me? Of course, I'm delighted that you did."

"I'm rather desperate, sir. No idea where to turn. I've made no real friends in New York. Without a job, I'll be sent back to London and I don't want that. I thought, perhaps, you might know somebody who requires a first-class butler."

"I don't, offhand, know anyone who employs a butler. Americans don't have many servants these days. I promise to keep you in mind, in case I hear of something."

"Very kind of you, sir."

"There are several things I'd like to ask you about Madame . . ."

"Certainly, sir."

"Do you have any idea where she ate dinner last night?"

"No, sir. She always dined out Monday nights. Never told any of us where she went."

"The police found an empty pill bottle. It had contained sleeping pills. Did Madame Amadoro take drugs?"

Nair hesitated. "Yes, sir. We all knew about that. Every member of the staff could tell when Madam had taken—something, but we never knew what it was."

"Do you have any idea where she obtained these drugs?"

"No, sir."

"None of the staff supplied her?"

"Certainly not! We, none of us, would have anything to do with drugs. The chef, Carl, is a health nut. Always cursing people who take pills. Except vitamins. He's on a strict diet. Madam hired him to help her keep her figure and he's done that."

"Did you see any drugs in the apartment?"

"Never."

"Didn't know where she kept them?"

"The housekeeper has talked about that. Says she's never seen a trace of drugs anywhere. I used to think I knew who brought her drugs, but I've not seen this person lately. Madam told us he'd gone back to France."

"Was his name Marnat?"

"That's the one! Monsieur Clement Marnat. He frequently came to see Madam late at night. Always with a small parcel. None of us ever found out what was in those packages or what Madam did with them."

"Didn't you know Marnat's dead?"

"God! No . . . What happened?"

"He was murdered, last week, in his apartment. You knew he was employed at Amadoro Associates?"

"I had no idea, sir. None of the staff ever went there. We knew nothing about Madam's business affairs."

"Who pays your salary?"

"Our checks come in the post from Amadoro Associates. Including a nice bonus at the end of each year. We all hate to see it end. Especially Carl. Madam had promised to help him open his own restaurant in New York someday. It was to be called Chez Amadoro and she was going to bring her friends to dine there. Carl doesn't want to go back to Europe, either. We all prefer to stay here."

"How many others are on staff?"

"Only the housekeeper—Mrs. Dainley—she's Scotch, and the maid, Teresa, who worked for Madam in the palazzo she maintains in Venice. We're all here on special permits Madam arranged because we had worked for her abroad. She brought me to New York when her previous butler retired."

"Have you always been a butler? Isn't there something else you could do?"

Nair shrugged. "I trained to be an actor."

"My wife's an actress."

"Unfortunately, I had no talent for the stage. I studied at RADA and played in rep, but only small parts. Mostly butlers. Madam saw me in a West End comedy. Had a secretary send me a note to come to her office. I went, not knowing what to expect, and she asked if I would like to be a butler for real. Her butler was retiring but he would teach me everything he knew. Which he did. I never liked acting but I enjoy being a butler. Madam said, later, it had been difficult finding a young butler." He smiled for the first time. "She told me I was the best butler she ever had!"

"I suppose Inspector McCorkle questioned you, with the others, last night . . ."

"Each of us. Separately. But there wasn't much we could tell him. Madam didn't confide in any of us." He stood up abruptly. "You've been extremely kind, Mr. Hendrie. I had to talk to someone, other than the police . . ."

"As you may know, I'm writing a portrait of Lyli Amadoro. I'd like to talk to you again."

"Certainly, sir."

Ash rose from the desk. "Do you recall who signs your salary checks from Amadoro Associates?"

"Oh, yes! The name's always the same. Carlo Ricci."

"Carlo Ricci?" He studied the young Englishman again, saw that he seemed more relaxed now. "Tell me . . . how well did you know Madam Amadoro?"

"Know her, sir?"

"Did you know her, perhaps, better than any of the other staff members? You're a very presentable young man."

"I don't quite understand . . ."

"You've had an affair with Lyli Amadoro, haven't you?"

He smiled again. "You might say that, sir."

"Frequently slept with her?"

"At least twice a month."

"Did you tell Inspector McCorkle this?"

"He didn't ask. If he had, I wouldn't have told him. Although no harm, I suppose, now."

"Thanks for confiding in me."

"None of the others on staff ever suspected. There is a hidden passage, from the servants' wing, into Madam's boudoir. I was the only one knew it was there."

"Are there other secret passages?"

"I wouldn't know. Madam herself showed me this one."

"I'll contact you if I hear of any sort of position."

"Thank you, sir. That's very kind."

"Will you be staying at the apartment?"

"For the moment. We're all waiting for word from Mr. Ricci about our future. He phoned Mrs. Dainley this morning and said we might be moved to a hotel. I'll let you know what happens, sir."

"By all means, keep in touch."

"Thank you again, sir. I'm terribly grateful." He turned and, walking more purposefully, went toward the door.

Ash sat down again. This unexpected interview had been decidedly fruitful. McCorkle hadn't learned that Amadoro slept with her young butler at least twice a month! He wondered if he'd discovered that the staff's salary checks were signed by someone at Amadoro Associates named Carlo Ricci. Very likely he hadn't thought to ask. It was the sort of thing a detective wouldn't be interested in during a first interview.

He reached for the phone and pressed the button under his desk.

"Yes, Mr. Hendrie?"

"Greta, would you call Amadoro Associates and ask for a Mr. Carlo Ricci? I'll talk to him . . ."

chapter twenty-four

THE SWARTHY YOUNG MAN AT THE RECEPTION DESK WAS not the one who had been here when Ash paid his previous visit to Amadoro Associates. Curly black hair, gray suit and dazzling smile were the same, but the face was different.

"I'm Mr. Hendrie, and I—"

"Mr. Ricci's expecting you." He reached under the desk and the same glass panel slid open in the mirrored wall.

"There will be someone to show you the way, sir." He picked up the phone.

Ash passed through the opening into the long inner corridor. The closing panel, behind him, reminded him of Amadoro's passion for secret passages. He hesitated as another young man came hurrying toward him, not the one who had escorted him to Marnat's office. He wondered if that office was empty.

"Mr. Hendrie? Mr. Ricci will see you immediately."

He followed the expensive gray suit through a side corridor with more paneled walls and closed doors to a smaller office than Marnat's where another swarthy young man, wearing black-rimmed spectacles, looked up from a computer.

The young man pushed himself back from the computer and got to his feet. "Mr. Hendrie?"

"Yes."

He bowed and turned toward a pair of inner doors, knocked on one and opened it. "Mr. Hendrie's here, sir."

Ash entered and heard the door close, behind him, as he walked toward the small man seated behind a large desk. This was a working office with a minimum of furniture, expensive but functional. The only decoration was an enormous photomural of Venice covering one wall. The man at the desk also appeared to be severe and functional.

Ricci rose, extending a hand. "Sit down, Mr. Hendrie."

He shook hands and sank onto the aluminum-and-black-leather armchair as Ricci resumed his seat.

"I was surprised when you called and said you wished to see me."

Ash studied him as he talked. A tiny man but impressive. Carefully brushed black hair, silvered at the temples, black eyebrows over hawk eyes, dark complexion and darting Latin hands moving constantly. Silver-rimmed spectacles and, as he had noticed on the phone, a barely perceptible Italian accent.

"You said you're preparing a portrait of Contessa Amadoro for *Metropole* magazine . . ."

"That's correct. I saw the Contessa twice, shortly before her death, to discuss what I planned to write."

"Twice? I was informed you had seen her several days ago but she refused to grant permission for your portrait."

"We talked a second time, last Friday night; in fact, I dined at her apartment. The two of us."

"Did you, indeed? I had no idea!" He shrugged. "But then, I'm frequently the last to be informed."

So Amadoro hadn't told her associates, before she died, that she had turned him down again. This was good to know. "We had a pleasant supper and I discovered that she had decided to cooperate, fully, in the preparation of her portrait."

"Lyli has been known to change her mind, frequently, on important matters. When she told me, after your first meeting, that she had refused to give her permission, I ventured to suggest that such a portrait in *Metropole* might be quite desirable. I suggested she read your current portrait of Sandra Saunders, the parapsychologist. Perhaps I may have helped to change her mind." He smiled smugly. "I've been able to do that in the past." He frowned, dramatically, gesturing his despair with both hands. "It is unfortunate that the Contessa died so suddenly. Unfortunate, most of all, for Amadoro Associates. So much left undone and undecided!" He shrugged again. "None of us know what will happen now. The attorneys and the bankers will have many conferences settling the Contessa's affairs. Personal and business. I suppose you plan to complete your portrait . . ."

"I'm determined to do that. The portrait will be even more important now. In spite of the newspaper stories that will be published these next weeks. Mine will be a study, in depth, of her entire life. I plan to visit London and Paris and talk to people who knew her."

"And what, sir, do you wish from me? I am curious. How did you hear of my name? Know of my existence?"

"I learned that you sign checks for Amadoro Associates. Which makes you a very important person."

Ricci smiled, smugly again.

"You must know many things. About the Contessa's personal life, as well as her business affairs."

"I suppose there's no reason why I shouldn't answer your questions. Unless they seem to be indiscreet."

"How long had you known Madame Amadoro?"

"Ah! I was a banker in Venezia and, for many years, had handled the fortune of Conte Alfredo Amadoro before he married Lady Craydon. After the Conte's most unfortunate death, I helped the Contessa settle his estate. She was, of course, already a wealthy woman from two earlier marriages. I advised Lyli when she was forming her own corporations—Amadoro et Cie, Paris; Amadoro Limited, London; and Amadoro Associates here in New York—so, you see, I've known her for many years. Lyli persuaded me to leave Italy and become treasurer of this vast organization."

"Was there anything suspicious about the death of Conte Amadoro?"

"Most certainly not!"

"He died in a skiing accident but he was an expert at the sport. Practically a professional."

"Many professional sportsmen are killed because of simple errors in judgment. Alfredo misjudged a turn and shot over the side of the mountain into a deep crevasse. His body wasn't recovered for days."

"Was there an autopsy?"

"That wasn't necessary. Twenty people saw the accident and testified at the inquiry."

"Both of Madame's previous husbands died in accidents. One drowned in a storm, the other crashed a racing car."

Ricci shrugged again. "Accidents are common at sea and in racing cars."

"I'm aware of that. What will happen with Madame's personal staff? Her butler and chef, for instance, are first-class."

"No decision has been made, as yet, as to their disposition. Lyli has provided for each of them with generous bequests."

"I imagine she provided for her daughter even more handsomely."

"Daughter?" Ricci looked startled. "Nicole will be a very wealthy young lady."

"I would like to talk to the daughter. Could you tell me where I can reach her? Where she's living?"

"That, I'm afraid, is impossible. Lyli never permitted anyone to interview Nicole."

"Was the daughter ever married?"

"I believe not."

"Does she live in the United States?"

"She has spent much of her life in Europe. Mostly Switzerland."

"Will she be coming to New York for her mother's funeral?"

"There was a meeting this morning and Lyli's attorneys informed us that she had specified in her will that, in the event of her death, there would be no service of any kind. No memorial ceremony, nothing of that sort. So there is no reason for her daughter to inconvenience herself. One of our executives will take any documents requiring her signature to Switzerland."

"What will happen with Madame's penthouse?"

"For the moment, it is to be kept intact, in case the daughter ever decides to make her home in New York."

"Have the police been here to question your office staff?"

"Not to my knowledge. A reporter contacted our night operator and wanted to talk to someone in charge. He was told to phone back today. The operator reported his call to her superior. Someone, no doubt, has been assigned to handle all inquiries from the press and the police. You are the only person to contact me. I agreed to see you, at once, because I was certain it concerned your proposed portrait of the Contessa. That you would, certainly, wish to go on with the project. And I agree. An honest portrait of Lyli should be given to the public. I believe you can do that portrait, Mr. Hendrie."

"Thank you."

The phone rang on the desk and Ricci picked it up. "Yes . . . ? I'll be with you in a moment." He set the phone down. "I trust, Mr. Hendrie, you will come straight to me if you have further questions."

"I'll certainly do that." He got to his feet. "You've been very helpful."

Ricci rose, smiling, holding out his tiny hand. "Call me anytime."

Ash shook his hand and headed for the door.

Walking back to *Metropole*, keeping to the shaded side of the crowded streets, he considered what he had learned.

When he reached his office, he jotted down brief reactions to everything Ricci had told him . . .

"Am I interrupting?"

He looked up to see Mandy with clippings in her hand. "What have you there?"

She came toward the desk. "Greta said you were alone. These are the first brief newspaper reports on Amadoro's death." Handing them across the desk. "Early evening editions. Old pictures of Amadoro and distant shots of the skyscraper where she lived."

Ash glanced at the pictures and read the headlines.

"One says accidental death and another says possible suicide. Take your choice."

"Which means the police know nothing, as yet, from the coroner's office and are being cagey with the press." He let the clippings fall onto his desk. "I've talked to an executive at Amadoro Associates—Carlo Ricci—and he's willing to help, any way he can, with our portrait of Amadoro."

"That should be useful."

"Claims he tried to persuade her to cooperate with us. I asked about Lyli's daughter and he claims she's in Switzerland. Won't be coming here for her mother's funeral. In fact, there won't be any kind of ceremony. Lyli ordered that in her will."

"She was smart."

"Get all the stories on Amadoro's death and her obituaries from London and Paris. Something of interest might turn up in one of them." The phone rang and he snatched it up. "Yes, Greta?"

"Inspector McCorkle's here."

"Send him in." He put the phone down. "McCorkle."

"Shall I vanish?"

"Soon as I introduce you."

The door flew open and McCorkle lunged in and, without closing it, came toward the desk, his eyes on Mandy. "You keep some mighty classy dames in this place. That one you have on guard outside and now . . ." Facing Mandy. "I'm Inspector Desmond McCorkle."

"Known as Mac the Cork to friends and criminals." Ash waved his hand in a gesture of introduction. "This lovely lady is Amanda Kwong, head of our research department."

"Head of research! I don't believe it."

Mandy giggled. "It's not a terribly large department."

"Miss Kwong, I trust . . ."

"Ms. Kwong, if you please."

"I do please."

"And I mustn't hold up whatever important information you've brought Ash. Nice meeting you." She headed for the door, her cheongsam flapping.

McCorkle glanced down at the delicious leg that was revealed and smiled as Mandy departed.

Ash motioned to an armchair. "Ms. Kwong has been pursued by every man on our staff without success. She may have been waiting for you."

"I shall investigate, after giving the little lady at least a week to anticipate that possibility." He sank into the armchair. "Stopped by on my way back to Amadoro's apartment. We were there until dawn. Went home for a fast nap and a shower, then spent the morning downtown. Several developments, and I wanted to bring you up to date."

"Anything from the coroner?"

"No final report as yet, but I talked to him after they finished the autopsy. They have to do further tests. The results, so far, are inconclusive. Could be suicide or an accident. She'd drunk several glasses of white wine with dinner and at least two brandies afterward. Then she'd taken sleeping pills and a large amount of some liquid drug made from hashish."

"My God!"

"There also was an amount of residual cocaine in the body. This dame liked everything! They have to analyze the quantities of each to find which, actually, caused death."

"How long will that take?"

"He didn't say. There was no bottle containing the liquid hashish. I've a hunch she got that somewhere while she was out for dinner. We may never trace it. There were no drugs in the apartment. Nothing in her medicine cabinet. Fanciest john I've ever seen! Has everything but drugs."

"Were there fingerprints on that pill bottle and the water glass?"

"None. Both were checked."

"Isn't that odd?"

"Frequently happens. Glass doesn't always take a print. The servants swear they didn't touch anything. So now you're up to date and I'm on my way." He got to his feet. "Busy day ahead. Until the coroner says it's not murder, I've gotta operate as though it is."

"But you still don't think so."

"Not until the lab finishes its tests."

"Sandra Saunders thinks it's murder."

"You're kidding!"

"Talked to her on the phone."

"I'd better take another close look at everything." He started toward the door."

"You'll let me know about those tests?"

"Sure will." Looking back as he opened the door. "I'm on my way back to that apartment. Got a feeling there's something there I overlooked." He went out, closing the door.

Ash frowned as he unlocked his desk and brought out the Amadoro file again. Spread the pages out and studied them once more. Making several additional notations.

His phone didn't ring until the middle of the afternoon. He picked it up. "Yes, Greta?"

"Miss Saunders on line two."

He pushed the button. "Good afternoon, dear lady."

"Any news about Amadoro's death? There was very little in the evening papers."

"Coroner's final report isn't completed. McCorkle says it could be suicide or accidental death. Overdose of drugs. She had taken several. They have to find out which one actually killed her. Sleeping pills, some kind of liquid hashish or cocaine . . ."

"How very sad! I've just talked to Fernand Maudru in Chicago. He stopped off to visit a client but he'll be in New York tonight. He's anxious to meet you tomorrow. I'm seeing him tomorrow evening to go over the details for his lecture. I'm told most of the seats have been sold. Your ticket will be waiting at the box office. Come around, backstage, afterward. Fernand's giving a small supper at his hotel. You can be my escort."

"My pleasure!"

"Miss Cassie's trying to persuade me not to go to Town Hall."

"Why not?"

"She says my life could be in danger."
"Shouldn't you listen to her?"
"I always listen to her, but I must be there with Fernand."
"Did you tell him about this?"
"Certainly not! He's aware that Cassie is psychic, but I don't want to worry or distract him before his lecture."
"Do you see danger for yourself?"
"I can seldom see anything in relation to myself. I've checked my charts and they do indicate some vague sort of threat for Friday. This city is dangerous every time you step outside your door."
"That's true."
"See you at Town Hall!"
"Be careful."
"I most certainly will. See you then . . ."
"Right." He put the phone down.
So Miss Cassie had warned Sandra her life could be in danger if she attended Maudru's lecture.
What possible danger?

chapter twenty-five

THE UPSTAIRS CORRIDORS OF THE PLAZA ALWAYS REminded Ash of the Ritz in Paris.

He pressed the button beside the door and heard a discreet buzzer respond inside.

No sound of footsteps before the door was opened by a short middle-aged man in a tan summer suit, white shirt and patterned brown silk tie.

"Ah, Monsieur Hendrie! Welcome . . ." He stepped aside for Ash to enter. "Maître Maudru has been looking forward to this moment."

"And I, to meeting him."

"I am Jean Clair." Leading him across the small foyer. "Le Maître's assistant. We always stay here because the Plaza is quiet and like a corner of his beloved France in the heart of New York." He flung open an inner door. "Here he is, cher Maître! Monsieur Hendrie . . ."

Ash went into the handsome sitting room as a man in a black silk robe rose from a small sofa and stood, his head against the light from an open window, holding out a hand.

"Monsieur Hendrie, how delightful . . ."

Ash was unable to see Maudru's face but realized that he was tall and thin. Saw that the outstretched hand was fragile with long, delicate fingers, but his grip was firm. "I am honored, monsieur, that you would see me. Knowing your time is very precious."

"Time is precious for every human being. Unfortunately, most people do not realize that." Motioning to a striped fauteuil. "Please . . ."

The assistant withdrew, closing the door.

Ash sat down and was able to see Maudru's face in the light from the open double windows, as he sank onto a small sofa. The face was, indeed, that of an ascetic, pale against the aureole of white hair, clear blue eyes, sensitive mouth, but the line of the jaw was strong.

". . . and, of course, I no longer have a great amount of temporal time remaining. Only eternal time. And that, apparently, will continue on for another life or so. I believe that we do continue, far beyond this present existence. I've found sufficient evidence to convince me of that. Proof that I have lived in this world several times before. At various periods of mortal history . . ."

"You mean reincarnation?"

"That is one word for it. There are others. I call it, more simply, conviving. Continuing to survive. We are convivors, you and I. Many, unfortunately, are not."

"Convivors?" Ash smiled at the idea. "Does one know if he is a convivor?"

"I believe so. You know, don't you?"

"Well . . ."

"Well?"

"Yes. I do know that."

"You see! Sandra tells me that you, too, are psychic."

"She has convinced me that I am. But in a very modest way."

"I want to congratulate you on the superb portrait of my beloved friend which you have written for *Metropole*."

"Thank you. She told me you had seen it."

"In Vancouver, last week. I saw her face on the cover, at the airport, when I was purchasing newspapers. Jean began to read it to me in the taxi and finished it after we reached our hotel. You treated Sandra with such complete respect and honesty. So many reporters try to make a joke of parapsychology and astrology. A thoughtful account like yours helps to balance dozens of less perceptive ones. I, for instance, dread being interviewed by representatives of the press. Certain they will prove to be antagonistic. In fact, these days, I rarely give interviews to anyone. But to get back to your portrait of Sandra. She says it's the best account of her work and her aims that has ever appeared."

"I enjoyed writing that portrait as much as anything I've ever done."

"And it shows! You have helped the entire profession of parapsychology. A positive report, such as yours, tells the public we are not cultists but apostles spreading the word of eternal life, the next life beyond this one. And the peace of knowing that it is life which survives death. Not the contrary. You've helped thousands of people, with your portrait of Sandra, to comprehend what it is that we believe. Their understanding will enrich their present lives and offer them hope for a future one. It should convince many who have not believed in the past." He smiled. "You'll be at Town Hall tomorrow night?"

"Mais certainement!" Ash realized, to his surprise, that he had been speaking French for several minutes.

"I suspect this may be one of our most successful lectures. My own personal horoscope indicates that something extraordinary will take place. I've no idea what that might be, however. So I shall not anticipate but will accept." He peered at Ash. "You, of course, are about to ask me about Lyli Amadoro."

"Sandra said you knew her in Paris."

"I saw Madame Amadoro only once. An old client persuaded me to meet her. Brought her to my villa, outside Paris, one afternoon. Meeting a person only one time tells you very little about that individual."

"But you must have had certain perceptions about her. Even from a single meeting."

"I most certainly did. I sensed that she possessed great powers for achievement and for—destruction. Self-destruction, as well as the destruction of others."

"Did you ever know a Frenchman named Clement Marnat?"

"I believe not. Who is he?"

"He was an employee of Amadoro Associates. He was murdered in his New York apartment, last week, by two men I suspect were sent there by Madame Amadoro."

"For what reason?"

"She learned that he had talked to me. Had told me things from their mutual past. Marnat had known her, for many years, in Paris . . ."

"What sort of things?"

"That she had murdered her second husband—Lord Robert Craydon."

"She told me she was having frightening dreams about her English husband. That he had died in a horrible accident—burned to death. She had not been present when this happened, but she constantly saw the accident, again and again, in her dreams. Begged me to help her put an end to them. I assured her there was nothing I could do."

"She told this same dream to Marnat."

"Did she? I suggested she visit a psychiatrist who might help her with hypnosis to wipe the past from her memory. She said she had seen several in London but their hypnotic sessions had not helped."

"What about her third husband—Conte Amadoro—who died in a skiing accident? Was that also murder?"

"She did not mention him to me. Only the Englishman."

"Could both those accidental deaths have been murder?"

"I cannot say. Lyli Amadoro certainly had the capability of causing physical death—if she wished someone dead—quite able to arrange for them to die." He closed his eyes. "I cannot tell you that she actually did such a monstrous thing. Taking another person's life, for any reason, is evil. Despicable . . ."

Ash studied the old man's face as his eyes remained closed. Not a wrinkle. He had seen such faces in ancient religious paintings of saints and martyrs. "Her first husband also died in an accident."

"Is that so?" The eyes slowly opened. "How curious . . ."

"She was never present when any of these three deaths occurred."

"And you think all three were murders?"

"I don't know."

"I hope what you suspect is not true. Anyone who kills another carries guilt in the depths of their soul. Throughout their life on planet Earth and in any other future life they are permitted. The evil of murder remains with them until they pay for what they have done with their own soul."

"Amadoro told Sandra that you had helped her."

Maudru shrugged. "It was impossible for me to help her. There was nothing I could say that might give her any peace. I never saw her again."

"Did she tell you why she had come to you?"

"Oh, yes! She wanted to know, specifically, about her future—business and personal. She said that, in spite of her wealth, she was completely unhappy. She wanted me to tell her the secret of happiness."

"What did you say to that?"

"I told her there is no secret for happiness. Never has been and never will be. It doesn't exist."

"She accepted that?"

"Certainly not! She insisted there was such a secret and I knew what it was. Offered to buy it from me."

"This sounds familiar."

"She, unfortunately, thought there was a price on everything and she was able and willing to pay for what she wanted. I assured her that every human being held a secret for happiness within himself. The only secret he would ever know."

"Did she understand?"

"She called me a charlatan. Stormed out of my villa to her black Rolls-Royce. I never saw her again, although, perhaps a month later, she telephoned several times. I had told my assistant, Jean Clair, that I would neither see nor talk to her again, so she was unable to get through to me. And now Lyli Amadoro is dead . . ."

"The police think it might have been an accidental overdose of drugs or it could be suicide."

"What do you think, Mr. Hendrie?"

"I'm trying to learn the truth, in order to write my portrait of Amadoro for *Metropole*."

"Sandra has told me about that."

"Sandra doesn't think Amadoro's death was accidental."

"Oh? What does Sandra say?"

"She says it's murder."

"Lyli Amadoro was one of the few completely evil human beings I have ever encountered. I suppose she did many terrible things in her brief life on planet Earth. Her death may have been retribution."

"The police would call that murder."

"Yes, Mr. Hendrie. They would."

"Who is the murderer? Can you tell me?"

Maudru closed his eyes again. "I cannot see a face. I only hear a name . . ."

"What name?"

"Alfredo . . ."

"That was her husband's name. Conte Alfredo Amadoro! But he is dead!"

"I do not accept death."

chapter twenty-six

ASH PAID FOR HIS TAXI, MADE HIS WAY BETWEEN THE groups of people clustered on the sidewalk and went into Town Hall. More people crowding the lobby and going up the marble steps on either side of the central entrance to the orchestra. As he approached the box office he saw a "Sold Out" sign that explained why there was no line to buy tickets.

He gave his name and paid for the ticket. Made his way, slowly, through the crowd, aware of voices but not hearing what was said. He always did this in a lobby, looked at faces but blotted out the sounds.

These people seemed older than the average theater audience. Some were dressed for the evening, women in smart gowns and their husbands wearing dinner jackets, but many of the others were shabbily dressed. They were the ones climbing to the balcony, while the dinner jackets and their ladies headed for the orchestra.

His parents had brought him here, years ago, to hear Vivaldi for the first time and he had returned, frequently, for concerts by the world's greatest artists. He and Mara had attended concerts whenever there was a famous pianist.

Tonight's crowd was not the sort that turned out for concerts. Several of the people looked eccentric or worse. Odd clothes, ridiculous hats, weird jewelry. Some, quite obviously, were crazies. Parapsychology had brought them out of the woodwork. It attracted the knowledgeable but also drew the eccentric.

As he passed the foot of the staircase, careful not to jostle anyone, he became aware of Amadoro's perfume. The now familiar scent was unmistakable. Was he being psychic?

He glanced at the nearest faces but none of the women looked familiar. Strange that someone here, tonight, would be wearing Amadoro's perfume.

Obviously other women did buy and wear it. Nothing psychic about that!

As he edged toward the entrance he wished that Mara were beside him. She would be preparing for her first entrance, only a few streets away, in a play that would soon be closing. Too bad she couldn't skip one performance, but she had great loyalty to the other members of the cast and wouldn't desert them at the end of their long run.

Would McCorkle be here tonight, as he planned? Hadn't heard from him all day and hadn't attempted to contact him.

He gave his ticket to the attendant and carried the stub inside.

The auditorium seemed to be filled, but more people were moving down every aisle. He'd never seen this large an audience unless a famous singer was performing. No young people tonight who looked like music students.

An usher took his ticket stub and led him to an aisle seat in the sixth row.

He sat next to an old man in an old-fashioned dinner jacket. The white-haired lady in the third seat, obviously his wife, was wearing a flowered gown, and they were conversing in whispers.

The curtains were closed across the stage. In the past when he attended concerts, they were always open when he arrived and a grand piano waited, expectantly, on stage. The auditorium lights remained lighted during most concerts.

He glanced around and wondered if Miss Cassie was here. She would, more likely, be backstage with Sandra.

A small waving hand caught his attention. Waving at him? He saw that it was Mandy Kwong. She had said she was a member of the Parastro Society and would be here tonight. He raised his arm and saluted her. Mandy Kwong, whose mother was Irish and mystic.

The lights in the auditorium were dimming.

He turned toward the stage and saw the curtains stirring in a movement of air from behind.

There was a small stack of magazines and pamplets at the apartment which had arrived since he and Mara joined the Parastro Society, but he hadn't, as yet, had a chance to read them. As a result of knowing Sandra, and now Maudru, he was determined to read more about parapsychology and attempt to understand, more clearly, the part that psychic phenomena had played in his own life.

The auditorium was completely dark, except for small red lights above the exits.

All conversation had stopped.

No footlights, so even the curtains were invisible, but you could sense their presence in front of you, their weight and massive folds.

There was that hushed moment of anticipation which always happens before curtains rise in any theater.

No more late arrivals coming down the aisles.

Then, very slowly, the curtains began to part.

The stage was in darkness, except for an overhead spotlight shining down on a table. A row of three chairs waited behind the table, one thronelike carved chair in the center between two gilt chairs, all upholstered in red velvet.

The audience remained silent but you could feel everyone leaning forward slightly.

Sandra Saunders hurried out and the audience applauded with enthusiasm. She walked into the glow from another overhead spotlight and stood at a lectern near the side of the stage.

Ash saw that she was wearing a simple gown. Some sort of dusky rose material with matching slippers, a strand of pearls around her neck. She looked relaxed and elegant, smiling and bowing.

The applause continued, growing then diminishing but rising again.

Sandra continued to smile but, after a moment, raised her hands in a graceful gesture for silence.

The applause stopped immediately.

She folded her hands on the sloping lectern. "Good evening, ladies and gentlemen." Extending both arms in welcome. "My dear friends!"

More applause.

Her voice was amplified but Ash couldn't see any microphones.

"We are here, all of us, for another meeting with Fernand Maudru."

Applause again, heavier now.

"Yes. We all love Fernand Maudru." The applause faded as she continued. "As president of the Parastro Society, I am privileged tonight, as I have been for the past several years, to bring this great man to you once again. Tonight Town Hall is sold out, which means that you are contributing to the maintenance of the Institut Parapsychologique, whose president and founder is Fernand Maudru. His American lecture tours are made every year solely to raise funds for this internationally renowned and respected institution. There is nothing like it in this country, although our Parastro Society is now an affiliate. Monsieur Maudru has appeared, during the past week, in several major American cities, as well as in Canada. He has flown here after giving a lecture in Beverly Hills. I'm sure that all you wish to hear from me is a very brief introduction. So! Here he is—our beloved friend and mentor—Fernand Maudru!" She gestured, gracefully, toward the opposite side of the stage.

There was a moment of silence as the spotlight dimmed on Sandra and, at the same time, another spot revealed Maudru entering from the other side of the stage.

He walked slowly, leaning on the arm of his assistant, Jean Clair, who was barely visible in a dark gray suit.

There was a tremendous burst of applause.

Ash found himself applauding enthusiastically as he got to his feet like everyone else. Standing, he could see the stage better over the heads of the people in front of him.

Maudru had paused in a spot of light, halfway across the stage, holding himself erect, head high.

Ash saw that he was much taller and even thinner than he had seemed yesterday. The white hair made a soft silver halo under the spotlight. Clear blue eyes raked the dark auditorium. His face was even more striking, lighted from overhead. Cheekbones now had dark shadows underneath which made his face seem gaunt, the nose even more impressive. This rather forbidding look was softened by the sensitive smiling mouth. Maudru was wearing a black suit with a white shirt and muted yellow cravat. There was a small yellow rose in his lapel. Now he was bowing, graciously, before taking Jean Clair's arm again and continuing across the stage to sit in the center chair behind the table.

Sandra came from the darkness to occupy the chair at his right, and Jean Clair took the other one.

Ash sat down as the audience sank into their seats.

Like them, he leaned forward slightly. They reminded him of some huge animal, crouched to pounce, waiting for Maudru's first words, but he sensed that all these people were friendly, not antagonistic.

"*Bon soir, mes amis.*" Maudru smiled. "Good evening, my dear American friends. I am always happy when I return to New York. We have survived the unspeakable threats of this Atomic Age for another year. As I have told you in the past, we are convivors. We continue and we survive . . ."

There was a tremendous response, cheers and more applause.

"And, once again, I wish to welcome members of the Parastro Society who are present here tonight and, especially, their founder-president, my dear friend Madame Saunders." He turned to smile at Sandra, who bowed as an even larger surge of applause rolled toward her.

Ash applauded with the others.

"Later, as always, I will be happy to accept questions from the audience, which I shall attempt to answer. But first, I would like to talk to you—speak directly to each person—particularly those who are with us for the first time. Tell you something of our aims. Of both the Parastro Society and the Institut Parapsychologique. We do, of course, have identical goals and beliefs. We are searching for answers to the same important questions. Questions about life and death and life beyond death . . ."

Ash settled back, captured by the warmth and sincerity of Maudru's voice. The Frenchman spoke excellent English.

"So many of us have been intimidated, confused and overpowered by what is taking place on this planet—happening beyond our control or comprehension—bewildered by the conflicting reports we are given by the politicians, the newspapers and television. We live in fear that our families—our children—will, in the future, face even greater problems. Children already suffer doubts because they are aware of their parents' insecurity. Some of us believe that parapsychology is the only answer to surviving what is happening today. But it is not a substitute for religion. I, for one, am a devout Catholic, and there is nothing in my lifelong and continuing study of psychic phenomena that conflicts with my religion. Quite the contrary!

"Some of you may not understand the term parapsychology. It is, quite simply, that branch of psychology which investigates and questions all psychic phenomena. Nothing more. That includes what has come to be called extrasensory perception, telepathy and clairvoyance."

Ash realized there wasn't a sound coming from the spellbound audience. No coughing, whispering or moving about in seats.

"Parapsychology was discussed, publicly, for the first time early in this century. It had been investigated for hundreds of years, but that was the first time it was given a name. Today more than twenty of the great universities in the United States, including Princeton and Duke, are involved with psychic research. We have, finally, been recognized and are accepted as—legitimate."

Laughter from the audience.

"Some of what has been said about parapsychology is true, but much is not. Unfortunately, the psychic attracts both lunatics and charlatans. As well as honest men, including some of the world's great scientists and psychiatrists. Lack of scientific proof must not be accepted as a reason to condemn parapsychology. For centuries there was no proof that the world is round. There is no scientific proof for any of the world's religions. And none is needed."

Ash wondered if McCorkle was in the audience and what he was thinking of this.

"I am the greatest skeptic here tonight. But I also am the greatest believer in psychic phenomena. Each of us has unknown and untapped potential beyond those called the five senses. There is, for instance, an acknowledged sixth sense which is our power of intuition. Each of you knows about intuition. That is your psychic sense.

"Some of you, I am sure, have experienced precognition. Many of you have had paranormal experiences, as we shall hear in a few moments. We have, all of us, had intimations of the future. So each of us has psychic powers within us—you as well as I—and have all had personal experiences which can only be explained by parapsychology.

"So each of you is psychic. Some more than others. Just as some of us are better singers than others. Some become opera stars. Most do not. But all can sing. It's as simple as that!

"*Eh bien!* I have talked enough for the moment. Later we will have discussions, back and forth, and explore various aspects of the psychic. Madame Saunders will tell us something about her recent work in New York. Many of you must have read her portrait in the current issue of *Metropole* magazine. The author of that fine portrait, Monsieur Ashton Hendrie, is present in our audience tonight."

Applause.

Ash hunched down in his seat, but smiled.

"Now is the time for your questions, *mes amis!* I beg you, as in the past, for serious questions. Anything about the psychic that you do not understand. Questions about phenomena you personally experienced. I will be happy to answer those, but please, do not demean yourselves by asking stupid or foolish questions. You will be wasting a precious moment of your life—and mine."

More applause.

Maudru pulled back from the spotlight into shadow.

His assistant, Jean Clair, leaned forward into the light. "If you please, ladies and gentlemen. The first question. Stand up, if you will, and speak clearly."

Ash straightened and looked around the dark auditorium. He could see faces floating in the reflected light from the stage.

"Who will ask the first question?"

A man stood up in the orchestra. "I will, sir."

"Thank you, monsieur. Give your name and tell us where you are from. But no address. Only the city."

"My name's Manning. George Manning. I live in New York City."

"Yes, Mr. Manning?" Maudru's voice came from the darkness as Jean Clair moved back out of the light. "What is your question?"

"I work for a brokerage firm on Wall Street and I'm constantly taking phone calls. Why is it, several times each day, when a phone rings I know who's calling and say their name when I pick up the phone? Before I hear their voice . . ."

"You are experiencing simple precognition, Mr. Manning." Maudru's face came into the light again. "These are customers who call every day."

"That's true."

"You get psychic vibrations from them. They call at the same time each day and you are expecting their calls."

"They do. Yes."

"This is a common form of precognition." Maudru's face withdrew into darkness again.

"Thank you, sir." Manning sat down.

The assistant's face came into the light. "Next question?"

A voice came from overhead. "I'm Mrs. Jerry Cassidy from Brooklyn . . ."

Brooklyn, as always, caused laughter.

Ash looked up at the balcony but was unable to see Mrs. Cassidy.

"Yes, Madame?" Maudru's face moved into the light.

"Would you tell me, sir, do you believe in Tarot cards?"

More laughter.

"That depends," Maudru responded, "upon who is shuffling the cards. Tarot cards have frequently been used for experiments in extrasensory perception. There have been reports in various scientific journals as to the frequency of the appearance of each symbol. I do not, however, know of any evidence that the future can be predicted by such cards. The future can be told only if the person handling the cards is a true psychic. That person makes the predictions from vibrations he receives from the person seated across the table. Not from the cards."

"That's what I told Mrs. Doyle!"

More laughter from the audience.

"Another question?" the assistant asked.

"I would like to ask about my daughter . . ."

Ash saw a woman standing in the orchestra.

"Your name?" Maudru asked.

"Mrs. Charles Norris. I come from Pittsburgh."

"What about your daughter?" Maudru's face came forward into the light again.

"She ran away from home last month. I'm trying to locate her."

"Have you reported this matter to the police?"

"Oh, yes. They haven't found any trace of her."

"Why do you come to me?"

"I read about you in the paper after I arrived in New York, that you had located many people who were missing."

"Tell me, Madame, why did your daughter leave home?"

"She didn't get along with my husband. He wanted her to find a job but she wanted to be a dancer. She'd taken ballet lessons until her father found out I was paying for them from our savings."

"Tell me your daughter's name. Her age . . ."

"Her name's Julie. She's eighteen."

"Let me try to help you, Madame. Be very quiet." His face pulled back out of the light.

There wasn't so much as a whisper in the auditorium.

"Your daughter is well and happy . . ."

"Thank God!"

"She has been rescued by two people. The man is an artist, his wife a teacher. They noticed your daughter on the street. Questioned her and took her into their home. They have fed and clothed her. Given her affection. She is treated like their daughter."

"I must see her!"

"Would you be willing to let her stay with these kind people? They plan to arrange for her to attend ballet classes."

"Stay with them?"

"If she remains in New York she will, eventually, become a successful dancer. Can that happen if you take her back to Pittsburgh?"

The woman hesitated. "She can stay with them. I'll even send money to her!"

"Your daughter has never told these people her true name or that she had run away from home. That's why they haven't reported her to the police. They think she has no family."

"She can stay with them, but I must see her. Know for myself she's safe and sound."

"They live in an apartment on . . ." He paused. "St. Luke's place. If you will come backstage after we finish here, my assistant will give you their name and the address."

"Thank you, sir. I'll do that."

Ash watched the woman sit down again.

"Another question?" Jean Clair leaned into the light, peering into the orchestra, then up at the balcony. "Who will be next?"

"I have a question for Mr. Maudru." A man's voice from the far side of the orchestra.

"Your name, sir?"

"Thomas Stark. I'm an executive with an insurance company in Scarsdale."

"What is your question, Mr. Stark?" Maudru's voice out of the dark.

"It's about a dream I have. Ever since I was a boy I've had this dream where I'm living in a strange city. From books I've read, I'm certain it's London in the last century. The people look and dress like those in pictures I've seen. I see the same people over and over again in these dreams. There's one young woman—her name is Cora—whom I've come to love. There are others, especially one man, whom I detest."

"How frequently do you have these dreams, Monsieur?"

"At the moment it's maybe once a month. Sometimes they stop for a year, but they always return. Can you tell me what they mean?"

"We have many cases of such dreams in our files. You are experiencing post-cognition. Recalling scenes from a past life."

"Who are these people?"

"They could be relatives or friends."

"I speak to them, but it's as though they don't hear me."

"They can't hear you. Enjoy these dreams. The young woman—Cora—may have been your sweetheart in that earlier life."

"How long will I continue to have these dreams?"

"Possibly as long as you continue in this life. The post-cognition may leave you when you go on to your next existence."

"Then you do believe in life after death?"

"We are convivors. We continue to survive. There is extensive evidence—chiefly of near-death euphoria—recording hundreds of persons who actually left this life for a brief time—and returned—which confirms that there is, indeed, another life after this one."

"Thank you, sir." He sank out of sight into his seat.

There was a scattering of applause.

"Quiet, please!" Jean Clair raised his hand for silence and the applause died. "What is the next question?" He looked around again.

"My name is McCorkle. I live in New York City . . ."

Ash saw the detective standing at the far side of the orchestra.

"Your question, Mr. McCorkle?"

"I would like to ask Mr. Maudru what he can tell me about a woman named Amadoro . . ."

There was a murmur of recognition from the audience.

"Lyli Amadoro?" Maudru's voice responded.

Ash faced the stage and saw Maudru lean into the light.

"What can you tell me about her death?"

"Her death . . ."

"Was it an accident or suicide?"

"No. Not suicide . . ."

"Then was it murder?"

"It was . . ."

There was the sudden explosion of a gun fired. The sound echoed around the auditorium.

Ash sprang to his feet.

Women were screaming.

McCorkle had disappeared and, glancing toward the stage, Ash saw that Maudru, Sandra and Jean Clair were on their feet. The two men were staring at Sandra.

She was holding up an arm, as the curtains closed. Her right arm. And it was dripping blood.

Ash turned and ran up the aisle, past the gaping ushers, toward the rear and pushed a door open into the brightly lighted lobby.

It was empty. Nobody on the staircases to the balcony.

He started across the shallow lobby toward the open entrance doors but stopped dead as he caught the scent of Amadoro's perfume again.

It was unmistakable.

Was he having a psychic experience? Or was this only coincidence?

Had someone gone through here ahead of him?

The person who fired that shot!

Ash went outside and hesitated on the deserted sidewalk in a blaze of light from the marquee.

He could see the electric glare of Broadway at the end of the street.

No trace of Amadoro's perfume here. Only a stink of fried food from a nearby restaurant.

He turned and headed for the alley that led to the stage door.

chapter twenty-seven

ASH KNEW HE WOULDN'T SLEEP TONIGHT.

The hot shower had done nothing to relax him.

He had turned off the air-conditioning before he got into bed and opened the windows of his bedroom. Hadn't put on his pajamas or pulled the sheet over his body and could feel humid air across his flesh.

Somebody was having a party in one of the other apartments. Loud music and a hum of voices with one woman who squealed. Friday night. No one would be calling the manager.

He closed his eyes and, immediately, returned to Town Hall.

When he went through the stage door, he'd faced bright lights and an uproar of voices. All the lights in the auditorium were turned on and hundreds of people seemed to be talking at once.

The curtains had been opened and McCorkle was standing in the center of the stage, telling the audience to remain seated. Nobody would be allowed to leave.

A door stood open into a lighted dressing room.

As he went toward it, he passed a man who was shouting into a wall phone. Telling somebody to send an ambulance.

When he reached the open door he saw that the dressing room was large and handsomely furnished.

Sandra was relaxing on a chaise, her bleeding arm wrapped in a scarf, with Maudru seated beside her. Jean Clair was hovering as Miss Cassie told him she had warned Sandra something terrible was going to happen tonight.

Sandra had noticed him in the doorway and assured him that she was fine. Only a flesh wound in her right shoulder. She had even laughed as she said somebody was a terrible shot. Thank God, they had missed Maudru.

He had told them an ambulance was coming and returned to the stage where McCorkle was assuring the audience that Maudru's lecture would continue.

People settled down in their seats as the detective hurried up a side aisle toward the lobby.

He had watched McCorkle moving about in the balcony, questioning people, examining the area at the rear—behind the rows of seats—where the person, apparently, had stood to fire his gun.

When he returned to the dressing room, two medics were with Sandra. One had placed a temporary bandage on her shoulder before taking her to a hospital. The other medic was cleaning blood from her arm and hand.

Fernand Maudru still sat beside Sandra, his eyes closed.

The sound of more voices had drawn him back to the stage.

Reporters had crowded through the unguarded entrance doors and blue-uniformed policemen were pouring down the aisles, followed by men, obviously detectives, in rumpled sport jackets.

For several minutes there had been chaos.

McCorkle, again, had ordered the audience to remain seated and told the policemen to guard all doors to prevent anyone from leaving.

He realized, now, that nobody remembered it was McCorkle who had asked Maudru the question about Amadoro.

He had walked to the ambulance with Sandra and Miss Cassie before finding a taxi for Maudru and Jean Clair . . .

Ash turned over in bed, facing the open windows, aware that the party had stopped. Must be past eleven.

Another hour and Mara should be here, unless she had gone somewhere for supper.

He could hear distant sirens. Probably in Central Park. Another mugging or a murder . . .

If only he could close his eyes—shut them tight—and that window in his mind would open. He would see something that might solve the death of Amadoro.

The window of his mind never opened when he was awake. Never opened when he wanted it to open.

His thoughts returned to Town Hall.

The manager had finally announced to the audience—with McCorkle's permission—that the lecture would not be resumed. Fernand Maudru was no longer in the building, and Sandra Saunders had been taken to a hospital.

McCorkle had wanted to have another look around the rear area of the balcony after the audience departed.

That was when he walked up to Times Square and found a taxi to bring him home.

He was glad he hadn't told McCorkle about "Alfredo" or about those hidden passages in Amadoro's penthouse. He wasn't obliged to tell the police what he turned up in his own investigation. Those secret passages were there for them to find.

He heard Mara's high heels in the hall.

If she hadn't eaten supper with friends she would head for the kitchen to see what Rosie had left her in the refrigerator.

Instead, to his surprise, he heard his door open.

"Ash? You asleep?"

"Too warm to sleep." Should he tell her what happened tonight? Better not.

"I'm not feeling too well."

"What's the matter, love?"

She plumped down on the edge of his bed. "We went out together. The whole cast! After the performance."

"Have fun?"

"It was a great mistake. We all drank too much. Like an Irish wake."

"Who died?"

"The play. They told us. The show's closing tomorrow night."

"You knew it was."

"But not this soon! You never believe it until they say the closing notice is going up. I'm feeling very lost . . ."

"I am sorry."

"We were all crying at Sardi's." She sniffled. "Could I sleep with you tonight?"

"Of course."

"That would be simply lovely! Let me get a fast shower." She jumped up and ran across the hall to her room.

His mind, at once, returned to Amadoro . . .

When Mara came back, warm and fragrant from the shower, he held out his arms to her.

She snuggled up to him, leaning against his shoulder.

He saw that she had covered her ears with quilted pink satin pads to deaden all sounds. "You are a love," he whispered.

She didn't hear what he said.

Ash smiled as his mind returned to Town Hall and, within moments, realized his wife was asleep.

He edged away from her, to the far side of the bed, in order not to disturb her if he was unable to sleep.

Town Hall . . .

Someone had tried to kill Maudru to prevent his naming Amadoro's murderer.

Would Maudru have said "Alfredo" again?

McCorkle hadn't planned to ask Maudru anything when he came to Town Hall. In fact, he had had no idea that members of the audience could ask questions.

Who was Alfredo? He would call the Plaza tomorrow and ask Maudru for the rest of the murderer's name.

Had Alfredo come to Town Hall with a gun and stood at the back of the balcony waiting for the right moment to aim and fire?

Alfredo had to be someone who was aware that Amadoro knew Maudru in Paris and suspected there might be somebody who would ask him about her death.

He settled down to what he knew would be a sleepless night.

His wife wakened, hours later, and, without a sound, returned to her own room.

Ash smiled, as she departed, not moving.

Then rolled over to sniff her scent on the other pillow and stretch out where her body had been.

chapter twenty-eight

HE WAS STILL AWAKE WHEN A TRUCK CLATTERED through one of the side streets. There was another skyscraper going up in the next block.

Saturday . . .

Maybe he should spend the day at the office. It would be quiet there and he could go over his Amadoro notes again. And again and again . . .

He got out of bed slowly, aware of the humidity in the air.

This was going to be another warm day.

Who was Alfredo?

Better not call Maudru, at the Plaza, before noon.

He showered, dressed and wrote a note telling Mara to phone him at the office before she left to do her matinee. Propped it on her bedtable and kissed her on the forehead, without waking her.

When he opened the front door to their apartment he found the morning *Times*. Picked it up and left it inside for Mara. He would buy another one as he went downtown.

The morning, after he passed the doorman and started down Fifth Avenue, was sunny and slightly cooler.

He had decided in the elevator to walk. The exercise in the fresh air would clear his head.

After a few blocks he turned east to Madison. Took a *Times* from a vending machine and looked through it as he waited for breakfast at the counter of a favorite coffee shop.

There was an old photograph of Fernand Maudru and a more recent studio portrait of Sandra on an inner page.

The heading above the story was precise.

Gunman Shoots at French Psychic
Hits Famous American Astrologer

The story was brief. Unidentified gunman fired one shot at Fernand Maudru, during Town Hall lecture. Reason for attack unknown. Bullet grazed shoulder of Sandra Saunders, well known astrologer. Police had no clue, as yet, to gunman's identity. Fernand Maudru unharmed, but not available for interview. Miss Saunders, after emergency treatment, had been taken to her home.

Nothing about the question McCorkle had asked Maudru prior to the shot. In fact, no mention of McCorkle. He had probably asked his reporter pals not to print his name and they would comply, hoping for a later break on the story.

Ash folded the paper and left it on the counter when he finished his breakfast.

Continuing on, down Madison, he had noticed a flower shop that was open and went inside. Selected some fresh yellow roses and had them sent, with a brief note, to the mansion on Gramercy Park.

To avoid the sun on Madison he turned, at the next corner, and went back to Fifth. Taking the shady side of the street, across from Central Park, to his office.

Not many people out this early. It was a pleasure to walk down the avenue. Another hour and it would be crowded. Everybody walking their dogs.

The lobby of his building was empty except for one attendant at the information desk.

The sound of his heels echoed on the marble floor in the vast expanse of marble and glass.

He saw that the attendant was an old acquaintance.

"Morning, Mr. Hendrie. Working today?"

"At least until noon. Possibly later. My office is quiet on Saturday. Not even a secretary." He passed the information desk and headed for the bank of elevators.

In a matter of minutes he was upstairs, unlocking the entrance door to METROPOLE with his master key. No blue-eyed blonde at the reception desk. She would arrive later. He hurried through the inner corridors to his own office, unlocked the door but left it unlocked. Passed through his secretary's kingdom and into his private office, which was not locked.

He closed the door and went straight to the row of windows. Opened the curtains and glanced down at Central Park before going to his desk.

Sat down and unlocked the drawer containing his pages of notes for the Amadoro portrait and the file of material from research.

Laid out his pages of notes in their usual order and began to read them again. Page by page.

Read every word but had no fresh thoughts.

He rose from his desk and began to pace around the room. Did this every time he was working on a new portrait.

With the exception of the last. There had been no problems when he wrote Sandra's portrait. That was, surely, the easiest he'd ever done.

And, apparently, the best!

This Amadoro portrait had to be even better.

He continued to walk, pausing to look down at the green grass and trees in the park, then circling his desk again.

He wondered if his wife was still asleep. Sometimes, on Saturday, she slept until noon because of the two performances she had to do.

The final two performances would be difficult for her. Actors would forget their lines, even though they had been doing them for months. The last performance, tonight, would be brilliant, or a catastrophe.

If only he could come up with the name of Amadoro's murderer . . .

Before McCorkle found out who it was.

Perhaps he could risk calling the Plaza before twelve. Say eleven-thirty . . .

The phone rang on the desk.

He hurried back and sank into his armchair, wondering who would be calling on Saturday. Maybe McCorkle would have some news. He jabbed the button for the outside line. "Yes?"

"Sweetie? It's me."

"Was thinking about you. This very minute."

"That's nice. I'm up early. Had breakfast and looked at the morning paper. You didn't tell me about Sandra. What happened at Town Hall . . ."

"Didn't want to worry you. You were upset enough last night."

"But it's terrible! That person shooting at Fernand Maudru and hitting poor Sandra. Do they know who did it?"

"They didn't last night. The bullet only grazed Sandra's shoulder. They took her to the hospital and sent her home."

"I'm going to phone her."

"She won't be talking to anybody until this afternoon."

"I'll be doing the matinee. Our last matinee!"

"Why don't I pick you up for supper? After the final performance tonight."

"That would be lovely. There'll be a closing party, onstage. But I'll manage to slip away."

"We'll go somewhere and celebrate."

"Celebrate our closing?"

"No. Our vacation in Europe."

"If you're able to get through to Sandra, tell her I'll see her next week. And tell her she was right, about the show closing."

"I'll do that. Give a good performance tonight."

"We'll all be as nervous as we were opening night. See you after the show."

"Right." He set the phone down and stared at the pages of notes spread across his desk.

If he were really psychic, why couldn't he, somehow, sense the truth about Amadoro's death. The identity of "Alfredo" . . .

He squeezed his eyes tight until lights danced in the blackness.

This was how he saw the window.

He'd never been able to force it to appear. It always showed up when he was half asleep or coming out of sleep. Never when he tried to make it happen.

The window of his mind . . .

He had thought Mandy might call in this morning. After being present for what happened at Town Hall last night. In the excitement, he hadn't looked for her in the crowd. Mandy didn't like noise. The sudden shot would have frightened her.

Mandy was one of the few people who had his private number. If anyone called *Metropole* over the weekend, they got a taped voice saying the offices were closed until Monday.

Actually, Maggie Delaney was the weekend receptionist, but she took no phone calls. She was there only to admit anyone with an appointment. Carrington liked to see people Saturdays, when he could talk without interruption, and some of the editors came in to catch up with their work.

Should call his parents. Tell them Mara's play was closing and they would be free for that trip to Europe. Do that tomorrow . . .

He was aware, as he looked at the circles of lights, within his eyelids, that he was extremely tired.

No small window opened to reveal the secret of Amadoro's murder.

Somehow he must find "Alfredo" . . .

What a break that would be!

For *Metropole* to have the solution to Amadoro's murder in their September issue and publish it before the police knew the identity of the murderer.

They might never find him . . .

Although everyone said McCorkle was New York's smartest detective.

The only way he could beat McCorkle would be to uncover more facts to which the detective had no access.

McCorkle still didn't know the whole story about Clement Marnat. Had gotten nowhere against the vast bulwark of Amadoro Associates . . .

And he hadn't told McCorkle about Mrs. Winston . . .

The window had opened suddenly.

He was looking into a large, brightly lighted room. Amadoro's drawing room! Columns of glass bubbles reflecting shafts of light. One column had been smashed, its globes scattered across the carpet. Parts of bubbles still clung to the columns, yet the globes on the carpet were unbroken. They were like translucent balloons that would rise at any moment and float toward the ceiling.

As he watched, more of the globes dropped, silently, leaving shards of glass hanging from the column. Yet the fallen globes remained whole.

Someone was smoking a cigarette.

He looked around but there was nobody in the room. No one seated on the white sofas.

Would he be able to find that secret passage Lyli had used for her sudden disappearance? Was there something hidden there that would reveal the secret of Lyli Amadoro? Her life and her death . . .

The image went black as though he had switched off a television set.

His eyes opened, reluctantly, as he realized that he'd been asleep.

Ash straightened. Someone was seated, facing him across the desk. Smoking a cigarette.

"You were asleep, pal."

It was McCorkle.

"Guess I was." He sat erect, blinking his eyes.

"Girl out front said you were in. I knocked but you didn't answer. So I came in. When I saw you were asleep I sat down to wait."

"How long was it?"

"Maybe ten minutes."

"Can I offer you a drink?"

"Not at the moment. I'm working today. Just came from a session at the Plaza with Maudru. Stopped off here on my way downtown to see Ms. Sandra."

"You learn anything from Maudru?"

"Claims he has no idea who fired that shot at him. Says he knows nothing about Amadoro's death and doesn't wish to become involved in a murder investigation. He and Ms. Sandra claim they didn't see who fired the shot. On the other hand, Ms. Cassie says she did."

"Saw who held the gun?"

"Only a dark blur moving across the rear of the balcony. Saw it against the light in that upstairs corridor when the person opened the door to leave."

"Man or woman?"

"She couldn't tell."

"When did Cassie tell you this?"

"At the hospital, while I was waiting to take Ms. Sandra home."

"You drove her home?"

"Siren sounding. Thought the ladies might enjoy that, and they did."

"I must have another talk with Maudru."

"Too late. He was checking out of the Plaza when I left him. Some friends are taking him to their home in Old Greenwich. He'll rest tonight and they'll drive him back tomorrow to catch a plane for Paris. I gave him permission to leave the country. Don't think there's anything more he'd be able to tell me."

"I'll contact him when I'm in Paris."

"When will that be?" He crushed his cigarette out in an ashtray.

"Week after next, I should think. I'm flying over to try and dig up material on Amadoro's past."

"The old Frenchman seemed exhausted. He was very upset about what happened. Especially that Ms. Saunders had been wounded."

As McCorkle talked, Ash thought about the broken column he'd just seen in Amadoro's drawing room. Lights glittering on the glass bubbles.

He realized that McCorkle had stopped talking. "Any further word from the coroner?"

"Nothing today."

"I'd like to have another look around that penthouse."

"What the hell for?"

"So I can write about it. Describe it in my portrait of Amadoro. I've only seen the place at night. I need to see it by daylight. Spend some time there and make notes."

"That could be arranged. When would you want to do that?"

"This afternoon?"

"I'll fix it. Let me make a call."

Ash shoved the phone across his desk.

McCorkle picked up the receiver and dialed. "McCorkle speaking. Who's this?" He grinned. "Thought I recognized your voice, pal. Is a man in blue guarding that private elevator? . . . Tell him Mr. Ashton Hendrie's coming there this afternoon, and he's to be allowed upstairs. You know Mr. Hendrie? Then you can see he gets up okay. And nobody else! I'll be back, first of the week. Thanks, pal." He put the receiver down. "Guy on the information desk. Says he knows you."

"You have a man on duty at the elevator?"

"Both elevators. Front and rear. Impossible to seal off a penthouse. I've put guards on twenty-four-hour duty, now the staff's gone, to question anybody who tries to get upstairs. You'll have no problem."

"Thanks, Mac. What became of the staff?"

"They've moved into the Waldorf, expenses paid, until Amadoro Associates decides what to do with them. I've told 'em not to leave the country without permission. I want to question them again."

"What's happened to Amadoro's dog?"

"They put him in a kennel." Getting to his feet. "Did you see that crazy woman at Town Hall last night?"

"What crazy woman?"

"The manager from Marnat's apartment."

"Mrs. Lacey?"

"That's the one!"

"She was at the Maudru lecture?"

"Grabbed my arm in the balcony when I went up to look for anyone who'd seen the gunman."

"Had she seen him?"

"Claimed the shot was fired from behind her and she hadn't seen anything. That dame's an alcoholic. I had to push her out of the way." He hesitated, facing Ash across the desk. "I'm getting nowhere on this Amadoro investigation. Ms. Sandra says it's murder, but I've found no evidence to prove that. If it's murder, there's a whole lot missing. Including motive and suspect. You find something in that penthouse we missed, I trust you'll let me know."

"Doubt I could turn up anything you guys overlooked."

"I'm calling the coroner this afternoon. Gotta pin him down—suicide or accident." He turned to leave. "I'll contact you after I talk to him."

"Right." He watched McCorkle leave.

Was it Mrs. Ferne Lacey who had worn Amadoro's perfume last night at Town Hall? Clement Marnat could've given it to her!

Had Mrs. Lacey fired that shot at Fernand Maudru?

Not likely.

The dame was an alcoholic.

She would've hit somebody in the orchestra . . .

chapter twenty-nine

THE ATTENDANT RECOGNIZED HIM AS, STEPS ECHOING, he crossed the empty lobby.

"Afternoon, Mr. Hendrie. McCorkle said you'd be in this afternoon." He motioned toward the elevators. "You know how to get up to the penthouse."

"Thank you." Ash continued on without pausing.

"Too bad about Miss Amadoro. Such a fine lady! They say it was an accident . . ."

He didn't bother to respond but headed for the private elevator.

The young officer on duty saluted. "Mr. Hendrie?"

"That's right."

"Been expecting you, sir." He ran two stubby fingers up the metal column and the elevator doors slid open.

"I may be upstairs for an hour or so." He stepped into the elevator and faced the officer again. "Was here last night, with McCorkle, but want to look around by daylight."

"You'll be alone. Nobody else permitted to go upstairs."

"Thanks." He jabbed the Penthouse button and the elevator doors closed.

What did he expect to find in Amadoro's penthouse?

Hopefully some clue to her death. Maybe a cache of drugs . . .

She must've kept them in one of those secret passages.

Or hadn't she used drugs in her own home?

Perhaps she'd taken the hashish before she returned Monday night from some disco or friend's apartment.

Marnat said she'd been on opium in Paris. Had he sold her drugs then?

The butler, Nair, said the staff had Monday nights off because she always dined out that night . . .

The murderer must've been aware that Amadoro's servants had Monday nights off. Knew that when the staff returned, the maid wouldn't check the lights until one o'clock . . .

The elevator doors opened silently.

Ash hesitated, facing the dim central corridor of the penthouse.

A spill of daylight, in the distance, came through the open drawing room doors.

He left the elevator, reluctantly, and waited motionless in the entrance foyer. Listening for some sound of life.

Sensed the elevator doors closing behind him.

No butler to lead him to the library today.

He must contact Nair at the Waldorf. Have a drink with him in Peacock Alley and question him again.

Right now he would take another look at that drawing room, then go upstairs to Amadoro's boudoir.

He moved forward, cautiously, until he reached the drawing room which he had seen, earlier this afternoon, through the window of his mind. Paused, inside the doors, and glanced around the incredible room.

The columns of gleaming bubbles were intact, none broken, the room unchanged. Daylight poured through tall windows open onto the terrace. The harsh light revealed that all the flowers in the crystal bowls had died, their petals scattered on the glass-topped tables.

As he crossed the room he saw that daylight made it look like a badly lighted stage set. Even the Picassos were crude and vulgar.

He walked the length of the room and went out onto the sun-baked terrace. Stood in the shade, under a yellow awning that extended far out, like a canopy, above the windows. Elegant white patio furniture with several tables under yellow-and-white-striped parasols. Chairs and chaises piled with striped cushions. Huge green plants in white pots, several lemon trees lush with fruit. White and yellow roses in sunken beds edged with tiles.

No other tall buildings visible from where he stood, only blue sky. Some kind of bird flying in the distance. Probably one of the Plaza's fat pigeons.

There was a whisper of sound behind him.

He whirled but could see nothing moving in the drawing room.

Returning inside warily, he paused, facing down the length of the room. After the glare of the terrace, the interior seemed dim.

Was someone here?

Ash had a sudden and surprising rush of fear.

Amadoro's murderer could have returned.

He felt beads of perspiration break out on his forehead and wiped them away with his handkerchief.

There was an odd scuttling noise which seemed to come from behind one of the white sofas placed between the glittering bubble columns.

He moved toward the sound slowly, around the end of another sofa, but there was nothing there.

The sound had been like the scurrying of a small animal.

Amadoro's dog?

"I will kill you . . ."

Ash stiffened.

The words were whispered, barely audible. Or had he imagined them?

He circled the oval of glass columns, behind the row of sofas, peering in every direction. "Is someone here?"

Again that rodent-like scurrying.

"Who is it? Where are you?"

There was a sharp crash of glass.

Ash saw one of the far columns, near the stairs in the corner disintegrate. Glass tinkled onto a table and scattered across a sofa but most of the bubbles remained intact.

This was how the room had looked through the window of his mind. What he had seen must've been precognition!

He approached the shattered column, cautiously, and saw that a solid cube of crystal had been tossed at it and dropped onto a rug. Reaching down, he picked it up and discovered that it was a crystal flower holder. He rested it on the table and looked around again.

Someone had come in here while he was on the terrace. They must have used that passage Amadoro had disappeared through last week. He had turned away from her for a moment, and when he looked back she was gone.

He went toward the paneled wall, behind the sofa where Amadoro had been seated, and saw a vertical opening. One glass panel had been pushed out from the wall. Far enough for a small animal to get through.

Not large enough for a man.

He moved closer and opened the panel far enough to enter the passage.

It was narrow, with a row of small electric bulbs lighted in the ceiling. Accoustical walls, painted gray, floor padded with cork tiles to deaden the sound of footsteps.

On a metal table near the entrance was a neat row of small flashlights.

Then, quite clearly, he heard footsteps hurrying up a flight of steps. The sound was muffled by distance.

Ash felt the yielding cork surface underfoot as he hurried down the passage.

Within moments he came to a staircase with a light in the ceiling at the top.

As he went up the steps his shoes were silent on the cork padding. Whoever came through here ahead of him must've been running to make that much noise.

Would they be waiting for him at the top?

Or would there be a blank gray wall with no visible exit?

Suppose all these bulbs went dark! He had no lighter or matches in his pockets. Should have picked up one of those flashlights.

What if he returned the way he'd come and found that panel closed and locked with no other way to escape?

He had an overpowering sense of claustrophobia.

There was another passage at the top of the staircase.

He looked from side to side and saw more gray walls.

Which way should he go?

He started toward the right, hurrying now, anxious to escape.

A blur of brighter light straight ahead.

Ash went toward it and found another partially open panel.

Left open for him? This could be a trap . . .

He pushed against the panel and looked into Amadoro's boudoir.

Stood there, for a moment, listening.

What a curious woman! Living in a luxurious penthouse with a honeycomb of hidden passages.

Perhaps one passage would lead to an exit into a public corridor through which her lovers had departed undetected!

This woman had been like a sorceress at the heart of Amadoro Associates and here in the center of this penthouse. The center was, of course, her boudoir. Her bed . . .

He stepped out into bright daylight from a row of floor-to-ceiling windows which, the other night, had been hidden behind closed curtains. More blue sky beyond a smaller terrace.

This boudoir, he now realized, must be directly above the drawing room.

The golden moiré-covered walls were intact, but everything in the boudoir had been pulled out or turned over. The bed that had held her body was taken apart, sheets tossed across a chaise, expensive mattress propped against a wall. Nothing appeared to be broken or damaged, only pawed over and desecrated.

He stood at the foot of the enormous antique bed and wondered how many male bodies had joined Amadoro there . . .

"Going to kill you . . ."

He had heard that voice before!

Ash turned, slowly, to face the small boy with the black curls and strange eyes he had first encountered at Amadoro Associates. He'd been hiding behind the chaise. "So it's you! Who are you to threaten people?"

The piercing dark brown eyes were staring at him.

"I am a demon." He shook his small clenched fist. "I will kill you."

"Don't make me laugh."

"I can kill anybody I don't like."

"Good luck!"

"I don't like you."

"What are you doing here?"

"I live here."

"Live here?"

"Sometimes. This is my kingdom. In the sky. I am the king!"

"And what's your name?"

"Won't tell you. What's yours?"

"Ashton Hendrie."

"That's a silly name."

"Where are you, Fredo?" Woman's voice, from the distance.

The child turned, in a flash, and glared toward the salon beyond the open doors.

"Who's that?" Ash asked.

"My mommy."

"Where's my baby?" The voice was coming closer.

"I'm not a baby." He scowled.

Ash moved toward him. "How old are you?"

"I am six."

"I know you're here somewhere . . ." The voice again.

"He's in here," Ash called, going toward the salon, aware of the boy running out onto the terrace.

The young woman with long brown hair appeared in the corridor and came into the salon.

He saw that she was startled by his presence. Her face younger and more attractive than he had realized before. Instead of a dowdy hat and coat, she was wearing an expensive dress.

She walked past him, into the boudoir. "Who are you? What are you doing here?"

"I could ask you the same thing."

She disregarded his reply and looked around. "Where did he go?"

"He appeared to be heading for the terrace."

She went toward the windows. "Come in here, Fredo! You hear me? Come in here at once . . ."

Ash followed her. "I'm Ashton Hendrie."

She faced him. "You're the one! Writes those portraits for *Metropole*."

"My next one's to be a portrait of Lyli Amadoro."

"She was afraid of you. Terrified . . ."

"Why?"

"Of what you were going to write about her. She thought you'd discovered the truth."

"And what is that?"

"The truth?" She appeared to be confused. "I—I don't know. Nobody ever told me . . ."

"Mommy!" The boy darted in from the terrace. "Mommy! Mommy!" He clutched her around the thighs with both small arms, burying his face against her hip. "I was only playing. I love you . . ."

She leaned down and kissed the top of his head. "Yes, Fredo . . ."

Ash realized that she was wearing Lyli's perfume. "This is your son?"

"Of course he's my son." The reply was sharp, her voice harsh. "My name is Towson . . ."

"You're Nicole Towson?"

"My father was Toby Towson, my mother—Leola Martin."

"I met your grandparents, last week, in New London."

"Did you?" She looked at him, for the first time, with interest. "I have never met them."

The boy turned abruptly and ran, squealing, back onto the sunny terrace.

"Be careful out there!" his mother called after him.

Ash frowned. Amadoro's scent was overpowering. She had used it with less discretion than her mother. And, suddenly, several things came into focus. "It was you, last night, at Town Hall . . ."

"Was I?"

"You tried to shoot Fernand Maudru."

"I'm a lousy shot." She giggled. "I wounded Ms. Saunders. Didn't mean to do that. Though Leola would approve. She didn't like Ms. Saunders. Was afraid of her . . ."

"Why did you want to shoot Maudru?" he asked quietly.

"Lyli told me, last week, that the Frenchman knew many things about her past. She was afraid he would reveal them to anyone in the audience who questioned him about her."

"Who would do that?"

"She thought you might."

"It didn't occur to me that I should question Maudru about Amadoro."

"I didn't fire the gun until that man asked about my mother."

"That was a detective. He's trying to find out if her death was an accident or suicide. Or murder . . ."

"It was an accident. Lyli would never have taken her own life." She frowned. "The police terrified her. Leola told me a detective followed her into a restaurant and questioned her. Lyli didn't tell him anything, but Leola was frightened."

"Perhaps you'd be willing to help me with this portrait I'm writing about your mother . . ."

"I couldn't do that. Lyli wouldn't want me to tell you anything."

"You must know the true facts about Amadoro. Things nobody else would be able to tell me."

"I know nothing about Lyli." She moved away from him, toward the open windows. "My mother was Leola Martin. I loved Leola but I hated Lyli. They were different persons."

"You have a son, so your name can no longer be Towson. What is your husband's name? I was told you married Mrs. Winston's son."

"Laurie? She never had a son . . ."

"What's the boy's name?"

"Fredo . . ." She turned toward the windows again. "Where are you, Fredo?" There was no reply. "Fredo!" She raised her voice. "You hear me! What're you doing out there?"

"Nothing!" The boy popped into view on one of the patio chairs. "Here I am!" Bouncing up and down on the cushions. "See me? Watch!"

"Be careful. Don't get near the edge. Get down from there."

"Okay!" He hopped down from the chair and scampered out of sight.

Ash resumed his questioning. "Your father was Toby Towson . . ."

She faced him again. "He died before I was born."

"You were born in Paris . . ."

"That's why I was named Nicole. My mother's best friend, in Paris, was called Nicole. I never knew her because we moved to London when I was three. That was after Leola met Robbie Craydon. I thought, for years, that Robbie was my father." She frowned. "How could you know I was born in Paris?"

"We've done a considerable amount of research on your mother's past. Even have a copy of your birth certificate."

"Why would you want that?" She sank onto the chaise, pushing the rumpled sheets out of her way. "What possible reason?"

"To check the date of your birth, the name you were given. I must have every possible fact about Lyli Amadoro—and Leola Martin— before I can write their portrait. It has to be a portrait of both."

She frowned again.

"Won't you tell me what you know? About both of them . . ."

Her eyes narrowed. "I suppose you found out things about me. This research you've done . . ."

"Very little. I didn't even know you were in New York."

"Nothing about my face?"

"It's a very attractive face . . ."

"I was born with a disgusting birthmark down the side of my cheek . . ."

"I see no mark."

"Look closer!" She pushed the soft brown hair away from her right cheek. "Can't you see it? Under all this pancake Lyli made me wear."

There was a faint shadow from forehead to chin under what, he realized, was heavy makeup. "I see nothing."

"This is why Lyli hated me. Even when I was a child!" She let the hair fall, covering her cheek. "She wouldn't look at me. Said I was ugly." Her voice was bitter with old memories. "But it was she who bore me with this obscene purple stain on my face. That's why she kept me hidden all those years in Switzerland."

"You lived in Switzerland?"

"Behind high stone walls. Lyli married Conte Amadoro before I was allowed to be seen in public. He insisted. But even then, when we lived in Paris again, I never met her friends."

"Did you come to America after your marriage?"

"I have never been married, Mr. Hendrie."

"I see." He didn't see, but he would avoid any further questions about her personal life and the small boy squealing on the terrace. Say nothing that might antagonize her. Keep to questions about Amadoro. "Did you know," he asked gently, "that your mother took drugs?"

"Lyli took drugs, not Leola," she protested. "Leola wouldn't touch drugs. I begged Lyli, again and again, to stop, but she said she needed them to live."

"Did she keep drugs here?"

"In a secret passage off her bathroom. There are passages behind most of these walls. Lyli used them all the time. Going from room to room . . ."

"You know where they are? These passages . . ."

"Not all of them. Fredo knows more about them than I. Lyli showed them to him when he was smaller. Told him they were like a game. Later, she wished she hadn't. Fortunately, he isn't tall enough to open some of them. Sometimes, at night, he hides in the passages for hours and I can't find him. He doesn't come out until after the staff's gone to bed. They don't know about the secret passages . . ."

"How often did Lyli take drugs?"

"Most nights, I guess. She had trouble sleeping. So do I, but I would never take drugs. I hated the drugs they gave me at the clinic."

"Which did she use most frequently?"

"Cocaine, I suppose. She served it to her guests at parties in Paris, but not in New York. Do you take drugs, Mr. Hendrie?"

"Never!" The question surprised him. "I've never used any kind of drugs." He was getting important information about Amadoro, but he must be more guarded with his questions or he would lose her confidence. "Why did you move out of that apartment on Seventy-third Street?"

"Because of you."

"Oh?"

"Fredo and I were living there with Laurie Winston until last Friday.

Laurie was frightened, the day before, when you came to the door. She phoned Lyli. Told her you'd found us. Lyli ordered us to move."

"The boy forgot his bear again."

"So that's what happened to it!"

Better not mention the knife in its back. "I saw it Saturday, when I returned. I had seen it before, in the elevator at Amadoro Associates."

"I knew your face was familiar!"

"Why were you there?"

"To persuade Lyli not to send us back to Switzerland. There had been an incident the night before, when Lyli came for dinner. Fredo was naughty at the table. She said he must be disciplined. We would return to Zurich and place him in a strict school. I begged her to let us stay in New York."

"Did you succeed?"

"No. We were to leave tomorrow."

"Where are you staying now?"

"We have an apartment next door."

"Next door?"

"Another building. Lyli owns both of them. We enter from another street, through a different lobby. Take the public elevators, but there's a hidden passage between our apartment and this one. We've lived there several times. Two years ago Lyli decided we should move to that apartment on Seventy-third Street. Fredo had been naughty, as usual. Constantly upsetting her as he got older."

"How old is he?"

"He was eight this year."

"Eight? I thought . . ."

"I know. He's unusually small for his age. His father was only five feet tall. Lyli has sent us off before. Usually back to Europe, but this time she wanted us to stay in New York."

"You were in your apartment Monday night, when your mother died?"

"Yes . . . But we didn't hear from Leola all day and we went to bed early. Had no idea what had happened until Mrs. Winston read about Lyli's death in the paper. Tuesday afternoon."

"And you don't think it was suicide?"

"I told you! Leola would never have taken her own life. I'm sure it was an accident. Lyli forgot how many sleeping pills she'd already taken and took some more. She's done that before. And, of course, she'd had wine and brandy for dinner."

"How could you know that?"

"She always did."

"You knew where she dined Monday night?"

"I've no idea. No . . ." Glancing toward the terrace. "Fredo!" She screamed his name, rising from the chaise. "Come away from there!"

Ash saw that the boy had pulled a patio chair toward the parapet edging the terrace.

"You hear me, Fredo! Come here! At once."

The child turned to look toward her, impishly, as he climbed onto the chair. "Watch, Mommy! Going to fly . . ."

"No! I've told you not to do that again!" She hurried toward the open windows. "Stay right there! Don't climb any higher."

Ash followed her, across the boudoir, onto the terrace.

The boy was standing on an arm of the heavy metal chair, hoisting himself onto the parapet.

"No, Fredo!" Nicole was crossing the terrace, walking slowly now. "Don't do that! No!"

Ash was behind her, his eyes on the boy crouching on the parapet.

"Hold still, Fredo!" Nicole ordered. "Don't move . . ."

"Don't go near him," Ash ordered. "The slightest motion and he'll lose his balance."

"What can I do?" She had stopped a few feet from the parapet.

Ash stood behind her. "Don't move, boy." His words were an order. "Get down from there. Very slowly and carefully. You climbed up and you can get down."

The child's brown eyes were enormous, as though the pupils were enlarged.

"Get down from there!" Ash commanded, his voice harsh. "Get down."

Fredo laughed. "Going to fly!" He disappeared, suddenly, over the edge.

Nicole screamed.

chapter thirty

ASH REACHED THE PARAPET AND LEANED FORWARD, slightly, across the ledge. Felt instant vertigo, his guts wrenching, as he looked down into the dark canyon far below.

The small body would still be falling.

Nicole continued to scream.

Ash turned from the parapet, placed an arm around her and, gently, took her inside. Guided her to the chaise, where she sank onto the tumble of sheets.

She buried her face in her hands and sobbed.

He stepped back, away from her, unable to say anything that might calm her grief.

"What is it, Nicole? What's this man done?"

Ash turned to see Mrs. Winston coming through the open wall panel.

"What's happened?" she asked.

"Fredo's gone." Nicole raised her head, face streaked with tears. "He climbed onto that parapet. And fell . . ."

"Not again!" She turned and hurried across the boudoir toward the open doors. "You stay there. I'll get him."

Ash turned back to Nicole. "He's climbed onto that parapet before?"

"Fredo has no fear of heights. Or of death. He's tried to kill himself. Several times!"

"What?"

"Ran in front of a car on Fifth Avenue. The driver saw him and swerved. Then he cut his wrist with a knife but the cut wasn't deep . . ."

"Those were accidents, surely."

"Fredo did it purposely. Each time. Told me he did. To get back at Lyli." She brushed tears from her eyes. "One psychiatrist, in London, said many children take their lives when life becomes unbearable. Leola loved Fredo, but Lyli made his life impossible. She hated him because she was afraid of him. Said he was possessed by a devil. Perhaps he was. I'm not possessed by any devil but she hated me, too. Because of my face. This face she had given me! Did everything she could to destroy both of us. Fredo never knew she was his mother."

"Lyli was his mother?"

"His name is Alfredo Amadoro."

"Alfredo?"

"That's what's on his birth certificate and his passport. Named after his father. Born a month before his father was killed, so he has no memory of him. He's always been told I'm his mother. Lyli gave him to me because she didn't want him. She hadn't meant to get pregnant again, but the Conte was determined to have a son and heir. Now they're both dead." She began to sob softly. "Lyli never felt love for anyone. Only for money . . ."

Ash sat on the chaise beside her as she pushed her hair back, saw she had smudged the pancake on her cheek and the birthmark was more visible.

"She never knew love with any of her husbands because she wasn't capable of affection. Except for those damned dogs! She loved them. All of them named for Prince, her first dog, the one she killed . . ."

"I know about that. It was an accident. She didn't mean to kill it."

"And I killed Lyli. Meant to kill her . . ."

"What?"

"I gave her those sleeping pills. And put the liquid drug into that water glass on her bed table. Knowing she would drink it. Killed Lyli and Leola. I loved Leola. But I hated Lyli because of the way she treated Fredo. Killed Lyli the same way she killed her husbands . . ."

"She murdered her husbands?"

"Not my father. His death was an accident, I think, but that was what gave her the idea to kill the other two. Told me so herself. I've had to live with that—as well as everything else—the fact that my mother was a murderess—"

"How did your father's death give her the idea to kill the others?"

"My father had been drinking and, foolishly, went on deck during a storm. He'd drunk so much he lost his balance and was swept overboard. That's what gave her the idea for the other two. She put sleeping pills into Robbie Craydon's brandy flask. He always drank brandy when he tested a new motor. Put sleeping pills in the hot punch Conte Amadoro drank before he left the chalet to ski with his friends. She wasn't present either time. When Lord Craydon crashed his car or when Conte Amadoro went over the side of the mountain. They were sweet and loving husbands. So kind to me. Both of them! And she destroyed them. All she wanted was their fortunes. That's how she became the rich and famous Lyli Amadoro. Killed two husbands but nobody suspected because they died in front of witnesses. Their deaths were declared, officially, to be accidents, but she told me she killed both of them."

"When did she tell you this?"

"I was in my teens. She hoped that telling me would bring us closer. Instead I hated her even more. She was drinking, of course, when she confessed. I loathed that! The drinking and the drugs . . ."

"And this is why you killed her?"

"This, and much more. I had to do it before she destroyed me and Fredo. Especially Fredo! For the way she kept us hidden. Sending us to psychiatrists in Paris and London. When all we needed, both of us, was love and affection. Not money. That's all she ever gave us. Money . . ."

Ash glanced toward the sunshine on the terrace as he listened, afraid to interrupt the flood of words.

"I've never married. And never will! Who would want me for a wife? So I'll never have a son of my own. Only Fredo. He believes I am his mother. He's always been told I was Mrs. Towson and he is Fredo Towson. Lyli forced me to do that. Poor little Fredo! I've loved him as though he really were my child, but he never was. He was always Lyli's son. But I've done everything I could to protect him from her. Kept them apart. She hated him because he reminded her of his father. She never loved Conte Amadoro and never, really, loved his son. Or me . . ."

"Mommy! Mommy!"

Ash got to his feet as the boy came running across the salon followed by Mrs. Winston.

"I flew, Mommy! Did you see?" He flung himself into her arms. "I flew again!"

"Fredo! Fredo, my love." Nicole stroked his black curls and tears flowed from her eyes as she hugged him. "My sweet boy . . ." She held him to her, kissing him on the forehead. "Please, God! You'll never do that again."

He squirmed, trying to free himself from her embrace.

"Next time he may not be so lucky." Mrs. Winston's voice was stern.

Ash faced her. "Where did you find him?"

"The lower terrace is wider. He lands on a cushioned divan. Discovered he could do this last year. He's been lucky so far. Next time he might not be."

"But he won't do it again. Not ever!" Nicole released the boy and got to her feet. "Come, my love. We'll go home."

"Okay, Mommy!"

"We'll go through the other passage. You know the way."

"Me first!" He darted toward the open doors to the salon.

Nicole followed, glancing toward Mrs. Winston. "We'll be in the apartment. I'll go on with our packing." She looked at Ash. "Goodbye, Mr. Hendrie. Everything I told you was in confidence, you realize. I trust you."

"But, Miss Towson, I . . ." He didn't finish the sentence because she had hurried after Fredo through the salon.

"Whatever Nicole told you, Mr. Hendrie . . ."

"Yes?" He faced Mrs. Winston.

"I can assure you it was not the truth."

chapter thirty-one

"BUT YOU CAN'T KNOW WHAT SHE SAID."
"She told you it was she who killed Lyli."
"Yes. She did."
"Nicole told you that to protect—someone else . . ." She walked toward the open windows. "We had better have a talk, Mr. Hendrie. You and I."
"I've been trying to talk to you since last week. I'm sure there's much you can tell me."
"I prefer not to remain in this room, Lyli's boudoir, because it holds such unpleasant memories." She went ahead of him, onto the terrace, and sat on one of the cushioned patio chairs shaded by an enormous parasol.
Ash sat, facing her, and waited for her to speak. He realized that her face was not as forbidding as it had seemed last week. White hair, firm lips in a strong face, intelligent gray eyes which were studying him. Wearing a simple white-and-gray-striped linen dress.
She sighed. "I will tell you the truth, Mr. Hendrie, about what I know. Now that Lyli is dead. I will tell you everything."
"You met Leola Martin when her parents engaged you to be her companion?"
"Then I won't have to explain all that."
"I talked to her parents last week."
"Such fine people! Glenda and Happy. Unfortunately, Leola detested both of them." She shrugged. "But then she hated everyone. I'm one of the few people she trusted. I don't know why . . . What her parents couldn't have told you is that, after the death of Toby Towson, I went to Paris with his widow. I was with her when Nicole was born."

Unfortunately, from the moment Leola saw the baby's disfigured face, she couldn't bear the sight of her."

"Nicole has told me."

"I took the baby to Switzerland. Leola rented a villa for us near Zurich, and that was where we lived, with a staff of servants, for many years. I had all the mirrors removed from every room, and as long as we remained there, Nicole never saw her face. Never knew . . . until after we went to England, where Leola married Sir Robert Craydon. He adored Nicole! She was happy there and deeply disturbed by his horrible death. After that we moved to Paris, where Lady Craydon met Conte Amadoro. Moved on to Venice, where Leola married again, became Lyli Amadoro—the Contessa Amadoro. Alfredo also loved Nicole. She was shattered, mentally and physically, when he died. It was too much for her to comprehend. Those two violent deaths."

"I can understand."

"By that time, Lyli had told Nicole about her father's death. She was unable to accept a third one. I took her back to Paris, where she had long months of psychiatric treatment. Then specialists in London . . ."

"She told me, a moment ago, that Lyli murdered her second and third husbands. Caused them to have those accidents . . ."

"That's true. Lyli told both of us. I'm surprised that Nicole confided in you. After Conte Amadoro's death Lyli packed us off—with the baby—to Switzerland again. A larger villa and more servants. Nicole seemed happier. She loved little Fredo, and as soon as he could talk, he called her Mommy. Those were good years for both of them. Except, slowly, I began to realize there was something very strange about the boy. He had a wild look in his eyes, at the age of two, that disturbed and frightened me."

"Wild look? A two-year-old?"

"As though he saw things nobody else could see. He was a sad child, rarely smiled. Lived in a private world which Nicole and I were unable to enter . . ."

As she talked, Ash noticed the shadow of the parasol creeping across the terrace as the sun edged higher.

"At the age of four—this was after we came to New York—Fredo began to hear a voice speaking to him that we couldn't hear. He claimed it was the voice of his stuffed tiger. One night I found the tiger with its skin ripped open, the stuffing torn out. Fredo said he had to destroy the tiger because it was threatening to kill him . . ."

Ash remembered the teddy bear in the cupboard.

"Told me he was a demon. He could destroy anything. Even people."

"How could he know about demons?"

"Children's books have lurid pictures of devils and demons."

"That's true."

"Before that, in Switzerland, there was an aviary in our garden, filled with birds. The gardener found all of them dead one morning. Poisoned with pellets he kept to kill snails. I knew Fredo had killed those birds but he denied it. I took him to a psychiatrist in Zurich who specialized in troubled children. He seemed more sympathetic than any of the others, but during that period Fredo became violent for the first time. Would kick and bite strangers. And it was then he began to talk about killing himself . . ."

"Suicide?"

"The first time was when we were preparing to visit his mother in New York for several weeks. He said: 'I will kill myself after we come back to Switzerland.' He didn't mention it while we were away, but after we returned he swallowed most of a bottle of aspirin tablets. His stomach had to be pumped and he survived, but for several days he was very ill."

"Did you tell his mother about this?"

"We didn't dare! Nicole and I never told Lyli anything about Fredo or, for that matter, about ourselves. Anyway, she didn't wish to hear about him. Good or bad. He was permitted to eat dinner with her—he, Nicole and I—but if he became naughty she would order him from the table. I would take him to his room, in our apartment, and Lyli would rage for hours . . .

"At that time I threatened to leave, but Lyli doubled my salary and I finally agreed to stay. Not for the money. That went into my savings account for the future. Not for myself but for Nicole and Fredo. Without me they would have nobody. I knew I could never leave them. I'd feared, for years, that Lyli might decide to put both of them in some private clinic for the rest of their lives. She threatened to do that many times. Told them she would. I knew that in an institution, with bars at the windows, Fredo would certainly take his life. He has no fear of death, of course, because the word has no meaning for him. And Nicole, in an asylum, would fade into the shadows. She suffers from acute melancholia. No danger of this happening now. Lyli is dead. Thank God . . ." She clasped her hands together in her lap. "She told me, many times, I would be their guardian in the event of her death." Straightening in the chair. "We're leaving for Europe tonight. I'd hoped we would get away before we were discovered here. We have our own apartment on this floor, but in a public wing of the complex with a hidden passage connecting the two apartments."

"Amadoro seems to have had a passion for secret passages!"

"She learned about them in England when she lived at Craydon Castle. She wanted us to have a New York apartment convenient to hers, so our apartment was included in the first plans for this penthouse. We stayed in our apartment whenever we came to New York. Lyli joined us for dinner every Monday night."

"She was with you the night she died?"

"We had a pleasant evening. The four of us. I always cooked special dishes I knew she would enjoy. Unfortunately, after dinner, Fredo was naughty and Lyli slapped his face. I took him to his room and she came back here . . .

"We moved to the apartment on Seventy-third Street two years ago, because Lyli didn't wish to see Fredo. It was impossible to keep him away from her after he learned how to open some of the secret passages. Including the one between our apartments."

"How did he find out?"

"One evening, after dinner, it amused Lyli to take him on a tour of all the passages. That was a mistake! Fredo knew more about them than Nicole or I and would hide in them for hours. Unfortunately, he would go through the passages at night while I was asleep. Creep in here to visit his mother. She wakened and found him staring at her. That's why, last year, she moved us to the apartment on Seventy-third. Had us return here, in a panic, after you turned up last week. Afraid you'd find out about Nicole and Fredo. Terrified that you would learn anything about her personal life." She hesitated. "I must tell you the complete truth, Mr. Hendrie. And this is very difficult . . ."

"What is the truth?"

"Leola Martin—Lyli Amadoro—was an evil woman. I should know! Better than anyone. Both her children are the result of that evil. They are extensions of Lyli. She was an evil, destructive force. They, too, are destructive. Especially Fredo. Nicole is more passive. She only destroys herself. They can't help what they do. Either of them! Their evil is inherited. They are innocent victims. The evil is in their genes. It was Fredo—not Nicole—who killed his mother."

"How could a child . . ."

"Nicole blames herself for everything, as usual, but she would never have harmed her mother physically. Fredo would—and did."

"Eight years old? I can't believe it!"

"I knew he was furious when Lyli slapped him, Monday night, at the dinner table but I hoped, next morning, the incident would be forgotten. While we slept—Nicole and I—Fredo got up and went into the passage where Lyli kept all her sedatives and drugs. He took a bottle down from a shelf. I found the stool, later, he'd dragged from our kitchen and used to reach the bottle. He carried it into Lyli's boudoir. She was asleep. There was a glass on her bedside table, as always, with a thermos of water. She took two sleeping pills every night."

"Nicole said she gave her the sleeping pills."

"She's lying. She might've given her mother a glass of water, nothing more. Fredo filled the glass from that bottle he found in the drug cabinet. Roused Lyli and held the glass for her to drink. He'd seen me do that many times. She must've been half asleep because she drank quite a lot . . .

"I went in, around midnight, to see if she was asleep. Did that every night, before the maid came to check the lights, to be sure Lyli was all right."

"You knew she took drugs?"

"Oh, yes! She had for many years. When I saw that the panel to the passage where the drugs were kept was open, I knew Fredo had been there. I saw, at once, that Lyli wasn't breathing. There was a bottle on the bed table. The water glass was almost empty and the liquid in it was darker than water. I smelled the glass and realized it must be some kind of drug. Picked up the bottle and read the label. Oil of hashish. There was very little left . . .

"I forced myself not to panic. Carried the glass into the bathroom and washed it. Dried it with a towel. Put on rubber gloves, to avoid fingerprints, before I took the glass back and put it where I'd found it beside the bed. I knew where Lyli kept her drugs—in another of her secret passages—so I took the oil of hashish bottle there and returned to Lyli's bedroom with a bottle of sleeping pills that was nearly empty. Knowing she always took one or two before retiring. I looked around to be sure nothing was out of place before leaving. Carefully closing the hidden door in the wall. For the next half hour I removed all the drugs from her hiding place and carried them to our apartment in the other building. Scoured the wall cabinet in case anyone discovered it. Closed all the hidden doors. Spent another half hour washing all the bottles before I dropped them into the incinerator. Knowing they would be destroyed without a trace . . .

"Checked that Fredo was asleep before I returned to my own room. Nicole, unfortunately, was wakened by the sound of the incinerator. I was forced to tell her what Fredo had done. She will help me protect him. That's why she told you she had killed her mother. To protect Fredo."

"The police suspect Amadoro's death was suicide or an accident."

"Let them think what they please."

"Nicole said she would be packing."

"Yes."

"You're taking them—Nicole and the boy—back to Switzerland?"

"No. Not Switzerland. I can't tell you where we're going." She clasped her hands in an unconsciously beseeching gesture. "Our passports are in order and our tickets are waiting at the airport. No one knows we've been in the United States. And nobody suspects that Fredo exists. No announcement was made when he was born."

"There's been no mention of a son in our research."

"You won't attempt to stop us, Mr. Hendrie?"

"No. Certainly not."

"Won't tell the police anything of what I've confessed to you?"

"I see no reason to tell anyone."

She got to her feet. "I'm very grateful."

Ash rose. "Is there anything I can do to help you?"

"Everything's done." She hesitated. "You are a good man, Mr. Hendrie. Lyli said you were one of the few honest men she'd ever met. That's why she feared you . . ."

"Nobody, I suspect, is entirely good—or bad."

"That is certainly true. I suppose the police may stumble onto one of these secret passages. And that will lead to all the others. They will discover Lyli's hoard of drugs. Poor Lyli! By that time, we shall be far away. We'll be traveling for several days to reach our final destination. A peaceful island we've visited before. Nicole and Fredo have always been happy there. The boy will, eventually, forget Amadoro. And so will Nicole and I. Fredo has no idea that he killed Lyli. In a few years he won't remember any of this."

"No, I suppose not." He hesitated. "I wish you peace."

"I believe you really do." She smiled for the first time. "Perhaps some tourist will leave a copy of *Metropole* on the beach and I will find it. I shall read your portrait of—Leola Martin and Lyli Amadoro. But I won't let Nicole see it. In fact, after I've read it, I shall throw the magazine into the sea." She turned, abruptly, and hurried inside.

He followed, slowly, out of the warm sunlight into shadow.

chapter thirty-two

ASH WAS AWARE OF THE SILENT OFFICE AROUND HIM AS he wrote, page after page, in longhand.

He had hurried back here, from Amadoro's penthouse, unaware of the people in the streets.

He'd been writing for several hours. Getting everything down on paper and correcting all the previous notes, which now had new meanings.

He finally squeezed his aching eyes together before checking the desk clock. After five-thirty!

Realized that his back was aching. Got to his feet and walked around, briskly, circling the desk for several minutes.

Nothing he had to do before he picked Mara up at the theater.

He returned to his desk, dialed Costigan's and made a reservation for eleven-thirty.

Leaned back in the leather armchair and stared at that same blue sky beyond his windows. Still not a cloud.

He knew who had killed Amadoro, but he would never be able to tell anybody. McCorkle or anyone else . . .

How would he end her portrait? With whatever the police finally decided was the cause of death? Accident or suicide . . .

Maybe he should start a first draft. Write it as though, at the end, he would reveal the murderer. Fit in all the facts leading to murder. Fly over to London and Paris, as planned, next week. Whatever he discovered about Lyli's past, he would insert into the rough first draft when he returned. Including everything he could dig up on the deaths of Lord Craydon and Conte Amadoro . . .

He frowned at the waiting typewriter.

Damn complicated piece of cold machinery!

The phone rang.

First time this afternoon! Who the devil would be calling him at this hour, on his private line?

As he reached to pick it up, he knew who was calling. "Yes, McCorkle?"

"How the hell could you know it was me?"

"I'm psychic."

The detective chuckled. "So put your psychic powers to work on this. I decided to drop by Amadoro's penthouse again."

"Did you?" He straightened in his chair, alert.

"Calling from there now. Want to know, was one of those glass bubble columns smashed, in the big downstairs room, when you were here?"

"Don't think so." He answered without hesitation.

"And did a section of wall paneling stand open in this same room?"

"If it did, I wasn't aware."

"It's open now and there's a passage behind the wall that leads upstairs to the dame's bedroom, where another panel's been opened."

"I'll be damned. Who do you think opened them and smashed that column?"

"Guy downstairs, at the desk, says nobody's been here. Only you. Police security says the same."

"You don't think I did it?"

"That hadn't entered my mind, pal. But, now you mention it . . . Did you?"

"Certainly not."

"I've talked to the coroner again. They've finished their final report."

"What did they find?"

"The dame only took two sleeping pills. Not half a bottle. In addition to that, they found a small amount of residual cocaine and a large amount of hashish that had been ingested in liquid."

"What, exactly, does that mean?"

"The coroner thinks she had it while she was out for dinner. I'm not so sure. I'm beginning to agree with you and Sandra. It could be murder."

"Are you?"

"It was the hashish caused her death. Coroner still thinks it could've been an accident. He's not so sure of suicide, because there was no hashish here in the apartment. The guy's driving me nuts! Can't make a final decision. He's not signing his report until next week. If it is murder, pal, there's not one goddamn clue or suspect. And no motive! Except when drugs are involved you can always find motives. Which reminds me. Couple of developments in the Marnat investigation."

"Yes?"

"We had a report from the Préfecture in Paris. Marnat was known to be involved with drugs when he lived there. Under suspicion, never arrested. He was thought to be furnishing cocaine to wealthy women, but they never caught him at it. I've suspected, all along, he was mixed up with drugs. Those two guys he saw, watching his apartment, were sent to collect money from him.

"I'm having a pal from Narcotics go over Amadoro's apartment. Go over these wall passages. And I'm paying another visit to Amadoro Associates next week. Question some of those executives I wasn't able to locate before."

"Good luck, Mac!"

"This smashed glass column and these open wall panels mean somebody else was here this afternoon. But how did they get in? I've gotta lot of questions to ask somebody. Okay, pal. Talk to you next week."

"You know where to reach me." Ash put the phone down and stared at the pages of notes in front of him.

McCorkle wouldn't start to look for more hidden passages until next week, but he would, eventually, find them.

Mrs. Winston would get away with Nicole and the boy. By the time McCorkle found the passage leading to their apartment—if he ever did—they would be safe on their island.

There was nothing to connect Fredo with murder. No prints on that water glass, and the bottle that held the hashish had been destroyed.

He would do a first draft of the Amadoro portrait at once. Make changes after McCorkle decided whether or not Lyli was murdered.

Many things he still had to find out.

He'd never learned why Leola had changed her name to Lyli!

Ash pulled his armchair closer to the electric typewriter. Snapped it to life and heard a low humming inside its gray metal carapace.

He began to type.

PORTRAIT OF LYLI AMADORO
(rough first draft)
by
Ashton Hendrie

She was reputed to be the most beautiful woman in New York City, some said in the world.

Her name was Leola Martin when she was born, but forty-three years later, when she died, she was known as Lyli Amadoro.

Most people called her Amadoro.

As a result of three marriages, she was also known, briefly, as Leola Towson, Lady Craydon and Contessa Amadoro.

Her three husbands died in what appear to have been accidents.

Were they?

As I type these words, the Manhattan police believe that her own death may have been an accident.

Was it?

I shall give you all the facts I have been able to uncover.

This is a portrait of the life and death of an incredible and mysterious woman.

Amadoro . . .

He stopped typing and stared at the words. Startled by a totally unexpected thought.

Could Mrs. Winston have lied?

Had she told him Fredo put the liquid hashish into the glass because she knew a child could never be tried for murder?

What if it was Nicole who had done it, and Mrs. Winston was protecting her?

Or was it Mrs. Winston herself who murdered Amadoro?

No!

Sandra Saunders said it was murder . . .

And Fernand Maudru said Amadoro's murderer was named Alfredo.

Fredo . . .

His fingertips, resting on the plastic typewriter keys, were suddenly ice-cold.